Praise for *Never Coming Home*

"Told with pitch-perfect pacing and unrelenting tension, McKinnon explores the darkest corners of the human heart in this highly entertaining, bone-chilling must read."
—Heather Gudenkauf, *New York Times* bestselling author of *The Overnight Guest*

"Fiendishly clever and deeply chilling, *Never Coming Home* is psychological suspense of the first order. With dark wit, searing prose, and a plot that twists like a strangling vine, McKinnon will lure you in and hold you breathless until the final page. Don't miss this propulsive, hypnotic thrill ride."
—Lisa Unger, *New York Times* bestselling author of *Last Girl Ghosted*

"A bold and original thriller, with a narrator you'll love to hate. I tore through it."
—Clare Mackintosh, internationally bestselling author of *Hostage*

"A diabolical tour de force... Exquisite tension, fearlessly drawn characters, and sharp-as-knives prose make for an unforgettable thriller that will both terrify and implicate you... Nobody stress-tests the human heart quite like Hannah Mary McKinnon."
—P.J. Vernon, author of *Bath Haus*

"Hannah Mary McKinnon is the queen of dark thrillers! *Never Coming Home* captivates, horrifies...and it will make you laugh. Impossible to stop reading until you get to the final page."
—Samantha Downing, *USA TODAY* bestselling author of *For Your Own Good*

"A clever, riveting psychological thriller. Hannah Mary McKinnon delivers a witty, dark and totally absorbing edge-of-your-seat novel that is sure to leave you breathless, shocked and shouting from the side-lines."
—Adele Parks, #1 *Sunday Times* bestselling author of *Both of You*

HANNAH MARY McKINNON

NEVER COMING HOME

mira

ISBN-13: 978-0-7783-8610-0

Never Coming Home

Mira
22 Adelaide St. West, 41st Floor
Toronto, Ontario M5H 4E3, Canada
BookClubbish.com

Printed in U.S.A.

To Becki—through thick and thin!

Also by Hannah Mary McKinnon

You Will Remember Me
Sister Dear
Her Secret Son
The Neighbors

NEVER COMING HOME

If you want some lies to be believed wrap them up in truths.

—Danish Proverb

SUNDAY

1

The steady noise from the antique French carriage clock on the mantelpiece had somehow amplified itself, a rhythmic *tick-tick, tick-tick*, which usually went unnoticed. After I'd been sitting in the same position and holding my ailing mother-in-law's hand for almost an hour, the incessant clicking had long wormed its way deep into my brain where it grated on my nerves, stirring up fantasies of hammers, bent copper coils, and shattered glass.

Nora looked considerably worse than when I'd visited her earlier this week. She was propped up in bed, surrounded by a multitude of pillows. She'd lost more weight, something her pre-illness slender physique couldn't afford. Her bones jutted out like rocks on a cliff, turning a kiss on the cheek into an extreme sport in which you might lose an eye. The ghostly hue on her face resembled the kids who'd come dressed up as ghouls for Halloween a few days ago, emphasizing the dark circles that had transformed her eyes into mini sinkholes. It wasn't clear how much time she had left. I was no medical professional, but we could all tell it wouldn't be long. When she'd shared her doctor's diagnosis with me barely three weeks ago, they'd estimated around two months, but at the rate of Nora's decline, it wouldn't have come as a surprise if it turned out to be a matter of days.

Ovarian cancer. As a thirty-two-year-old Englishman who wasn't yet half Nora's age I'd had no idea it was dubbed the *silent killer* but now understood why. Despite the considerable wealth and social notoriety Nora enjoyed in the upscale and picturesque town of Chelmswood on the outskirts of Boston, by the time she'd seen someone because of a bad back and they'd worked out what was going on, her vital organs were under siege. The disease was a formidable opponent, the stealthiest of snipers, destroying her from the inside out before she had any indication something was wrong.

A shame, truly, because Nora was the only one in the Ward family I actually liked. I wouldn't have sat here this long with my arse going numb for my father-in-law's benefit, that's for sure. Given half the chance I'd have smothered him with a pillow while the nurse wasn't looking. But not Nora. She was kindhearted, gentle. The type of person who quietly gave time and money to multiple causes and charities without expecting a single accolade in return. Sometimes I imagined my mother would've been like Nora, had she survived, and fleetingly wondered what might have become of me if she hadn't died so young, if I'd have grown up to be a good person.

I gradually pulled my hand away from Nora's and reached for my phone, decided on playing a game or two of backgammon until she woke up. The app had thrashed me the last three rounds and I was due, but Nora's fingers twitched before I made my first move. I studied her brow, which seemed furrowed in pain even as she slept. Not for the first time I hoped the Grim Reaper would stake his or her claim sooner rather than later. If I were death, I'd be swift, efficient, and merciful, not prescribe a drawn-out, painful process during which body, mind, or both, wasted away. People shouldn't be made to suffer as they died. Not all of them, anyway.

"Lucas?"

I jumped as Diane, Nora's nurse and my neighbor, put a hand on my shoulder. She'd only left the room for a couple of minutes but always wore those soft-soled shoes when she worked, which meant I never heard her coming until she was next to me. Kind of sneaky, when I thought about it, and I decided I wouldn't sit with my back to the door again.

As she walked past, the air filled with the distinctive medicinal scent of hand sanitizer and antiseptic. I hated that smell. Too many bad memories I couldn't shake. Diane set a glass of water on the bedside table, checked Nora's vitals, and turned around. Hands on hips, she peered down at me from her six-foot frame, her tight dark curls bouncing alongside her jawbone like a set of tiny corkscrews.

"You can go home now. I'll take the evening from here." Regardless of her amicable delivery, there was no mistaking the instruction, but she still added, "Get some rest. God knows you look like you need it."

"Thanks a lot," I replied with mock indignation. "You sure know how to flatter a guy."

Diane cocked her head to one side, folded her arms, and gave me another long stare, which to anyone else would've been intimidating. "How long since you slept? I mean properly."

I waved a hand. "It's only seven o'clock."

"Yeah, I guess given the circumstances I wouldn't want to be home alone, either."

I looked away. "That's not what this is about. I'll wait until Nora wakes up again. I want to say goodbye. You know, in case she…" My voice cracked a little on the last word and I feigned a cough as I pressed the heels of my palms over my eyes.

"She won't," Diane whispered. "Not tonight. Trust me. She's not ready to go."

I knew Diane had worked in hospice for two decades and had seen more than her fair share of people taking their last breaths. If she said Nora wouldn't die tonight, then Nora would still be here in the morning.

"I'll leave in a bit. After she wakes up."

Diane let out a resigned sigh and sat down in the chair on the opposite side of the bed. A comfortable silence settled between us despite the fact we didn't know each other very well. I'd first met Diane and her wife, Karina, who were both in their forties, when they'd struck up a conversation with me and my wife Michelle as we'd moved into our house on the other side of Chelmswood almost three years prior. Something about garbage days and recycling rules, I think. The mundane discussion could've led to a multitude of drinks, shared meals, and the swapping of embarrassing childhood stories, except we were all what Michelle had called *busy professionals* with (quote) *hectic work schedules that make forging new friendships difficult*. My Captain Subtext translated her comment as *can't be bothered* and, consequently, the four of us had never made the transition from neighbors to close friends.

Aside from the occasional holiday party invitation or looking after each other's places whenever we were away—picking up the mail, watering the plants, that kind of thing—we only saw each other in passing. Nevertheless, Karina regularly left a *Welcome Back* note on our kitchen counter along with flowers from their garden and a bottle of wine. Not one to be outdone on anything, Michelle reciprocated, except she'd always chosen more elaborate bouquets and fancier booze.

My wife's silent little pissing contests, which I'd pretended to be too dense to notice, had irked me to hell and back, but when Nora fell ill and Diane had been assigned as one of her nurses, I'd been relieved it was someone I knew and trusted.

"I'm sorry this is happening to you," Diane said, rescuing me from the spousal memories. "It's not fair. I mean, it's never fair, obviously, but on top of what you're going through with Michelle. I can't imagine. It's so awful…"

I acknowledged the rest of the words she left hanging in the air with a nod. There was nothing left to say about my wife's situation we hadn't already discussed, rediscussed, dissected, reconstructed, and pulled apart all over again. We'd not solved the mystery of her whereabouts or found more clues. Nothing new, helpful or hopeful, anyway. We never would.

Silence descended upon us again, the gaudy carriage clock ticking away, reviving the images of me with hammer in hand until the doorbell masked the sound.

"I'll go," Diane muttered, and before I had the chance to stand, she left the room and pulled the door shut. I couldn't help wondering if her swift departure was because she needed to escape from me, the man who'd used her supportive shoulder almost daily for the past month. I decided to tone it down a little. Nobody wanted to be around an overdramatic, constant crybaby regardless of their circumstances.

I listened for voices but couldn't hear any despite my leaning toward the door and craning my neck. I couldn't risk moving in case Nora woke up. Her body was failing, but her mind remained sharp as a box of tacks. She'd wonder what I was up to if she saw my ear pressed against the mahogany panel. *Solid* mahogany. The best money could buy thanks to the Ward family's three-generations-old construction empire. No cheap building materials in this house, as my father-in-law had pointed out when he'd first given me the tour of the six bedrooms, four reception rooms, indoor and outdoor kitchens (never mind the abhorrent freezing Boston winters), and what could only be described as *grounds* because *yard* implied it was manageable with a push-along mower.

"Only the best for my family," Gideon had said in his characteristic rumbly, pompous way as he'd knocked back another glass of Laphroaig, the broad East Coast accent he worked hard to hide making more of a reappearance with each gluttonous glug. "No MDF, vinyl or laminate garbage, thank you. That's not what I'm about. Not at all."

It's in the houses you build for others, I'd thought as I'd grunted an inaudible reply he no doubt mistook for agreement because people rarely contradicted him. As I raised my glass of scotch, I didn't mention the council flats I grew up in on what Gideon dismissed as *the lesser side of the pond*, or the multiple times Dad and I had been kicked out of our dingy digs because he couldn't pay the rent, and we'd ended up on the streets. My childhood had been vastly different to my wife's, and I imagined the pleasure I'd find in watching Gideon's eyes bulge as I described the squalor I'd lived in, and he realized my background was worlds away from the shiny and elitist version I'd led everyone to believe was the truth. I pictured myself laughing as he understood his perfect daughter had married so far beneath her, she may as well have pulled me up from the dirt like a carrot, and not the expensive organic kind.

Of course, I hadn't told him anything. I'd taken another swig of the scotch I loathed, but otherwise kept my mouth shut. As satisfying as it would've been, my father-in-law knowing the truth about my background had never been part of my long-term agenda. In any case, and despite Gideon's efforts, things were working to plan. Better than. The smug bastard was dead.

And he wasn't the only one.

2

My mother-in-law's hand twitched again, shifting my focus away from the memories of her dead husband and back to her. When Nora's eyes fluttered open, I waited a while for her to get her bearings. What was it like, I wondered, in the split second after she woke up, before she remembered she was dying, and Michelle was missing? Perhaps she found some relief in the fact her misery would soon be over. Maybe she was glad her fight would end.

"I fell asleep again," she said when her gaze met mine, her voice croaky, the soft West Country accent still noticeable even after living in the US for decades. "I'm not the best company, am I? You should've gone home."

As she patted down her short silver hair, the thin and wrinkled skin on the back of her shaky hand reminded me of the crêpe paper we'd used for arts and crafts in school when I was a kid. An image of a spider flashed through my mind. Bits of gold paper triangles painstakingly cut out one at a time and glued to a set of pipe cleaners. When I'd proudly carried my creation home to show Dad, a big kid called Tony had grabbed it, thrown it into a puddle and stomped on it with his size-ten feet. The black eye and bald patch I'd given him earned me a badge of honor from my cohort, and a three-day suspension from the headmistress. Both had been worth it, but it had been one of the last times I'd laid a hand on anyone publicly.

"I didn't want to go yet," I said. "You can't get rid of me that easily."

"Apparently not." Nora attempted a smile which looked more like a grimace as her bloodshot and watery eyes searched the room. "Where's Diane?" she said, her voice a little panicked. "She didn't leave, did she?"

"No, there was someone at the—"

On cue, the bedroom door opened, and as Diane walked back in with Detective Anjali Dubal behind her, my spine straightened. Nora's eyes went wide. When she tried to push herself up, I reached for her arm to steady her, but she shook her head.

"Detective," she said with a gasp. "Do you have news?"

Anjali—who'd insisted from the start we use her first name—walked to the foot of the bed, her long dark hair cascading over her shoulders. She was somewhere in her mid- to late-thirties, about a head shorter than me and the kind of person who'd never let her height, or lack thereof, hold her back. She was ambitious, determined. One to watch.

"I thought it best to stop by," she said. "It's good to see you both. How are you?"

Nora grabbed my hand, bones digging into my palms. "Hanging in there, aren't we?"

"Barely." I got up and turned to Anjali before repeating

my mother-in-law's question but in a far more clipped tone. "Do you have news?"

The detective thrust her hands deep into the pockets of her knee-length charcoal-gray coat, her feet hip-width apart. From what I'd learned about Anjali during our conversations, she was single, didn't have kids, and hadn't taken more than a week's vacation in nearly two years. It hadn't been a complaint. She loved her job, was good at it, and seemed completely in her element standing in Nora's bedroom, gun strapped to her hip, confidently in charge. There was no doubt her instincts and skills were impressive. They just weren't quite good enough.

"We got the forensics back on the stolen van." Anjali's features transformed into an apologetic look. I'd long noticed her facial expressions were more public library than open book, and I hoped for her sake she never played poker. Still, her words filled my veins with curiosity. A little bit of trepidation, too, if I'm being honest.

"What did you find?" I said, trying not to hold my breath as I waited for the answer.

She shook her head. "Nothing helpful, regrettably."

"Nothing?" I said, heart thumping harder. "In the entire van? How?"

"We knew it would be difficult seeing it'd been burned out," Anjali said. "And, unfortunately, the blaze wiped all traces of DNA. There were no usable fingerprints or footprints, either. Not even a stray hair or fiber." She burrowed her hands so deep into her coat, I wondered if her confidence had disappeared, and she was searching for a magic escape route in there. "It pains me to say we're at an impasse when it comes to forensics, and there's no CCTV or any other footage we haven't already combed through."

"And still no witnesses?" Nora whispered.

"No," Anjali said. "Whoever took Michelle knew exactly what they were doing."

"Professionals," Diane said, and the detective agreed.

Nora's voice turned shaky. "How hopeful are you Michelle will come home alive?"

Anjali took a step and waited a moment before answering. "From the start I promised I wouldn't lie," she said. "The fact her abductor didn't show up for the ransom drop can mean many things. Cold feet—"

"You agreed they were pros," I said.

"Yes, but there might have been logistical issues—"

"Logistical?" I snapped. "Michelle isn't a bloody Amazon package. They knew you were there, it's as simple as that. They knew the cops were watching." When Anjali opened her mouth, I continued, "The ransom note made it crystal clear I wasn't to involve you, but *you* insisted. You said you knew what you were doing, and had everything under control."

"Lucas, please." Diane jumped in. "We're all on the same side here."

"Maybe." I pressed my lips together, getting myself back in check. "But what if… What if they *hurt* her because I went against their demands? If I hadn't, she might be here."

Anjali put up a hand. "We can't—"

"It's been thirty-one days since Michelle was taken. *Thirty-one.*" No doubt everyone could hear the rising tension, the waves of frustration in my voice becoming a rolling crescendo, a verbal tsunami on the loose. "Twenty-eight since the ransom drop went wrong for reasons nobody can, will, or wants to explain."

"I understand," Anjali said.

"Do you really? Was the love of your life abducted?"

"No, Lucas. But I promise we're—"

"Working hard?" I let out a bitter laugh. "You've said that so often I've lost count. Meanwhile time's running out for Michelle and for—" I pinched the bridge of my nose, but it was too late. They all knew who I meant. I exhaled and shook my head. "You didn't answer Nora's question. How hopeful are you my wife will come home *alive*? And don't give us some logistical nonsense this time."

Anjali lowered her eyes and as she tilted her head to one side, I prepared myself for the answer I knew was coming. "Given the fact there's been no communication from her abductor, and no demands for four weeks…well, the statistics are against us."

Nora let out a small cry as she sank back onto her pillow, while Diane wrung her hands together so hard, I thought they might burst into flames. I blinked three times, my jaw making tiny sinewy movements as I processed what the detective had said.

"We can't lose hope." Anjali glanced at each of us in turn, pausing as she made direct eye contact. "And yes, I know I've said this before, but finding Michelle is and will remain my top priority. I asked for this case. I fought for it. And you have my word I'll keep on fighting."

"Thank you, Anjali, we're grateful." Nora's disappointment sounded thick enough to spread on toast. "Is there anything else you can tell us?"

"No." Anjali gave her head a small, subdued shake. "I wish I had better news."

Nora raised her chin, her stiff British upper lip rushing to the forefront. Despite my mother-in-law's warm personality, she wasn't one for public displays of emotion, except for the day I'd married Michelle. Not a dry eye in the room back then, including my own, although my mini waterworks display had been for different reasons.

"Diane," Nora said quietly. "Would you mind seeing Detective Dubal out? I need some time alone with Lucas."

Diane hesitated, but after Anjali had said goodbye and we heard them moving down the staircase and into the hallway, Nora looked at me, her face determined. She gestured to the chair next to her and waited for me to sit before speaking again.

"You've always been the perfect son-in-law," she said.

I pulled a face and shifted my body around. "Oh, I don't think—"

"Yes, you have. And you won't know this because you're not a parent, but when you have children you always fret about not making the right decisions. About being too soft or too hard, giving them too much freedom or not enough."

"And hearing them complain no matter what you do?"

"Exactly, and you try to guide them as best you can, but you still feel each and every failure they experience as if it were your own." She paused, catching her breath. "But when you got married I knew I'd done something right. She'd picked a good man. We couldn't have wished for a better choice for Michelle."

"How can you say that?" I let my gaze drop to the floor. "If I hadn't been in England the week she was taken, if I'd been here, or if I hadn't given the police the ransom note, maybe—"

"Don't do this to yourself," she said, her voice surprisingly stern. "Don't you dare spend your time and energy on feeling guilty when I need you to keep pushing the police." She reached for my hand. "Lucas, I need you to do whatever you can to bring Michelle home."

"Of course, I will."

"Whatever it takes. If you need money—"

"I don't, I'm fine." My shoulders slumped and I mumbled, "Financially, anyway."

Nora leaned over a little. "There's something else I have to ask of you."

"Yes?"

"Keep an eye on Travis when I'm gone. He'll lean on you more than ever."

"The spare room is his for as long as he wants or needs."

"And I deeply appreciate it. Believe me, I know how much of a handful my son can be. His relapse is a huge problem, but I need you to watch out for him. Get him back into rehab. Help him recover. He's done it before and I'm counting on you. You'll have access to whatever funds you need—"

"Nora, I don't need money—"

"Maybe not, but Travis will." She paused. "Except I may tell him I'll be donating most of his inheritance to addiction charities if he doesn't seek help again."

My eyes went wide. "Oh?"

"Not all of it, but a good chunk, I think. It's something I talked to Michelle about in confidence a while back, before…" She pressed her lips together and blinked. So did I. My wife hadn't mentioned any of this. "In any case, I don't think I'll leave money to him, not directly. If his recent backslides are anything to go by he might put it up his nose faster than you can say substance abuse." She closed her eyes, her small burst of energy already seeping away, and I waited for her to feel strong enough to continue. "I'm thinking about making you and Michelle administrators of his trust fund and any inheritance. I don't want some anonymous person making decisions about his money if he can't look after it himself, that kind of thing needs to stay in the family. But, Lucas, you and…and Michelle, when she comes home, you must help him. Can I trust you to do this for me?"

"I promise," I said, mind spinning. "You have my word I'll do whatever's best."

She sank back down and sighed. "Thank you, thank you. I knew I could count on you."

"Always. Has Travis been to see you today?"

"No, he hasn't."

Her response didn't come as a surprise. Travis had pretty much bailed on his mother since the diagnosis, and the only thing he did with any reliability or regularity was show up when he needed one thing—her cash. It was good to know he might no longer get his hands on it without going through me first, a problem he couldn't sweet-talk his way out of. Nora's trust fund administrator intentions were perfect and all it had taken were a few nudges to get Travis using, and some subtle hints in my mother-in-law's direction, seeds I'd sown months ago about what she might do if he got back into drugs. I'd said nothing about a charity donation though, and I didn't like the idea. Not one bit.

A bit more small talk with Nora and Diane, and a short while later I left the house, pulling the custom-made ten-foot-high front door closed, not for the first time wondering if its size had something to do with sentiments of male inadequacy Gideon may have harbored.

The cool, crisp November air carried with it the promise of another long winter. Hopefully my last on the East Coast. A year from now if I wanted to be subjected to snow, ice, and ridiculous wind chill temperatures, it would be by choice, and somewhere more exciting. Aspen, Chamonix, Verbier, Whistler. Hell, I'd make my way through the alphabet of best places to ski.

Buoyed by the thoughts of how my not-too-distant future would be, I felt my smile broaden into a full-on chuckle. Snowy holidays of my choosing weren't fantasy, speculation, or wishful thinking. They were a certainty. Soon I'd be able to spend my wife's money on whatever I wanted. Because with what I'd done, I already knew Michelle was never coming home.

3

It took a bit of effort to keep the spring out of my step as I walked to my car, a brand-new Mercedes C-Class Coupe Michelle had surprised me with on my last birthday. It hadn't been a milestone celebration and I'd protested, insisting I was happy with the used Audi I'd bought when I'd arrived in the US a few years earlier. I'd said the new one was too extravagant, the price tag too outrageous, and I'd meant it, but Michelle had thrown her head back and laughed.

"Extravagant and outrageous are what trust funds are for, honey." She pressed the keys firmly into my hands as I tried *very* hard to not think about yet another large sum disappearing from her account, although I'd known it would be one of the last excessive purchases she'd make. My plans had been set in motion at that point. The countdown was on.

"Need I remind you," she continued in her persuasive voice

that brought most of her opponents to their knees, "to never look a gift horse in the mouth, let alone put a bullet in its head? And, well, I haven't been the easiest person to be around lately. Hopefully, this'll make up for it, among all the other things I've got planned…"

She'd slid her arms around my neck as a sly smile played on her heart-shaped lips. It was the kind of embrace I knew would lead us to the bedroom, the back of the sofa, or the kitchen floor. I'd kissed her harder, not only for the promise of sex, which was always spectacular, but also to avoid saying she hadn't been a pain in my arse *lately*, it had been since the day we'd met.

But the car… Holy hell, it was a beast of a machine, and as the door shut now with its heavy metallic clunk, leaving the birthday memories outside to blow away with the winds, I relished the fact of being in a silent and masterfully engineered cocoon alone. After allowing myself a moment of sitting peacefully in Nora's driveway, I fired up the engine and reached into the glove box for the pack of Marlboros I'd stashed in there.

Michelle had detested smoking, said the smell of it turned her stomach, but she'd never known it to be one of my vices, however regularly I partook. I was good at hiding things—my history, true thoughts, emotions, and habits. There were so many things about me my wife had never known.

As I drove out through the Ward family's wrought-iron gates, I drew another satisfying puff, grinning some more as I thought about never again having to wear gloves to mask the smell when I smoked, or listen to Michelle tut-tutting whenever we walked past someone on their cigarette break. With the evil eye she'd insisted on giving them, her head practically doing a one-eighty, it was a wonder none of her victims had turned to stone.

Listen, I didn't *hate* Michelle, and I should probably make that perfectly clear at this point. How could I when she would give me everything I'd ever wanted? Besides, when I was a kid my dad always used to say *hate is a strong word, son*, and there had been more than a few people in my life who conjured up those emotions far more intensely not to mention more quickly than Michelle ever could. No, I didn't *hate* her, but I certainly didn't *like* her very much. To put it mildly, my wife annoyed the bollocks off me.

I'll bet your partner does it to you, too. Or are you really going to pretend when you're in your darkest of dark and private moments, say after another massive row about a continual and baseless jealous streak, the split of household chores, the state of the family finances, or another of the in-laws' backhanded compliments, you've never imagined your other half…*gone*?

Fine, so you might not think about slicing them with a Santoku knife while they sleep, or perhaps you do, in which case who am I to judge? But what about something out of your control? An unfortunate *incident*. Them keeling over from a sudden heart attack at the supermarket, face-planting into the bags of frozen peas. Their car skidding on a deadly patch of black ice and wrapping itself around a century-old oak tree. Maybe your approach is more cartoonish—a piano or an anvil falling from the sky, so it feels less Machiavellian. Either way, all these scenarios would be tragic, but after an adequate period of grieving, you'd be free to continue your life exactly as you please. No more maddening habits to put up with. No idiosyncrasies to grit your teeth through. No ugly divorce with extortionate legal fees and heated arguments about who gets the cat.

Never crossed your mind? Not once? Yeah, that's what I thought.

My wife was a curator for an art gallery in the Back Bay area of Boston. The kind of *über*-pretentious place that hosted elaborate *vernissages* where everyone air-kissed, left hungrier than when they arrived because of the thimble-size canapés, and sipped expensive champagne while pondering what the latest darling of the art world had meant to convey in their abstract pieces. *Gimme yer money*, was the message I typically saw, and the glitzy crowd would happily oblige. They'd boast to one another about how far they'd opened their wallets, and how much their collections had increased in value year-over-year, trying to outdo one another simply for the sport of it.

In contrast, I worked in IT recruitment. Less glamorous, for sure, but still lucrative if you put in the hours. It was equally as boastful, could be a thousand percent more cut-throat, which meant my set of virtual knives always stayed sharp.

I'd been in the business for years. The staff turnover was steep because many people couldn't deal with the rivalry, the deadlines, the frustration of unreliable candidates, and all the flaky HR team leaders. Me? It was an environment in which I thrived. Constantly changing, increasingly difficult. Never boring. Unlike the colleagues I'd left eating the dust *on* my dust, I didn't care about work-life balance, what my employer gave me in terms of flexibility, whether I got free snacks. I was in it for the win, my fiercest competition was my past self, and I excelled.

Michelle never understood why I loved it so much.

When I'd first met her, I'd intended on us being married for quite a while longer, a few years more, at least. Being in a relationship where her money was plentiful and she wasn't afraid to spend it had its advantages, and yet, there were downsides. Receiving lavish gifts ad nauseam was as fun as I'd imagined at first, but the lack of financial control grated on my nerves, as did Michelle's frivolous spending. We'd changed the sofa twice since we'd moved into the house, despite there being nothing wrong with either of them. Their shape and gray hue had been practically identical but according to my wife they *didn't look right*. Then there were the new cars, the jewelry, the expensive meals, and dear God, the *shoes*. How many pairs of identical black heels did one person need? It wasn't as if my wife had spare sets of feet she could parade them around in.

The whole point of putting a ring on her finger had been to ultimately get her cash. I'd initially planned a divorce, but things hadn't worked out that way thanks to an ironclad prenup a pair of meddling hands had convinced her to sign. I'd had to rethink my strategy, mull things over before making a move in a different and less desirable direction. If I hadn't, there may not have been enough money left to bother with.

I'd toyed with getting things started for a while, debating whether I could actually go through with it. Part of me had considered somehow stealing her money and disappearing, but I didn't want to glance over my shoulder for the rest of my life. I wanted to be free. And rich. Not cowering somewhere waiting for the authorities to catch up with me. What I'd done hadn't been a snap decision. I'd spent eons going over a multitude of scenarios, one more outlandish than the next so we wouldn't end up here, but then the pandemic hit, throwing the mother of all accelerants over my plans.

Both Michelle and I worked long hours in separate parts of the city, so when our respective bosses implemented social distancing measures and working from home policies, from the outside it seemed we were so fortunate. Our jobs were secure, home offices already set up, our whirlwind romance the stuff of legends among our small circle of friends, which was made up entirely of people Michelle knew. We were the perfect, adorable couple in which everyone knew my wife wore the trousers and she let me believe I did. Or so they thought.

So, the pandemic was when my patience wore less than razor-thin. Honestly, you spend months on end cooped up in a house with someone you've pretended to love, and it makes you imagine things, lots of things, including the music you'd play at their funeral.

Not that we'd had one for Michelle yet. There was no body to bury and we still had (insert forlorn, shiny puppy-dog eyes) *hope*. As a side note, hell's bells, funerals are expensive, and when we got around to having one whenever she was officially declared dead, I'd have to go all out. Probably get an expensive-yet-empty coffin to give the service some sense of normalcy. There would have to be flowers, and no doubt an elaborately catered wake for her chichi art gallery brigade. It would all be for show, but I could hardly fashion a symbolic container from aluminum foil and plonk flowers from the petrol station on top. Well, I would if I thought I could get away with it.

I finished my smoke and dropped the butt out of the window as I pulled into the cul-de-sac and drove to the last house, which had been a wedding gift from Gideon and Nora. Not my wedding gift because my name wasn't on the deed but Michelle had wanted to live close to them. Not once had she aspired to be anywhere but the leafy suburb of Chelmswood.

My wife had never enjoyed experimenting much outside of the bedroom. Our vacations typically consisted of a week or two at a five-star hotel in the Caribbean where she lay on the beach, snapped her fingers at the waitstaff and worked on her tan while I tried all the sports on offer. She wasn't the exploring, spontaneous type, so my quip about wanting to backpack around Asia and Australia had been met with a snort because she'd thought I was kidding.

"Backpacking?" she'd said, eyebrows raised. "What on earth

for? You'll say you want to stay at bedbug-infested youth hostels next. Gross. Why don't you just kill me now?"

Oh, if only.

Putting fantasies of potential trips on hold, I parked the car in the driveway instead of the three-car garage. Michelle would've complained about that, too. We were the same age, so her teenage years weren't in the long and distant past, yet she seemed to believe, if given half the chance, the local youths would at best key the car, at worst steal it and sell off the parts by sunrise. Never mind the vehicle's fancy anti-theft and tracking systems, the gated community we lived in, or its proud neighborhood watch members who met once a month to gossip over cocktails rather than to discuss the incident rate, because there was none to talk about. It wasn't as if the kids in Chelmswood needed the cash from a boosted car. Most of them were on an Ivy League school list before they were conceived, for God's sake.

I never told Michelle this, but if you'd taken my Merc to my old estate in Manchester, odds were someone would try to nick the wheels while you were still driving. To prove the point to myself, I got out, left the car unlocked and headed to the front door before changing my mind. I'd tempted fate enough in the last little while. Best not become too much of an arrogant bastard about it. Not when there were still so many things to take care of.

4

I walked up the path to our two-story house, a four-bedroom, four-bathroom colonial which, while more than adequate before, had been reimagined and renovated under Michelle's watchful eye and my assumed agreement. The exterior hadn't escaped the magic makeover—*first impressions are so important, honey,* she'd said—and the landscaped path with its expertly clipped Japanese maples standing guard either side a mere prequel to the delights within. A lovely house, if you liked that kind of thing, which I did, especially when I thought about putting it back on the market. At that point, every dollar spent on the renovation would make its way back into my pocket along with another twenty-five percent. I knew a good investment when I saw one—the house…and my wife.

I hoped Travis wouldn't be inside. No lights were on at the front of the house, and his BMW wasn't here, both of which meant nothing. He might have sold the car, lost it on a bet, or hit a taco truck. It wouldn't have been the first time for any of those.

While I'd told Nora her son could stay with me as long as he wanted, it wasn't the truth. My houseguest was on a time limit, one in direct correlation with how much longer his mother had to live. I could only put up with Travis for so long before I'd be searching for a place to hide the body. Kidding, sort of. After all, it wouldn't be the first time I'd *disposed* of someone. However, something happening to Travis when I'd promised to help get him into rehab would shatter my heroic image. He'd relapse again, I'd make sure of it, but it would make me look good if I convinced him to try, and I'd been truthful when I'd told Nora I'd do what was best. What was best for *me*.

And why the hell not? I felt zero obligations to the guy.

Although book smart, Travis was the epitome of lazy, not to mention unreliable these days. A twenty-nine-year-old who, much like Michelle, grew up so steeped in privilege he failed to see it or put it to good use. He used my spare bedroom as it suited, came and went on his own schedule. I dutifully played the supportive brother-in-law when what I really wanted to do was beat him to death with the dirty socks he left lying around. He couldn't even be bothered picking up after himself or washing a cup, because some underling had always done it for him. Wouldn't have surprised me if he'd had a minion hold his cock when he'd taken a leak.

Thankfully, there was no sign of him when I pushed the door open. Not a hint of his acrid aftershave either, which I found particularly unpleasant, but didn't seem to have the same repelling effect on women. Instead, a scrappy furball the size of a small pony bounded up to me, barking, and wagging his tail.

"What's up, Roger?" I said, bending over and patting his giant head.

The dog collapsed on the floor and held up his front paw, his mouth in what can only be described as a ridiculous smirk, tongue hanging out lopsided as he begged for a belly rub. Crouching, I obliged, called him a daft bugger as he licked my hands.

Roger was of indeterminate breed. At a guess I'd have said some of his ancestors were wolfhounds because he had a scraggly scruffiness about him, but whatever his lineage, it had been significantly diluted. I'd seen him hanging around the house the week before Michelle disappeared, spotted him at the end of our garden, which backed onto a ravine. He seemed to need a good scrub, brush, and copious meals, but when Michelle saw me head for the back door with a plate of fake bacon in my hand, she hadn't been impressed.

"Don't you dare. It'll stick around if you feed it. I'm calling animal control."

"Way to roger the dog, Michelle," I'd muttered.

"What?"

"They'll put it down, sweetheart."

She shrugged and clicked her tongue, patted her chin-length blond bob she spent at least half an hour on every morning, straightening and preening every strand. It was naturally wavy, and while I liked it, she loathed it. My wife was stunning, no question, and always had been. A classic beauty from the time she was born. Not a hint of a gangly, puppy fat, braceface, awkward stage when she hit puberty, either. I'd seen the photos.

"Euthanasia is the best thing for it," she said, as she picked up her phone and walked over to give me a peck on the cheek. "I mean, seriously, who on earth would want a mutt like that?"

I looked out the window. The dog sat facing me, his head

to one side and an expression I'd seen countless times when I was growing up and happened to glance in the mirror. The ugly mug of a misfit, a reject. Someone everyone thought was a loser. Someone everybody not only judged but underestimated as well. Someone who'd for the longest time felt unsafe, unworthy, and looked down upon. Not anymore.

"No answer," Michelle said, dropping the phone into her bag. "I'm heading out, but that thing might be sick or have rabies or something, so call animal control. Please? If you do, I'll let you take me to bed early tonight..."

Her kiss was soft and lingering this time. Suggestive. Not that long ago my wife had presented me with a brand-new car and told me to not look a gift horse in the mouth, so no, I didn't call animal control, and yes, I lied about it.

I didn't see the dog for the rest of the week, but within days of Michelle vanishing and my return from England, Roger made a reappearance. It was uncanny, almost as if he'd known she was gone, and the threat of a fatal needle had disappeared along with her. Clever boy.

He'd cleaned up nicely over the past few weeks. A trip to the groomer, another to the vet, a couple of shots and anti-worming stuff. Clean bill of health. Roger was way better company than most humans I knew. More loyal, too, and whenever I felt a sneaky bit of guilt about what I'd done or I found myself missing my wife's companionship in a big house I rattled around in mostly alone, I reminded myself she'd wanted him dead.

"Fancy a walk?" I said to Roger, glad he'd come out on top.

Before I grabbed his leash, he bounded up with a loud bark and not long after we were outside. The street was empty, most of the neighbors already settled in for the evening, flashy cars parked in their driveways—they didn't appear to have as many trust issues as my wife—the lights from their front rooms spilling over their manicured bushes and lawns, casting a golden, lavish glow.

I saw our paper courier, a kid called Katie who always wore a fluorescent yellow beanie, up in the distance. She was a few houses ahead, pulling her newspaper-filled red-and-green trailer behind her so I slowed my pace and hung back, not in the mood for conversation.

From what I knew, Katie was twelve and had delivered the free weekly local newspaper along with bundles of flyers, whatever the weather, for the last two years. Her parents hadn't inherited their fortune like so many others on our street but had earned it by starting up a juice-bar business, which they'd franchised and sold for millions before the pandemic.

At some holiday party I'd overheard them talking about how they were old school, had told Katie she needed to save for college, so she didn't graduate with student debt up to her eyeballs, and she'd decided to get a head start. Michelle thought they were draconian, joked she should call child services which I wouldn't have put past her, but their stance had made sense to me. At Katie's age I'd been making money too, and a lot more of it by the sound of things, primarily by hacking into my teachers' computers, downloading test papers, and selling them for a fiver each. It was a solid business, and I'd never got caught. I'd been too smart, making the papers available on an anonymous website I'd put together in a few hours rather than selling them face-to-face. That had been my first little baby step into the life of a trickster, a career criminal. I may not have made it to university, but I'd always had an entrepreneurial spirit, no matter how I'd chosen to apply it.

I kept on walking, stopping for Roger to have a sniff'n'piss whenever he wanted. For the benefit of the curtain twitchers, when we reached the little parkette on the corner, the one with the yellow curvy slide and a pirate ship, I sat down, hung my head, and covered my eyes with my hands. Anyone watching would think I was crying and attempting to keep my composure. If questioned by the police, they'd no doubt confirm I appeared upset, haggard, and in distress—same as I had been since Michelle had gone missing.

This was without a doubt my biggest, most important performance. As far as everyone else knew, I'd stopped acting when I'd played a donkey in a primary school nativity play when I was ten, and shoved Stevie Pritchard off the stage after the little shit had poked me in the back five times with his plastic sword. The fight had earned me another suspension and had been a turning point. Nobody had witnessed Stevie's actions, and while I wrote *I will not push people* two hundred and fifty times, a task assigned by my father, I'd come to understand I needed to find more cunning and discreet ways to deal with any future problems.

Sitting in the parkette, I knew, this time, my role was more complicated than nodding, braying, and propelling Stevie into the crowd. I had to remain consistent in my portrayal of a man whose partner had been abducted, one who blamed himself for not being able to protect her. Initial suspicions always landed on the husband when the wife went missing, and statistically for good reason. In this case the statistics were accurate, except nobody but me knew the whole story about what had really happened to Michelle, and I intended on keeping it that way.

5

I'm no fool. I knew Detective Anjali Dubal and her colleagues had investigated me, probably still were. They'd crawled through my entire background and financial history while pretending to be on my side. Good luck with that because I knew how this game worked. I'd spent the last decade reinventing myself and covering my tracks, which meant they only saw what I'd left for them to find. I may not have blown out thirty-two candles on a birthday cake that long ago, but I was way ahead of them, and light-years removed from being naïve.

In their eyes, did I have motive to kill Michelle? Everybody told them what a great couple we were. Never fought, rarely disagreed, and I'd never cheated on her. So, on the surface things appeared to be great between us, but what about money? Michelle had far more than I did, so of course this provided motive, one of the strongest there is. Means? Yup. But what about opportunity?

The night Michelle went missing I'd been in England visiting my father. I wasn't even in the US and I'd made sure I had plenty of witnesses over there to prove it, not to mention travel documentation. It wouldn't have been enough of an alibi to convince the authorities I wasn't somehow involved in my wife's disappearance, but the cops had searched through the house and the cars, had gone through our laptops and iPhones and iPads, which I'd all willingly provided, and they'd found nothing. Not a single fissure in the façade of our perfect marriage. I hadn't lawyered up because there was no need. No sense looking like I had something to hide, or lining someone else's pockets with my wife's money, thanks very much.

There'd been a lie detector test I offered to take so they could exclude me and focus on the real criminal, which I passed not so much with flying, but death-defying, trapeze-artist colors. Those machines aren't difficult to mess with providing you know what you're doing.

Then there was the consistency of my story and behavior, which I'd planned and practiced to perfection for months and months. Years. Cops search for patterns, home in on any irregularities but they found none with me. My habits were more regular than a Swiss train. Add on the great relationship I had with Nora, the one I'd allegedly enjoyed with Gideon before his *accident*, the support I provided Travis with, plus all the other small details and gestures I'd carefully planted during the three and a half years Michelle and I had been together… well, there had been nothing for the authorities to go on.

Had the cops suspected me? A hundred percent guarantee I'd landed at the tippy-top of their shit-list. Did I remain suspect numero uno? Not a chance.

"Come on," I said to Roger as I got to my feet, deciding

I'd put on enough of a show for anybody who happened to see us out tonight. "I'm freezing my nads off. Let's go home."

He let out a bark of what I assumed was approval, and as we walked up the road, I looked around, making sure Katie was gone. She was a good kid, but I also had no intention of getting sucked into committing to another half-dozen boxes of Thin Mints and Lemon-Ups. I'd had no trouble munching my way through the last lot and had forced myself to run extra miles to burn the buggers off.

Back at the house, standing on what would soon be referred to as *my* doorstep, I grabbed the bundle of papers Katie had left. Michelle had rarely read this newspaper, and never touched the flyers. Whether things were on sale or not was of no interest to her. If she wanted something, she bought it, not caring about getting it a ton cheaper by waiting a week. I'd once suggested we donate the money saved by using coupons to charity. I didn't think for one minute she'd go for it but the look she'd given me—as if I'd told her to cover herself in honey and walk through bear-infested woods. She'd blinked, and with a laugh said, "I'll write a check like normal people. I don't have the time or energy to scour for deals. I've got better things to do with my life."

My wife's ridiculous spending habits were no longer relevant or important, but as I went inside and hung my coat in the closet, they still bugged me. Clipping coupons and poring over the weekly deals as if they were the holy grail had been my life for years, the only way to ensure I got enough food for Dad and me, and we didn't end up living on the streets again. It was one of the many skills I'd mastered when I was a kid, same as talking my way into bars when I was underage or stealing a pack of smokes for Dad, which had inevitably become mine.

I could still picture the blustery Christmas Eve when we'd

finally moved into the council flat on one of Manchester's dodgiest estates when I was eleven. The air stank of a combination of old fried food and animal pee. Judging by the depth of the scratches in the laminate flooring of the tiny, rank hallway, it looked like the previous tenants might have had a pet lion.

The social worker had shoved the keys into Dad's hand and hurried off, no doubt keen to celebrate the holidays with her family, stuffing her belly full of turkey, roast potatoes, and brandy pudding while I popped down the corner shop for a couple of Pot Noodles. Dad and I had eaten them sitting on the floor of our new kitchen, the one with wobbly, black-and-white checkered cabinet doors that could've triggered an epileptic fit. Some of them hung so precariously, I wondered if they might fall off and crack my toes, so I curled my feet under my arse and tried to remember if we had a screwdriver.

The rest of the flat wasn't in a better state. Mold had crawled up the bedroom walls in an abstract pattern, which Dad proclaimed to be *nothing a bit of bleach can't fix*, and we couldn't open the windows at first because the frames were painted over. But it felt safe, I had my own room for the first time in years, and every night I crossed my fingers and wished for it to be permanent this time. No more dossing in Dad's car or on somebody's sofa, my belongings crammed into a couple of Tesco bags. No more having to put up with classmates pinching their noses and loudly complaining of how I reeked of week-old body odor. As I lay in my bed that first night, I didn't wish for piles of presents to open the next morning. I willed my weeks of sneaking into the school showers and lying about my wet hair being from swim club, an activity we'd never been able to afford, to be over.

The day after we'd moved in, I'd stolen a tiny plastic Christmas tree from a neighbor's front doorstep and fibbed to Dad about finding it in a dumpster. We hadn't spruced the place up much over the holidays, not until my father's next late-night escapade at the pub, which ended with him losing control of his bladder over the carpet in the bathroom. I'd bawled as I'd ripped it up. Cursed as one of the self-adhesive fake tiles I'd bought got stuck on the toilet bowl. Good times they were not, but they'd turned my backbone and determination to platinum. Nowadays I didn't shoplift anymore, but I always popped a couple of bucks into any children's charity donation boxes I came across at the corner stores. My way of making up for past and plentiful misdemeanors. And more recent not-so-*mis*demeanors.

Stepping into my massive Chelmswood hallway, and with Roger on my heels, I checked the house's Ansa phone and my cell for messages, deleted the one from a friend inquiring if I was okay. Over the past weeks I'd signaled I was too distraught to talk and would let everyone know if there were any developments in Michelle's case. Most of them left me alone now. They'd scuttled away from my perceived grief, perhaps thinking it was contagious, relieved to shutter themselves off from what had happened to my wife, and what they imagined I must be going through. And while they were wrong, I hadn't expected to miss Michelle, but I did, at times. Although I'd relished the thought of having the king-size bed to myself, I didn't particularly enjoy sleeping alone, much preferring the warmth of another body next to mine. Had circumstances been different, had *she* been different, I wondered at times if we may have made a proper go of it.

A bit too late for that now.

I meandered to our—*my*—fancy, color-coordinated kitchen, which Michelle had filled with stainless-steel appliances and subway tiles. Stomach rumbling, I opened the fridge and pulled out the leftovers from the vegetable casserole Karina had dropped off a day earlier. I bunged it in the microwave before opening a bag of dog food. Roger sat down behind me, panting, patiently waiting to be fed. I hadn't bothered trying to find out to whom he'd belonged—as far as I was concerned, he was mine. The vet said he'd been well cared for but probably abandoned quite recently, an all-too-common occurrence especially in the run-up to the holidays.

"There you go, mate," I said, putting his bowl down. "Let's dig in."

As I settled at the table to eat, I picked up the flyers, flicking through the offers of new TVs and hot tubs. I rolled my eyes at the price of beef, glad I no longer had to ration the meat intake to once a week, as had been the case when I'd lived with Dad. It had been years since my diet predominantly consisted of fast food because it was cheap. No wonder I'd barely fit into size-XL clothes at age fourteen, tugging at the waistband of my jeans as the sweat flowed south of my back when I walked to school. Downhill. I'd never forgotten one of the popular kids making up a chant about my needing a bra or attempting to shove me into a locker, howling with glee when he couldn't make me fit. I didn't punch him, push his head down the toilet or take a swing at his knees, but swore I'd wait for the perfect opportunity to get revenge. Years later I came across the arrogant wanker in a bar in London. He arrived with his girlfriend. She left with me.

Fork poised midair, I grinned as I caught sight of my reflection in the glass cabinet. How things had changed. *Chiseled* is how I'd once overheard one of Michelle's friends describe me when we were at a party. Michelle had snickered and said, "From top to bottom. *Especially* the bottom."

Damn straight, I was. I'd worked hard for it, spent hours running and doing body weight exercises at the park when I couldn't afford a gym membership, researching the best diets and making every healthy lifestyle change I could. Some of my effort had been to leave the lumpy, spotty kid I'd once been behind. Another part because I needed to make sure I'd never be found. And the rest? Well, because in this superficial world, appearances combined with a certain charm could get you what you wanted—and where you wanted to be—far more quickly, regardless of what anybody said about looks not mattering. I hadn't forgotten where I'd come from, though, or who I'd been. The insecure kid I used to see in the mirror wouldn't let me.

I flicked through another of the flyers, was about to pile them together and stuff them in the recycling bin, making a mental note to take the rubbish out before I went to bed, but as I picked them up, a single, postcard-size advert fluttered to the ground.

Roger, who'd wolfed down his food before I'd taken three bites of mine, lifted his head an inch. His interest waned, and as he rested his chin on his front paws again, I grabbed the card and turned it over. It wasn't a flyer, not a proper one. There wasn't a single word advertising anything, not even a website, social media handle or phone number. Instead, it was a partial black-and-white photo, grainy and indistinct. Abstract, almost. Like some art project my wife would've gone crazy over while I'd stifled a yawn.

There wasn't anything on the back of the card except for the Roman numeral one, scribbled in thick black felt-tip pen. I flipped it frontside again, was about to chuck it in the discard pile when my face contorted itself into a deep grimace. The realization of what I might be seeing crept up my back with long, spindly fingers and whispered in my ear I'd best take another look.

I blinked a few times, hoping I'd imagined it, but I hadn't. The photo was a partial picture of a neck and earlobe, and while I couldn't see any hair, from the shape and curve of the person's jaw I knew it was a woman. Not *any* woman.

Michelle.

6

I stared at the flyer, flipped it around as if I were a magician practicing sleight of hand, pretending I couldn't feel or see the tremble in my fingers. Heart thumping hard, I brought the paper closer to my face before holding it at arm's length, moving it back and forth, trying to decide if it really was my wife's neck and earlobe, or my imagination playing tricks on me.

The earring seemed identical to the set I'd given her last Christmas and I remembered them well because Michelle had dropped hint after unsubtle hint. She'd left a picture of them open on my browser when she'd used my computer under pretext of hers crashing a few times, yet when I'd checked her laptop, I'd found nothing wrong. A week later, Michelle had complimented Karina on her jewelry when we'd crossed paths outside, and then told a story about almost losing one of her earrings in the snow.

This was one of the contradictions about my wife. She was wealthy, smart, and assertive, could've strode into the store and bought a dozen pairs for herself, but she also wanted to be treated, looked after—when it suited, the timing of which was as mysterious as the Bermuda Triangle. No wonder men said they didn't understand women. Kids weren't the only ones who should come with a handbook.

As my wife was used to receiving what she desired, and ever since we'd met I'd made it my primary job to keep her happy no matter how much I grumbled to myself about her wishes, I'd bought the coveted earrings the next day. Basked in her praise Christmas morning when I handed her the elaborately gift-wrapped parcel, letting her believe once again that she'd manipulated me when in fact it had been the other way around. They cost me three and a half grand. Yup. Three and a half large for a pair of sodding diamond Tiffany earrings which, truth be told, weren't too dissimilar from the multiple other sets my wife kept in her overflowing, sparkling jewelry box. I'd bought her a bigger one of those for Christmas, too, without being asked. "For all the things to come," I'd said as I'd kissed her on the lips, cupping her face with my hands and wondering what might happen if I slid them a little farther down, put them around her dainty neck and squeezed.

Michelle hadn't had a clue, but the jewelry was my parting gift of sorts, something I'd reassured myself I could sell later, but after she'd been taken and I hadn't spotted the earrings anywhere around the house, I'd assumed she'd worn them on the night she was abducted, had even referred to it as *sod's law* in my mind as they were now money lost. Yet here they were, or a reminder of them at least, staring up at me from a grainy black-and-white photograph buried in my pack of weekly flyers.

I examined the picture again, trying to work out if it really was Michelle. I was unable to see anything else in the photo, it was too zoomed in and blurry. As I studied it once more, the obvious reality of what I was looking at made my shoulders drop.

Of course this wasn't Michelle. It was my mind being over-active, veering dangerously close to paranoia. I'd been thinking about lying in bed next to her and my brain had gone into overdrive. The flyer was a misprint, a production error, which had somehow made its way into my papers by mistake. Hell, most likely every house on the street had one. It was part of an advert.

"That's settled then," I said. Brushing away any lingering doubts, I tore the misprinted flyer in half and flung it with the rest of the papers into the recycling bin.

I moved to the living room and parked myself on the sofa for the evening, ready to binge on some episodes of a spy series I'd saved because Michelle thought it was rubbish. She had a somewhat unhealthy obsession with true crime stuff instead, which I had naturally pretended to enjoy as much as she did.

My downtime didn't last—the damn flyer continued searing a hole straight through the kitchen cabinet door and into the back of my skull.

I didn't need this. Didn't want a reminder of Michelle's earrings or any other part of her. It was bad enough still having all her belongings in the house, and knowing they'd remain here for a long while. I had no choice but to leave everything exactly how it was for the time being, almost shrine-like, to keep up the pretense of my desperately wishing for her safe return. Everyone would find it uncouth, far too early, not to mention overtly suspicious for me to even consider doing away with her stuff. They all still thought there was a chance she'd be found alive and clung to that hope as it slipped through their fingers, turning to dust. Much like my wife's gorgeous body, I imagined.

Even so, no matter how much I told myself to stop being paranoid about that bloody flyer, thinking of Michelle and still being surrounded by all her things got the better of me. I pushed myself up with a grunt. Roger trotted behind me as I walked back to the expansive kitchen, retrieved the postcard from the bin, grabbed a lighter from the drawer next to the six-burner gas stove, and set the piece of paper on fire in the sink.

As the blackened sides curled, for a moment it made me wonder how my wife had been disposed of. It wasn't something I dwelled on, and while I had the option of knowing exactly where she was, so far, I'd resisted the temptation to find out. Sure, there was some morbid curiosity going on, but the less I knew, the better. My lack of knowledge was part of the reason I'd passed the lie detector test, and I had no intention of getting caught because I didn't follow the strict rules I'd set myself from the beginning.

Some may wonder, if I didn't know where Michelle's body was and had been out of the country the day she'd been abducted, how I killed her. I didn't. Not directly. The saying about not bothering to bark yourself when you have a dog? I got a dog, and I don't mean Roger.

It's surprising how easy it is to find someone willing to make another human being disappear. Relatively inexpensive, which isn't as astounding as it should be terrifying. Warning: this fact may cause some sleepless nights, but right now, the disgruntled colleague who was so sure they'd get the big promotion that went to you, the short-tempered ex you abandoned for a better suitor, even the neighbor you're having heated arguments with about who'll pay for the repairs to the fence separating your properties—every single one of them could be plotting your demise for a few grand, maybe less, and those are only the ones you can list off the top of your head.

Would they do it themselves? Probably not, but that doesn't mean they can't find someone who will. These are desperate times for many, which leads some to be willing to do almost anything for a bit of cash, including eliminating another person's nemesis. Although, to be fair, I never saw Michelle as such. Yes, it's crude, but she was my meal ticket, a means to an end, the Golden Goose, and all those other clichés. It wasn't personal. It was business. When she, quite literally, stumbled into my life one evening it took no time at all to know she was the one I'd been waiting for, but not for the reasons I led her to believe.

We met at an art gallery on an abnormally hot end-of-May evening. A private party in London I'd wangled my way into. It had been a spur-of-the-moment thing as I'd walked past the building, watching two men wearing well-tailored suits and white gloves at the front door take black-and-gold invitations from the guests. The cards seemed posh, expensive, and I fancied myself a challenge. I was well-dressed and hungry, so I decided I'd go inside and sample whatever was on offer. I had nothing better to do, and pretending to be someone else, making up a persona on the fly, was always good for a laugh. I enjoyed seeing how far I could push it, how much I could get away with. When you said something with conviction and a straight face, it was incredible how gullible people could be. With excitement building in my stomach, I headed to the back of the short line.

A willowy woman in front of me, who wore a spaghetti-strap, curve-skimming, emerald-green silk cocktail dress, was having a hushed argument with her partner, a broad man who suffered from a bad case of dandruff. He'd taken off his suit jacket and slung it over his shoulder, the telltale corner of the black-and-gold invitations peeking out of the pocket. Within a heartbeat, one of the thick cards had disappeared into my hand, and I slid it inside my own jacket. Neither of them noticed. They were too busy arguing about who should be allowed to booze it up seeing as they'd driven here because Emerald had arrived home late from work, and Dandruff had forgotten to pick up the babysitter. As we neared the front of the line, I waved a couple of new arrivals ahead of me, insisting they take my place while I waited for my *plus-one*. In contrast, Emerald and Dandruff held everybody up.

"You told me you had both invitations," she said, her voice rising.

Face turning red, Dandruff dug his hands into his pockets. "I did."

"Well, obviously you don't. Did you leave the other one in the car?"

"I don't know. Maybe."

"God, honestly. I told you I should've put them in my bag."

"You couldn't fit a stamp in that thing," Dandruff grumbled, turning his attention to one of the white-gloved men at the front door. "Our names will be on the guest list. Look them up, would you, old chap?"

"I'm afraid we must have the invitations to—"

"Excuse me? Now listen here. I'm—"

"Oh, for goodness' sake, don't make a scene, people are waiting." Emerald pushed Dandruff away from the entrance. "Run to the car and I'll wait here. I'm not walking there and back again in these heels."

Not long after, I was inside the gallery where I slid the invitation into another man's blazer in case anyone happened to check, and made my way further into the dimly lit room. The exhibit consisted of framed sketches of people in various states of undress playing sports, and abstract wire sculptures set on top of gilded columns. I wandered from item to item, taking a flute of champagne from one waiter, and a perfect square of bruschetta from another, neither the bubbly nor the food particularly satisfying.

I'd almost reached the end of the room when I saw her. A woman wearing a long scarlet dress, her blond hair smoothed back and tied in a small knot in the crook of her neck. She stood surrounded by a gaggle of people, mostly men, all of them guffawing loudly at something she'd said. Intuition and experience told me she had money and I wondered who she was. A celebrity, maybe, the latest darling of the film world, perhaps. Gorgeous. Definitely wealthy.

I made my way around the outside of the exhibition, inched closer to the woman in red. When I got within earshot, I noticed she had an American accent. It wasn't pronounced enough for me to tell from which part. Despite being a US citizen by birth—my mother and father were visiting the Grand Canyon when I made an impromptu arrival eight weeks early—I'd only ever been to New York for a few days.

I moved toward the group, observed her a little longer, watched as she threw her head back and laughed, her eyes sparkling when she spoke, and the way she leaned in when she listened to whomever was talking, making them the center of attention. I wondered if she worked in sales, thought she should, because she'd be a natural, until I saw her take a beverage from the tray one of the servers held toward her. She removed the glass without as much as a glance his way or a word of thanks but continued the conversation with her admirers as if it were her God-given right to be waited on, and whoever did so was invisible. I added *entitled* to my description of this woman, an important trait to be aware of when you're already thinking of how to manipulate someone.

Looking closer, I noticed the set of freckles on her left

shoulder, shaped like a kite, decided I'd tell her they resembled a diamond but wouldn't make it cheesy. She didn't seem the type who'd fall for flattery so easily. This lady would require work.

She was my challenge.

If she happened to be in the UK on holiday or a business trip, I knew she'd be a much simpler mark. Tourists and out-of-town suits, I found, were far more open to one-night stands than the locals. Less risk of bumping into them again, which was better for the both of us.

Was this woman married? She didn't have a ring on her finger, which didn't mean much. If she had a spouse or partner it would complicate things in one way but make them easier in another. I'd targeted several wealthy married women in the past, and they'd usually been the ones to first suggest falling into bed. Before the next morning I'd be gone, and they woke up to find I'd disappeared along with their cash, valuables, or both. I always got away with it. They were hardly going to alert the police if it meant admitting to their partner they'd had an affair. I never stole enough for it to make sense for them to destroy their relationship by confessing they'd been unfaithful, and had been played.

I continued studying the woman in red, hoping this might be more of an opportunity than making a quick buck. For a while now I'd been thinking about a different plan, one to set me up for life, and which would allow me to take care of Dad properly. He'd been in long-term care after suffering from—or, more accurately, being made to have—a massive stroke a few years before, and I'd recently read about experimental treatments, which would be coming on the market at some point in the future. Expensive therapies that cost hundreds of thousands of dollars and which would only be available in clinics in Switzerland and Singapore weren't something I'd be able to afford from the money I was making in recruitment and my illicit side hustles. If I wanted to secure a better future for my father, I needed to find someone with money. A ton of it. The mother-fucking-lode.

When I heard the woman excuse herself and head to the bathroom, I grabbed a full flute of champagne and stopped around the corner, pretending to admire one of the exhibits. As she came back into the room and was about to walk past me, I took a step back. She slammed straight into me, spilling the cold liquid down the front of my shirt.

Within minutes of a profuse apology (mine, not hers) we were locked in conversation, her other suitors sulking and long forgotten once I'd passed what I identified as her *is he worth talking to* test. That fun ten minutes consisted of a thinly veiled investigation into my pedigree—where my family was from, what and where I'd studied, and what I did for a living. It felt like a classist cross-examination rather than a normal exchange of pleasantries, but I made sure to be the perfect candidate. Told her exactly what she wanted to hear and sank my carefully baited hooks deep into her moneyed pockets.

Later that night, as Michelle and I lay naked in her hotel room, her head resting on my chest, I solidified my plans on how I'd marry her, divorce her because I had no intention of being tied down, and get a large chunk of cash in the settlement. Earlier in the evening, as I'd traced the outline of her diamond-shaped freckles with my fingertip, she'd told me our meeting at the art gallery had been serendipitous. To this day, it was one of the only things we'd agreed on.

7

No matter how much you dislike a person and want them gone, finding someone to do the job isn't something to be rushed. Well, I suppose it can be, and impatience is the prerogative of whoever's footing the bill, but it's also synonymous with stupid. You may save a few bucks if you pick your killer-for-hire off the street, but what's the point when they'll get caught and rat you out faster than you can say *jumpsuit*? Whoever doesn't put the proper amount of time and effort into their research to find the best person for the job had better ask themselves if their complexion looks good in orange.

I'd started this journey on the dark web. A largely nasty, despicable place for all kinds of nefarious deeds and supplies. Drugs, weapons, computer viruses, hard-core pornography, and human trafficking. It's not somewhere anyone in their right mind wants to spend even a little bit of time, but I'd needed to go in deep.

The dark web wasn't the only thing I'd learned to navigate. Most people are aware of digital and hard-to-trace crypto-currencies unless they've been living under a rock. Not that I'd have blamed anyone for avoiding the news in recent years because most of it had been depressing as shit. Anyway, put the dark web and crypto-cash together and not only did you have illicit resources at your disposal, but also anonymity, providing you had the guts and willingness to decipher how it all worked. And the wiliness to not get caught.

It wasn't easy. As I said, there are plenty of whack jobs ready to do your dirty work, but my choice had to be infallible, the selection process meticulous and precisely thought out, picked over, examined, and quadruple tested. Nobody wants to hire a fuck-up. When I thought about it, searching for a hit man was an extreme form of recruitment. We might not have been talking about skill sets that included in-depth knowledge of Sarbanes-Oxley, experience in SAAS, or someone who was fluent in Mandarin, but the principles of finding the best person for the job were identical. Turned out my work experience truly was versatile.

Still, it took months and months of meticulous planning, detailed screening, and encrypted chats and messaging, working my way from one lead on one message board to another, and I was more than a little surprised to see the dark web had a rating system similar to eBay's with positive and negative feedback for buyers and suppliers alike. Plus, it did a fairly good job of blacklisting anyone who'd been exposed as law enforcement. Every little bit helped. I couldn't be too careful.

All my research was carried out miles away from home, on a laptop I'd paid for in cash almost a year prior to starting my search, when I'd visited the UK. Since then, I'd stored the device in a locker at a bus station where CCTV was nonexistent. Reduced budgets in small towns carried consequences, which I used fully to my advantage. I'd picked up a few burner phones, and only ever used each one once. A voice-altering gizmo was added to my arsenal, but it wasn't enough. On the rare occasions I talked to anyone, which was as little as possible, I spoke with a different cadence, put on an array of convincing accents, varied my tone, and never used British slang.

I knew technology, as great as it is in so many ways, could also be my downfall. It's everywhere—there are cameras all over the place, watching our every move. We think we're avoiding them until someone snaps an innocent selfie and bang, our face is in the background in a place we claimed never to have visited, and don't get me started on facial recognition software. This was where disguises came in handy. Whenever I picked up a new burner phone, or when I went to the bus station, I wore different clothes and hats. The odd wig. A fake sleeve tattoo, or a water-soluble one—things easy to get rid of because I couldn't leave them in the house for the cops or Michelle to find before she went missing.

The last piece of my duplicity was walking a little differently, changing the way I moved to consciously modify my gait. Not as easy as it sounds.

All this effort was to stay miles ahead of anyone looking in my direction, cover my tracks (better still, not leave any), and reminded me to never, ever be in a hurry. Speed breeds carelessness. Show me a prison, and I'll show you a bunch of people who should've been less impulsive. And so, I took my time as I went through the hit-man selection process. Wheedled out the show-offs and the cons from my list of potentials. Those were most of the interactions, to be honest. Many people were voyeurs or all mouth and no trousers, as they say, so it took me a long while before I'd whittled it down to the perfect killer: W00ds47, who I simply called *Woods*.

Woods had no idea who I was, and vice versa. I didn't know their gender, not that it mattered. What I needed was the best person for the job. The payment, half up-front, half upon completion, had been made in an obscure cryptocurrency from some funds I'd stashed away well before Michelle and I met. Although it had increased multiple-fold in value, unfortunately it was only a fraction as much as Bitcoin had soared, but it was something the tax authorities had no knowledge of. Enough to cover the fee, which was high, but still less than the cost of the Mercedes Michelle bought me.

I'd left the details of the day of the week, time, and place the task would be carried out entirely up to Woods, but I'd made the rest of the instructions crystal clear. Make it seem like an abduction. Ensure Michelle's passing was swift and painless. I may have been after her money, but I wasn't a complete monster.

Why go to all this trouble when I could've arranged an accident for my wife instead? Maybe a hit-and-run, a tumble down a flight of steep stairs, an unfortunate drowning or that piano falling from the sky (kidding, that one's incredibly complicated to pull off—it's all in the timing). Anything that concluded with the discovery of her body.

Why not one of those? *Optics*.

Like I said, I knew from the beginning I'd be suspect number one. Not only did I have to make sure they could never prove it, but I also wanted their doubts about me to fade and disappear. Michelle had been abducted, but her body would never turn up. It could take years before she was officially declared dead, which meant a long time before I'd inherit her money.

Most individuals who are after their partner's cash aren't willing to wait. They get greedy and impatient. They think they can increase their spouse's life insurance policy one week, shove 'em off a cliff the next, and get away with it. Not me. I kept my eye on the horizon and worked my way there in slow, meticulous fashion, dealt with any surprises that came my way.

For example, when I'd made my plans for Michelle, I'd hedged my bets on Nora leaving a small part of her fortune to me at some point, although I'd imagined my mother-in-law living to a much older age. I never had plans to hurt Nora, like I said, I *liked* her, and I'd therefore regarded any of her cash a future tidy bonus, and not something I'd rely on. Before her cancer diagnosis, I'd had no clue I'd suddenly be looking at another large inheritance. Actually, when Gideon died, I'd hoped Nora would meet someone who'd appreciate her, but now she'd unfortunately pass before Michelle was declared dead, and half of her money would go to my wife. And if Travis happened to meet his maker not long after Nora, then my still missing spouse would inherit all his cash. A triple whammy that would eventually flow to me.

Good things come to those who wait was a total pile of crap. Good things come to those who make them happen…and then wait for the payoff. Mine was on its way.

8

I stood at the kitchen sink, staring at the charred remains of the misprinted flyer. The paper had long turned to ash and I washed the flaky pieces down the drain. Decided I had to stop worrying about the bizarre misprint that had ended up on my doorstep. Even if it wasn't a production error but a proper photograph of someone, plenty of other people had those earrings. When I thought about it, the picture could've been of anyone with pockets deep enough to shop at Tiffany's, which meant almost everyone in our neighborhood alone.

I pulled my shoulder blades together and stretched. There was nothing to worry about, I was on course, and however long it took to obtain my wife's official death certificate, it would be time well spent playing the grieving husband. I assumed Detective Anjali Dubal had long subpoenaed my phone records, tapped my cell and home line if they'd got the FBI involved—which they told me they hadn't—and had maybe followed me for a while.

I imagined them digging through my recycling and rubbish bags in the middle of the night, hoping to find evidence of some kind, maybe the telltale signs of a mistress, or that Michelle had a lover. Not a chance. I'd been faithful and so had she. I wanted Michelle's money, and I'd never been stupid enough to risk it by sleeping around. Anyway, and as I said before, there was nothing wrong with our sex life, and cheating on her as well as planning her death really would've taken my arseholery to a whole other level.

After pouring myself a gin and tonic I watched some TV, the clear liquid swimming around my gut and warming my insides. Half an hour later, and the booze had done little to rid me of my remaining jitters. I wished I hadn't burned the flyer now, so I could take another look. I could've compared the angle of the chin to another photo of Michelle, held up a pair of different earrings she still had in her jewelry box in the walk-in wardrobe upstairs. I let out a snort. Walk-in? More of a send-a-search-party-if-you-don't-see-me-in-an-hour affair. The bloody thing was gargantuan.

I went to the front room and kept the lights off as I glanced at Diane and Karina's driveway. Diane's car wasn't there but I saw Karina walk down the path, a bundle of newspapers in hand. She threw them into the recycling bin and made her way back to her front door.

"Fancy another airing?" I said to Roger. He let out a whine and rolled on his side. "Come on, lazybones, I need you. Let's go."

After I'd dumped our bins on the curb, we walked toward the parkette but doubled back seventy-five yards in. Roger made up for his less than enthusiastic start by yanking on his leash to chase a squirrel, and as we approached my house again, I stuck my nose in my phone, set myself on a direct collision course with Diane and Karina's recycling containers, and knocked two of them over.

Loudly chastising my apparent clumsiness, I bent over to pick up the bottles, cans and papers strewn across the sidewalk. Karina had flung the newspaper and flyers on top, hadn't even taken off the blue elastic band holding them together, which I swiftly removed, letting the flyers flutter to the ground.

I searched through the papers as I picked them up, shaking them out to see if the same grainy postcard had made its way into their pack. If I found one, I'd immediately walk back inside my house and let this whole thing go. Maybe I'd allow myself to sleep for a whole five hours instead of the usual four. Not that I had much trouble staying asleep, but I always set my old-fashioned alarm clock with the Superman logo—a gift from my father and the only possession I'd kept from my childhood—to the early hours of the morning. It wouldn't do to appear well rested when my wife was missing. I needed those dark circles and puffy bags under my eyes to maintain the illusion I cared as much as people thought I did.

I heard a door open and saw Karina come back out of her house and walk to me. She wore a pair of plaid pajama bottoms and a T-shirt with a picture of Ripley from *Alien*, and as she came closer, she wrapped her green cardigan around her middle.

Karina was originally from South Africa, had a job as a jet-setting movie and celebrity makeup artist. After training with the best, she'd worked with the best and had become the best. Over the past decade and a half, she'd made a fortune because her expertise was in such demand and she had clients willing to pay enormous sums for it. She was a smart and savvy businesswoman, and I admired her greatly for it, liked her even more when I once overheard her saying my wife could be *a bit of a Karen*. Not quite sure how Karina had ended up in Boston. An ex-partner or something, I think, then she'd met Diane on a blind date. Love at first sight.

"Brr, it's chilly," she said, in her distinctive husky voice, bending over to give Roger a pat. "I saw you from the house. Is everything all right?"

I stuffed my hands into my pockets, rocked on my heels and did the head bob thing, the universal message for *I'm okay*. "Knocked over your bins," I said, rolling my eyes in a self-deprecating way. "Wasn't looking where I was going."

"Here, let me help." Karina reached for the last two flyers and tossed them on top of the others, but neither of them was what I wanted. "Diane sent a text. Told me the detective stopped by Nora's. I gather there are still no leads."

I closed my eyes for a beat. "No. Nothing."

"If there's anything we can do…"

"I wish there was, but you and Diane have been incredible." I meant it. Their generosity and empathy after Michelle went missing had been extraordinary. Food, company, comfort. They'd returned some library books for me and had suggested they take care of Roger when I took him in, should I be too busy, and I knew neither of them was keen on dogs. In a strange way it made me think some small sense of universal balance had been restored. Their omnipotent kindness counteracting my darkest deeds.

"You've done plenty," I said. "Thank you."

Karina waved a hand. "I don't think we've done enough."

"You have." I gave her another head bob. "How's work?" I said, because good neighbors ask that kind of thing. "Weren't you supposed to be in France or somewhere?"

"Monaco, which would've been lovely this time of year, but the film schedule got delayed. Clooney broke his ankle, poor guy."

"Uh-oh."

"Don't repeat this but frankly, I'm glad for the time off. Stay home for a few weeks and see Diane, do some cooking.

Speaking of, I'd best get inside. I'm browning some onions for a cottage pie and don't want them to burn. I'll bring some over for you. It's vegan."

At the mere mention of gravy and potatoes, my stomach rumbled. I'd made myself drop ten pounds since Michelle disappeared and, Christ almighty, I was sick to death of nibbling on lettuce and apples like an oversize rabbit. Still, the image of the black-and-white flyer flashed in my mind—a warning sign from my deceased wife, a reminder not to get complacent. The show wasn't over yet.

I hung my head. "Thanks, but my appetite isn't what it used to be."

"I understand. You can always pop it in the freezer."

As she walked to her front door I stood there, watching until she'd disappeared inside her house. When I turned, I noticed the side gate leading to my back garden was a few inches ajar. I frowned, certain it had been closed when I'd pulled up in the Mercedes earlier in the evening. Sometimes the wind blew the gate open if it wasn't latched properly, except the air was calm, not a hint of a breeze. I walked over and pushed the gate open the rest of the way, peering down the path and into the blackness, searching for movement.

The garden was ninety feet deep, and I couldn't make out the tree line from where I stood. With the flashlight on my phone and Roger by my side, I made my way to the back of the house and onto the wooden deck, tripping the motion-activated lights. I let my gaze sweep from left to right, scanning the entire garden. That's when I saw it. Trampled-down grass in the shape of footsteps leading all the way from the trees, and down the left side of my fence, straight to the gate. A prickle zipped up the back of my neck, making every single hair stand on end.

Someone had been at the house. Somebody was watching.

9

A minute later I was inside the house with Roger. While I hadn't noticed anyone resembling a cop or any other kind of investigator outside, and no random cars were parked on the road, it didn't mean they weren't out there. In case someone was trying to spy on me through the window, I stabbed a finger at the buttons for the automatic living room blinds and heavy silk curtains, urging them to go faster, wishing I could yank them closed by hand instead.

Being vigilant was paramount to my plan but apparently, I may not have been careful enough. Among other preparations, I'd kept tabs on the comings and goings of cars on this street for months before going ahead with the hit on Michelle, memorizing vehicle makes, models, and number plates to distinguish visitors from regulars. With it being a cul-de-sac, it wasn't difficult to do, especially since I had a real knack for visual memorization. I'd boosted the ability with other techniques I'd found on the web. It was incredible how much information you could retain if you were willing to put in a bit of effort, except none of it helped answer the question of who the hell had traipsed across my grass.

Perhaps it had been a hiker who'd taken a shortcut out of the ravine, it had happened before, but I couldn't help thinking those weren't the boot prints of someone with blisters hopping a fence. Over the past week or so I'd been quietly confident the cops were now entirely focused on finding the stranger who'd taken Michelle. At the beginning, Anjali had always come to see me with at least one other officer, but now when she visited, she came alone, a sure sign she didn't see me as a potential threat. Still, I couldn't exclude them from potentially creeping around the outside of my house.

Maybe someone from the life insurance company had come snooping. However unlikely it was at this early stage of the game, some bright-eyed-and-bushy-tailed prat might have tried to stick their nose where it didn't belong. No matter because they'd be sorely disappointed. They'd find the policy was a generous two million, but when Michelle and I got married we'd taken out an equal amount and had listed each other as sole beneficiaries, something she'd always believed had been her initiative. Actually, she'd suggested five, and I'd told her it was too high. A mistake, but in my defense at the time I'd thought of divorce, not murder. In any event, my wife hadn't been declared dead, so there was no reason for me to make a policy claim yet but that didn't mean those sneaky insurance investigators weren't on the prowl.

Michelle's abduction had been all over the local news. If the insurers' interest hadn't been piqued by the on-air reports, alarm bells may have gone off when the cops had spoken to them, which I presumed they had if they were remotely good at their jobs. Those discussions would've led to another unsuccessful fact-finding expedition. I wasn't in a hurry to cash in the policy. The insurance would need Michelle's death certificate before they released the funds. That wouldn't happen until the courts were petitioned, and I'd make sure *that* wouldn't be the case for ages, not until I felt certain all suspicions directed at me had long vanished. The only thing able to change those plans was if Michelle's body was discovered, which Woods had assured me would never happen.

Whoever Woods was, I admired his handiwork and methodology. Structured, thorough, and precisely planned. Not much of a sense of humor though. When I'd asked him if he had a satisfaction guaranteed refund policy he hadn't been amused. The recruiter in me couldn't help wondering if he disposed of people full-time or as a side hustle, and if it was the latter, what his regular job was. My bet was on something highly detail-oriented, organized, and painfully boring. Accounting or risk management, maybe. I imagined him lining up his pens in a straight row on his desk every morning. He probably didn't start work until he'd had a coffee and an acceptable bowel movement.

Whatever his occupation, Woods was resourceful, introducing me to an app called *what3words*. It's simple enough: a map of the world broken down into nine-foot-by-nine-foot squares. Each square was assigned three random words corresponding to the exact geographical location of said square. Think GPS coordinates but way easier to remember, especially when under duress. Lost hikers have been found thanks to the app, and the lives of crash victims saved because rescuers located them more quickly. Clever stuff, although Woods and I used it for less noble things. Okay, despicable, wicked ones.

I'd sent Woods the details of where the target lived via the app (making sure he didn't think the victim was me, which would've been quite the balls-up), and he gave me the location of the body once things had been taken care of. I committed the three words to memory and highlighted them in one of Michelle's novels, just in case. The less I knew, the better. I didn't often adhere to the ignorance is bliss adage, but I couldn't argue this time.

Truthfully, I hadn't known what to expect when I got on the plane to visit Dad in England. All I knew was by the time I returned to Boston, Michelle would be gone forever, and I had a few gin and tonics on the flight to bid her farewell. Four days into my trip, and my wife was no longer answering her phone. I made a point of calling her every day whenever either of us traveled, which wasn't often for me, but quite regular for her, and as soon as I woke up, I sent her the same message.

Good morning, Sunshine!

I added two sun emojis—his'n'hers—had done so forever. I thought it was tacky as hell, she and her friends thought it was adorable, so I kept sending them. Michelle usually responded with hearts and a smiley face, but there was a time difference of five hours, so I didn't expect a reply straightaway. When she hadn't responded by 8:00 a.m. Eastern Time, little wings of freedom flapped in my chest. I sent another message two hours later, my excitement building.

Hey Sweetheart. Everything okay?

Nothing.
I waited a little while before calling the art gallery. Michelle's assistant told me they hadn't heard from her either and had been debating whether to phone me.

"Yes, you should've," I snapped, lacing my voice with worry.

Missing work wasn't Michelle's style. She was hugely proud of not having taken a sick day for years, going in with a heavy cold on one pre-pandemic occasion despite my concerned husband stance of insisting she stay home. She wasn't bothered about spreading her germs to everybody else, including those who didn't have medical benefits.

"I can't give them an excuse for slacking off, I have to lead by example," she told me once, eyes red and nose running. No matter what I said, it hadn't changed her mind. Michelle thought it made her look like a trooper when she set off for the gallery, even when she sounded as if she might cough up a lung, so it was highly doubtful she was wrapped up in a duvet at home, sipping honeyed tea. Something had happened.

I wondered if she'd had car trouble. Broken down by the side of the road somewhere, but she'd have answered my texts and let work know she was running late. There was no chance of her deciding to take a day off without telling her assistant. It was something else she'd placed near the top of her list of seven deadly office sins. I'd never forgotten how she'd once told me she'd fired someone for printing flyers at the office. For a multiple sclerosis fundraiser.

"She should've asked first," Michelle said. "It's the company rule. Give them an inch and they'll take fifty miles. You know how it goes. People should know their place and stay in it."

People think I'm cold. In comparison, my wife could be downright glacial. I bet a few people at her work breathed a sigh of relief when she disappeared. If you look at it that way, I did them a favor, too. Ding, dong, the bitch is gone, and all that.

I won't lie, after speaking to her colleague, both my exhilaration and nerves escalated. Choosing to be in the UK while

Woods did his job had been the best decision. Not only did it give me an ironclad alibi, but also time to practice my reactions now the plans seemed underway. My messages on Michelle's voice mail became increasingly frantic, and I had no doubt they sounded genuine because I was desperate to know with absolute certainty she was gone.

There had still been one call to take care of, and I'd known this one would make my gut contract. Nora. My mother-in-law didn't deserve what was about to happen to her and a little guilt crept in, but my father's needs were more important and so I brushed the feeling away. I guess if my wife was glacial, I was Antarctica pre–global warming.

"What do you mean she's not answering her calls?" Nora said as soon as I phoned. "We spoke last night. She was heading to a Zumba class. What's going on?"

"I… I don't know where she is," I said, as one of my burner phones buzzed with an incoming text from a private number. I stared at the three random words accompanied by a single picture. My wife, lying on her back, clothed, face drained of color, eyes closed, her head surrounded by leaves. Woods had fulfilled his end of the bargain.

It's hard to explain what I felt. Guilt, certainly, followed by an undeniable rush of relief mixed with panic. After all, I'd planned this for so long, but I immediately questioned whether Woods had done a good enough job. Yes, I'd done my research. No, this wasn't his first time (quote) *conducting this kind of business*, but humans are fallible, things get miscalculated, errors are made, and his part was entirely out of my control—and I didn't like not being in control.

"Lucas?" Nora said. Her voice had traveled down the phone line, snapping me out of my thoughts. "Are you there?"

"I don't know what's going on but I'm calling the cops." My voice had trembled as I understood the rest of my plans had to be set in motion. No going back now, no matter how I felt. "And then I'm getting on the first plane back to Boston."

Unsurprisingly, the police didn't take the case seriously at first. We were told adults go missing all the time, many of them by choice. A lot of bad stuff happens in the Boston area, and investigative resources are stretched thin, but when Michelle's abandoned car was located in the parking lot near the fitness studio, their curiosity bloomed.

Inquiries were made, security footage scrutinized, and when Detective Anjali sat Nora, Travis, and me down in a room and showed us the footage of a masked person bundling Michelle into a dark, unmarked van, well, let's say we were all surprised. I'd rehearsed my reaction as much as possible, but although I'd coordinated it, knowing this was the last time I'd see my wife was, I don't know, *odd*.

Three days after she went missing, a ransom note arrived, which, along with a day, time, and location, said:

It was one of those old-fashioned notes made up of cut-out words and letters from newspapers and magazines, like the ones they had in the classic '80s movies I'd watched with Dad when I was a kid. You don't see that kind anymore, it's almost a lost art, so I'd taken my time to construct one months before I put it to use. Dad always said they seemed so ominous and making it had given me a sense of nostalgia. I threw out all the supplies I'd used, and which I'd bought new and kept away from the house. Dumped them in different bins outside various schools so they wouldn't seem out of place with the other discarded art project materials. Same with the pack of envelopes, of which I used only one. It was a generic brand you could buy anywhere. Something nobody could ever trace.

Half a million bucks for Michelle's safe return seemed reasonable. A decent but not ridiculous sum, and one which wouldn't take Nora and me days to come up with.

"We have to tell the police," she begged, despite the note clearly stating not to involve them, and after I put up a decent fight, I gave in.

Unfortunately, the *abductor* never showed, had been incommunicado ever since, and the argument whether the note had been genuine, the cops had scared off the kidnapper or something terrible had happened to Michelle before the exchange could be made raged on. Either way, the money, which Nora had insisted she withdraw in cash from one of her savings accounts, was safely returned. No financial harm done to anyone. I took some comfort in that.

Now, almost a month later, no further ransom demands had been made. Nor would they. I'd made the second crypto payment to Woods after he'd sent me the photo of Michelle on the burner phone. The deal was done, our business concluded. We'd never cross paths again unless he got caught, in which case he still wasn't a threat. Woods could spill his guts all over the police station floor, the investigation into who'd hired him could continue, I might even unofficially become more of a suspect again, but they'd never link anything back to me. I'd play the part of the innocent, shocked and grieving husband perfectly for all to see, sit in the audience while attending his trial and watch him being sent down for a murder he had indeed committed. Perhaps it wouldn't be a bad thing.

My intention had always been to get rid of one person. Sure, circumstances had caused my plans to change but I was hardly a serial killer. Woods, on the other hand, made a living from it. The thought made me wonder…had he come to spy on me at the house? Snoop on his victim's grieving spouse for some bizarre kicks?

We didn't have any security footage I could check to identify my trespasser. This was entirely my fault because I thought those private surveillance cameras were a nuisance, a double-edged sword. Michelle had wanted a set for the driveway when she'd bought me the Mercedes. I'd kept putting her off, promising I'd take care of it, stalling and delaying for as long as I possibly could, showing her my research periodically as I allegedly debated the best options. The thing was, cameras didn't only record what others were doing, but everything their owners were up to, as well. People didn't seem to think about that when they installed them, but I had. Hence no video recording, a decision which had come back to take a sizable bite out of my arse.

I tried to ignore the uncomfortable sensation sneaking its way into the pit of my stomach, but it sat there, refusing to budge. The flyer and the footprints in my garden were a combination I didn't like. One that spelled trouble.

MONDAY

10

When Roger let out a loud yawn and stretched, I glanced at the time. A few minutes after midnight, and much as I'd have loved to follow the dog's example and crash for the night, my nervous energy didn't agree. Not such a bad thing. I needed to stay up a little while to continue looking like crap. I'd found one way to ensure I didn't fall asleep was working out, and the fact I'd become slightly addicted to keeping fit in recent years was a definite advantage.

It hadn't been until I'd fled Manchester and moved to London ten years prior that I'd started losing weight. At first it had been without trying. I couldn't always afford public transport, so I'd walked everywhere, slowly dropping a noticeable number of pounds. I had to invest in a belt, didn't sweat as profusely, and as I'd walked to work one morning, and passed a group of people running, I vowed in the not-too-distant future

I'd be able to do the same. I swear I almost had a heart attack the first time I gave it a go, but in time it had gone from a near-death experience to jog twenty yards, to my comfortably running six miles five days a week for most of the year, never mind my cigarette habit. Although not in Chelmswood. The frigid temperatures and snow kept my sneakers from pounding the streets for at least part of the winter, sometimes well into the spring, so I'd had to find other solutions.

Michelle didn't enjoy working out from home, something she'd been vocal about during the pandemic because it didn't offer enough *social time*, aka gabbing with people, but I'd invested in one of those water rowers, and it had fast become one of my favorites, even in the summer. Now it was something I could do on the quiet, away from all the empathetic smiles and judgmental stares. I mean, your wife goes missing and you're still pumping iron at the gym? Douchebag alert.

I headed upstairs to change, walked past the three other bedrooms to the main. As well as the massive walk-in wardrobe, there was an en suite bathroom almost as big as the council flat I'd lived in with Dad. Claw-foot tub, oversize shower with a rain head and the best full-body jets money could buy, and which Michelle and I had used together on a regular basis, getting down 'n' dirty before we got clean. Ah, good times. All in all, though, the house was far too big for two, and I couldn't wait to be able to sell it and move to an apartment. Or two apartments. Maybe even three. Smaller but in different countries, places I could run my six daily miles all year round.

Dad didn't seem to register much when I saw him, but whichever clinic I moved him to, I'd visit regularly, it was the absolute least I could do. Nobody else went to see him. He was an only child, and after Mum's death he'd alienated the rest of the family. We hadn't seen them in years.

Tragedy struck us early when Mum died giving birth to

my baby sister, who'd passed away from complications two days later. That's what kicked off Dad's drinking. I'd been six, and we'd gone from a happy family of soon-to-be-four to a shattered mess, with Dad's alcohol and gambling habits digging our broken souls into a bottomless financial and emotional hole.

I'm not sharing all this for sympathy. We all have our demons. Reasons for being the way we are or doing the things we do. Everyone has secrets. Everybody has done at least a few things they're not proud of. Stuff they'd rather keep quiet because it could cost them their job, family, or reputation, perhaps all three, maybe even land them in prison. We're all a little evil on the inside. Different shades of gray depending on circumstance, character, and predisposition.

"Tragedy changes you," Michelle once said, nodding sagely as if she'd ever experienced any herself. I almost told her the fact her parakeet escaped its cage and made a bid for freedom through her open bedroom window didn't count, but she had a point. Losing my mother and a sibling I'd never met was bound to have an impact. I'd never lied about what had happened to them to Michelle, but it wasn't something I talked about much. It was private, personal. She'd never understand.

As I stripped down and changed into my workout gear, I considered calling the nursing home in the morning to check on Dad. The state his stroke had left him in didn't bear thinking about, and so I avoided it as much as possible. I tried hard not to imagine him needing twenty-four-hour care or being confined to a wheelchair and his bed before he was fifty-five. Him knowing he had years and years ahead of himself, and during which he couldn't do anything alone, not pick up a piece of toast, roll over or wipe his backside, let alone hold a conversation because his speech and memory had mostly gone, too. After Dad's stroke I vowed I'd take care of him financially, especially because I couldn't be there in person, and I'd made good on the promise. I was a con, a thief, a crook, a liar. A murderer. But when it came to that pledge, it was the one promise I'd never break, and I had to do whatever I could to make it up to him.

I was about to head downstairs to the home gym when I doubled back on a whim and went to Michelle's side of the wardrobe. It was filled with clothes, not all of them designer, which had surprised me when we'd met. Michelle may have been a snob in other ways but when she saw something she fancied on the high street, she didn't care about the absence of a luxury brand name. Her jewelry was a completely different story. Nothing fake about any of that stuff—no costume pieces, or imitation pearls. When it came to adorning her neck, earlobes or wrists, my wife had expensive tastes indeed.

I peered at the different items, my eyes scanning the silver, gold and platinum, the colorful sapphires, rubies, and emeralds. Rings, necklaces, bracelets—the value of it all more than enough to rival a small country's GDP. My gaze landed on a diamond-encrusted jaguar-shaped pendant and it made my stomach turn. Not in a *oh, jeez I miss my wife* way, but because it reminded me of the time I'd slightly opened up to Michelle after speaking to one of the nurses at Dad's home, when he'd had a particularly rough day.

"I wish I could move him to Boston," I said to her. "I could see him more."

"But you can't afford it. I guess you should be thankful for small mercies. From what you've told me your dad wouldn't know the difference anyway."

She was right. I couldn't afford to move my father to the US with the cost of health care here but I remember staring at that bloody jaguar pendant she'd splurged on days earlier *just because.* I'd never expected her to write me a blank check, wouldn't have taken it even if she had for fear of how it would look, but that damn cat's value alone would easily have covered a month or two of Dad's care and she'd never offered a dime. Simple truth was my father wasn't important to her. She'd never met him or expressed an interest in doing so. Unlike Nora, whose charitable work was discreet and went unnoticed by anyone who wasn't directly involved, whatever my wife spent money on had to be *seen*. My father was invisible to Michelle, and I loathed her for it.

I shook the memory away, pulled open another drawer with the vast collection of Michelle's earrings, and peered inside, searching for the ones on the flyer I'd found earlier. Nothing.

Sometimes my wife left her jewelry perched on the side of our double sinks, apparently not overly worried about a two-carat something-or-other disappearing down the plug hole, although I'd have noticed by now. I still went to the bathroom to check but there was no trace of the earrings in the cabinets above or under her sink, either.

I inspected my side in case the cleaning lady had moved them over but still came up empty-handed. I noticed my comb and razor had been put back at different angles, but that was typical after the place had been cleaned. Michelle had exacting standards. Things couldn't be dusted *around*. They were to be picked up, wiped under, and wiped down. Twice a week, three if we had guests staying over.

I walked to the spare room which Travis now occupied and had a good poke around. He'd been here at some point during the day because he'd left a set of crumpled clothes on the floor, basically a giant *screw you* to the cleaners. The way some rich people treated others appalled me, and Travis was no exception. Much like my wife, he was a spoiled trust-fund brat who didn't care about anything or anyone but himself. *Mostly* himself, because he'd fallen apart when he'd watched the footage of his sister's abduction, and when Nora told him about the ovarian cancer, he'd lost it again. Cried like a baby for days.

Once I was sure there was nothing in Travis's room that interested me, I went to the gym in the basement, was about to get on the rower. I wrinkled my nose. When Travis wasn't high, he occasionally went on a health kick, which invariably didn't last, but he might have worked out in here, sweating like a pig and not cleaned up after himself. There was no knowing where he'd placed his clammy hands or plonked his soaking butt.

I ambled over to the supply cabinet for the bleach and paper towel, happy to find the pump on the bottle wasn't sticking anymore. Maybe Travis had used it to clean up after all. Shame he hadn't drank the bleach though. My expression eased into a grin. If he had, it would've made things easier in the long run.

For the both of us.

11

I'd been rowing for a solid half hour, had found a steady rhythm, and was working up a good sweat to my new playlist when the lights in the stairwell came on. I slowed my pace, popped out an earbud and listened to the footsteps. Heavy, labored, with a bit of a stumble—classic Travis—and I didn't need to see him to know he was drunk, high, or both.

"You're up late," he said as he slunk into the room, bringing with him the pungent smell of stale booze mixed with dope. Michelle would've had a field day if she'd been here. Marched him upstairs and shoved him into the shower before he'd been able to take off a shoe. My wife had lost count how many times we'd tried to get Travis sober again. *We* might be a bit of an exaggeration. *She* tried. *I* meddled. Introduced Travis to people from the office who I knew partied hard and shared a liking for his guilty pleasures. He'd lost a few jobs because of me, including a more recent one as manager at a high-end restaurant, which everyone thought had helped him turn a corner. Except the booze had been too tempting, especially when I'd given him a push from the wagon.

I stepped off the rower and gave Travis a clap on the shoulder, ignoring the fact his pupils had gone AWOL. "How's it going? How was work today?" I looked at the time. "Yesterday."

Travis sniffed and wrinkled his nose. "They fired me."

Shocker. "What? Why? When?"

"Soon as I got there. Said I'd been late four times and I was out." He sniffed again, rubbed a finger under his nostrils. "Didn't care when I told them I'd spent ages looking for my car keys. It wasn't my fault."

As much as Travis laid the blame for everything that happened to him squarely on anyone but himself, in this instance he was correct. Losing his keys wasn't his fault. It was mine because I'd dropped them behind the sideboard in the hallway, pretending to help him in his search as he tore through the place like a mini tornado on speed.

It had been a tactical move on my part as I'd known the fast-food joint forced accountability through tough love and strict rules. I was clued into this because I'd made some calls after seeing their handwritten HELP WANTED sign in the window. I'd posed as a helicopter parent trying to find a job for his fifteen-year-old daughter who was saving up for college and determined to find a cure for cancer. Feed people a feel-good story and they'll tell you almost anything.

"Punctuality is a sign of respect," the owner had said. "We don't take tardiness lightly. I fired my last manager because of it."

Duly noted. I'd made Travis call them for the manager role, which reflected well on me and I knew how to get him fired later and derail him. I hadn't felt quite so bad about my sabotage plans when the ungrateful sod hadn't wanted to call at first. He'd wrinkled his nose and said the place was *beneath him* but hadn't had a choice in the end. His references were shot, and Nora said he had to, or she'd cut him off.

Now, giving Travis a well-honed sympathetic look, I sighed, crossed my arms, and adopted a concerned-parent voice, the one I knew he hated. "Uh-huh. They let you go, what, sixteen hours ago? Where have you been?"

"Out."

"Clearly. Where?"

"Mind your business."

He may have been twenty-nine, but with the combination of his stuck-out chin and surly attitude he could've easily passed for someone half his age. It made me want to slap him. Instead, I let out another long sigh, genuine this time.

"Travis, level with me here, bud. I know you've been drinking. What else did you take?" When he didn't answer straightaway, I threw my hands in the air. "You said you'd stop. How many times do we have to do this? Your mother's going through hell. Can't you consider her even for a split second?"

I meant every word about Nora. She'd begged Travis to stop abusing a multitude of substances for years, before he'd managed to get clean until I'd arrived. It hadn't started with anything too serious, Michelle had told me one night as we lay in bed, her head nestled on my chest. I kept wanting to roll her out of the way because my arm had gone numb, but my wife enjoyed a cuddle after sex, and sensitive guy I pretended to be, I obliged, ignoring the stabbing pins and needles.

"He'd have beer or wine, mostly, smoked a bit of weed sometimes," she said. "Fairly typical teenage behavior, especially considering the amount of money he had at his disposal, and the company he kept. It got really bad when he was about seventeen."

She was wrong, but I didn't say so. Travis had told me on the quiet he'd tried coke for the first time at the tender age of thirteen, and almost any drug had been on tap at his private school.

"Whatever I wanted, whenever I needed," he'd said with a wistful smile. "Top quality."

He hadn't graduated from university, but chopped and changed programs on his parents' dime as often as he pleased before dropping out completely. It didn't make me angry as much as it made me resentful. The guy had been handed his life on the proverbial silver platter and he'd taken a dump all over it. He really was a selfish bastard.

"Think about your mum for a change," I said, driving my point home again.

"Lay off me, man," he said, and from the change in his expression I could tell the guilt had gripped his gut nice and hard.

There were still elements of the handsome guy he'd been before he'd relapsed. Blond hair and blue eyes. Surfer type. Sharp features, a diminished but still reasonable set of biceps, and abs he'd managed to maintain despite his extracurricular activities. The kind of jock who'd have despised me in high school, jeered at my ludicrous attempts to climb a rope, my blubbery body too heavy to lift with my puny arms.

We'd both undergone a makeover. Mine for the better whereas he'd slowly been sliding downhill for years. Michelle tried to help him however she could, she'd pleaded, bribed, and threatened, tried smothering him with love and withholding it to coerce him into rehab. Neither Nora nor Gideon could work out where they'd gone wrong with their son. My mother-in-law's words, not mine, although Gideon had never accepted any kind of responsibility for Travis's attitude, certainly not in public, and our relationship had never fostered a discussion that personal. In the relatively short time I'd known him, Gideon had been incapable of showing any kind of vulnerability.

I knew addiction was a complicated beast, had wrestled with it enough when Dad still had the ability to down enough booze to flood a distillery. My father had loved me, as Travis did Nora and Michelle. But they both loved the high more.

"I'm worried about you," I said. "My concern's coming from a good place."

"You don't need to be *concerned*. I said I'm fine."

"What about financially?" The abrupt change of subject made his scowl deepen. I'd hit a nerve. I took a step forward, invading his personal space. "I need to ask you something. It's important so don't get upset."

"What?"

"I know cash is tight for you but…" I waved a hand and took a step back. "No, never mind."

"*What?*" The mention of money had piqued Travis's curiosity, his first thought perhaps I might offer him some so he didn't have to ask his mother. Time to press a few more of his buttons while I went looking for truths.

"Okay…well, did, uh, did you take some of Michelle's jewelry?"

"Are you asking if I stole something?"

"Did you?"

Travis exploded. "What the hell? Why are you accusing me of—"

"I get it if you did, I do," I said quickly, putting a hand on his shoulder, which he immediately shrugged off. "I'm not blind. Maybe you pawned some stuff for quick cash." I grimaced, made myself appear apologetic as I seemingly struggled to find my next words. "It's, well, uh… I can't find the diamond earrings I gave her last Christmas, and—"

"I didn't touch them."

"If you did—"

"I *didn't*."

"*If* you did, tell me now so we can get them back. They mean a lot to me." I blinked a few times. "They were one of the last gifts I gave her."

"I said I didn't touch them." Travis stood so close now the rancid smell of his breath made me want to retch. "I wouldn't, and it seriously pisses me off you think I would."

Experience had taught me Travis was a crappy liar and I was almost certain he was telling the truth this time. If he hadn't taken those earrings it meant Michelle must've worn them the day she went missing, but the image of the stupid partial flyer hadn't yet faded. I wanted to be sure, and the fact I wasn't made my anger resurface. I used it to give Travis another verbal shove.

"I'm not sure I believe you."

"Then fuck you. I'm outta here."

"You can't go back out in this state, Travis. It's late. Stay here and sleep it off."

"What are you, my mom?"

As soon as he said the words, I saw his face fall, but he let out a cold laugh and walked out of the room, muttering a string of expletives. As I followed him upstairs and into the hallway, past the living room from where Roger observed us with one eye, I insisted again Travis stay home. He ignored me and grabbed his keys until I marched past him, stood in front of the door, and held out a hand.

"Give those to me," I ordered. "You're not driving. You'll kill someone."

He opened his mouth, probably with another round of insults at the ready before appearing to change his mind. Even through his brain fog he must have known he needed me as an ally, especially if Nora had given him any indication about her plans to tighten his financial belt. Although she'd pressed him to stay with her, I knew he didn't want to, and this house was his best bet for a comfortable place to crash. Without another word or as much as a muffled grunt he dropped his car keys into my palm. And then he grinned. A full-on charmer that lifted all the self-abuse from his face.

"I'll get an Uber," he said. "See you, Grandpa. Don't wait up."

I let him push past me, open the door, and slip out, his fingers already tapping on his phone. Despite his alleged nonchalance, I knew he was still worked up, which meant he'd be out late, getting into all kinds of trouble. If I didn't have any morals or principles, I'd have let him take his car, but I'd meant what I said, he could kill someone, which was an unacceptable outcome, plus, if he died before Nora, his money would go back to her, and she might decide to donate it.

I watched him leave, debated whether I should force him back into the house. "Hey," I called out instead. "Were you in the back garden today?"

Travis turned around. "Huh? What for?"

"Forget it."

After he'd disappeared into the darkness, I closed the door, resting my head against it. As the house fell silent around me, I tried to ignore the whispers about something not being quite right, and went back to trying to convince myself I had nothing to worry about.

12

When my Superman alarm clock went off a few hours later that morning, I toyed with flinging it across the room before remembering my plan of looking exhausted. I forced myself up, staggered to the bathroom where I splashed icy water over my face, and brushed my teeth before pulling on some sweatpants and a T-shirt.

Upon stepping into the hallway, it took less than a nanosecond to ascertain Travis was home. The discarded sweater left in a pile at the top of the stairs was my first clue, the reverberating sound of his snores another, and from the stale-air smell smuggling its way up my nostrils as I approached the bedroom door, I figured he'd been back a while. I wasn't happy I hadn't heard him come in, but whether he'd made it here in one piece was another question.

I glanced inside the room and regretted it in an instant.

He'd left the bedside table light on, lay on his back with his hands above his head, his stark-bollock-naked body sprawled on top of the covers, every detail of his anatomy on prominent display.

"Jesus," I muttered, slamming the door shut in the hope it would startle him. Not a chance. If the past couple of weeks were anything to go by, Travis would be out cold until well after lunch, possibly still in bed when I returned from work this evening. Not that it mattered. At least this way I'd be here when he started with his usual antics of roaming around the house.

He'd make a rubbish burglar. I could always tell where he'd been and what he'd done when I came home. From the open kitchen cupboards to the empty cereal box abandoned on the counter, the dirty dishes strewn about the main floor to the TV he couldn't be bothered turning off in the den, Travis left a trail of mayhem in his wake.

I'd banned him from using any bathroom other than his en suite and I'll spare the graphic details as to why I made that decision. I was a tidy person, always had been. Some shrink might say it was a form of control, psychological remnants from when I'd had to clean up after Dad. I'd counter it's no more complicated than my not being a pig. Michelle was forever mocking me because I couldn't sit down until the kitchen was spotless after dinner whereas she could happily leave stuff stacked for the cleaners to take care of the next time they came to the house, which drove me nuts.

Would I have someone come in wherever I ended up once I got Michelle's cash and inherited the rest from Nora's estate? Yes, but I'd still put my cups in the dishwasher for God's sake, which was a damn sight more than Travis could manage. He wouldn't have recognized the bloody machine if it had clunked over and given him a kick in the crotch.

After he'd stormed off in a pubescent huff last night, I'd debated whether I should hide all Michelle's jewelry in the safe in case I'd given him an idea on how to get his sticky mitts on some cash. I decided against it. As much as it would irk me if he stole any of the stuff, it would provide me with more arsenal against him if he did. Even if he cleared out Michelle's entire collection, it wouldn't make a significant enough dent in the money I'd be getting when she was declared dead.

There were other advantages to letting him plunder his missing-and-presumed-dead sister's jewelry box. He'd turn whatever money he got into drugs. His near-constant high of late made him unreliable, and not only when it came to managing his money. In turn, this would make it less probable for Nora to reconsider her wishes of having me manage his affairs. I could also use it as leverage, threaten him with telling Nora about what he'd done, suggest I ask her to double the charity donation she was considering once he knew about it. It would get him nice and pissed.

I cleared up the plate and peanut butter Travis had dumped on the counter, and emptied the half-full container of milk, which felt warm and smelled sour, down the sink, cursing him for causing so much waste, squandering money so many of us could put to better use.

In my case, when I got Michelle's fortune, I'd make sure Dad had the best care money could buy and I never had to worry about the monthly payment for his nursing home fees again. He'd love having a view of the Alps, and Switzerland would be a cool place for me to live. When I'd worked in London, I'd placed a ton of IT contractors in Zurich, Lausanne, and Geneva, and many of them ended up staying permanently. I closed my eyes, imagined the mountains, the clean air, the skiing. It would be perfect for at least part of the year, and I'd be close to Dad. I could try to make up for what had happened to him. For what I was responsible for.

I forced myself to stop thinking about the future or the past and tidied the rest of Travis's mess. Once I'd taken Roger out for a walk despite his melodramatic barks and sloth-like enthusiasm, I checked the side gate was locked, and scoured the garden for more footprints, but found none. Back inside the house I made myself a cup of coffee from the fancy built-in machine and settled at the marble kitchen island where I flicked through the news on my phone.

Still nothing new on Michelle's disappearance. There hadn't been a mention of the case for over two weeks, and the public had already moved on to fresher events, bigger scandals, and gossip with more salacious details. With the current state of the world and the abundance of information, the alleged abduction of a rich suburban woman didn't hold people's attention for long, especially when the trail had gone cold.

In the days after Michelle was taken, I'd given all the radio and TV interviews I'd been asked for, which, much to my astonishment, hadn't been many. I'd begged for more to keep the case in the public eye for as long as possible. It had been a calculated risk, a strategic move. A demonstration of my full cooperation for the benefit of anyone watching, but mostly a show for Detective Anjali and her colleagues.

Now, a month later, when I made calls, sent emails and social media messages to the local and national newspapers offering to speak to them and asking them to run an update, my pleas were met either with silence or muted disinterest. Frankly, if I'd had nothing to do with Michelle's situation, my disgust and anger would've been genuine because neither the press nor the public gave a toss about her.

I surfed the net for a while and passed the time with another round of coffee and a few slices of whole-wheat toast.

Shortly before eight thirty I was at the front door, pulling on my coat and giving Roger a pat on the head.

"See you later," I said. "Hold down the fort for me, and don't let the slob upstairs give you any grief. Bite him in the arse if he does." When Roger let out a low grumble I chuckled, grabbed my keys and workout bag before heading outside, my bonhomie disappearing as I got closer to my Mercedes.

There was a deep scratch, long and snake-ish, down the entire length of the driver's door, all the way from left to right, an ugly metal-on-metal gouge.

"Come on!" My voice bounced off the garage doors and back out into the street. I cursed again and crouched to inspect the damage, already doubting it had been caused by the local teenagers Michelle had obsessed about. If I were a betting man, I'd have placed my entire upcoming fortune on the culprit lying in my spare room, his naked bum cheeks on top of my Egyptian cotton sheets, the ones with the astronomically high thread count and price tag, and which I'd still burn once he'd left the house.

Travis had walked by my car three times last night, so he'd left this mark either because he was pissed or pissed off, and it made me seethe so much I wanted to march inside and throttle the vindictive prick, whether he was birthday-suited or not.

What was the point? He'd be too off his face to hear any of my yelling, and it was time to get to work. I wanted to finish at a decent time tonight so I could go for a swim at the gym. I wouldn't start my day off by having a pointless, one-sided argument with Travis. I had to focus. I was meeting one of my largest clients about a new software implementation project this morning, a company I'd worked on reeling in for over six months, and I wanted a clear head. It was no secret multiple competitors were vying for the deal and I wasn't about to let Travis's behavior interfere with my success.

I pondered whether I should ride my motorbike instead, a 1980 Triumph Bonneville I'd restored and equipped with an aftermarket exhaust to make it far quieter. I longed to take it out another few times before the weather turned too cold. The thick, dark clouds billowing and swirling in the sky made me decide against it. The last thing I needed was to get drenched midroute. Although if I did, it would put me in a much sourer mood, and might have been enough to make me turn around and bust Travis's balls after all.

I arrived at the office shortly after nine, where Agnes, the near-retirement receptionist, made big eyes at me as she waved me over. "I was about to call you," she said, grabbing my arm and pulling me to one side. She was a member of an amateur dramatics troupe and aside from her baby-blue twin sets, liked nothing more than demonstrating her acting skills at the office. She wasn't bad at it, either. I'd seen her outperform a Greek tragedy when she got a paper cut.

"Jeffreys is already here," she said in a lowish whisper.

"What? He's early. The meeting isn't for another half hour."

Her eyes widened again, the huge (also baby-blue) glasses magnifying them further. "He said it was set for nine. Apparently, you agreed to the time weeks ago."

"No, it wasn't." I swiped a finger across my phone, but Agnes was right. The meeting *was* scheduled for nine o'clock. I must have misread my calendar last time I looked. Shit. I was never late for anything, in fact, I was always early as a matter of principle. Being late meant you began with an apology, weakening your position from the start. Arriving early, on the other hand, afforded the opportunity to choose where to sit, and I always took the chair with my back to the window, so my counterpart's face was clearly illuminated, ready to read, and mine remained a little obscured by the brightness shining into their eyes. One of the oldest tricks in the book. And one of the most effective.

When I walked into the meeting room, Victor Jeffreys stood looking out the window. He was the heir and sole owner of a near hundred-year-old sporting goods retail empire his grandmother Elsie Jeffreys had set up. While rumored to be worth millions, it desperately needed some help when it came to IT security, which meant he needed a crack team of specialists I was about to convince him only I could provide.

Jeffreys was a tall man with a copious amount of thick gray hair. He didn't have much of an appetite for sugar, judging by the plate of Danish pastries Agnes had brought in, and which sat untouched in the middle of the table. I scanned the seats, spotted half a cup of black coffee, a briefcase and phone in the exact place I'd wanted.

"Good morning, Mr. Jeffreys. I—"

"Spare me the apologies, Lucas," he said, despite the fact I'd offered none. Holding up a hand, and with his back still facing me, he continued, "I'm a busy man. I expect you to value my time."

"I understand." I tried not to grit my teeth. "As your future HR business partner—"

He let out a low chuckle and turned around, a bemused and patronizing smile dancing on his lips. "Don't be presumptuous. And you can dress it up with whatever fancy corporate term you want, son. I'll call you a supplier. I demand. You supply. Providing you can be bothered to do so on time."

His tone reminded me so much of Gideon's it made me want to tell him to shove it—or walk over and shove *him* out the window. Maybe I'd have given it more serious thought if the office hadn't been located on the ground floor. But, damn it, I could almost taste victory. I wanted this account, wanted the win for the glory and the bonus waiting for me at the finish line. Now he'd increased the challenge, I had to reel him in.

I bowed my head. "I apologize for my tardiness. Let's take a seat."

We settled around the table as I prepared to feast on humble pie, and gobble I did. I listened to him drone on about his business, all the different areas they *utterly dominated*, particularly when it came to hiking, camping, and skiing equipment. How they'd pivoted online and not only survived but thrived during the pandemic, watching their competitors die, and picking through their bones.

"I've spoken to a number of suppliers like you," he said. "Seems to me most of your competitors don't know their asses from their elbows and I doubt this meeting will be different."

Off he went on another round. I let him speak, listened intently, didn't interrupt once. It's something salespeople don't do enough of. *Listen.* Such a simple way of successfully conducting business. I let the prospective customer talk and they told me exactly what they wanted. No need trying to work it out for myself. All I needed were my ears, and Jeffreys was warming toward me because of it, I could tell. As we neared the end of the meeting, and while we weren't about to go down the pub for a pint, I knew I had him. Time for the final strike.

"Let me leave you with this." I leaned in, mirroring his body language. "You haven't worked with Taylor and Strong Recruitment before, and I understand you have other *suppliers*." I smiled, as did he. Prat. "Add us to your list and benchmark us against them. From what you've told me we'll do better. I guarantee it. And if we don't—" I tapped the table with my fingertips "—you'll have the pleasure of saying 'I told you so.'"

Jeffreys grunted. "Something tells me you're not the type to let that happen."

"I won't argue with that."

This was my favorite part of the job. The conclusion, pulling in another big whale for the account managers to feast on. Jeffreys would sign the contracts I'd asked Agnes to prepare on Friday within the next twenty-four hours, possibly sooner.

Hunters like me were a rare breed. Most of my colleagues were farmers—great at working their way through a company like wildfire once they got in, but they hated the cold calls, the initial approach, the vast amount of rejection. Me? I loved that part. Lived for it. Deciding which company I'd break open, and doing whatever I needed to find a way in. The harder, the better. It wasn't about the praise my boss, Richard, would reluctantly give. I didn't give a toss about him. I loved the glory and the money, but the best part was the pure, unadulterated satisfaction from succeeding at something I'd been told I couldn't do. "Don't waste your time," Richard had said when I'd told him I was going after Jeffreys. "He'll never work with us. Forget it." Who would eat the humble pie, now?

After accompanying my *almost* new client back to reception where we shook hands and he thanked me profusely for my time, I made my way to my office at the far end of the building. I stopped to talk with a few of the associates about what they'd done over the weekend, and the IT specialist profiles they were looking for. While they engaged in some chatter, I knew they didn't see me as one of them, never had since I'd come in at a senior sales level when I'd moved to Boston. Some of them asked how I was doing, and I knew they were circling the waters, hoping Michelle's disappearance would cause me to crack and leave, in which case they'd be splitting my accounts between them before you could say Shark Week. In that sense, recruitment hadn't changed much in the near decade I'd been in the industry. If you didn't watch your back, someone had you for lunch. Not today, my friends, I thought, not today. Or tomorrow. Or the day after.

I flexed my fingers and drew my shoulder blades together, ready for the rest of the day to go without another hitch. As I sat down at my desk and was about to switch on my computer, I noticed a small orange envelope placed on top of my regular mail. It was addressed to me, but had no stamp or postmark, meaning it had been hand delivered. The sender had marked it CONFIDENTIAL.

Curious, I pulled out the contents. It was a single page about the size of a postcard. Black-and-white, a grainy, blown-up, partial image of a woman. Not the same picture as the one which had arrived in my pack of flyers last night. This time it was the bottom left side of the woman's face.

Blood whooshed in my ears. I flipped it over, read the single word marked in thick, black felt-tip pen. Four letters that made my insides turn to ice.

KNOW.

13

Dropping the photograph, I propelled myself backward. My feet scrambled to gain traction as my chair slid across the floor and ended up in the bookcase behind me, the impact rattling the salesperson-of-the-year awards displayed on top. It wasn't enough distance, so I leapt up, heart racing, as I ran a clammy palm through my hair and over my face.

I read the word over and over.

KNOW.

My pulse accelerated, my heart beating so hard I thought it might rip itself straight out of my chest. Eyes closed, and gripping the armrests of the chair, I forced myself to breathe in through my nose and out through my mouth, again and again. And again.

"Hey, Lucas. How did it go with Jeffreys?"

Agnes's voice made me jump. I hadn't heard her come in.

Hadn't heard her knock. My eyes flew open as she took a few steps farther inside my office.

"Are you okay?"

"All good," I croaked, swiftly sliding some papers over the photo. "I'm fine."

Agnes's hands went to her hips. "You don't *look* fine. I'll get you a glass of—"

"I said I'm fine," I barked, and it was Agnes who jumped this time. I'd never raised my voice in the office, not to her, or anyone. Not even when the new guy sent the wrong contract to a client, or when he spilled his barista nightmare of a special-order coffee over my brand-new shirt and tie minutes before a client meeting. I fired him. But I didn't shout at him. Lucas Forester didn't have a temper.

"Sorry, Agnes."

"Forget about it." She lowered her voice. "But, kiddo, you're under so much stress. Maybe you shouldn't be here? You haven't had much time off since...you know."

"The meeting with Jeffreys was good. It's a done deal."

Agnes gave me a slow nod and a neutral smile, indicating she understood my desire to sweep whatever was going on under the proverbial carpet. "Why am I not surprised you turned him?" she said. "Congratulations, how fabulous. Is there anything you need? Can I help at all?" When I declined, she added, "I'll leave you to it then. But promise me you'll take care of yourself? We need you here."

There weren't many people I'd miss when I left Boston, but Agnes was one of them. She was a hard worker. Should've retired by now so she could enjoy her weekly pool tournaments and astronomy club, but when her husband had left her for another woman, he'd cleared out their joint savings account along with his wardrobe. Agnes had no idea where he lived, but over lunch one day she'd told me if she found him, she'd put rat poison in his food, and I'd almost considered putting her in touch with Woods. Instead, and before my departure, I'd give her a bonus from my own pocket.

"I will," I said.

As she turned to leave, my gaze dropped to my desk, where the corner of the photograph stuck out from underneath the papers I'd put on top. I swallowed hard, called out to Agnes and as she spun around, I forced my voice back to a normal tone. "Do you know where the orange envelope came from this morning?"

"It was here when I arrived. Someone slipped it under the door. Why? What was it?"

"Uh, a thank-you note from a candidate, but I can't quite read the handwriting."

She held out a hand. "Let me take a peek."

"Never mind, I think I know who it's from." I pulled my cell out of my pocket and looked at the blank screen with a pretend frown. "I have to take this. I'll catch you later."

Once she'd pulled the door closed behind her I let my phone drop on the desk and sank into my chair. My pulse thumped again as I picked up the photo. It was Michelle, not a doubt in my mind. I'd know the curve of her chin anywhere. Flipping the picture around made my gut lurch. Neither of the two photos I'd received were part of a flyer. They weren't misprints. This was deliberate and intentional, and yesterday's picture hadn't been marked with the Roman numeral one. It was the word *I*. Part of a message.

I KNOW.

Someone had hand delivered both photos. But who? And what did they think they knew? Whatever it was, I needed to get rid of this picture immediately. I jumped up, stuffed the photo into my pocket and headed to the copy room, planned on shoving the partial image of Michelle's face deep into the shredder where I'd watch it be ripped into tiny pieces. I changed my mind before I got there, took a detour to the bathroom where I closed the stall door and pressed my forehead against the cool, tiled wall.

I had to keep calm. Dispose of this...*problem* at home. This wasn't the time for me to panic, not yet, or to start leaving any evidence lying around. I couldn't get sloppy.

Mind whirring, I walked back to my office on autopilot, stopping only when Davinder, one of the up-and-coming sales reps who openly nipped at my heels, called out my name. I didn't respond until he'd said it at least three times. It seemed as if I were underwater and couldn't hear properly. I watched his mouth move, had to arrange the words in some logical order when they entered my brain, as if they were on a jumbled-up time delay.

"You got the Jeffreys account," he said, sounding congratulatory but looking anything but. Under normal circumstances I'd have rubbed his face in it, made a joke about chucking him some scraps once I'd had my fill, but I barely managed a head bob as I kept walking.

Back at my desk, my brain continued to race ahead as it tried to connect the dots to whomever had sent the photographs, what they meant, and what I'd do if another arrived. What would the next word written on the back be? How did whoever was sending them *know* anything? I ordered myself to regroup. Process of elimination was how I needed to approach this. Who had motive, means, and opportunity?

A thought flickered in my mind. *It's always the husband.*

The cops didn't have anything on me. I knew for sure because of the way I'd orchestrated Michelle's disappearance. Dark web, encrypted messages, payment by cryptocurrency, burner laptop and phones. Planning for months, taking even longer to implement the perfect series of events. Being out of the country when it happened. Passing the lie detector test. They had *nothing*.

Another thought grabbed me by the throat. Detective Anjali. Had she done this? A theory started to emerge, and part of the crushing weight slid off my shoulders. Was this her way of trying to unsettle me? Force me into making a mistake to see if I was guilty of something?

I leaned back in my chair, wondering if I should give this photo to her, an open demonstration of having nothing to hide. It didn't sit well. They believed I thought they'd bungled the ransom drop, and I put myself into the shoes of the distressed husband. Would he run to the cops with this, or wait and see if another ransom note followed?

I frowned, thinking there may be a very real possibility of that happening. This could be the work of some random person thinking they were clever by posing as the abductor and trying to make a fast buck. It wasn't unheard of. The whiff of another person's misery could turn humans into animals. But why the message on the back? Maybe it would be I KNOW WHERE SHE IS. Yes, that made sense. Instead of sending Michelle in pieces—a finger here, a toe there—they'd used a photograph to insinuate they were the abductor and still had her.

Either way, I decided if this was Anjali trying to get me worked up, or some lowlife hoping to cash in, I wouldn't share the photo with the cops. I didn't like the idea of waiting to see if another arrived, but strategically it was the better play. In the meantime, I'd destroy this one in case it wasn't the police behind it, and they somehow got wind of what was going on.

"Bloody hell," I whispered as I thought about them potentially receiving a copy. No. If they had, Anjali would've shown up at my office by now, cheeks flush with excitement as she told me about the new lead.

My next thoughts went to Travis, more specifically to the memory of one of the first nights he'd ended up staying at the house after Michelle went missing. He'd been spiraling for a good few months and that night he'd practically drunk himself halfway to unconsciousness before announcing he'd drive back to Nora's, where he was staying after being kicked out of his apartment because he couldn't make rent. It wasn't the first time I'd taken his car keys from him, and after insulting me for two minutes straight, using every combination of cuss words he could seemingly think of, he finished his tirade with, "My dad always said you weren't good enough for Michelle." He let out a guttural belch before continuing with one finger pointed at me, words slurred. "If he were here, he'd say you had something to do with this."

"I'm going to ignore that," I'd said, grabbing Travis by the arm and marching him upstairs, where I shoved him into the spare bedroom. "Get some rest. Sleep it off."

The next morning he'd woken up with a colossal hangover, but he'd never mentioned what he'd said again, and I hadn't brought it up, either. That didn't mean he wasn't thinking it. Was it possible he suspected me of being involved in Michelle's disappearance? Had he sent these two pictures either to find out the truth, or for leverage so he could bribe me into giving him money because he was broke? I let out a snort. No. The guy wasn't smart enough.

My grin faded. Perhaps the cops had talked him into getting involved in this ruse. Then again why use a man as unreliable as Travis? Anyone could've delivered the envelope to work, and while I'd been at the park with Roger last night, the bundle of papers had sat on my doorstep for at least twenty minutes, ripe for tampering with, but Travis hadn't been around. Surely there was no way Anjali would trust him to do anything with a degree of efficiency or discretion.

I picked up my phone, flipped it over in my palm. About five months ago, Michelle and I had taken Nora out for dinner. Over dessert, my mother-in-law had mentioned watching a program about tracking software on cell phones, and how a woman who'd stalked her ex-husband had installed a secret app. She'd been able to switch on his microphone and camera remotely, patch herself into his calls, track his every movement.

"She did it for six months," Nora said, shaking her head. "He had no idea."

"What a disgusting invasion of privacy," Michelle said. "Isn't it, Lucas?"

"Terrible," I'd offered.

"I can't imagine," Nora continued. "She knew where he was at all times. She was listening to all his private conversations. What a despicable human being."

"Don't get any funny ideas about doing that to me, will you?" Michelle joked. "You know I'll cut your balls off."

"*Michelle,*" Nora said as she looked around. "That's a little uncouth."

I gave my wife's leg a squeeze and grinned. "What's the world coming to, eh? What about honest to goodness old-fashioned trust? I didn't even know those apps existed."

Lie. I knew all about them, had toyed with the idea of installing one on Michelle's phone but discounted the thought. With Woods taking care of business, I didn't need to follow her, and if the app had been discovered—which it most certainly would have once the cops had combed through her phone—all fingers would point at me. I hadn't needed to know what Michelle was doing, who she saw or talked to, because it didn't matter. Now though, I wished I'd installed one of those apps on Travis's cell.

I needed to talk to him so he could be eliminated from my list of suspects, and to do that I had to catch him off guard, ascertain if he'd had something to do with these photos. I grabbed my coat and headed for reception.

"You're right," I called over to Agnes as I walked past. "I'm not well, so I'll work from home. Will you forward any calls to my mobile?"

"Will do. And don't forget what I said. Take it easy."

Take it easy.

Depending on what I discovered next, I wasn't sure when I'd be taking it easy again.

14

Stepping outside into the drizzle I yanked the collar of my jacket up to my ears and hurried to the car, fists clenching when I noticed the scratch in the door again. My hands clenched even harder when I registered another problem. Flat tire, driver's rear.

"Piss it," I said, taking a step closer.

As if someone had flicked a switch, the heavy clouds above burst open. Light rain morphed into an instant downpour, forming an icy rivulet sneaking its way down the back of my neck. Another cuss word escaped my lips, louder this time, and with superhuman effort I stopped myself from kicking the wheel hard enough to shatter a couple of toes. I reminded myself I'd changed tires before, no big deal, and set to work, pulling my coat tighter as I went to locate the spare before remembering this model didn't come with one.

I had two options: drive the car to the nearest garage or phone roadside assistance. The former would lead to more damage and delays, and whichever I chose meant figuring out if Travis had a hand in photographic subterfuge would have to wait. Decision made, I whipped out my phone and searched for the assistance number as I climbed into my car, soaked to the core.

The call center agent informed me it would take about forty-five minutes to get someone out to help, so I tried to calm down, listened to the rain's rhythmic symphony as it pattered against the windshield. Cigarette in one hand, my mind sped around in circles. The only thing I could think of was who'd sent those photos, if the footprints in the garden had anything to do with them, and what the hell might happen next. In my experience, coincidences were rare. I believed in them about as much as I did Father Christmas, love conquers all, and ghosts.

I had to do something to distract myself while I waited for the service truck, thought about calling my father's care home for an update but was certain the nurse would say, "Nothing new," in a tone as bright as if she were announcing I'd won the lottery.

With time on my hands my mind wandered, thinking of how the only good thing about Dad's condition was the fact he didn't know what I'd become because there was no doubt he'd at least partly blame himself for my exploits.

Those with children might say I'm talking out of my arse because I don't have kids, but I don't adhere to the logic parents are responsible for their offspring's mistakes for all eternity. Yeah, when they're small because of a lack of discipline, and the whole monkey see, monkey do thing, but can we adults blame every bad decision we've made on the way we were raised? Should I blame my father for the fact I gave up on my childhood dreams of becoming a doctor? After all, I had eleven top-notch GCSEs, which I hadn't needed to work particularly hard for, could've gone on to take A levels and head off to university, but it cost money, and we didn't have any. Even before Dad's stroke, I needed to work to support the two of us given he was drinking himself into oblivion most days.

Maybe I should've blamed him, but I didn't. It was my decision to quit school. I also wondered if I'd have been cut out for heavy studying, not to mention getting a regular job and doing things on the up-and-up. I wasn't sure I'd have it in me. I'd always loved the game, the thrill of getting away with something ever since I'd stolen my first pack of gum, which was probably why I didn't think twice about getting involved with Manchester's home-grown mobster, Bobby Boyle.

Whoever hadn't heard of Bobby could count themselves lucky. Nasty piece of work, that one. Those who'd had the pleasure of making his acquaintance didn't always live long enough to regret it fully, especially when they got on his wrong side. As for me, a decade later, I still wished I hadn't looked at him, spoken to him, let alone taken him up on his job offer.

I met Bobby when I was twenty and working for Wright Space, a self-storage company not far from the estate where I lived with Dad. The owner, Justine Wright, had relented and hired me after I'd bugged her for a job every day for three weeks straight.

At first, I was her lackey. Running errands, answering phones, cleaning out lockers. Within a few weeks she not only understood I'd hold my tongue about the many cash deals she arranged under the table, but that I also had what she called the *gift of the gab*. She wasn't wrong. Sales had always been my thing since I set up shop at school when I was a tween. I saved the cash my grandmother had given me the final time I'd seen her, and which I'd hidden from Dad. I'd used it to buy chocolate bars, pop, and crisps in bulk from the supermarket and sold them at more than twice the cost.

The kids went crazy, descending on me daily. A bunch of locusts, stopping me in the hallways to ask if I had a Mars bar up my sleeve. My little tuck shop empire grew, and I roped in a couple of friends who set up satellite locations, and I took a third of their profits. This went on for weeks, and I could barely keep up with demand. The glory days lasted until one of the parents squealed, phoned the headmistress, and my inaugural venture got shut down. I'd never forgotten how Mrs. Martin first educated me about the school's strict rules before finishing in a softer tone, one eyebrow raised and whispering, "You might want to consider a career in sales at some point, young man."

So, there I was a few years later, selling locker leases for Wright Space, when a tall guy with a head full of dark hair and a face that belonged in a Calvin Klein advert walked in. He was dressed in black from head to toe, except for the brown leather jacket he'd slung over his shoulder. I pegged him at around forty, and as he complained about how he couldn't get into his unit because some idiot had dumped three heavy wooden crates directly in front of it, I immediately considered him a wanker. Still, Mrs. Wright had told me the customer was king, so in no time I'd found the crate-culprit and demanded he come in immediately to move them. At the same time, I'd accessed the details of the complainant, and had learned his name was Bobby Boyle. I'd never heard of him.

"The owner is on his way, Mr. Boyle," I said as I put the phone down, and Bobby was impressed for all of a second until I told him it would take about half an hour to get the crates shifted.

"Are you pulling my leg?" Bobby barked, baring his teeth

so fiercely I took a step back, thinking he might head-butt me if I didn't move. "How about I set fire to the lot of them? Throw you on top for being a useless little flit? Half a clucking hour? Give me a break."

Going back to what I said earlier about parents not being responsible for their descendant's behavior, there are some exceptions to the rule. Although I didn't know it then, Bobby's obsession with substituting obscenities with other words—cluck, flap, hiss, flit—had come straight from his mother who'd rapped his knuckles with a wooden spoon when he was young and happened to let out a cuss word.

I met her once a while later; a charming white-haired elderly lady who invited me in for tea and cucumber sandwiches (*with the crusts cut off, dear, they're much nicer*) when Bobby instructed me to stow a box of *stuff* in her immaculately kept garage. I swear Beverley Boyle was the only person in the world who'd made me instinctively change my usual *yeah* to a clipped and Received Pronunciation *yes*.

Anyway, to stop Bobby from setting fire to the crates blocking his way, and quite possibly torching the entire storage facility in the process, I gave him a cup of tea with two chocolate biscuits, sat him down in the waiting area, and told him I'd move the crates myself.

"Don't bother, kid, you'll slip a disc." Bobby gestured for me to sit on the plastic chair opposite him. It was less of a request than a direct order, and while I didn't yet understand his *colorful* background, I did as I was told. He was that kind of guy. Got you to do stuff simply by breathing.

As I plopped myself down, I made a comment about the weather and the previous night's football match before switching gears and asking if he'd considered leasing an end unit.

"It'll reduce the chances of one of your neighbors leaving their stuff in front of your space by half," I said. "And I know for a fact the unit on the end of your row is about to be vacated. It's bigger than the one you have, but I can do you a good deal."

A smirk spread over his face. He held his arms up, gesturing around the little entryway as if he were holding court. "As I live and hissing breathe. You're trying to upsell me. You're that kid Justine's been telling me about."

I shrugged, feigning nonchalance about the fact he knew who I was. Watching Dad play cards had taught me a thing or two about facial expressions, and I'd always been a fast learner. "I wouldn't hang around to make a decision. Those units go fast, and there's a waiting list. But I distinctly remember signing you up ages ago. You must be at the top by now…"

I still can't believe I gave him a deliberate and exaggerated wink. I thought I was being clever. Reckoned Mrs. Wright wouldn't notice because I managed the spreadsheet. It would give me a bit more commission, which Dad and I desperately needed if we wanted to eat properly and on a more regular basis.

Looking back, it was the one time in my life when I miscalculated and misjudged someone entirely. Upselling Bobby Boyle turned out to be the biggest mistake of my life.

Seeing the service truck arrive, I gave my head a shake to dislodge the memories. By the time the tire had been replaced, and I made it home, it was already after twelve. Travis's car was no longer in the driveway.

As I surprised Roger with a quick stroll, I dialed Travis's phone, but he didn't pick up, so I called Nora, but much as I'd suspected, he wasn't there. Simple enough to figure out where he might be. Another of Travis's more recent indulgences was frequenting strip clubs so I checked online, saw quite a few of them were open.

The hunt was on.

15

I headed off to the closest club, but Travis's car was nowhere to be found. More unsuccessful stops and a few miles south west, I arrived at a joint called Eden. Bingo. Travis's BMW was sprawled across two spaces, demonstrating his driving habits were about as uncourteous and obnoxious as the man himself could be.

I parked the Mercedes and walked inside, eyes adjusting to the dim lights as I craned my neck, searching for my brother-in-law, hoping he wasn't in the middle of getting a lap dance. Although it wasn't a place I patronized, Travis had once told me Eden had been taken over by a consortium of ex-strippers who'd got sick of the previous owner's wandering hands. They'd had him arrested for sexual assault, bought out his business and cleaned the place up. Nowadays it was renowned for its dancing talent, strict no-touch policy, and upmarket clientele.

Strip clubs had never been my thing. While watching a woman take off her clothes could be undeniably erotic, knowing they were doing so for money spoiled the mood. Absurd how most men thought they were the ones in control when it was the complete opposite, and they were being cajoled into emptying their wallets. I respected the women here, and what they did. After all, I'd changed my identity and adapted my behavior multiple times over to get what I wanted, and I hadn't always kept my clothes on either.

Eden was all purple velvet and gold lamé décor, and about a quarter of the two dozen tables were occupied. I scanned the room a couple of times before I found Travis sat within arm's reach of the stage. Judging by the quarter-full bottle of beer in front of him and the glint in his eyes as he watched the lithe, body-glitter-covered woman writhing a few feet away, he didn't have a care in the world, didn't even glance my way until I slid into the opposite seat.

"What the…? *Lucas?*" He had the decency to blush. "What are you doing here?"

"Drove all over town searching for you." I narrowed my eyes, gauging his reaction to my sudden appearance. While an expression of surprise and obvious embarrassment had registered on his face, he didn't seem in the least bit nervous. I searched for the slightest of twitches to indicate he'd left a surprise envelope at the office for me this morning, or he'd messed with my newspaper last night, be it of his own accord, or as an errand for someone else. I couldn't tell and wondered if he might be a better liar than I'd thought.

"You were looking for me? Is it Mom?"

"No, she's fine. I tried calling you."

"Battery's dead. Keep forgetting to plug it in."

He tapped his chest and burped as his eyes wandered back to the stage where another woman in five-inch transparent heels spun around a pole. Her abs rivaled mine, and her athleticism, stamina, and dedication were astounding. When Travis caught my eye, he winked.

"Hot, huh?" he said, before finishing his beer and pulling a face. "God, hair of the dog doesn't always work, does it? Maybe the next one will help." He signaled to the waitress and I shook my head at her. Him not asking again why I'd come here and glossing over last night's argument wasn't surprising. Travis avoided conflict as much as he'd been skirting regular work. I needed to get him outside where I could assess his face and reactions properly. I got up, grabbed his arm.

"You've had enough. Time to get you sober. I'll drive."

He shrugged me off. "Nope."

Christ alive, was he *pouting* again? Never mind hair of the dog, it was time for a few helpings of guilt cocktail. "Nora asked me to take care of you—" I crossed my arms, towering over him "—and you haven't been to see her in days so I'm going to take you later, which means you need to get sober. Show her some respect."

This time, the mention of his mother got his attention. Travis stood, and with a wobbly flourish, bowed to the stage before blowing the dancers a dramatic series of kisses, which one of them pretended to catch and hold close to her heart. I shoved Travis to the exit, both of us squinting when the doors opened, and the gray light hit us full on. As we approached my car, I steered him to the driver's side.

"You're letting me drive?" he said.

I pointed to the deep scratch in the door. "Know anything about this?"

He looked at me. "What?"

"*This.*" Hell, my patience levels were so low, I considered slamming his head into the door a few times, not that it would've knocked any sense into him. "Is it your handiwork?"

"Why does everyone blame me for everything? Money goes missing from the cash register. Blame Travis. Michelle's earrings disappear. Travis's fault. Scratch in your car. Travis again. *Whatever.*" He threw his hands into the air, almost losing his balance in the process.

"You didn't do this? You're sure? Maybe it happened when you walked past."

He mumbled, "I don't think so. Not intentionally, anyway."

"And have you been anywhere near my office?"

"Huh?" He scrunched up his face. Travis wasn't that good an actor, and most definitely not when he had multiple beers in him on top of whatever else was still in his system. If he'd delivered the envelope with the photograph, it was a safe bet I'd know.

"Get in the car."

"Can we stop for breakfast?" he said, bouncing back.

"It's noon."

"Call it lunch, then. I'm starving. How 'bout pancakes? Or waffles?"

I pinched the bridge of my nose. "Travis. Get. In. The. Car."

He headed to his bathroom for a shower when we got home. I let him go, hoping it would help sober him up. I also wanted to use the time to my advantage. After the water upstairs had run for a bit, I searched through the jacket he'd dumped on the hallway floor for any other pieces of the photograph of Michelle but there were no signs of them. Frustrated, I crept to his room and rummaged through his jeans, but again, nothing but a couple of crumpled up phone numbers, which I put back.

I slid out of the room when the shower shut off and waited for him to go downstairs. Knowing Travis, he'd head straight to the kitchen where he'd forage for food. Sure enough, I heard bags rustling and the clink of silverware. As soon as the sound of the TV floated up from the den, I went back to his bathroom to search for more clues.

Along with alcohol, drugs, and women, Travis enjoyed boiling hot showers, as demonstrated by the amount of steam fogging up the room. I looked in the bin, found nothing, but as I straightened up, I froze.

A smiley face had been drawn on the upper right-hand corner of the mirror. A goddamn *smiley*. Michelle had always drawn them on the mirror when I had a shower. Always in that exact place, upper right-hand corner.

"It's my way of showing you I'm thinking of you," she'd said.

Quite frankly I'd thought it meant the woman had no concept of boundaries, but of course I'd given her a hug, and reciprocated the next time.

But we hardly ever used this bathroom.

I stared at the drawing, told myself it must've been there for a while. Or Travis had drawn it. I grabbed a towel while trying not to think about which of Travis's body parts it had last touched and wiped the smiley off the mirror before jogging downstairs, ready to ask him a couple more questions. Too late. He lay on the sofa, mouth open and snoring, a half-finished bowl of cereal balanced precariously on his stomach.

I removed the dish and grabbed his arm. "Hey."

"What?" He swatted me away, opened and closed his eyes a few times, blinking slowly.

"Travis." I shook him again. "God, did you take something since we got back?"

He smacked his lips. "Might've."

Maybe him being high would mean getting to the truth. I grabbed his collar. "Wake up."

He let out a small groan. "Yeah, man. Whaddayawan'?"

"Did you put something in my newspapers?"

"Don't read newspapers."

"What did you leave at my office?"

A shake of the head, a mumble. "Never been to your office."

"Did you draw on the mirror upstairs?"

"Huh?"

I balled my fists, wondered if breaking his nose would help. "Did you draw a smiley?"

"Michelle does that." He rolled over and buried his head into the back of the sofa, his next words muffled. "Always did it when we were kids."

I stood watching him, my jaw making tiny sinewy movements, pulse thumping in my forehead. We were done here, and depending on what he'd taken, Travis wouldn't be coherent or capable of holding a conversation for hours. I made myself take a few steps back, headed to the kitchen where I sat at the island thinking about having a shot of vodka. Decided against it.

Logic prevailed. Didn't seem like Travis had dropped off the photos of Michelle, and as for the smiley, it was simple: my wife had drawn it on the few occasions we'd used the bathroom or maybe for Travis when he'd stayed with us before she'd been taken. Hopefully she hadn't done so when he'd been *in* the shower. Most likely though he'd drawn it himself. Whatever the case, the cleaning service hadn't buffed the mirror all the way to the top. The drawing certainly wasn't Michelle's recent handiwork. Not unless I suddenly believed in ghosts, after all.

16

Despite my scoffing at signs from beyond the grave, a shudder snuck down my spine. I strode to the cupboard, retrieved the bottle of vodka I'd hidden behind the tub of organic quinoa and knocked some back. I could forget about the smiley face, but the mystery of the partial photographs needed an explanation. If my other theory was correct, and the police were trying to provoke a reaction, I had to stay calm, not give them what they were hoping for. And if it wasn't them...

I screwed the lid back on and stashed the booze away. My jaw clenched as I wondered if Woods had somehow determined who I was. Perhaps he did this all the time—found and extorted his clients to get another payout. Maybe I'd be next on his hit list if I didn't come up with whatever cash he'd demand. Although how would he know for sure it was me who'd ordered his services? He was guessing because there was no other way he'd have been able to tell.

Sitting in the home office, I spent the rest of the afternoon staring at the wall or wearing down the carpet with my incessant pacing as I calculated my next possible moves. Time seemed to slow down—cold treacle on a frozen spoon—as I processed every scenario and potential outcome I could think of. I went over each interaction I'd had with Woods, combed through the details from beginning to end, and then did it again. I hadn't made a mistake, hadn't slipped up and revealed my identity to him. It was impossible. I'd planned Michelle's misadventure too well, and with every step I'd checked each communication, encrypted or not, at least five times before I sent it to ensure nothing could ever be traced back to me.

Anonymity was everything on the dark web, but my privacy was only as secure as my last interaction, and a single error could bring everything down faster than a house of cards in a hurricane. Humans are creatures of habit, and the more comfortable we get, the less we pay attention. Many people can't stand the inconvenience of having different passwords for the websites they log into or apps they use even if it's highly recommended. Hell, plenty are those who leave the preset 123456 and believe they'll be okay, and as we familiarize ourselves with technology, we get sloppy and lazy, all too often using similar handles and logins, providing clues to anyone who knows what they're looking for.

Not me. Sloppy and lazy I was not, especially on the dark web. No way had Woods got hold of my identity, which meant he was taking his chances. At least if he was the one behind all of this it meant he wouldn't go to the cops. We'd put out a fifty grand reward for any information on Michelle's whereabouts, but if Woods was trying to make more cash on this job, he could hardly stroll into the police station and ask them to cut him a check. They may not have found any trace evidence on the van he'd burned out, but what if he gave them a concerned citizen tip that led to the discovery of her corpse, and they found his DNA or prints? He wouldn't take that risk, not if he was as smart as I thought he was.

I picked up a green rubber stress ball and crushed it in my palm, pressing down as hard as I could as I wrestled with what I knew, which was frustratingly little. Maybe it wasn't Woods at all. Perhaps it really was some other fuckwit who thought they were being clever, and who was working their way up to extorting me by pretending Michelle was still alive.

Her face had been splashed all over the news, people knew she was missing, and she was wealthy. Cases like this one made all kinds of weirdos crawl from the shadowy woodwork. It wasn't much of a stretch to picture some hoodie-clad, zit-faced kid in a basement rubbing their hands together in the hopes they'd hit the jackpot.

Deep breath. If that was what was going on here, and another demand was made, I'd have to play along, be the broken husband who pleaded we pay up never mind what the cops thought. Nora and I could come up with cash, no problem. Even if they asked for four times the initial amount I'd falsely demanded, we could get our hands on it within twenty-four hours, maybe sooner. Nora had her bank manager on standby ever since the abduction. But I'd been the one who'd crafted the ransom note. I'd known for certain no money would exchange hands, and I refused to be screwed out of any cash which was ultimately supposed to go to *me*.

I threw the stress ball against the wall, repeating the motion again and again, harder and harder. The next time I launched it my aim was off and when it bounced back on an angle it torpedoed into the framed wedding photo of us, knocking it to the floor and shattering the glass with a crunch.

I picked the picture up and examined it. Professionally taken, expertly edited. Michelle in a long white dress which hugged her curves, me in a black tux with a price tag that had made my eyes water. We'd had a fun day. A sunny Saturday in early November, almost three years ago to the day. Michelle hadn't wanted a huge wedding, which had been easy to agree on. We'd settled on a ceremony on the grounds of Nora and Gideon's house. A marquee, caterers, and about fifty guests, most of whom I didn't know. Gideon had wanted to put on a much larger affair to display his wealth, no doubt, but surprisingly, Michelle declined, and Nora had backed her up.

I'd hardly been involved in the planning, had been happy to let her take the lead, giving enough input to seem interested, but not enough to meddle with her desires. She'd looked perfect the day we got married. To be honest, she looked perfect every day, even when she had a cold, but I'd still lied my way through the vows, promising I'd love her through sickness and health when I had no intention of doing either, and all the while I'd tried to decide how I'd get my hands on her money now Gideon had messed things up.

When I repeated the *'til death do us part* bit, I tried to ignore the obvious solution, the voice whispering in my head if she were dead, the problem would be solved. I shoved the thoughts away, told myself I couldn't. But things had changed. Dad needed innovative health care. The pandemic hit. My patience ran out.

Everyone has a breaking point. Everyone has a price. I guess I found both of mine.

This was the truth: when I met Michelle at the art gallery that balmy spring evening, it didn't take long to determine the play. Turned out she'd come to London on a business trip and vacation combo and was staying another week. We spent every minute we could together, and before she got on the plane home, she'd invited me to Boston. We talked on the phone every night, and when I surprised her by showing up a couple of weeks later, I had a ring in my pocket.

"I've never felt this way about anyone," I said as I got down on one knee in the little Italian restaurant I'd taken her to, which I knew was her favorite because I'd *listened* when she'd mentioned it the first night we'd met, and gone through her social media to check for inspiration on how to propose. "I know this is sudden, and crazy, but will you—" I didn't finish the sentence because Michelle threw her arms around me and the place had erupted in applause.

Well before the wedding four months later, I'd established Michelle wasn't sure she wanted kids, said if she did, it wouldn't be until she was at least in her midthirties. Suited me fine. I had no interest in fathering a child and complicating the situation. I decided to bide my time, but predicted we'd stay married for four or five years at most before telling her I wanted a divorce, at which point I'd take a sizable chunk of cash with me. Or I'd siphon some off each month and build a nest egg.

So, stealing and divorce had been my plan, not murder, but, like I said, situations change, and when they do, you either stay ahead by shifting gears or you get run over.

I never knew for sure what prompted my father-in-law to convince Michelle she and I needed a prenup. He was a shrewd man, I'll give him that. Could've been a simple gut feeling as Gideon had no doubt come across swindlers and crooks during his long career in construction, but I doubted he'd ever met a chameleon like me. How would he have known?

Perhaps his suggestion stemmed from being suspicious of the Englishman who'd seduced his daughter while she'd been in Europe, and the whirlwind romance which had culminated in a proposal. Maybe it was because he knew I didn't have a

ton of money, although he believed I'd come from it originally. I'd been careful to include some truths. For example,
while I hadn't lied about my mother's and sister's deaths, I'd
spun a sad tale about my wealthy father getting caught up in
a Ponzi scheme, losing all our money before having a stroke
and ending up in a care home. Who would contradict me?
Michelle never bothered meeting Dad, and even if she had,
he couldn't have told her any different.

Whatever the reason for Gideon's wariness, three weeks before the wedding, Michelle sat me down because we *needed to
talk*. In my experience, those words were rarely a good pre-
amble for a conversation.

"Dad says we need a prenup," she said, matter-of-fact. I forced
my face into an interested expression and as I gave her a nod, she
continued. "Basically, whatever assets we bring into the marriage stay our own, whatever gains are generated on the money
while we're married is also ours. Same with any inheritance. A
clear delineation of his and hers." She stared at me, as if searching for a negative reaction. She didn't find one. "This is only if
we got a divorce, babe, so it's a formality, obviously."

"Obviously, sweetheart. But then…should we bother at all?"

She shrugged. "Dad says it's smart, you know, particularly
as I have the trust fund and I'll inherit part of the business
one day. He says it's a safeguard." She put her arms around
me, pulled me close and slid her hands up my chest. "His attorney, a guy called Philippe Danton is drawing up the contract. I know Philippe, he's lovely."

"Sounds like it's all under control."

Michelle kissed me, long and slow. "I knew you wouldn't
mind."

I did mind. I minded a whole damn lot. Especially when I
saw the document, which was so watertight it would've kept
the *Titanic* afloat. I could've left Michelle. Broken things off

125

and manipulated my way into some other woman's fortune, but my future wife was rich, and I was close. So *bloody* close.

I'd thought there had to be another way of getting my hands on her money, not quite yet realizing how OCD she was about her cash. She liked spending it, but she also kept an Excel spreadsheet detailing what on, and she checked every single payment and withdrawal. Something else Gideon had suggested, apparently, the meddling toad. So much for my siphoning off any dollars. She'd have noticed if I'd taken enough for a Boston cream pie.

And so, as my beatific bride walked down the aisle toward me, my mind buzzed with how I'd get my payout, and as I'd repeated *'til death do us part*, the whispers in my head got stronger.

Not going to argue with anyone who throws a ton of insults my way. I knew exactly what I was and wouldn't waste anyone's time by claiming my moral compass was in fine working order. It was wonky and I was okay with that. Those pointing fingers also shouldn't forget one thing—people marry people for money. All. The. Time. They spend hours scouring online dating apps, searching for the perfect, wealthy catch. My situation wasn't that different.

As all these thoughts about Michelle, Gideon, our wedding day, and the blasted prenup swirled in my mind, I was still pacing the home office, trying to ignore the broken picture frame with our wedding photo. I needed to give myself a good kick up the backside. Do something to manage the unpleasant predicament I found myself in.

I glanced at the computer, was overtaken by the sudden urge to find out where and when the photograph of Michelle that was being delivered to me in segments had been taken. If whoever sent it had found it on the web, it might narrow things down a little, particularly if Michelle had limited the privacy settings of her posts. Granted, it wouldn't be much to go on, and someone could've sent it to someone else, and so on and so on, but it was better than chucking a stress ball or walking around in circles.

My own social media profiles were almost nonexistent by design, but I knew how to use the platforms, and got to work on her Twitter feed. I scrolled down, eyes darting across the screen. She didn't use the app much, and her tweets mainly consisted of retweets or short replies, some with the odd GIF. Many of them were sharp and witty, making me chuckle a few times. That didn't surprise me as much as what came next—a small and sudden pang somewhere deep inside my gut. Uncomfortable. Mostly unexpected. Hard to believe, but for a second there, I *missed* her.

"Don't be daft," I said, giving my head a shake. The last thing I needed was to sit here reminiscing about the good ol' times, pretending our marriage had been anything other than my future piggy bank, never mind the fun we'd had.

I refocused, but after almost an hour of digging and scrolling I'd found nothing, so I moved on to Facebook. As I entered her login credentials and was about to hit Enter so I could access all her photo albums and messages, I froze, my fingers a fraction of an inch away from making my first mistake.

While I knew Michelle's passwords for all the social platforms, I'd told the cops I had no clue. During our initial interviews I'd spouted random possibilities in an apparent attempt to help. I didn't want to tell them I had all the details, which I'd got hold of in secret. I had no intention of letting them think I was a control freak who demanded oversight of his wife's online presence. Now though, the decision meant I couldn't log in as her. The cops were keeping tabs on how and from where her accounts were being accessed, and it wouldn't do for them to see they'd been logged into from my house. Consequently, I'd only be able to see what she'd posted and made public or shared with online friends, but nothing she'd restricted further, or anything she'd sent in Messenger.

Muttering a few choice words, I got back to work and this time my progress was slower. Examining her Facebook feed and available photo albums took forever, but after my back had gone stiff and my legs were almost numb, I'd still not located any sign of the photograph, and my frustrations mounted.

Time to regroup. After a bathroom break, a quick walk with Roger that allowed me a smoke, and checking in on Travis, who was still out cold on the sofa in the den, oblivious to my foul mood, I settled back in the home office for round three. Instagram.

The last post she'd ever shared was of the two of us, a cute-couple selfie, our faces smooshed together to fit the frame, one of her hands on my chest, both of mine around her tiny waist, all stylishly composed, and posted with a black-and-white filter and the caption, Forever yours, forever mine #made-foreachother #soulmates.

I had to admit, we looked good together, and judging by the comments her followers had left, they agreed.

OMG! You guys!

U2 r made 4 each other.

Lovebirds!

Jealous!

Cue multiple heart-eyes, high-fives, and wide-smile emojis. Once Michelle had gone missing, those comments had turned into desperate messages asking for her safe return, pleading for her to be found alive.

Good grief, was that another of those pangs in my gut? What was causing them? Loneliness? Maybe. Regret? It had better not be, I decided, as I buried it deeper. It was beyond too late.

I scrolled down. Michelle used Instagram the most by far, posting at least twice a day. The books she read. The food she ate. The coffee shop she went to. Sunrise workouts. Sunset hangouts. A perfect diary of her daily activities and where-abouts prominently displayed for all to see. Were I a stalker, I'd have been in heaven, and I bet Woods had used the infor-mation to help decide from where he'd snatch her.

Another twenty minutes of scrolling and zooming, and my hand froze on a second black-and-white photograph of my wife. I retrieved the picture I'd received at the office this morning, glad I hadn't disposed of it yet, and held it up to the screen. An exact match. Instead of elation building from my successful treasure hunt, my shoulders dropped. Finding what I'd been looking for on Instagram meant anyone could've downloaded it. The number of people who could be trying to use it to get money from me was exponential.

As I swore again, my phone rang. Detective Anjali. My mind raced. Did she know I was searching through Michelle's social media? Was there a team watching me now? I'd bought a webcam with a lens cover, so I knew they couldn't be spy-ing on me that way. Even if they were somehow tracking key-strokes on my computer, my activities were easy enough to explain. "I miss Michelle, Detective," I'd say, wringing my hands for emphasis. "I miss her so much. Her social media posts make me feel close to her." I wondered if I should men-tion what I'd been doing this afternoon, decided I'd wait and see what Anjali had to say first.

"Detective." I kept my tone flat, bordering on fearful. The husband hoping for the best but expecting the worst. "Have you found something?"

She waited a second, and I heard her take a deep breath. "I'm afraid not. I wanted to reassure you again we're doing everything we can. And I wanted to see how you're doing. Are you okay?"

As I thought about the partial photos and their cryptic messages, the scratch on my car, the meeting with Jeffreys that had almost derailed, my flat tire, and the smiley on the mirror, I had to grit my teeth. "Not the best," I said, glad she couldn't see my face.

"I'm sure this is really difficult for you."

Was she fishing? Expecting me to bring up the photos because she'd planted them? I couldn't tell. She continued talking about the case and how I had her personal guarantee she'd keep working on it until Michelle was found. I made all the right noises and uttered all the appropriate thank-yous. I wanted to tell her I had a client call or make up another excuse to cut our chat short but giving her the impression I was rushing wouldn't do me any favors. Finally, we said our goodbyes and hung up, still leaving me wondering why she'd really called.

Back in my home office, I sank into my chair, going over the facts, realizing with a sharp intake of breath I *had* made my first mistake. The orange envelope—I'd asked Agnes about it. Not only that, but I'd lied and pretended there'd been an illegible card inside. I made a note to self—if ever questioned why, I'd say I'd been shocked and couldn't bring myself to tell Agnes the contents had something to do with Michelle. I'd been stunned, too anxious. It was why I'd left the office and gone home.

Snatching up the partial picture of Michelle, I walked to the kitchen, set fire to the photo, and dropped it in the sink. As I watched it burn, I vowed I'd make sure whoever had left it, whoever thought they were oh-so-much cleverer than me would live at least long enough to regret it.

TUESDAY

17

By five thirty the next morning my stress levels hadn't dropped much so I decided I had to get out of the house, needed to do something to help me stay focused and sane. This would be my first time back at the gym since Michelle had gone, and I'd missed my routine of four weekly swims at the club. I'd allow myself a couple of training sessions a week, I decided, but that was it for now. Any more wouldn't reflect well on me, but a limited amount could indicate I was trying to re-gain at least some form of control over a hopeless situation by returning to my old habits.

The drive to the gym took fifteen minutes and I parked the car, staring up at the brown, stone building with sparkling nine-foot silver letters which spelled *Invicta*. The place was as pretentious as its name sounded, and if you asked me, a total waste of cash. Then again, for those who had the money, dropping a few thousand bucks a year so they had a place to show off their latest Lululemon gear probably didn't seem indulgent.

Michelle and I had joined a few months before the pandemic hit and had shut everything down. When the place reopened, she'd convinced me to keep my membership despite the fully kitted-out home gym, so we could work out together. I'd agreed, not because I wanted to have a *sweat-sesh* with my wife, or because of my mission to make her happy, but because of the center's pool. Twenty-five yards, brand spanking new, and with barely anyone in it at any time of the day, let alone first thing in the morning. Michelle had never as much as dipped a toe. According to her, the water was too cold, she couldn't stand how her eyes went red and puffy from the chlorine, and it was too much of a pain to get ready for work afterward.

Inside the sleek white granite reception area, I greeted the new guy at the front desk. André according to his shiny red-and-silver badge. I always made a point of knowing everyone by their first name, not only because it was good manners, but you never knew when someone you befriended even on a superficial level might tell you something useful. I'd made a few great business deals off the back of conversations I'd had in this place.

André gave me a wide smile and bid me good morning as I asked how his day was going. I pulled up my membership card on the gym's phone app and held it close to the scanner, almost walking into the opaque glass doors when they didn't swing open. I tried again, and a third time after wiping my cell down on the cuff of my jacket.

"Let's see what's going on." André's deep, rumbly voice came from somewhere within his huge neck. If his body was any indication, he spent his free time at the club, although I'd heard the staff was only allowed to work out during off-peak hours lest they disturb the elite.

"Tech gremlins, probably," I said.

"I'll enter the details manually. Can you please give me your membership number?" His fingers darted across the tablet as I reeled off the digits, but when he glanced at the screen, he said, "I'm sorry, sir—"

"Lucas."

"Lucas. Uh, I'm afraid your membership was canceled."

"Huh?" I shook my head, as if the gesture would somehow make an automatic adjustment to my hearing. "No. Can't be. When?"

He grimaced and flipped the tablet, pointed at the screen. "Ten days ago."

"I haven't canceled anything."

"Must be a mistake. I'll find out what happened. Won't take long, and I apologize for the inconvenience, Mr. Forester. Can I offer you a power juice while you wait? On the house."

I passed, hung around the entrance, and flicked through the pages of the latest edition of *Men's Health* until André came over.

"Apparently we received an email from you canceling your membership," he said.

"Impossible. I never sent one, and isn't there a month's notice or something?"

"We waive it for our triple platinum-level clients."

"Ah, yes. I remember. Can you show me the email?"

"I can't see the message in my system, only that it was received."

"Except I didn't send it."

"Yes, uh, well, you paid up-front for the year and a refund for the remainder is in progress. It should come through any day now."

"But I don't want a refund," I said gently. "I'd love to go for a swim."

"I'll reactivate everything while you work out," André said, visibly relieved I wasn't freaking out. I wondered what percentage of members either straight up ignored him or talked down to him when their power juice wasn't the exact mix they'd requested. No clue what André earned on a weekly basis, but it was without a doubt a fraction of any club member's income, triple platinum-level or not. How many times a week did he want to tell people to get lost?

"Appreciate it," I said. "Thanks, mate."

André pressed a button and the access doors slid open. "Have a good workout, sir."

A few minutes later I was silently slicing through the water—no earphones, no music, zero distractions—trying to find the usual sense of calm I'd lost over the last two days. My brain wasn't having any of it and darted off in multiple directions no matter how badly I tried to ignore everything or how hard I pushed myself physically.

Yesterday evening, the farce of pretending everything was normal had been as much for my own state of mind as it was to combat the expectation of whomever had sent the photos of Michelle. Whoever it was, and especially if it *was* Travis, something I couldn't fully discount without proper evidence to the contrary, I wouldn't let them see me react. After downing another shot of vodka, I'd called Nora, told her I wouldn't be visiting with Travis after all because he'd lost his job and had ended up in a bit of a state.

It took forever for him to sleep off whatever he'd taken and so I'd left him in the den and had gone for a walk with Roger to clear my mind, which hadn't worked. The highlight of the evening had been installing the tracker app on Travis's cell.

He'd been too out of it to feel me lifting his finger to access his phone, and now I had the ability to spy on his every move.

Once satisfied the app worked perfectly, and despite not being hungry, I'd cooked enough dinner for the two of us, ate mine, and got an Uber to pick up Travis's car, which we'd left at the strip club. By the time I returned at around eight thirty, he'd woken up and sat at the kitchen table stuffing his face with the curry I'd made, a yellow outline of sauce around his lips.

"Hey, Lucas." He ducked his head and wiped his mouth on a napkin before launching into his usual brand of apologies. He said he was sorry, promised he'd stop getting high, get help, and be sober by year's end. He'd done it before, he'd do it again.

On some level, deeper than the Mariana Trench perhaps, I was sure he meant it. But he already knew he'd never follow through. And I wouldn't let him.

"We were supposed to see your mother today," I said, putting his car keys on the table.

His fork froze midair, a splat of sauce landing back in his plate. "Yeah."

"I spoke to Diane earlier. Today hasn't been good."

"What do you mean?"

"Your mum's not doing well. She's suffering. I said we'd go tomorrow."

Travis pushed his plate away. "I won't mess up this time. I promise."

"Good. I'll meet you there. Five o'clock, sharp."

We hadn't spoken again until I'd headed to bed and left Travis to gorge himself on his mountain of guilt for the rest of the evening, wishing he'd choke on it.

As I reached the end of the pool, I flip-turned and upped my pace, arms and lungs burning. Chances were, Travis wouldn't visit Nora with me today either. He'd intend on going but instead of driving around, filling out job applications like he'd promised, he'd end up in some dive bar or a strip club instead, finding solace for all the rejections at the bottom of a few bottles. He'd get wasted beyond his eyeballs, lose track of time and the cash he spent, of which he surely didn't have much left. He couldn't handle what was happening to Nora, and I fully understood that. Most never wanted to see their parents suffer.

When Dad had his stroke I didn't think I'd be able to cope, especially as it had been my fault, and I'm not just saying that. I was coming up for my twenty-second birthday, had worked for Bobby Boyle for over eighteen months, ever since he'd walked into Wright Space and I'd successfully upsold him a bigger locker. While I didn't have intricate knowledge of his operations, I'd quickly come to understand my perception of him hadn't been as harsh as the reality. He was a calculating, hard bastard and made sure everyone knew it, thought nothing of breaking people's wrists with a meat mallet or popping their kneecaps with a baseball bat if they as much as thought of crossing him.

I'd heard the screams once, a guy who hadn't kept up his end of whatever dodgy bargain he and Bobby had agreed. I'd been told to keep watch outside, but even through the door I could hear the man begging for mercy, pleading for his life, and when his cries had finally stopped, Bobby had strolled out with a grin on his face as if he'd attended a Sunday picnic. I never saw the screaming man again, and for the longest time I told myself it was because he'd settled his debts and stayed out of trouble. My boss scared the hell out of me as much as I was in awe of him. As long as I remained on his good side, I reckoned nobody would ever touch me.

Bobby also had more fingers in pies than he had fingers or

pies and I was an errand boy. Delivered messages. Picked up packages from his accountant, dry cleaner, and various other operations I assumed weren't all legit, but I never asked questions.

"No point keeping all your eggs in the same basket," he'd said one day when I came back from another round of deliveries. "You have to have a diversified portfolio, son. I'm going to teach you all about it."

I knew Bobby wasn't talking about stocks, bonds, and precious metals. He was balls-deep in drugs, stolen cars, illegal gambling, and money laundering, to name a few of his so-called *eggs*. He sounded so much wiser than his forty-odd years, and I hung on his every word, wished my father were as gutsy as him, even despised my old man a little for losing his backbone somewhere along the journey of life.

Despite his well-earned reputation for being tough, Bobby could turn on the charm in a nanosecond. When he cracked a grin, he looked nothing like the ruthless criminal we all knew him to be. But when he was upset with you, when he stared you straight in the eyes, that's what scared me the most. Not because of what he was capable of, but because he didn't seem to have a soul, and he didn't care, because a soul would've meant emotions. According to Bobby, those didn't just get in the way of business, they got in the way of life.

He'd already made his mark on the Greater Manchester Area, and a big one. Business had exploded, and rumor had it his fortune was big enough for him to retire multiple times over. Except Bobby didn't want out of the game. He loved the money, but it was the power that did it for him the most, and he was on a quest to expand his empire way beyond our city. Bobby took great pleasure of letting anyone in his way know they should either bow down or step aside, and always,

always keep their mouth shut. Nobody argued, and if they did, it wasn't for long.

Knowing all this about Bobby, it surprised me all the more when I learned he did have some scruples. Heinz, Bobby's second in command who'd taken me under his wing, had quietly informed me there were three things Bobby never touched when doing business, and which I'd best never bring up: child porn, violence against women, and prostitution. The former was considered *scum of the earth* for obvious reasons. The latter two were because of Bobby's older sister who'd worked the streets a decade earlier and had her throat slit by a john.

Heinz had shared these details with me one night as we were having a cigarette at the back of the dry cleaner's, waiting for Bobby, who didn't tolerate smoking inside any of his premises because his grandma died of emphysema.

"Hold on, you mean his sister was murdered?" I said. "What happened to the john?"

Heinz smiled, showing off his perfectly aligned teeth, and took a puff. He was German, with a thick accent, a road map of scars on his face, a body full of muscles, and a snake tattoo which curled around his little finger and traveled all the way up his arm to his chest. The guy also had a mad keen interest in meditation and Egyptian history, the latter of which was so borderline obsessive, he could cite the names, birthdays, and cause of death of all the Pharaohs and their spouses. He'd called his cats Apep and Ra, although according to him it should've been the other way around because Ra was a real *Arschgeige*, which I assumed wasn't a compliment. I liked Heinz.

"The guy was caught and convicted," he said. "Didn't spend much time in prison because he won an appeal. Technicality. Something the cops didn't do right."

"He got out? Damn, I bet he's looking over his shoulder."

Heinz smiled again and flicked the butt of his cigarette

onto the ground, crushing it underneath his boot-clad toe. "Not anymore."

"He's dead?"

"Uh-huh. Fell off the top deck of a ferry."

"Really?"

"Nasty accident, that's what the papers said so it must be true. By the way, yesterday I heard you laugh when Bobby said cluck instead of the eff word."

"Yeah. So what?"

"May I make a suggestion?"

"Sure."

"Don't. The last person who made fun of his habit had his fingertips peeled like grapes. Have you ever tried to peel a grape? It takes a long time, and it's not pretty. And don't swear around him either. He gets upset. Best stop altogether so you don't forget." He gave me a thunderous clap on the shoulder and went back inside while I made a silent promise to always stay in Bobby's good books, except it hadn't ended up that way.

Working for Bobby made things a lot easier financially. My dad hadn't held down a job for more than a month at a time for years, bouncing from one caretaker or cleaning job to the next, and I continued to manage the cash of the household. Dad still got his benefits, there wasn't much I could do to stop those being deposited directly into his bank account, and most of it regularly went on gambling and booze. He'd been on a losing streak again of late, griping and grumbling when he came home before opening a bottle of whatever he'd picked up on his way back.

Dad was a pleasant drunk. Always ruffling my hair as he did when I was a kid or pulling me in for a bear hug. Never foul-tempered or violent, and while I may have felt sorry for him, angry at times, too, I loved my father. In between his epic binge episodes, we'd have fun. When he managed to stay sober, we'd play video games or Monopoly together, and depending on the schedule Bobby gave me, I'd go to the movies with Dad to catch a double bill. He was an avid fan of comic books, which carried over into an insatiable appetite for everything in Marvel's and DC's worlds. The last time we saw a film together, we munched our way through a jumbo bucket of popcorn and an extra-large pack of peanut M&M's while cheering on Iron Man, Dad's favorite character.

"Imagine having Stark's money," he whispered, and for once his breath didn't smell of wine, beer, or spirits, but of chocolate, which almost made me weep. "Imagine being so rich you never had any problems again. I wouldn't mind his good looks while we're at it. Wishes are still free, aren't they?" He'd sat back in his chair with a contented sigh and chucked another handful of snacks into his mouth.

Instead of focusing on the movie, I'd thought about what he'd said. If I could make us rich, maybe he'd stop drinking. If he stopped drinking, perhaps he'd be well enough to get back to work properly, and eventually, possibly, find someone to share his life with. He'd had a few girlfriends in the fifteen years since Mum and my baby sister had passed, but nothing lasted, not with the lack of effort he put in, and his extreme unreliability. Sometimes I wondered if it was deliberate because he'd never truly let go of Mum, and he felt he'd betray her somehow if he tried moving on. He still carried an old photo of her in his wallet, and on occasion I'd watch him from the doorway as he held it in his hands, lips moving silently, as if in prayer. If we had more money, I decided, and he felt much better about himself, perhaps he'd finally lay her to rest and live his life as she'd have wanted him to.

The next day I approached Bobby, told him outright—my voice holding far steadier than my insides—I wanted more responsibility. I could do more stuff for him. Bigger deliveries, more important ones. I wanted to be in his inner circle, not the outer orbit. He'd laughed at first and told me to *run along*, but instead of scarpering out the door I planted my heels.

"What are your tiny testicles made of, son?" he growled. "Clucking steel?"

"Nah, clucking tungsten," I quipped, remembering the name for the strongest metal from *Who Wants to Be a Millionaire*, something else Dad and I would watch if he could stay awake long enough. Picturing my father strengthened my resolve to take care of him.

Bobby stared at me for so long I thought my guts might liquefy after all, but then he put his head back and laughed, deep and guttural. "Watch it," he said, but there was something else in his eyes. Respect, maybe? Perhaps not quite, but whatever it was, it was good. He tapped his index finger on the table a few times as he continued to observe me. I didn't blink, didn't move. In all honesty I'm not sure I'd have been able to lift a foot.

"Tell you what," Bobby said. "Pick up an order at Caz's. Five p.m. Bring it straight here. Do not pass *Go*. Do not collect two hundred pounds. And don't be late. Got it?"

I didn't need him to tell me twice. I was at Caz's on time, a hole-in-the-wall fish and chip shop a few miles away. It looked as dilapidated on the outside as it was on the inside, but the place served the best thick-cut chips and mushy peas I'd ever had. Except I wasn't there to pick up supper but a scuffed, blue-and-white Adidas sports bag. As I was on my way back, Heinz called.

"Do *not* come here," he said, his voice low, urgent. "Hold the delivery. I'll call you when we need it. Do you understand?"

No clue what was going on, but I wasn't about to ask or go against my orders. I hurried home and set the bag on the kitchen table, paced the room a few times, a thin trickle of sweat seeping into my track pants. Both Bobby and Caz had given me strict instructions not to look inside the bag, but I was twenty-one, curious, with a what's-the-worst-that-can-happen attitude. They'd never find out if I had a peek. After another little while of slight hesitation, I unzipped the bag, gulping hard when I saw the stack of cash. I dumped the contents onto the table and counted the bills. Fifty grand.

I'll admit I was tempted, dared to imagine what Dad and I could do with the money. Get out of Manchester. Hop on an easyJet flight to Spain, somewhere Dad had always said he wanted to visit. Except I knew if I was going to screw over a self-styled Mancunian mafioso like Bobby, I'd better have enough dough to run forever. Fifty grand might have been the most money I'd ever seen in one go, but that amount wouldn't cut it. Decision made, and with the images of the Costa Brava fading into the background, I packed the bills up and shoved the bag into my bedroom wardrobe, somewhere Dad would never look.

As I waited for Heinz's instructions, I thought about how Bobby would for sure give me bigger, better jobs now he knew he could trust me. I was one of the youngest working for him, and this would surely put me on the fast track. I wanted to make rank, work properly alongside Heinz at some point. The life of a criminal may not have been what I'd dreamed of, but I was good at it, and confident I could make decent money a lot faster.

I was hanging around the estate with some friends the next day when I got Heinz's all-clear to make the delivery.

"Four o'clock," he said. "And don't be—"

"Late? Yeah, yeah. I know."

I went home, called out a quick hello to Dad and headed to my bedroom, still confident about my future, right up until I pulled open the wardrobe door and saw the empty spot where the Adidas bag should've been.

"What the hell?" I yelped, dropping to my knees, scrambling to move everything out of the way, turning the contents upside down. I rifled through clothes and other bags, pushed empty hangers and boxes of old schoolwork aside. I checked under my bed in case I'd somehow misremembered what I'd done with the bag. I searched the top of the wardrobe and in the shelves of my old desk, which barely had room for a stapler let alone a stack of cash that size. Heart pumping, blood thundering in my ears as the realization of what had happened hit me full on, I rushed to the living room.

Dad sat on the sofa watching TV. Judging by the debris, he was in the process of making his way through a third packet of Monster Munch, his jeans and the Iron-Man T-shirt I'd given him speckled with orange dust. Without making eye contact and with a distinct waver in his voice he said, "Hey up."

"Where is it?" I gasped, my voice hoarse. Desperate, I hoped he'd stowed the bag in a safe place as a precaution in case we got burgled. I willed him to launch into a multitude of questions about where the cash had come from, what the hell I was doing with this much money in the house and demanding to know everything about what I'd told him was a *delivery job*.

He didn't. Instead, he murmured, "I'll get it back."

Fear rushed up my throat where it threatened to choke me. I wanted to lunge at him, pull him off his seat by his stupid shirt, and shake him until he passed out. "You don't understand. I need the money. I need it now. *Now*."

We argued. Our voices louder and louder as we engaged in a full-blown shouting match peppered with cuss words and spittle. He did ask where the cash had come from. Wanted to know if I was selling drugs, if there were any in the house. I deflected by yelling it was none of his business and I needed it back, *all* of it, *immediately*. I didn't ask again what he'd done with it, and he didn't tell me. We both knew he'd been gambling. We both knew he'd lost.

Two hours and plenty of missed calls later, as I sat slumped in the hallway with my phone in my hands, trying to plan how to best spin this, and what to say to Bobby, the doorbell rang. Walking those four steps felt like marching to the gallows, but I had no choice. It was too late to run.

Hands trembling, I opened up to find Bobby in the doorway, his expression tight, eyes narrowed, nostrils flared. Heinz was with him, and another of Bobby's inside crew, a nutter we'd nicknamed Vic Vicious because he was always up for a fight, hovered behind them.

"The bag," Bobby said. "Give me the bag. *Now.*"

I tried to explain, but Bobby wasn't listening. Before I got two words out, my left cheek connected with the wall so hard, I thought my head had popped out the other side. As Heinz twisted my arm behind my back he whispered, "Sorry, kid."

I heard Dad stumbling from the living room and into the hallway. *"Stop,"* he shouted, trying to pull Heinz away from me. "Get off my lad. Leave him alone."

"Dad, stay out of this," I said, my voice muffled. "They're here for the—"

"Get off my son," Dad bellowed. "He didn't take your money. I did."

"No," I yelled as Heinz loosened his grip a little. "It's not true. It was me."

"He's lying." Dad's voice stayed strong, which made me both proud of and terrified for him at the same time. He had no idea who he was up against. "I found the bag and I lost the money on the horses."

I was about to speak but Heinz squeezed my arm, a sign for me to keep quiet, and all I could do was wait for Bobby's next move. When he said my name, Heinz pulled me off the wall and turned me around. Before I could blink, the sharp sting of a slap spread across my face.

"Your orders were to keep my money safe." Bobby smoothed down the front of his shirt, stretched his neck and pointed to my father. "Which also included from him."

"I'll get it back," Dad said. "Every penny. I swear."

Bobby smiled. "Yes, you will, but let's make sure you don't forget."

I struggled and screamed as Vic lunged at Dad, making good on Bobby's word right there in our hallway as Heinz held me back. I'd never forgotten the sound of the punches, the kicks, the smell of blood. It was all over in a matter of a minute, but being forced to watch it happen, restrained and helpless, made it feel like light-years. Dad went down on his knees first before falling on his side, gasping for air, his entire body twitching as his eyes rolled into the back of his head.

A stroke, the doctor said later. Some pre-existing condition exacerbated by the beating. I never fully understood why. Never told anyone what really happened that day, either. Never mentioned Bobby's name.

He wanted his cash back. I couldn't give it to him, so I ran. Moved to London, where I could disappear. And my dad? He ended up in a care facility, a terrible place where the staff was overworked, underpaid, and too scarce. Over the next few years as I rebuilt my history and reinvented my background, I was eventually able to afford to move Dad to a private home where he was properly looked after. It was the least I could do.

So, as I cut through the water at Invicta's glitzy pool and thought about Travis, did I understand his pain at seeing Nora, someone he loved so deeply, suffer? Yes. But at the same time, I'd have given anything to hear my father speak again, even if they were his last words, rather than him sitting in a goddamn wheelchair, unable to mutter a cohesive syllable. If I were Travis, I'd have spent every moment Nora had left alongside her.

No amount of ruminating would help my situation, I decided, and I headed for the changing room from where I emailed Agnes, letting her know I wouldn't be coming in to work today. Given my mood, if I showed up there, I'd probably end up killing someone.

18

The rest of the day went by without any more strange envelopes arriving, or damage being done to my car, and Travis
kept his word, much to my surprise. He met me at Nora's in
the evening without smelling of booze or looking as if he'd
taken anything. After we'd spent an hour chatting about the
weather and politics, the latter of which Travis knew a surprising amount, Nora asked him to fetch her a glass of milk.

"I spoke to my solicitor today," she said as soon as he closed
the door behind him. "We discussed how you might become the
official trustee for Travis's money, how you'd determine what
he needs and how much. Basically, how you and… *Michelle*
might administer it all." She sank back onto her pillow. "You
do realize when I sign these documents and he finds out what
we've done, it will affect your relationship with him, but I trust
you to help him through it all. You make sure he knows that."

"You don't want to tell him about the decision before…
before you, uh, go?"

"I don't think so. I wouldn't want my last weeks with him
to be fraught with tension. I'm sure you understand."

"Of course. I'll do anything to help."

"Thank you, Lucas."

I did a fantastic job of hiding my excitement as I thought
about how my future had become even brighter, more lucrative. Once we'd buried my mother-in-law, and I was in charge
of Travis's cash, I'd make sure he got as little as possible, give
him the bare minimum to get by. Nora's death would affect
him greatly, probably enough to send him headfirst into a
final downward spiral without me having to give him much
of a nudge.

"Here's your milk, Mom," Travis said as he came back into
the room. I watched as he handed her the glass and helped
her take a sip, reminding me of how I'd assist Dad whenever I
made it to England, which hadn't been as often as I'd wanted
since I met Michelle.

Fifteen minutes later I made my excuses and left them to
it, slipping past Diane, who was in the kitchen having supper,
and who didn't see me head to Gideon's wine cellar, an ex-
tensive, climate-controlled room which would've made som-
meliers faint from desire.

My father-in-law had given tours of his cellar whenever
he could, including on Michelle's and my wedding day. He'd
drone on about bouquet, body, and tannins, his knowledge
regaling the crowd. The wine cellar was one of his favorite
places in the house and mine to discreetly plunder since his
untimely demise.

It had happened one afternoon in late August, ten months
after our wedding, when Michelle and I had come for Sunday lunch. Nora had gone all out in preparing a table on the

shaded terrace, and when we arrived, Gideon, who may have been a gigantic arsehole but also an excellent amateur cook, was in the throes of preparing a beef Wellington.

"Can I help?" I said in yet another attempt to get on his good side.

Gideon was about to answer when Michelle jumped in. "Oh, yes, and us ladies can have a game of tennis before we eat. Work up a real appetite."

Said tennis was to be played on the private court on the grounds. The one next to the swimming pool Nora and Gideon barely used but which they had serviced daily by a local company during the entire season.

Small talk wasn't one of Gideon's soft skills, so I made mainly one-sided conversation as I morphed into the role of sous-chef, my temper rising like a soufflé each time he barked instructions as if he were Gordon Ramsay.

"*Don't* touch it, it needs to rest," he sniped as he removed the beef from the oven and put the tray on the island before looking over my shoulder. "Haven't you finished blending the sauce yet? No, *no.* Stop—" Gideon pinched the bridge of his nose between his fingers, presumably for an extra touch of drama "—and fetch a bottle of Sauternes from the cellar. 2002. It's superior by far."

"Oh, that's interesting. I thought 2001 and 2003 were better vintages," I said, putting down the hand blender next to the sink. "I must be mistaken—you're the pro."

His eyes narrowed, making me feel as if I'd somehow walked into a trap. "Remind me, Lucas, where did you learn all about wine again?"

"When I worked in London. A few of us took a course offered by the bank." An utter lie. Much like everything I knew about art, history, and politics, my oenophilia was self-taught. I'd spent hours at the library hunched over books and in front of a computer screen, drinking the information in (pun intended), adding layer after layer of it around the well-educated and refined personality I was so carefully constructing, one fact at a time.

Heinz had once told me you could fool almost anyone if they thought you were well educated, especially if they believed you knew more than them, but you didn't overtly show it, so they saved face. A comment I'd never forgotten.

"Ah, yes," Gideon said. "Which bank was it again? UBS?"

"HSBC."

"Yes, of course. Canary Wharf, you said. Where you worked in HR for their global asset management team."

I kept my gaze even, didn't move. I'd thought I'd been sufficiently vague about my professional background, had fibbed about where I'd worked and what I'd done to make it sound more upmarket, and he hadn't seemed to care beyond making sure it was something with bragging potential.

What was he playing at?

"Yes, I was."

"How peculiar." His steely eyes bored into me. "Thing is, one of my friends at the country club has a son who lives in London. His fiancée works at HSBC, in that very department, in fact. Been there for almost ten years. Very senior." He raised an eyebrow, but I refused to respond, my mind sprinting ahead, trying to find a way to clamber onto this runaway train and steer it in a different direction.

"They're here for a visit," he continued. "We had lunch."

"Really? What's her name? Maybe I—"

"Know her?" he smirked. "As a matter of fact, I mentioned you. Told her my daughter had married a Londoner named Lucas Forester." I stayed silent, and when he understood I wasn't going to answer, he continued. "Can you explain why this woman, who has worked for the exact same department, at the exact same bank, in the exact same city as you, for *years*, didn't react at all?"

"I've no clue." I made sure my voice was smooth, my expression neutral. "There were quite a few of us. Maybe there are some crossed wires somewhere."

"See, I don't think that's true," he said. "There's something about you, Lucas. I've never been able to put my finger on it, but I think you're hiding something. I'm going to find out what it is." He pulled his cell phone from his pocket, waggled it midair. "I should call her now. You could talk about old times. What do you say?"

"I'm sure it would be quite lovely."

"Cut the crap, Forester," he said. "And let me assure you, if I find out you've misled Michelle and this family, there'll be hell to pay."

Wishing I could pick up the blender, push it into his eye and burrow all the way through to his brain, I bowed my head. "I may have exaggerated my experience a little," I mumbled. "I can explain."

"Yes, you'll do exactly that."

"Have you shared any of this with Nora or Michelle?"

"No, I haven't. Against my better judgment I thought I'd give you the opportunity to clarify things for me first."

"Thank you. I appreciate that."

"Don't thank me yet. After lunch you and I will have a conversation in the study. You'll tell me everything I want to know, after which I'll decide if I involve the women. Now, hurry up and get me the wine." He gave me a dismissive wave and turned on the tap.

I knew what he was doing. Trying to make me squirm, probably hoping I'd beg a little. Whatever I did, he'd share all the information I gave him with Michelle, and his wife. There was no way he'd ever let any of this go. And if he, by some miracle, decided to stay silent, it would come at a price. I stared at his back for a moment before heading to the hall, pretending to go to the wine cellar as I watched him through the doorway.

I'd had my history poked at before, but this was the first time I'd felt vulnerable, and I didn't like it. Ever since I'd met Michelle, my father-in-law had been wary of me, trying to trip me up with questions about my past, my education, my pedigree. Uncovering one loose thread would lead him to pick at it until everything around me had unraveled completely. Swift and decisive action was required.

I couldn't bribe Gideon unless I had some information on him, some dirty details that would lead to a mutual agreement of keeping our mouths shut. It would take too much time and telling him the truth about my résumé was a nonstarter. I'd be exposed as a liar, and all my plans would be in jeopardy.

I thought about what Bobby would do, decided I had no other choice, not if I wanted to reach my goal. Mind made up, I sneaked through the kitchen, taking a dishcloth off the rack as I walked, and wrapping it around my hand. In one fast move I swiped the still plugged-in blender off the counter and dropped it into the sink. I jumped back, watching as Gideon's body convulsed, his hands in the water, mouth and eyes wide open, the electrical current going up his arms and straight across his heart.

I'd never killed anyone before. Hadn't known for sure until then whether I was capable of doing so. There was no rush of excitement, no strange and perverse pleasure, and I did nothing when he finally slumped to the floor. Didn't move when the sound of his head hitting the expensive, imported Italian tiles reverberated around the room.

For the next few minutes, I stood perfectly still, making sure I didn't move my feet as I waited. From my vantage point

I could see Nora and Michelle in the distance, still midmatch. Even if they came to the house now, it would be too late.

Once I was certain Gideon would never get up again, I headed to the wine cellar for the Sauternes. For authenticity's sake, when I got back to the kitchen, I lunged toward him, letting the bottle slip through my fingers and explode all over the floor. Didn't matter. It truly wasn't the best vintage.

Much later when the police, paramedics, and coroner had left, I'd consoled Nora and Michelle, and Travis, too, after he arrived. Nobody questioned the tragic accident and I'd never regretted what I'd done. How could I, when I now live with the reassuring knowledge that all my secrets would remain intact?

19

Gideon's death had been necessary for my survival, and while I'd never intended on killing him either when I'd married Michelle, it did bring about various benefits, and not only for me.

Nora, Michelle, and Travis had been upset, of course, as was to be expected, although Travis appeared relieved he'd no longer have to see the near-constant disappointment in his father's eyes. Nora had seemed transformed in a way, less encumbered, as if she'd been set free. Michelle had made several comments about her dad being a bit of a tyrant, both in the way he ran his company and how he ruled his home as if it were the 1920s, which I'd witnessed plenty of times when he'd been subtly dismissive of, or had openly undermined Nora.

After his death, she'd no longer been subjected to her husband's antiquated, sexist views. She'd sold the company for a hefty sum, decided to hang on to the family home for now,

and spent her days traveling, getting involved with more charities, and joining three separate book clubs. When she'd shared
her cancer diagnosis with me, I'd been shocked and saddened,
and while I'd never wished any ill on her, I'd taken pleasure
in knowing I'd assisted in making her last two years on this
earth more enjoyable by far.

Hard to believe we'd got the news about her illness only a
few weeks ago, when all my plans were on track. That's where
I needed to be again and thinking about my father-in-law's
mishap had strengthened my resolve to make sure I got there.
I'd dealt with people who'd tried to screw with me before,
and I wouldn't hesitate in doing so again. But first, I needed
to find them.

When I got to my house, I parked the car, decided to hide
the bottle of velvety Bourgogne I'd taken from Gideon's stash
under the sink, and let Roger out into the garden. Cigarette
in hand, I scoured the grass for more footprints, relieved there
were none. In the office, I picked up one of Michelle's novels
and flipped through the pages for the seemingly innocuous
words I'd underlined in faint pencil. Three words Woods had
given me. The location of the body.

An uncomfortable sensation snaked its way to the pit of my
stomach, and although I tried pushing it away, it came back
twice as hard. If Woods was the one sending the partial photos, had he kept her alive? I'd wanted her *dead*, had clearly
specified there was to be no torture or rape, which Woods
had been indignant about because he wasn't *that kind of person*, but I'd trusted the word of a criminal, an oxymoron if I
ever heard one.

Woods had taken Michelle, a certainty based on the CCTV
footage the cops had acquired. The stolen van he'd used had
been burned, no DNA or other evidence recovered, but it
didn't mean he couldn't have held my wife captive for the last

month, waiting to see if he could make more money. Was he going to demand a ransom? Why wait so long? Had he hurt her in other ways despite his reassurances? What would I do if my wife was still alive?

More questions swirled. Could Detective Anjali and her team rescue her? I sure as hell didn't want them to, but was there a way I could botch any attempt made? I scoffed out loud. I was smart and manipulative, sure, but sabotaging a cop-led mission of that magnitude really did seem impossible and I was no Ethan Hunt.

Another option was for me to somehow become the hero who ensured her safe return. We'd be reunited, and happy. For a while. Nora would be delighted, and Travis, well, he'd continue partying himself to death. But I'd be back to square one. I supposed somewhere down the line my wife could suffer a tragic accident. In a car. On a lake. Skiing. All the possibilities I'd thought of before and had discounted because there were too many variables, too many chances of getting caught, and if she came back safe after being abducted only to die a short while later, somebody was bound to smell a big fat hairy rat.

Although it did happen. People survived tragedies all the time only to perish in another. How often had I read stories about the survivor of a shooting who'd gone on to die in a fiery crash a few months later? I let myself imagine—briefly— my personal *Final Fantasy* installment, but things weren't that simple, and I couldn't let myself get distracted. Somebody somewhere knew, or *thought* they knew something, which meant I was in trouble.

I needed to go to the location of her body. First, to ensure Woods had made good on our agreement, and second, because he might have left something there, a clue I could use to identify and find him with so I could sort him out if he was the one behind the photos.

Knowing Travis might come back to the house at any point this evening, I had to prepare before he arrived. I pulled an empty tea tin from the back of a top shelf in the kitchen. The container was filled with inconspicuous items—rubber bands, a couple of lighters, a few stray keys—what Dad would've called an *odds and sods* tin, and an ideal place to hide something in plain sight. I turned it upside down, emptied the contents on the counter, and dug through them until I found the key I needed.

Next, I left my phone on my desk in the office, grabbed my jacket and gloves, changed into my boots, and headed to the garage where I slid on my helmet and fired up my Triumph. I'd bought it over a year ago, when I was at the beginning stages of making my plans. The old bike was small, fast, and had no modern chips or inbuilt GPS technology like my Mercedes had, which could tell people my every move. Nevertheless, and as I had done for the past month whenever I took it out, I gave the bike the once-over, making sure the cops hadn't placed a tiny tracker somewhere.

At first, I took a few shortcuts and alleyways cars couldn't fit down. Next, I cruised around empty country lanes in a random, *riding to clear my head* pattern, stopping for a coffee. This was something else I'd done for the past year, and I had to ensure I didn't change my behavior now and stayed consistent in everything I did. Once satisfied there wasn't anyone on my tail and my escapade would be considered another typical ride, I headed for the bus station in a village a few miles away, the place I'd stashed my burner laptop and phones.

A homeless man sat on the front steps, holding a cardboard sign saying GOD BLESS. I slipped fifty bucks into his hand, thinking how Dad and I had ended up on the streets, and hoped he managed to stay warm for the night.

As usual, there were hardly any other people at the bus station, but I still yanked a baseball hat from my jacket pocket and pulled it low over my face before adding a slight limp as I walked to the dented sky-blue lockers on the left side of the building.

Once I'd retrieved the burner laptop from my unit, I went to the rank bathroom with the graffiti-covered walls, which had been painted a shade that could only be described as puke, and hit the computer's power button. Leaning against the wall, I waited to connect to the station's Wi-Fi, opened my VPN, and brought up the *what3words* app in the browser.

My heart rate sped up as I input the words Woods had texted me, and which I'd committed to memory before getting rid of the phone. Ignoring the shaking in my fingers and the trepidation in my stomach, I typed in *rise equal protection* and let my hand hover over the Enter key.

Hit the button, and it would reveal where Michelle was buried. I'd get my guarantee the job had been done as agreed. On the other hand, if the cops were somehow watching me despite all the precautions I'd taken, it would be almost impossible to get them to believe I wasn't involved. If they weren't following me, it still didn't mean I was safe. They might, at any time, ask me to retake the lie detector test. I could refuse, but it would be suspicious. If I agreed and they asked again if I'd had any involvement in Michelle's disappearance, I knew I'd be able to fool them. However, if they inquired whether I knew where Michelle *was*, and I'd been to the exact location, the results might not be so clear-cut. Yes, I'd beaten the system once, had extensively prepared for it, but this was a gamble. I made the calculation in my head, weighed the pros and cons and hit Enter.

The browser brought up a map of the area, overlaid with the nine-foot-by-nine-foot grid. I zoomed out a little, getting the lay of the land, recognizing the place instantly. A conservation area about a twenty-minute ride from the house, thirty from the place where Michelle had been grabbed, and in the complete opposite direction of where the cops had found the burned-out van.

Woods and I had never discussed location, but I knew this area quite well. Michelle and I had hiked there on several occasions, especially during the autumn when the colors on the leaves were spectacular reds, oranges, and yellows. She'd said many times how much she loved the serenity of the place, how she thought it magical, somehow. I didn't like the sudden pinch in my heart the memory generated, or how I thought it was some kind of destiny she'd ended up there.

Woods had chosen wisely. As well as a spectacle for the eyes and soul in autumn, the trees were thick, the brush dense and plentiful, and upon closer inspection, I saw the location of her body was a little over a mile from the main path. No random dog or kid would stumble upon her by accident. Quite the opposite. It was somewhere she could lay undisturbed and undetected. A place I could get to without being seen. Somewhere, I realized with an uncomfortable shudder, she'd had to walk to because there was no way Woods would've been able to lug a body that distance.

Satisfied I knew the general direction and landscape I'd be venturing to, I went to the dark web and flicked through the message boards. No trace of Woods, not a single message for me or anyone else. I didn't expect to hear from him. I also expected by now he'd switched to another username because when we'd first corresponded, I learned he never used the same one twice. There was no guessing which alias he'd taken, what he was doing, or where. I shut the laptop down and returned it to the locker. As soon as this nonsense with these partial photographs of Michelle was over, I'd get rid of it, and the phones. Chuck them into the Charles River and let them sink into the murky waters, lost forever.

Another ride down more country lanes reassured me I

wasn't being followed, which meant I could move on to the next part of my plan. While there was an outdoor equipment shop a fair bit closer to the house, I stopped at the one located in a large outlet mall instead, a place which belonged to my soon-to-be new client, Jeffreys.

According to him, they were having their annual everything-must-go blowout sale this week. An event so popular, with deep discounts and freebies galore, people descended on the store like ants on sticky bun. He wasn't wrong—the place was packed—and I was one face among dozens of others, inconspicuous and instantly forgotten by the harried staff.

I also knew from Jeffreys himself their overall IT security left a lot to be desired. For example, they only kept their footage for twenty-four hours before recording over it. It was something he said they wanted to upgrade. If the police ever asked whether I'd visited the store I could say yes, but there'd never be any visual proof of what I had or hadn't purchased.

Without fuss or asking for help I selected two handheld GPS navigators, a book of local hiking paths I'd never use, and two pairs of hiking boots, one that would fit, the other two sizes too big.

I paid for one of the navigators and pair of boots separately, handing over cash and declining the additional discount if I gave them my email address. "I don't need the boxes for the boots," I said to the cashier who sported shaggy blond hair, a pine-green beanie, and a beard which likely hadn't seen a trimmer in months.

"Dude, you sure? You can't return anything without the boxes."

"I'm sure."

Where I was headed, I'd never be bringing any of this stuff back.

20

The last place on my list was the library in Chelmswood where I made a point of talking to Antoinette, the French librarian with whom I regularly chatted whenever I stopped by. In a quiet and apologetic voice, I asked for recommendations on books about trauma and grief, and after telling me how sorry she was about what had happened to Michelle, and what I was going through, she led me to the section I could've found blindfolded. After pointing out a few books she thought might help, she touched my arm, told me she'd be at the reference desk if I needed anything, and left me alone.

I pulled some of the books from the shelves and flipped through them, selected the three with the most detailed sections about the impact and importance physical activity could have on mental health, and went to the checkout desk only to find my library card wouldn't scan properly.

"I still have my account though?" I said to Antoinette, wondering if it had been mistakenly canceled like my membership at Invicta.

"*Oui, oui,*" she said. "Sometimes the cards are a little temperamental." She tried the handheld scanner again, smiled when she heard the beep. "*Voilà.* You're all set."

I most certainly was. Everything I'd done this evening was foundation work. The boots, the GPS navigators, the books—all of it not only to prepare for my trip to the conservation area, but also in case Michelle's body was ever found as the cops would put the place under a microscope.

The boots because they'd lift whatever footprints they could find, but if compared to the shoes I had at home, they'd see they were the same model—giving them a little frisson of excitement—but the wrong size. My way of messing with them because when I'd researched how to get rid of my wife, I'd been astounded to discover how many criminals committed offenses, including murder, and didn't throw away their shoes. How bloody stupid could you be? People that sloppy deserved to get caught.

The library books were in case surfer dude at Jeffreys's store remembered my face. "I read physical exercise can help with stress," I'd point out, "and I picked up a GPS navigator because I didn't want to get lost." They'd have no clue I'd use only one of the devices a single time to find Michelle's location, after which I'd get rid of it. The other I'd take with me a few times over the next couple of weeks when I went for a hike in completely different areas. Smoke screen set. Job done.

It was all in the details. Hiding out in the open, wrapping lies up in truths so people couldn't see them. Lack of preparation and forethought was why so many people didn't get away with their crimes. They didn't plan enough. Weren't meticulous enough. Watching *CSI* reruns didn't make you an expert. They had no idea of or appreciation for what it really took. All things considered it was probably a good thing because if they had, the unsolved homicide rate would reach the stratosphere.

There was one downside to this legwork though. The best, most expensive lawyer in the world wouldn't be able to argue crime of passion or manslaughter, not with everything I'd done. Premeditated murder was what I'd be looking at. Exactly why I'd never get caught.

Satisfied I had everything, I rode home. Travis's car sat in the driveway, parked so far away from my Mercedes, it was practically hugging the bushes. I almost wanted to give the guy a standing ovation for actually listening, let alone remembering.

Once inside, I went straight to my bedroom and stowed the larger size boots in the wardrobe and plugged in one of the GPS navigators in the bathroom to charge. Back downstairs I put the remaining, regular size boots and the library books on the ottoman by the door and meandered to the kitchen.

Travis sat at the table, his head in his hands, the bottle of Gideon's Bourgogne three quarters gone. Making him nice and subdued before ensuring he was fully incapacitated for the night had been the final part of my preparation plan. Looked like he'd inadvertently got a head start.

Snotty-nosed, his cheeks pink, he swiped at his bleary eyes with the back of his hand, indicated to the bottle of wine, and muttered, "If you're going to give me a hard time for this, then let's get at it."

I dropped my shoulders in apparent defeat, forced out a sympathetic sigh and walked over, patting him on the shoulders before grabbing a glass from the cupboard. Travis watched, wide-eyed, as I poured myself a small amount of the wine and dumped more into his glass.

"Did you eat?" I said.

He looked like he wanted to ask why I wasn't busting his balls but must have decided against it. "Karina stopped by earlier. Came in for a chat and dropped off some cottage pie."

"How nice of her."

"Yeah. It's vegan but it's delicious. Your half is in the fridge." He pressed the heels of his hands over his eyes, his jaw clenched hard. "She reminds me of my mom, when I was little. Always kind. Taking care of others."

"Karina and Diane are great neighbors."

"She offered for me to stay with them."

"Did she?"

He put his head down. "Said she's at home for a few weeks, and because you're at work during the day. She was quite persistent, actually, thought I might appreciate the company."

More like she believed she and Diane could curb his substance abuse, and I couldn't let that happen. "What did you say?"

"That I'd think about it. I know you don't like having me around—"

"That's not true."

"Yes, it is. But the truth is, I know you're trying to keep me in line, and I appreciate it." When he swiped at his eyes again, I got up, retrieved Karina's grub from the fridge and shoved it in the microwave, giving him some time to compose himself.

I hadn't bothered eating today, I'd been too worked up, but now I had a plan of what I was going to do this evening, my hunger came back with a growling vengeance. I almost wished Travis had taken Karina up on her offer to stay with them, if only for tonight. I didn't want him to see me leave the house well before dawn. I also didn't want him waking up and noticing I wasn't home, not when he might unintentionally go blabbing about it to Nora or the cops. It would mean I'd have to explain why I was out, and the less I had to do that, the better.

"I can't believe she's dying." Travis stifled a sob, and for a flash there I felt bad for him. His dad, arsehole or not, was dead, Michelle was missing, and he was about to lose his mother. My sympathy didn't last, because his state of mind satisfied another part of me, the larger, darker side, the bit which easily justified my plans for him. The way I saw it, by not saving Travis from the inevitable drink and drugs once Nora was gone, I was doing him a favor. He'd probably kill himself with or without me, anyway.

I finished the little bit of wine I'd poured into my glass, then commiserated with Travis before telling him how angry and desperate I was about Michelle's disappearance. "If I find out who did it," I said, "I'll kill them." Didn't take much acting. Not when I thought about those partial photos of Michelle. I sighed. Deep and full of sorrow. "I need something stronger."

His eyes lit up as I hoped they would, and he smirked, making me an immediate accomplice. "I have a bottle of tequila. I'll get it. We'll have one shot. Only one."

Sure we would. As he bounded upstairs to fetch the booze, I walked to the mailbox with Roger to make sure I hadn't received a special delivery. There was no orange envelope. No random flyer. I exhaled, but as I was about to go back inside, a car turned into our driveway, and I spotted Detective Anjali inside. As I waited for her to get out, making sure my expression turned to a combination of gloom dashed with a sprinkling of hope, I wondered what the hell she wanted.

"Lucas," she said, walking over, hands thrust deep into her jacket. "How are you?"

I shrugged, trying to ignore the shiver zipping down my spine. I didn't trust her. The trick was to not let it show. "Have you found something?"

"No," she said. "I'm officially off the clock. Came to see Travis."

"Travis? He's inside." I indicated behind me with my thumb, remembering he'd gone for the bottle of tequila. Anjali knew all too well about Travis's recent downfall, and she wouldn't approve if she saw us drinking together. "I'll fetch him for you."

As I turned, she reached for my arm. "I hope you don't feel I'm intruding. I had another long chat with Nora, and I offered to talk to him. Try to scare him straight, or straight into rehab at least. Worth a try, no?"

I filled my expression with enthusiasm. Wide eyes, tentative smile, a touch of relief. "Really? That would be great. I've been trying but, well, he's not receptive. I hope you have better luck."

"I'll do whatever I can. Would you mind if we go inside? We probably shouldn't have this kind of conversation in your driveway."

As she headed in through the front door and waited in the hall, I saw her gaze fall on the bag from Jeffreys's store on the ottoman, along with the self-help books from the library. She looked up at me. "Please don't give up on Michelle. Or me. I'm not done with this case."

"But can you promise you'll find her?" I made myself choke on the words, forced tears into my eyes for some extra points. Crying on demand wasn't hard if you knew how, and it could be incredibly effective in a world where men were still trained to hide their emotions.

"You know I can't, Lucas. I'm sure you understand."

I blinked a few times, whispered, "I'll get Travis."

As I walked down the hallway, I allowed myself a small smirk. Whatever Detective Anjali did to find my wife and to help Travis, it would never be enough. It wasn't her fault she'd brought a lollipop to a gun fight.

WEDNESDAY

21

I'd set my old alarm clock to go off at one in the morning and had stuffed it under my pillow so Travis wouldn't hear it ring, but I needn't have bothered. I hadn't slept at all, the anticipation of what I was going to do far too intense to let me rest. Although I tried to distract myself by watching mindless TV and hopping around Netflix, I couldn't concentrate. I gave up and got up shortly after midnight, both body and mind fully alert and ready for my trip to the forest.

I hadn't set the security alarm when I'd gone to bed a couple of hours ago in case Detective Anjali ever consulted the log. It was preferable she believed I'd forgotten rather than her wondering why it had been deactivated. I supposed I could tell her it had been Travis, but I'd keep those excuses on reserve in case I needed them. I'd learned a long time ago a questionable lie was equivalent to a hangnail. People couldn't resist picking.

Without making a sound I dressed in the clothes I'd prepared before I'd gone to bed, pulling on an old, black, long-sleeve sweater, and black track pants. Next, I stuffed the large hiking boots, a few pairs of socks, and the fully charged GPS navigator in a backpack I retrieved from the depths of my closet. Once dressed, I slipped into the hallway and stood silently, listening.

Travis had downed a good helping of the tequila and, exactly as I'd planned, he was out cold, the sounds of his throaty snores audible even with the door closed. After Detective Anjali had spent time with him in the den last night, both speaking in voices too low for me to hear, he'd seemed more vulnerable than before. He hadn't wanted to go into detail about their conversation, only mentioned she had a sister who'd succumbed to her addictions, and Michelle would want a better life for him.

"She told me to hang in there," he said, blinking fast. "Tried to get me into rehab but I'm not going with Mom sick. What if she…" He waved a hand. "I'm not going, not now. Later."

Not the scared straight spiel she'd told me about. Travis had probably whined about how difficult his life had been, how he was finding it hard to cope but I hadn't expected her to fall for it. Regardless, after Anjali left it had been easy to fill him with enough booze to knock out a herd of elephants, but I'd added a crushed-up over-the-counter sleeping pill to his last two shots to ensure he wouldn't wake until noon. No way he'd think there was anything amiss either, not with the half-empty bottle of tequila I'd left next to his bed.

Pushing any lingering worries about Travis waking up aside, I put on my regular boots, headed to the door leading to the garage, and quietly slipped out before shutting it again. Aside from parking the cars in here, it wasn't used for much. A few boxes of Christmas decorations, several barely used tools, two

sets of winter tires. Nothing out of the ordinary. All seemingly
banal and innocent things until you put some of them together.

Nitrile gloves from a box of dozens. Michelle's headlight,
the one I'd bought her for when she jogged in the dark because I *worried for her safety*—even though her getting run over
would've saved me a lot of trouble. I'd scored extra *best husband
ever* points when I'd given her the light in front of her friends.
They'd put their hands to their chests, proclaiming I was *amazing*. Whoever said first impressions matter wasn't wrong, but
second, third, even tenth ones could be equally important.

I collected the other things I needed for tonight's trip. A
few disposable face masks, a small bottle of lighter fluid, and
a book of matches I'd picked up from some random restaurant I'd stopped at to use the bathroom while out on my bike
and never revisited. I added the collapsible shovel hanging on
the wall, which I'd bought over a year ago, and still looked
brand new.

"Why bother with yard work?" Michelle asked with one
eyebrow raised when I'd said I'd do some weeding. "We have
landscapers, and *they* know what they're doing. You might
pull out a real plant."

I'd gritted my teeth as she'd implied, incorrectly, I didn't
have a clue, and she'd completely overlooked the fact I enjoyed
gardening. I found it oddly satisfying and peaceful, and she
knew it had been something I'd done with my father when
I was a kid.

It was true—except it hadn't been in the charming garden
I'd fibbed about, but an allotment Dad had managed to get his
hands on for one season. I'd been twelve that summer, Dad
barely drank, had even managed to keep his latest job as a bus
cleaner for almost three months, and we'd grown so many to-
matoes and green beans we'd both gotten sick of them.

The two of us would stroll to the allotment almost every

evening, chat with the other people there and have a few sandwiches or fish and chips. It was the summer I had my first kiss with a girl called Cindy who was in Manchester to see her grandmother, and it was the point in my childhood where the blinkers had come off, and I'd begun to realize everything might not work out for Dad and me.

Michelle knew none of that part. She believed we'd had an elaborate vegetable patch at the back of the quaint cottage we'd lived in. Thought my father was a hardworking senior civil servant until his stroke. Not a complete lie. Dad had been a janitor at the town hall for a while.

My point is she knew I enjoyed gardening but when she told me to leave it to the landscapers, I never touched the shovel again. I let my wife and everybody else around us think her word was rule. It had been the same when she'd decided we were going vegan about three months ago. Not her. *We*. It hadn't been a discussion.

"We're killing the planet," she'd announced over dinner one night, a delicious meal of chateaubriand, homemade fries and béarnaise sauce I'd made from scratch to wow her, something she could brag about to her friends. I hated cooking.

"Huh?" I popped another piece of succulent steak in my mouth, thinking I'd misheard. Since when did my wife give an actual toss about the planet? It's not as if she particularly cared for animals or liked our fellow humans that much. I'd seen this behavior before. Give it a few weeks or months and she'd move on to something else she thought was trendy rather than devoting her time properly to a cause like Nora did. I stared at her, trying to resist the temptation of rolling my eyes.

"This planet's dying because of this—" she pushed away her plate "—because of meat."

"Assassination by cheeseburger?"

"You've been eating cheeseburgers?"

I laughed, mainly at her righteous expression, but also because I was about to tell her a big fat lie juicier than the meat on my plate. Fact was, before she'd run into me at the art gallery and spilled my champagne down my shirt, I'd listened. Overheard Michelle proudly declare she hadn't stepped into a fast-food joint since her sixteenth birthday when a pack of dodgy chicken nuggets had made her throw up. Imagine how surprised not to mention delighted she was when, a little later in the evening, I'd deftly steered the conversation around to dinner, and she discovered I hadn't eaten fast food in over five years. What a whopper. Actually, I'd had one of those the day before. My monthly treat.

"You know I haven't, sweetheart." I reached for her hand and gave it a tender squeeze. "Pathetic joke. What were you saying about burgers killing the planet?"

Honest to God, sometimes I wondered how she found me attractive, how she put up with someone so spineless, considering she was incredibly assertive. I presumed Michelle was so used to people bending to her will, to getting her own way all the time, she didn't notice. Or care.

"It's not only burgers," she said, and color me corrected because she launched into a detailed explanation about the link between meat production and global warming, sound science I'd read before but pretended I hadn't. I let her believe I was listening intently, and waited for her to finish. Finally, she announced, "...and so I've decided there'll be no more meat for us. No eggs or dairy either. We're going vegan."

"How exciting."

"I know. I'll do an online shop, make sure our fridge is fully stocked with almond milk, tofu and loads of different fruits and veggies. From now on we'll eat the rainbow."

"I'm guessing you don't mean Skittles."

"Har, har."

"Sounds fantastic, Mich. I bet I can find some great vegan cookbooks. I can't wait for us to try the recipes together." Pass me the sick bucket. I did wonder if I'd maybe given in too easily. Apparently not, because she got up to kiss me.

"You're such a great husband," she said as she made me push my chair back so she could sit on my lap. For goodness' sake, couldn't I enjoy my last official steak and chips in peace? "All of my friends are jealous. Did you know that? They think you're incredible."

She'd have taken it back, wouldn't have done any of the things that followed later in the evening if she'd known I'd be stuffing my face the next morning with a sausage McMuffin. Along with the occasional cigarette, a kebab or a burger had become something else I'd enjoyed in secret.

I shook my head. This was no time to be thinking about bacon butties. I had to get a move on and find the rest of my supplies.

The previous autumn, Michelle and I had decided to have our attic properly insulated with a combination of spray-foam and blow-in. Ever since we'd bought the place, we'd had to crank up the heat in winter, and the air-conditioning in summer, making my eyes water whenever I saw the electricity bill. When I'd suggested the upgrade to Michelle, she'd waved a hand and told me to handle it.

I couldn't believe how much of a difference it had made to the temperature in the house and to our utility fees, but there had been an ulterior motive to my plans. When the workers had packed up their materials at the end of the day, I'd swiped a couple of sets of coveralls from their van, still neatly wrapped in cellophane bags.

See, if your wife goes missing and you're caught on camera at the hardware store beforehand buying a suit that turns you into an extra on *NCIS*, you'll have a pair of brand-new bracelets faster than you can say Tiffany's. When there are a couple of them in your garage after she's been abducted, they're still in the bag and you've mentioned to the cops you were secretly hoping to convert one of the spare bedrooms into a nursery at some point, nobody raises an eyebrow.

After grabbing one of the sets of coveralls and stuffing it into my backpack I took a bottle of water from a stack in the corner and breathed in deep.

This was it.

And I was ready.

22

My breath filled the crisp air in a puffy cloud as I stood silent and unmoving in front of the garage's side door, listening into the night. There was no noise except for the slight rustle of wind in the trees and an owl hooting somewhere in the distance. I walked down the side of the garage to the driveway, staying close to the fence, and stopped behind an old oak tree that provided a generous vantage point over our cul-de-sac.

No cars. No people. I couldn't be absolutely certain nobody was watching, and a few of our neighbors had surveillance cameras pointed at the street, so I knew heading out at the dead of night might be a bit of gamble, albeit a calculated one. It wasn't the first time I'd taken a ride at this hour, and I'd been known to do so when Michelle was still alive. More regular and consistent behavior nobody could call into question, not even if I was spotted on somebody's door cam.

My wife believed my late-night trips were because I couldn't stop thinking about work when in fact I was solidifying my plans for her. Since her abduction I'd dropped a few comments to Travis, Nora, Detective Anjali, and some of my colleagues about how I'd often suffered from insomnia, and how Michelle's predicament had made things worse. None of that would change anything if someone followed me tonight. Being caught with a questionable assortment of supplies would result in all my diligently constructed intentions going belly up faster than a goldfish in an acid bath.

Satisfied I was alone, I returned to the garage, opened the door, and fired up my Triumph. Not long after I was out on the country lanes, where I rode around for almost half an hour, continuing to make sure there was nobody on my tail. The roads were dry and empty all the way to the conservation area, where I hid the bike behind a large stack of split firewood. My quest would take several hours, I wanted to be home before dawn, and so I made the final preparations for my trek. I opened my backpack, pulled on the pairs of socks to pad the large hiking boots, stepped into the coveralls, strapped on the headlight, and, once I'd input the coordinates of my destination in my GPS navigator, pulled on a pair of gloves. As I walked past a porta-potty I almost doubled back—something in my stomach didn't feel quite right—but I ignored it and set off into the brush.

It was eerie as fuck, I'm not going to lie. Traipsing through the forest under a fingernail moon with a light strapped to your forehead, knowing you're about to dig up your spouse's corpse and search for clues about her killer's identity would mess with most people's heads, including mine. Anyone who says different is either more of a liar than me, clinically insane, dead on the inside, or a combination of all three.

Like I said, I didn't believe in ghosts, but out there in the woods, moving toward Michelle's grave, I couldn't help but wonder what I'd do if her spirit suddenly appeared. Consequently, the smallest of noises made my head rotate as if on a swivel. The snapping of twigs and branches—not those caused by my clown-size boots which had turned hiking into an absolute chore—made me jump more times than I cared to admit.

There was snuffling and hooting, wings of birds or bats or whatever the hell flapping overhead. I'd never lived in the countryside. There weren't many trees on the built-up estates in Manchester and certainly no woodlands where I could hang out as a kid. I was used to navigating concrete jungles peppered with the sounds of car alarms and people shouting, not this haunting twilight chorus of insects and wild animals.

I pressed on through the undergrowth, aiming for the path of least resistance to ensure I left a trail as small and invisible as possible, trying not to think too much about how scared Michelle must've been when Woods forced her this way. She'd have been terrified, no doubt, and I took no pleasure in knowing this. I wished Woods had killed her quickly, and she hadn't had time to wonder what he might or might not do to her, and if she'd survive.

I shoved the thoughts away and kept going. When I got about three hundred yards from my target spot, I pulled out a face mask from the side of my bag and zipped the coveralls up to my chin. Now my eyes were the only thing remaining exposed and I wouldn't be leaving any traces of DNA here for someone to find.

Another snapping noise startled me, and I spun around, my headlamp only brightening a useless distance. I turned slowly from side to side but couldn't see anything. I had sudden images of being mauled to death by a wild animal. Wouldn't that have been ironic? Both Michelle and I lying dead in the forest, yards apart, never to be seen or heard from again. Some might have found poetic justice there. I wasn't one of them.

I scolded myself for not bringing a weapon of some sort, and as a makeshift alternative I reached into the backpack and removed the shovel, extending it all the way. If anything attacked me, I'd at least have something to fight back with, but if I got badly bitten and needed medical attention, how, where, and why I'd been injured would be an interesting story to spin.

Nothing happened as I stood still for a little longer, watching and waiting. No movement of any kind, and except for my guts letting out a piercing squeal, the noises in the brush seemed to have died down. Nevertheless, I had an unnerving sensation, the one you get when you feel you're being watched, and I forced myself to shake it away.

Turning around, I continued to my destination, heart racing, a damp patch of sweat forming under my arms. I didn't think I'd have this much of a visceral reaction to digging up my wife's body, but if the perspiration on my brow was anything to go by, I thought I might dissolve faster than candy floss in a hot toddy before I got there.

I walked on, ignoring my clammy palms and lurching stomach. Once I was sure I'd found the right place via my GPS navigator, I asked myself one last time if I was ready for this.

Other than Gideon, I'd never seen a corpse before, not even when I'd worked for Bobby. I'd never made it into his inner circle, never witnessed any of the multiple murders I knew had taken place, nor had I any intention of committing another of my own once Travis was gone. Confession time (honest): I hadn't hired a hit man to get rid of Michelle only because I didn't want any physical evidence tying me to the crime. It was also because I didn't like what killing Gideon had done to me—as if I'd taken a hit to the remains of my soul that afternoon. Not to mention it was messy, unsavory, and other people were a lot more willing to do these things.

But digging up Michelle's corpse...this was something I had to do myself.

With a stomach feeling as if I'd swallowed a basket full of rattlesnakes I got to work. Another crack of a branch filled the air, startling me, my eyes searching for the source, shoulders sagging when I caught a glimpse of a fox darting out from between the trees. The next time it happened I refused to let it disturb me. I had to get moving. I had a good look around, studied the area as best I could given the limited light, noticed how there was loose earth, some vegetation and twigs scattered about, and little new growth. This had to be it.

A couple of false starts thanks to the GPS navigator not being completely accurate, and two feet down, my shovel touched something harder than soil. I kneeled, started to scoop the soft earth with my gloved hands and dug up a plastic bottle caked in mud, the label barely visible. Drain cleaner. Weird. After briefly wondering if I was in the wrong place, I kept digging and as I worked, the pungent smell of decay and rotting flesh filled the air, making me gag.

Pressing my face into the crook of my arm, I tried hard not to retch. This was not the time or place to empty my guts. I dug around what I thought were bones of some sort, possibly the skull, but it turned out to be a layer of rocks. I lifted a few out, assuming Woods had added them to keep the animals away—I remembered seeing it when Michelle and I had watched one of her crime shows—and silently thanked him for being so meticulous.

Another foot down, and almost another, until I finally came across the glimmer of light-colored fabric. Bile rose to the back of my throat again and I forced it down. All I needed to do was open the sheet, examine her features and be certain

Woods had done his job. Then I could cover her face before moving along the rest of the body to see if he'd left anything I could use to find out who he was.

Grateful for my mask but wishing it would absorb the stench of death, I used my fingers to make a hole in the fabric, ripping it easily, working at the tear to make it wider. A frown formed on my face when I saw the first signs of shoes. Buggering hell. I'd started at the wrong end. I held my breath and leaned in a little closer. The sneakers looked like a pair of Michelle's, but I couldn't be certain because of the dirt.

Cursing loudly, I moved almost six feet to the left and dug, lifting the rocks out and working at double speed, tearing into the sheet as soon as I found it, trepidation and the dodginess rolling around in my guts be damned. I saw some hair first, sloughed off the scalp in clumps, matted and a strange, unnatural gray color. That was the moment I understood the presence of drain cleaner—like the rocks, the ammonia would help keep the animals away, and probably speeded up decomp, making a discovery less likely.

My revulsion at seeing and smelling a rotting corpse had to take a back seat as I brushed away more and more of the earth, allowing me to excavate what was left of the face, but the hollowed-out eye sockets and open mouth, both crawling with maggots, still made it impossible to tell for certain if this was my wife. Falling onto my heels, I took off my mask and allowed myself a few deep gulps of air, knowing I couldn't stop.

"Get on with it," I growled. *"Now."*

Pulling my mask over my face, I forced myself to examine the corpse again. I dug a little further around the body, spotted what looked like the remains of black yoga pants and a green T-shirt I felt quite certain belonged to my wife. Finally, a semblance of the proof I needed.

The shirt appeared to be covered in blood. A big, dried,

dark patch had formed a pattern on the belly, much like a bull's-eye, and from what I could tell, more insects were feasting on the flesh beneath. No clue how she'd died. Shot, or stabbed, maybe. Cause of death was of little interest at this point.

I dug a little farther, hit another item, this time a purse. My *wife's* purse, and I knew this for certain because her switched-off phone, wallet and keys were inside. I stopped for a moment, staring at the items as the certainty of what they represented grabbed hold of me.

Michelle was dead.

Woods had killed her exactly as we'd agreed. She wasn't alive. He wasn't holding her hostage. And if he was the one behind the partial photos, trying to get me to reveal myself as the person who'd ordered the hit, then he'd have a long wait. I smiled for all of a nanosecond.

What if he kept coming?

The hoot of an owl made me jump and look around, both cursing and thanking Woods for choosing such a secluded spot. When we'd corresponded, he'd said he didn't usually give location details, they were better left alone, but I'd insisted he tell me, threatened to cut off all communication and walk away if I didn't get what I wanted.

Another thought suddenly pinballed around my brain. Maybe this was Woods's habitual dumping ground. The place he got rid of all his local assignments. Was I surrounded by bodies? I shone the headlamp into the trees and across the ground, couldn't be sure nowhere else hadn't been disturbed, told myself it didn't matter how many bodies were here. They were dead. And dead people couldn't hurt me.

After a few deep breaths I dug around the rest of the corpse, found nothing else Woods had left behind and which might have helped identify who he was. That would've been too easy, and instead of managing to stay calm, I felt anger roiling within. While the trip had proved successful in terms of knowing Michelle was dead, I still had no idea who he was, or how to find him. Or what he might do next.

I wanted to put my head back and shout every single expletive skyward as loud and forcefully as I could, or use the biggest tree trunk I could find as a punching bag. Despite my reservations, my goddamn squeamishness, I should've had the balls to take care of Michelle myself. Now, Woods was maybe trying to flush me out, or worse. If despite all my precautions he'd figured out for certain I'd ordered Michelle's death, it gave him leverage while he remained invisible. If he came after me, I'd never see him coming.

As I took a breath and tried to calm down again, I piled the stones and earth back on top of the body, all the while promising myself no matter what happened, I'd be ready for Woods. Better yet, I'd hunt him down. And when I found him—if it came to it—I'd kill him.

23

I continued scooping up the dirt, using branches and fallen leaves, making sure everything looked the way it had when I'd first arrived. As I worked on blending the grave in with its surroundings, I kept on swearing at myself for not taking care of Michelle directly, before berating myself harder for using the dark web to recruit Woods. It had been the best choice to protect my anonymity—there wasn't a website called Hitmen'R'Us—but I may have underestimated him.

Whispered curse words escaped my lips as I finished up and surveyed the area. Nobody would know there was a corpse lying here, and I wasn't about to spend more time wondering if Woods had indeed got rid of more of his assignments in the area. I shone my flashlight on my backpack, making sure I had all the supplies I'd brought into the forest, and wasn't inadvertently leaving anything behind. The howl of an animal made me jump for the umpteenth time, reminding me I wasn't alone. Despite the layer of rocks I'd put back, I had a sudden image of a pack of coyotes digging up Michelle's body and tearing it to shreds, and this time I swore at Woods for leaving her out in the forest.

"You're going soft," I muttered as I hoisted my bag over my shoulder and stopped thinking about her, but at the same moment my intestines clenched, twisting themselves into uncomfortable knots. It was time to move, and so I walked away, never to return, stepping through the undergrowth the same way I'd come in. Two hundred yards later, the pit of my gut was on fire. I winced a few times, had to stop when my innards contracted as if I'd been punched.

By the time I got back to my bike it was almost 4:00 a.m., and while the parking lot was still empty, I knew I had to hustle to get to the house. I continued trying to ignore the stabbing pains in my stomach as I shoved my coveralls, gloves, extra socks, and mask into a nearby bin made from a rusty-red oil barrel. Once everything was drenched in lighter fluid, I struck a match and threw in the pack.

My next stop was a deserted bridge over the Charles River. Making sure nobody was coming, I flung the GPS navigator into the water. The hiking boots went into a clothes donation box at a homeless shelter, and my final stop was a self-serve car wash that didn't have security cameras. The last unit at the far end was angled away from the street, where my quest to destroy evidence could continue without prying eyes.

I'd almost finished hosing down the bike and shovel when I realized neither the discomfort building in my stomach, nor my sweaty brow and clammy hands, were from digging up my wife. My intestines made a sudden movement as the gut rot hit me full on, the point of no return where your entire body breaks out in a cold sweat because making it to a bathroom—any bathroom—becomes the most important thing on the planet.

Panic rising, I scoured the area. There was a garbage bin by the side of the car wash, and I'd be lying if I said using it didn't cross my mind. The hair on the back of my neck stood up. I let out a relieved groan when I spotted a 24-hour diner across the street, a greasy-spoon café called Mo's with an electric sign shaped like a bacon-and-egg-filled pan, the lime-green O of Open flickering sporadically. It was all the beckoning I needed.

I ran, full-out sprinted. Feet pounding as I prayed Mo's really was open and someone hadn't forgotten to shut off the sign. I yanked on the door, found myself being greeted by an ancient waitress and the smell of fried food. I ignored it all, hurtling past the woman and darting for the bathroom, from where I didn't emerge for the better part of half an hour. Once confident I'd be completely hollow for the rest of my life, I limped to a blue-and-white gingham Formica table in the back corner and collapsed, my torn-to-shreds insides burning.

The waitress came over, her wrinkled tortoise-like face full of concern. "Are you all right, darlin'?" she asked, setting the plastic menu she'd had clenched under one arm in front of me. When I didn't respond, she pulled out a notepad and a tiny pencil from the pocket of her shirt and raised her eyebrows in expectation.

I let out a feeble grunt. "I'll just have coffee, please. Black."

"Oh, honey, you gotta try the food. Mo's poached eggs are legendary, and the bacon's—"

"Just the coffee," I said quickly, the thought of runny yolks and grease making me want to run for the bathroom again. "Please."

She nodded, and as she shuffled off and I glanced at the clock on the wall, I blanched. Nearly six, still dark outside, but not for much longer. Diane and Karina would be up soon, if they weren't already, and my other neighbors would easily see me riding up the street on my bike. I wanted to pretend it didn't matter, but it might. I couldn't be sure what the cops were doing, who or what they were looking into, whose security footage they were still combing through, including that belonging to the people who lived on my road. Any one of the door cameras would have captured me leaving in the middle of the night, which wasn't unusual, but not coming back until the early hours of the morning meant stretching my *I went for a ride because I couldn't sleep* story to the max.

Coffee in hand, I took a scalding gulp, hoping it would settle my guts long enough to make it back to the house without having to stop. My stomach rumbled. Aside from some toast yesterday morning, I'd only eaten Karina's cottage pie. It had tasted rich and smoky, not in the least bit off, and Travis had devoured his, never mind it being made with tofu, which had actually been pretty tasty.

Thinking of my brother-in-law made me grimace. Even with the booze and sleeping pills I'd fed him, if something with Karina's food had been dodgy, surely he'd be up by now. And that was bad news for me if he'd noticed I wasn't home.

24

The sun graced the bottom of the pink skies when I finally made it back to the house. All I wanted was to collapse in a heap, preferably in bed, but I knew with Woods potentially on my tail, sleep wasn't an option. Pulling up in front of the garage, I saw Diane coming out of her front door. Too late to turn and speed off, she'd already noticed me and was walking over.

"You're up early," she said. "Couldn't sleep again?"

"No." My stomach contracted, making me wince. "Will you excuse me?"

As I dashed past her, her expression changed from concern to surprise, but I didn't have time to explain. Inside the house Roger greeted me with a wag of his tail and a small bark, and I had no choice but to ignore him and head to the main floor bathroom.

Another twenty minutes later and I was in the kitchen having more coffee, with Roger by my side, happily munching on kibble. Travis was still upstairs. Either those sleeping pills had really knocked him out, or the guy's insides were made of three-inch cast iron. I'd guzzled no less than four glasses of water, and mine were still a mangled wreck.

I ran a hand over my face, deciding I'd best take something for my upset stomach, and have a shower. A plastic box in the cabinet above the fridge held a variety of headache and other pills, including Imodium. I was in the process of popping a couple out of the pack when I noticed something else, more specifically that something was missing.

Laxatives.

I'd never used them, but Michelle had. Something to do with the unpleasant side effects of the iron tablets she'd been prescribed a while back when she'd been anemic. I hadn't asked for details but had never forgotten the brand name because of the TV commercials they played most often around dinnertime. There had been a few of those pills left over, and I knew this for certain because I'd needed a cough drop to ease a sore throat the week before, and when I'd spotted the laxatives, I'd considered throwing them away.

Instinctively, I turned my attention to the garbage bin under the sink, immediately finding the missing pack. Empty. My mind flashed to the night before. Karina had brought over the cottage pie. Travis had eaten his and he'd had access to mine. Had the little prick laced my food because I'd accused him of taking Michelle's jewelry? Maybe Nora had told him about her financial oversight plans for him after all and he'd been getting this childish revenge. The more I thought about it, the more convinced I became he'd done exactly that.

I marched up the stairs, straight to Travis's room where

I threw open the door and flicked on the light. "Hey," I shouted. "Oi, Travis."

He shot up, his eyes huge. "Whoa, man. What are you doing? What the hell's going on?"

"Did you put these in my food?"

He squinted at the box in my hand, his forehead crinkling. "What are those?"

"Don't take the piss."

"I don't know what they are. I can't see from here."

"Laxatives."

"Huh?"

"They give you the—"

"I know what they do. Eww. Why would I put them in your food?"

"You tell me." I flicked the empty box at him. It bounced off his skull and disappeared behind the headboard, giving me no satisfaction at all.

"Hey, what's up your ass today?"

If I hadn't been so livid, I might have found his choice of words at least somewhat funny, but in this instance, I could've drowned him in the bath. I took a few steps toward him.

"Have you been messing with me?"

My words came out quietly, with more than a hint of menace. I thought about the partial photographs of Michelle, the deep scratch in my car, the laxatives, even the canceled Invicta membership. Was Travis behind it? He'd have had access to my phone if I'd left it unlocked, but I wasn't stupid. I wasn't careless.

I took a deep breath and stared at him again. He was still sitting in bed, his face and body pale, his expression gormless. I reminded myself I was looking at a man who lived in his deceased sister's house because he'd lost his job and kept getting high. A man who didn't have the courage to be with his mother when she needed him most. I almost laughed, mostly at myself for thinking he was some kind of evil genius. It was ridiculous. Travis may have been smart when he laid off the drugs and booze, but he was no mastermind. He could have shoved some laxatives into my food after getting pissed off at me for accusing him of stealing Michelle's stuff, or because he'd learned of my soon-to-be financial chokehold over him, but there was no way he'd engineered anything else.

The lack of sleep and my midnight expedition were playing tricks on me, messing with my head, making me second-guess everything. Still, I thought about turfing him out, was about to open my mouth and order him to pack up his stuff and move next door when I remembered my promise to Nora. I was supposed to watch over him. Be his private guardian angel.

"Did you take these?" I said, softening my tone.

He shifted around. "Not that it's any of your business, but no, I didn't."

"Then how come the box was in the bin?"

"The hell do I know?" He reached for his sweats and pulled them on underneath the covers. "But what I do know is I'm tired of you accusing me of things I haven't done."

"Travis—"

"No. I get it, you're going through a hard time. We all are."

I needed him to calm down. Couldn't have him running to Nora, telling her I was making (according to him) random accusations. Thinking about it logically, it was possible my upset stomach had been caused by something else entirely, and Travis was too embarrassed to admit he was having trouble going to the bathroom, which was fair enough.

"Listen, man," I said, sounding surprisingly genuine. "I didn't mean—"

"Yeah, you did." He jumped up, grabbed his shirt, and yanked it over his head. "I know exactly what you see when you look at me. What you and Michelle said about me behind my back. Same as my mom."

"What do you mean? We—"

"I know I fucked up. I know I'm an addict. I'm not stupid. You all think I'm a loser."

This was interesting. Travis had never openly admitted he had a problem like this before, mostly talked about it when he'd gone overboard in recent months, promised he'd stop, it wouldn't happen again.

I considered my response. If his addiction hadn't suited my long-term plans, I'd have told him people would keep seeing him in this light until he kept his word, but I didn't want him to grow a conscience. Forcing my shoulders to drop, I held my hands up, palms facing him.

"No, I don't think you're a—"

"You do," Travis snapped. "And you know what? Get in line. Dad thought I was a failure and an embarrassment. My mother hides it well, but it's what she thinks, and trust me, I see it when I look in the mirror. I'm not blind."

"It's not like that."

"Ha, really? Funny, because since you arrived on the scene you've been my mom's golden child. And I can cope with that, but what tears me apart is the fact that Michelle's gone and no matter what I do, if I finally do stay sober, she won't be here to see it. It kills me—" he slapped a palm to his chest "—in here. I'm not perfect, but I didn't steal Michelle's things and I didn't mess with your food. So, you can take all your accusations and shove 'em."

He brushed past me and headed downstairs, where I heard him pull on his shoes and slam the front door behind him. Tires screeched as he backed out of the driveway, leaving me in the house alone, for once angry at myself for getting him worked up.

25

I opened the tracking app on my phone and watched the little blue dot representing Travis's cell move down the street. He'd left Chelmswood and appeared to be heading for Boston. No clue what he was up to or where he was going, but he obviously hadn't decided to visit his mother, which was a relief for me. I pressed a button, activated the mic on his phone and listened in, heard only the sound of hip-hop music blasting through the speakers. I switched it off again.

I doubted he'd be out looking for work. He'd end up either at one of his favorite clubs or find a bar where they were happy to let him drown his sorrows for the entire day. I knew Travis. His little speech, moving as it was, wouldn't cause him to have a sudden epiphany, let alone seek out an AA meeting. His solace right now lay in being hammered. Maybe he'd get in touch with his so-called friends, the ones he'd party with before Nora and I severely limited his funding and they realized he was broke.

While my stomach had finally settled, I had no intention of going to work. Instead, I made myself a pot of strong coffee and forced down a granola bar. A little before nine I sent Agnes an email, informing her I was taking the day off and didn't want to be disturbed because I wasn't well. Not two minutes later, my phone rang. I groaned when I saw it was the boss, Richard. It shouldn't have come as a surprise. Like Michelle, he didn't believe in sick days.

"Lucas, what's this about you not coming in?"

"I thought it was pretty clear," I said through gritted teeth. "I'm not well."

He exhaled his annoyance, which wasn't an unexpected reaction. Richard didn't have an empathetic bone in his body, either, and he couldn't hide it. In fact, a few days after Michelle had disappeared, he'd phoned to express his sympathies before reminding me to send him my monthly sales report. He was an oaf, and a harmless one, but he was also the regional manager's son and it had therefore proved difficult to maneuver him out of the way. I was already looking forward to telling him what he could do with his job when Michelle's money came through, providing I could force myself to hold my tongue until then.

"I need you here," he said, punctuating each word. "Jeffreys called last night."

"He called *you*?"

"Yeah, I'd left him a message in the afternoon. Thought I'd seal the deal for you."

"Richard, we've spoken about this. Jeffreys is my client—"

"Well, not quite yet, but you impressed him, which he said never happens. He wants to work with us. We're getting the contract. Congratulations to us. We did it."

No, *we* did not, arsehole.

"Here's the thing." He lowered his voice to a conspiratorial whisper, a pointless move considering he had a corner office to himself and always kept the door shut. "Jeffreys has another project." He waited a beat or two. "A bigger one."

I forced myself to loosen the grip on my phone before it broke. "What do you mean?"

"Aha! You don't know everything after all. He wants to come in today to discuss. Which means you need to be here so we can run some numbers and prepare."

I pictured my wife's body in the woods, could still smell the decay in my nostrils, see the sunken eyes, the blood on the shirt, the maggots, the flies. Thought about how Woods was out there, probably planning his next move to dick me around. "Put him off until Friday. Better yet, make it Monday."

"Lucas, this is a huge contract—"

"I'm not coming in."

"Uh-huh. Then listen up. You're probably forgetting Jeffreys is going on vacation. I'll get Davinder to stand in for you. You can split the account."

I knew what he was doing, and under normal circumstances I'd have already leapt into my suit and dashed out the door, upset stomach and corpse be damned. I didn't want Jeffreys to meet Davinder. Our *supplier* relationship wasn't solid enough, and while I knew I was the superior business partner by far and would deliver more and faster than any of my colleagues ever could, Davinder was a smooth talker. Except with everything happening over the past few days, I suddenly found I couldn't have given less of a toss and decided to call my boss's bluff.

"Be my guest. But don't say I didn't warn you when he fucks it all up."

I cut off Richard's protests and set my phone to silent after his third attempt to call me back. With the house now empty aside from Roger and me, I let out a puff of frustrated breath before heading upstairs for the shower and chucking the clothes I'd worn into the forest inside the washing machine for a high-temperature cycle. I needed to get my head around what was going on. More importantly, I wanted to find Woods before he did something stupid.

Dressed and ready, I got back on the Triumph, making sure I wasn't being followed. I rode to the bus station locker, from where I retrieved my burner laptop and, once again, connected to the Wi-Fi in the bathroom, opened the VPN and delved into the dark web. It took me a while to work my way through the message boards, but there was still no sign of him. I opted for an encrypted message but didn't want to reveal anything else, so I kept it simple.

Need 2 talk.

As I waited, hoping he'd reply immediately, I kept on scouring the boards for any signs of him. I searched for handles and coded exchanges similar to those we'd had but got nowhere. He'd never given me a phone number and had always called me. The guy was a phantom.

With a flash of inspiration, I created a different username and composed another message on the board where Woods and I had originally met, hoping he might take the bait. I didn't know how many jobs the guy carried out, or how frequently, but with the money I'd given him, and depending on his lifestyle, he wouldn't need to work again for at least a few months. Maybe he was on a Lucas-funded trip somewhere, throwing back cocktails on a beach, instructing someone else to drop off the partial photos to mess with me.

At least no more of them had arrived, except…how could I be sure when I wasn't at the office? What if there was another envelope—or two—waiting for my return? Worse, what if Agnes, Richard, or somebody else opened them? They might not recognize Michelle from the photo, but depending on the new cryptic, or not-so-cryptic message on the back they'd call the police before they reached me, especially as I'd left my phone at the house.

I gave Woods another sixty seconds to reply, thinking this wasn't the way things were supposed to work. This was my gig, these were *my* plans. I had to get a grip on the situation, not be sitting in a rancid-smelling public bathroom, at the mercy of a killer-for-hire's whim, damn it.

With the burner laptop safely stored in the locker again, I was back on my bike, cutting through traffic on my way to the office where I burst in through the front door. Agnes took one look at me, her mouth falling open.

"What are you doing here?" She rushed over and pulled me to one side. "You look like you haven't slept in a month."

I glanced down, took in my open jacket, my sweat-drenched shirt hanging over my jeans, my feet clad in dusty biker boots. Not once had I shown up here in anything other than an immaculate suit, and from the expression on Agnes's face, I could tell she thought either I was about to lose it, or I already had.

"Uh, Richard said Jeffreys—"

"Don't worry, I scheduled a video conference for Monday."

"But—"

"For goodness' sake, you can't let anyone see you in this state. If he was here, Jeffreys would rip up the contracts and feed them to you on a spoon. What's going on? Is it Michelle?"

"No. I need to get my mail."

"Your *mail*? You mean your regular mail?"

"Yes."

"Why on earth—"

"Do I have any?"

The vehemence and tone made Agnes take a step back.

"Not much. I'll fetch it. Go to the small conference room before someone sees you."

Agnes bustled me off and returned with a tiny bundle. I flipped through it. No orange envelope. Nothing suspicious. "Let me know if anything else arrives," I said. "Anything at all. Put it aside and call me."

"What's going on? What aren't you telling me?"

"Nothing, I'm fine."

Agnes sighed. "Hon, we both know that's not true. You really should take time off. A week, a month, whatever you need. I wish I could say with everything you've got going on, Richard will understand, but we both know it's a lie."

"I'm not worried about Richard."

"Well, no matter, because I'll keep him off your back."

"Thanks," I muttered. "I'm going home to get some rest and sort out my head."

"Don't fall apart, okay? We need you here when you're ready. Take care of yourself."

For the first time I wondered what she might say if I broke down and confessed what I'd done. The thought made me stumble out of the office before I did something stupid.

I got back on my bike, briefly thought about turning on the engine and riding off somewhere, not stopping until I ran out of petrol. I couldn't, and I wouldn't. It might be construed as an admission of guilt, or at least an indication I knew something. I took a breath. The cops had nothing on me. Woods had nothing on me. Even if they found Michelle's body and tied it to him, I would be fine.

"They've got *nothing*," I insisted as I rode on. "You thought everything through. Calculated every variation, went over every scenario. Stay the course. Just *stay the course*."

The words of reassurance didn't do much, and when I got home, I gulped down a glass of water while considering whether I should crack open something stronger. I folded, and was about to pour a double shot of whatever I could find when there was a succession of loud bangs on the front door. My brain went into overdrive as I imagined Anjali on the other side, fully kitted-out in SWAT gear, about to give the order to breach and take me down. I hesitated, wondering how far I'd get if I made a run for it out the back. A few yards, maybe, but I wouldn't get close enough to the ravine for me to disappear into it. They'd have eyes on all exits, shoot if I fled. Heart thumping, I walked to the door and yanked it open, bracing myself for a fight.

Except, it wasn't Detective Anjali or anyone from law enforcement. It was worse by far. A ghost from my past I'd been so certain I'd left behind. One I never expected nor wanted to see again. And yet, here he was, standing in front of me with a sly grin on his face.

Bobby Boyle.

26

It was him, no mistake about it. A decade may have passed and while Bobby appeared older, the hair on his temples a light shade of gray, the lines on his forehead somewhat deeper, he'd kept his body trim and lean. Although still good-looking, age and lifestyle had hardened his face, made his eyes even colder, heartless.

He smiled again slowly, revealing a set of straight white teeth. Those were new, and if this had been a happy reunion, I might have paid him a compliment. His grin broadened. It wasn't a *nice-to-see-you* expression but an *I-knew-I'd-find-you* smirk, and triggered bad memories, sending automatic and uncontrollable shudders throughout my entire body. Every single of my instincts screamed at me to run as fast and far away as possible because Bobby being here meant one thing: I was going in a hole in the ground like my wife.

My brain reminded me I was older, wiser. This was my house. I planted my feet. Refused to show the smallest of other reactions as he raised an eyebrow and spoke, his voice a low growl.

"Michael Cundy."

Michael Cundy. I hadn't heard or used my birth name in almost as long as I hadn't seen Bobby. It was something else I'd gladly left behind when I'd abandoned Manchester. I'd always detested the name and obviously my parents hadn't been thinking clearly when they'd decided to name me after my maternal grandfather. Mum, Dad, and all my teachers had called me Michael. The kids at school? Mike. Zero points for creativity when it came to my nicknames and I'd been happy to make an official change by deed poll a while after I'd arrived in London. It had been surprisingly easy, and I'd been certain it had given me another layer of protection as I morphed into a different person entirely. Until now, I'd believed I'd done enough to escape Bobby's clutches. Except he stood on my front step, his face still wearing that eerie smile.

"You look…*different*," he said. "No longer a fat little punt."

It took me a second to clue into his habit of substituting swear words with regular ones. *Punt* rhymed with… Nice.

"Where are your manners, Cundy? You're not going to ask us in?" He indicated to the man on his right, whom I'd never seen before, and who was a full head taller than me, and twice as wide, looking like he'd be most comfortable standing in a WWE ring dressed in tiny shorts. "It's been a long trip," Bobby added, as if he expected me to either throw my arms around him for a hug or roll out the red carpet.

"What are you doing here?" I wasn't sure where my voice came from, and I hated how strangled it sounded but I couldn't help it. Once again my heart felt as if it might jump out of my throat, which would please Bobby immensely because he'd step on it and squish it into the ground. "How did you—"

"Find you?" He tapped the side of his nose. "Ah, that's not what matters now, sunshine. Important thing is we're here. Now, be a good lad and invite me and Mel in. Before any of the neighbors see me making a fuss. Wouldn't want to ruin your reputation. But I will. Your choice, son."

I ran through my options, found two. Slam the door in his face or stand my ground. I wouldn't run, I decided. Not from him. In the back of my mind, I'd always known the possibility of this reunion had existed, and I needed to face it head-on because hiding hadn't worked.

For years I'd tried fading into the murky background and keeping a low profile. Take care of Dad at least financially as I couldn't be there in person at first because I'd never known when or how Bobby might be keeping an eye out so he could use my father to get to me. Once I'd been able to afford to move him to the different care home, I'd set up an offshore company for a few hundred quid and made the payments that way. As time had passed, I'd breathed a little easier, thought maybe Bobby Boyle's memory wasn't as lengthy or legendary as Heinz had once insisted. Clearly, I'd been wrong.

"Don't make this harder on yourself than it's already going to be," Bobby said, putting his foot over the threshold and leaning against the door with his shoulder. "It's been a long flight. We're cream-crackered, gagging for a proper brew and it's time for us to have a little chat, you and me. We've got lots to catch up on. Lots."

Mel didn't wait for my answer. He lunged and shoved the door with such force, I had to step back into the hallway to stay on my feet. I detested how it made me appear. Weak and pathetic. I hated them invading my home, my life.

There was no point telling them to leave. Now Bobby had found me he'd come back again and again—persistent punt that he was. Pointless calling the cops, not unless I wanted to do a whole load of explaining about my past.

I stood back as Bobby and Mel walked into my territory, part of my brain wondering if this might be a nightmare I'd wake up from, or if the lack of sleep was making me hallucinate. I blinked a few times, but Bobby and Mel didn't magically disappear.

Mel grabbed Roger, who'd only let out a feeble, semi-protective bark so far, shoved him into the office and closed the door. Bobby walked past me, and I watched as they both strolled to the living room, leaving me little choice but to follow.

Hands on hips and tilting his head to the ceiling, Bobby let out an exaggerated, high-pitched whistle before turning to me. "Ruddy heck.. Get a load of your pad. Not bad. Not bad at all. Although, it's a bit, I dunno—" he waved a hand around in a circle "—*American*, for my taste."

"American?" I said.

"Yeah, you know, loud, flashy. But overall, it seems congratulations are in order. You've done well for yourself, Cundy. Or should I call you Forester? I hear it's what you go by these days. *Lucas* Forester? Good name. Goes with your poncey accent."

"I could've sent you a brochure," I said, ignoring the questions. "Spared you the trip."

Bobby rubbed his goatee. I remembered him preferring being clean-shaven, and the presence of facial hair somehow made him more threatening. He flopped onto the sofa and put his feet on the coffee table, watching for my reaction. Mel remained standing a few yards away. Good job, really. He could've broken the couch with his heft. He hadn't said a word yet, and I didn't expect him to. Unless Bobby had changed, Mel's sole purpose was to protect and intimidate, much like a giant and vicious Rottweiler. It was working, and while I tried hard not to show it, I appeared to have tumbled through

205

a time warp and was in my early twenties again, scared shit-less of the man in front of me. I loathed him for that as well, although not as much as I loathed myself.

Bobby leaned back, put his hands behind his head. "Cut to the chase, shall we? I don't have time for niceties. You owe me money, Cundy. And a lot of it."

I let out a bitter laugh. "Yeah? Consider it your share of my father's health care bills."

"Ah, how is your old man? Still dribbling into his porridge?"

As Bobby sat up and put his elbows on his knees, steepling his fingers under his chin, I wondered how much damage I could inflict if I went for him, how much pain I could cause before Mel yanked me off with one hand. I was lithe, and my daily workouts had made me stronger than ever, but I wouldn't stand a chance against Mel, and Bobby knew it. My strength lay in strategy and planning, except there didn't seem much opportunity for those now. As my nails dug into the palms of my hands, I could feel my teeth clench. Bobby's dark eyes sparkled. He loved this part, the anticipation, waiting for his victim to make a move.

"You. Stole. From. Me." He enunciated each word as if I were a child. "Fifty grand, gone—" he snapped his fingers "—like that, and instead of coming to me so we could work things out, you clucked off. You *hid*." When I didn't reply, he continued, "It didn't look good, Cundy, you know? A snotty-nosed kid who fancied himself my protégé swindling me out of that much cash and getting away with it? People thought I'd gone soft. Any idea what I had to do after you left?"

I stayed silent, didn't move an inch. Didn't even blink.

"Damage control," Bobby said. "Because of you, a few oth-ers who owed me ended up a lot worse off than they would've if you hadn't put your tail between your chubby little legs. I had to send a message, see? Couldn't have people thinking I'd lost my touch. They'd have taken advantage." He grimaced, drew in air through his clenched teeth as he shook his head. "All that pain and suffering, well, it's all on you, lad. All of it."

What utter bull. Bobby didn't need me to justify his actions. He'd always known exactly what he was doing, to whom, and why. Any excuse for a fight had been good enough for him, and I doubted he'd changed.

I weighed my options again, my brain racing, figuring out how I could get rid of him. I thought about the money I had, more than enough to pay back my old debt. Did I want to give it to him? Hell no, but I needed him to get on a plane back to Manchester before he could interfere more. I wanted him gone.

"I'll give you the fifty grand," I said.

"Of course, you will." Bobby took his time, taking in the décor, head bobbing in appreciation. His eyes landed on a painting Michelle had been given by an up-and-coming Canadian artist. It was an abstract piece, multicolored splodges and rings that had always reminded me of a sliced orange. "Bet that one's expensive."

The fact he could tell didn't surprise me. When I'd worked for him, I'd learned the locker at Wright Space was a holding place for stolen art, among other things, property considered too hot to move, and which he kept there until the situations cooled down. Ironically, I always thought he and Michelle would've had a lot to talk about because he seemed to appreciate the items he stole rather than only take them for the cash.

"Let me gift-wrap it for you, and you can be on your way," I said.

"I doubt it'll cover what you owe."

"Like I said. I'll give you the fifty. It's what was in the bag, and don't pretend otherwise. Trust me, I counted. All of it."

"He says I should trust him." Bobby smirked, glancing at Mel who still hadn't budged. For God's sake, the guy had the emotional range of a sponge. "You disappear from the city, then the country, and you want me to trust you? You think this is a joke?"

"You know what I mean."

"How did you manage to get into the States, anyway?" Bobby said. "I heard immigration's a real witch."

"I was born here."

He rubbed a hand over his scalp. "Oh, yeah. I remember. Your mum and dad were here on holiday. Visiting the Grand Canyon or something and a sprog popped out early."

"I'm touched you recall."

He narrowed his eyes. "I remember everything, Cundy. But it seems you're forgetting how I do business. See, when you took the money from me it was a loan—"

"Piss off."

"Watch your mouth, and remember, my loans accumulate interest. You may have forgotten my rates, too, and they've gone up a tad but they're still less than those payday places." He shook his head. "And they call me a crook. Anyway, normally it's fifty percent. But tell you what, seeing as we have history and all, I'll make it forty, despite what you did. Mate's rates. Can't say fairer than that."

"You can have your fifty grand. *Today.* Then you leave."

Bobby looked up at Mel again. "He's not listening. Seems to think I'd fly all this way for fifty large when I have watches worth more. Cundy here must be having a laugh except I don't think it's funny. Do you think it's funny, Mel?" He didn't answer and Bobby went on. "After ten years without paying down the principle, it works out to one million, four hundred and forty-six thousand, two hundred and seventy-three quid and twenty-seven pence." His next smirk was slow and deliberate. "Trust me, I counted."

"Forget it, I—"

He waved a hand around. "Plus inconvenience and travel expenses. At the going exchange rate we'll call it two mil American, even. From what I've seen in here, and from what I've learned about your lovely wife and her family online, I can't see you having any trouble getting that amount." He slapped both hands on his thighs. "Which reminds me, sorry to hear about that nasty business with Michelle, by the way. Very…how shall I put this? *Unfortunate.* Although most convenient and profitable for you in the long run." He waited for my response, got none. "Come on, Cundy. Throw me a bone. You never did anything without an ulterior motive. I know because I made you."

"Fuck—"

"*Language.* But…ahh, the things we could've done together, young grasshopper. Right up until you stole—"

"You beat my father—"

"What do you think, Mel?" Bobby raised his voice. "Did he kill the missus to make a mint? I reckon he did. I wonder what the cops might say if I told them who he is. Or do they know already? Bet they have no idea."

"Fifty grand. Take it or leave it. Now. And get out."

Bobby raised his chin. "You're throwing out an old friend?"

"We were never friends, Bobby."

"Oof. I'm hurt." He cupped his heart and pulled a face, mocking me, taunting me. Sitting back, he crossed one leg over the other and dropped his hands into his lap, looking almost gentlemanly. "We're not going anywhere, so stop clucking about. Make us a cup of tea, there's a good boy. Then I'll tell you what you'll do next." He paused, smoothed his shirt down and smiled, his face full of malice. "And how much it'll hurt if you don't."

27

The desperation of being back in Bobby's clutches invaded every part of me, coursing through my veins, latching onto my bones. Everything I'd done to get away from him, every fail-safe I'd put in place, had been obliterated. Not only did I have the situations with continuing the pretense of Michelle's abduction and finding out who Woods was to deal with, but now Bobby was here, crawling down my neck.

In the space of four days, the life I'd so carefully built, lie by lie, and all the plans for my future, were threatening to crumble, fall to pieces. I couldn't let that happen. I'd been so diligent from the beginning. The night Bobby had put Dad in hospital, and the cops had arrived, I'd kept my mouth shut, said I had no idea who'd attacked my father or why. I'd told them I knew Dad had a gambling problem and suggested he might owe people some money. With a few swift sentences, and some genuine crying, I'd thrown my father under a row of double-decker buses.

It wasn't because I had any allegiances left for Bobby. I detested the prick with a vengeance I never thought possible. The expression *my blood boiled* wasn't an accurate enough depiction. My insides were on fire, my brain either melting or about to explode from all the hatred and guilt. For the following days I'd pushed it all down deep inside my gut. I'd had to. By demonstrating I wasn't a filthy scumbag of a rat I hoped Bobby would take pity, leave me and Dad in peace, especially after the doctors had confirmed my father's condition meant he'd likely need twenty-four-hour care for the rest of his life.

One morning as I was on my hands and knees cleaning Dad's blood off the walls in the hallway, choking on my tears and the stench of ammonia, Heinz showed up. He grabbed a brush and set to work, helping me remove the last sickening traces of what had happened in this house, the indelible point when my life had forever changed.

"The boss wants his money," he said, gently.

"You know I don't have it."

"I know, kid." Heinz put the brush down. "But you have to get it. What about relatives, friends? Someone you can borrow from? Your grandparents?"

"There's no one."

"Got anything you can sell?"

"Ha! See anything in here? Me and Dad are more than skint. I'll have to keep working for Bobby and get another job. Or three. Can you get him to agree to me paying small amounts?"

"You don't understand. The interest rate will kill you. You'll never be able to pay him back, and if you don't, he'll own you, do you understand what I'm saying?"

"I'll work hard. I'll pay him—"

"Michael, listen to me. If you thought it was bad being Bobby's employee, try being in his debt. He'll ask you to do things."

"What kind of things?"

"Things."

"Huh? I thought he liked women. I'm not—"

"That's not what I'm talking about." He flicked my scalp. "Pay attention. He'll tell you to take care of his *problems.* Permanently."

"You don't mean…?"

"Stop being naïve, Cundy. You understand exactly what I'm saying. You've heard the screams. And doing those things will change you. Give you nightmares."

"He'll want me to *kill* people?"

"You'll have no choice. It'll either be them or you." He put his brush down and lowered his voice to a whisper. "Trust me. I've been there, and Bobby won't care either way, so you must find the money, Michael. You must."

I weighed my options, instantly decided if I were ever to do something so sinister it would have to be for my benefit, not Bobby's, and most certainly not at his behest. I packed a bag that night. After a few stiff drinks, I called Bobby to buy myself, and Dad, some time. Told him to leave my father alone, if he touched a single hair on his head, I'd spill my guts to the cops. Tell them everything I knew about his operations. The reaction I got wasn't what I'd expected. Bobby laughed, a cold, hard sound, which froze my insides all the way to my core.

"Go on then, my son," he said. "Good luck figuring out which ones aren't in my pocket."

I retaliated, trying to keep my voice steady. "The press will be interested though," I said, sounding much braver than what was going on inside. "Your clients won't be happy, but your enemies will. Maybe I'll speak to them. Sell my intel."

"You wouldn't dare."

"I would, so back off."

"I'll make you a deal," he whispered. "And you know I'm a man of my word. If I hear you've as much uttered a syllable about me and my operations to *anyone*, I'll make sure your dad is worse off than now. Got it?"

"Got it."

"Good. Now, that means your father's debt is yours until it's settled. There's no going back, which means you can run, but you can't hide, not forever. Cockroaches like you always resurface, and I know every little hidey-hole in this city, and everyone in them."

"Just leave us alone."

"I'll find you, Cundy, and when I do, you either pay up or I'll dismember you one square inch at a time, starting at your toes. I'll keep you alive so you can see what I'm doing, then I'll sew you back up and start again. So, unless you want me to turn you into a steak tartare, you'd best get back here and—"

I barely managed to hang up the phone because I shook so badly. Some people made empty threats. Not Bobby. He truly was a man of his word and that meant I had to first disappear into the city before getting out of it as fast as I could if I wanted to keep on breathing. I dropped my phone into a passerby's shopping bag, hoping Bobby would waste time trying to get his cop friends to track it while I vanished.

I scrambled over the next week, sleeping rough, stealing, and pickpocketing as much money as I could, before bribing one of the admin staff at the hospital to change Dad's last name in the system, and push through paperwork so he was transferred to a different facility. It was the last time I'd lived in Manchester as Michael Cundy. I abandoned my father there, telling myself my plan would work, Bobby would stick to our agreement, and that it was the only thing I could do to save Dad, and myself. The constant fear none of it was true almost killed me.

I headed to London where I crashed on a friend of a friend's sofa for a few days before joining a squat with people I'd met in a bar, and who I'd never seen before. On a whim, I told them my name was Lucas. It sounded posh, and I loved the anonymity a different name provided, how I could pretend to be someone with an entirely different background and upbringing. My transformation had begun.

At first, almost everyone could tell I was from Manchester because of my broad accent, so I changed it, refined it, listened how others enunciated words which gave my origins away, and made sure I settled into something neutral but not snobby. The squat where I lived was damp and cold, and there was a library a couple of streets away where I'd go to warm up. Within weeks I spent most of my time there, much to my surprise lost in books, not realizing how much I'd missed education, and I inhaled everything I could.

A cash job as a busboy at a restaurant followed. I promised myself I'd work hard and stay on the straight and narrow, as Dad had always called it. It wasn't easy. I'd made good money with Bobby, something I'd got used to, and earning an honest yet minimum wage soon lost its appeal. London's an expensive place to visit, let alone live, and I swiftly found myself supplementing my income with petty theft—shoplifting and pickpocketing wallets and phones from unsuspecting tourists. That stuff came naturally to me, pretending to give them directions while I lifted things from their purses and backpacks.

Two years of working a variety of jobs passed, and one evening one of my squatter mates, Fred, who fancied himself the career advisor of the group, joked about me becoming a used car salesman. According to him, I could sell a turd if I polished it long enough. I remembered what the headmistress had said about my tuck shop enterprise, years back at school. Maybe they both had a point.

"Is there any money in it?" I said. "And I mean real money."

"Dunno. Maybe you should go into recruitment. My dad made a killing in IT. Ran his own company. Sold it when he was fifty. He's loaded."

"Why didn't you take it over?"

He inhaled deeply on his cigarette, blew a few smoke rings, and let the rest escape through his nose. "We had a falling-out. Anyway, last time I spoke to him he said the industry wasn't as good as it used to be, but some places still offer uncapped commission."

"What's that?"

He waved a hand. "You know, open-ended. No limits. The more people you place, or bums in seats, as he calls it, the more you make. He told me one year in the nineties, before he set up on his own, he made half a marigold."

"Huh?"

"Half a million quid."

"No way."

"S'true. I swear."

Two weeks later I had a job as a junior associate. A legitimate, proper job, I might add, working for one of the largest financial services recruiters in London as a trainee. I left the squat because I couldn't keep showing up smelling like damp, and moved into a dump of a bedsit miles away, which turned my commute into a painful hour and a half each way. I didn't care. It was dry, and I thought I was on my way to making a ton of cash and being able to take care of Dad properly, move him to a private care facility. All of it legally.

Trouble was, much like Mr. Dick Whittington himself, I found out the roads weren't paved with gold. Climbing the corporate ladder took too long. Despite my hunger, more than a year later I was still the tea-making minion, and my boss, an uptight arse who'd recently graduated from Cambridge, kept on promoting his university friends over me. Never mind I was willing, able, and worked harder than any of the other Muppets. Never mind I now sounded like them and kept educating myself with books from another library I'd discovered nearby. As far as my boss was concerned, I'd never make the higher echelons of anything because I didn't have the educational pedigree. Did it give me a giant chip on my shoulder? Too bloody right, it did.

As I was going through yet another résumé one day, I spotted a candidate, Samuel Cundy, and wondered if he'd been tormented about his last name as much as I had. Within an instant, an entire light bulb factory went off in my head. Without realizing it, I'd had the solution at my fingertips all this time. I searched the company database for the perfect match, the perfect candidate, and with the thousands we had on file, he didn't take long to find.

Lucas Forester. We shared a birthday, but unlike me he'd graduated with high honors in business from St. Andrews and had done so early because he'd skipped a year at school. I had copies of all his documents—personal details, degrees, university transcripts—all at my disposal. And so, I used them.

Changing my name by deed poll had been the easy part. Transforming from a sweaty, overweight lump less so, but as the weight came off, I got a proper haircut and changed my clothes, people's attitudes toward me shifted. They paid attention. Women, who had thus far been an alien species who mostly ignored me, began to take notice. Instead of it being me chasing them and getting rejected, they were after me and weren't often turned down.

With my newfound confidence skyrocketing, I made up not only for lost time, but also the few fumbles I'd had in the dark with the opposite sex. Even when I was making decent money, I'd take cash and jewelry from the married women I slept with. Hurting them wasn't deliberate, it wasn't my intention. It was a by-product of the actions I took to reassure myself my metamorphosis was working, that it was almost complete, and nobody could see the real me behind the curtain.

It was one of my legitimate dates who let slip her friend worked for an IT recruitment company in the city but was about to move to Australia. I called reception, invented a story to get the boss on the phone, and wangled an interview for the same day, exaggerating my expertise but knowing they wouldn't call my manager for a reference because I still worked for him. I needn't have worried. I had a job offer before I'd even left the building, in no small part thanks to my custom-tailored educational background, which I'd known would be exactly what he wanted to hear but wouldn't actually have anything to do with my job. I was finally going to be a full-blown recruiter with a portfolio of clients to grow and expand like they'd never seen before.

Within three years of leaving Manchester, I'd built myself a whole new history, and an entire new future. From here on out, I'd decided, things would be fine, and they had been, for a few years. I'd moved Dad to a private facility called Primrose in the south of England and set up the offshore company to handle the fees, which I could easily afford each month and live comfortably myself. Except, as I'd found out all too early in my life, good things didn't always last.

Two days before I was due a hefty annual bonus, Her Majesty's Revenue & Customs descended upon the office. Fraud and embezzlement. Money laundering. Company funds frozen. All of us laid off. The fancy car I'd leased? Gone. The fantastic apartment I'd rented? Couldn't afford it. Worst of all, Dad's care payments were in jeopardy.

The final kicker was when the owner of the IT recruitment company didn't end up going to jail but walked away a free man. We all suspected he had funds tucked away in the Caymans or the Bahamas somewhere; trouble was, nobody could prove it. I'd worked my arse off, lost everything when he got to keep it all, taking us for the mugs we were. I decided Bobby Boyle had had the right idea all along. Having a regular job would never enable me to get where I wanted, be *who* I wanted to be. I'd always be the underdog who got screwed over.

Not long after, I'd walked past the art gallery and met Michelle. A month later, with my brand-new emergency US passport in hand, I was living in Boston. An engagement ring on my future wife's finger. Gideon eyeing me with suspicion. Nora thinking I was the best thing to have ever happened to Michelle.

Now, Bobby sat waiting for me to get him a sodding cup of tea and I still hated the man with the same fierce intensity from all those years ago. But I wasn't a kid anymore, and I decided I couldn't fear him. I wouldn't let him scare me into any kind of submission.

All I needed to do was let him think he could.

28

"I'll get you that cuppa." I stood up, wishing there was a way I could ensure he'd choke on it.

"Go with him." Bobby indicated to Mel with his head, and as if reading my mind he added, "Make sure he doesn't slip cyanide in my brew. I don't fancy flying home in a box."

I moved toward the kitchen before turning around. "Where's Heinz? Didn't he want to come with you? It would've been nice to see him."

Bobby's eyes narrowed. "Creative differences."

"What do you mean? He left?"

He took a few beats before answering. "He wanted to."

I knew what that meant. Heinz was dead. There was no way Bobby would've let him walk away, not with all the information he had about Bobby's empire. If Heinz, who'd had a respectable relationship with Bobby, was no longer alive, there'd be zero hesitation when it came to my life. If I didn't find a way out of this mess, receiving partial photographs of my wife and damage to my vehicle were the least of my problems. Unless...no, I couldn't have. Had I by some coincidence contacted one of Bobby's crew when I'd searched for a hit man? Could they have recognized me when they researched the target? Was that how he'd found me? Sheer bad luck? That didn't make sense. They'd have come for me well before now.

Mel followed me to the kitchen and watched as I boiled the kettle and dropped a teabag into a mug. "Milk and sugar, dear?" I said with a fake smile, but he didn't reply. "Suit yourself. With that attitude you won't get a scone, either."

Back in the living room, I set the mug in front of Bobby and he gestured for me to take a seat. I desperately wanted to nip out for a smoke to steady my nerves. Probably not the best idea. He'd lecture me about the color of his grandmother's lungs, and my hands would shake too much to hold the cigarette anyway.

"Where were we?" Bobby said after taking a sip. "Ah, yes. The money. Don't bother saying you can't afford two mil. This place alone is worth loads." He tapped the side of his nose with his finger. "I did the comps."

"Then you weren't thorough in your research. It belongs to my wife."

"And like I said, I know who your wife is. Or was. Whatever. Michelle Ward-Forester has deep family pockets." When I shook my head, he laughed. "Cut the flap, Cundy. We both know you can ask your lovely Auntie Nora for help." He swallowed another mouthful of tea and sneered at the expression I hadn't been able to hide. "Surprise. I know all about her. She's sick, poor poppet, and if I'm not mistaken, that means you're about to inherit a ton of money."

"How the fuck do you know all this?"

"This is the third time I'm warning you about your choice of words. And do you really think I'm going to come all the way here without making it worth my while? Come on, lad. You know me better than that." He heaved a deep sigh. "Tell you what. Every day that goes by without you paying what you owe, your debt goes up another fifty large. Go on, drag your feet. Take your time. I could do with a holiday, and I'll gladly relieve you of your money. But know this—not only does your debt increase, so do the chances of me paying Auntie Nora and the cops a visit."

"Don't you—"

"How much have you told them about your past, anyway? Not all of it, I bet. Do they even realize you were Michael Cundy? Does anyone here know your big secret?"

I clenched my fists, and my teeth, speaking slowly and deliberately to make sure he heard every syllable. "You breathe a word, and I won't get a penny. Neither will you."

"You never answered my question about how your dad's doing." Bobby cocked his head to one side. "Nice place he's living at down in Brighton. Primrose is a great choice."

"How did you find—"

"Kudos for hiding him all these years, but if you don't pay up now, how about your debt reverts back to him? Mel here once told me he loves the south coast. Maybe I'll send him there."

"You leave my father out of this, you fucking wanker."

I barely got the words out before Mel took a giant step, grabbed, twisted, and shoved me facedown into the carpet. No time for me to blink, let alone react. He pulled my arm behind my back as he pushed a boot-clad foot onto my neck. Images of Dad's beaten face flashed through my mind. Blood spraying over the walls. Crunching noises reverberating in my ears as fists and feet hit him, again and again. The sound of my desperate yells, long after they'd disappeared. A neighbor arriving and calling the police. Lights and sirens. Someone pulling me away as I kicked and screamed because I wanted to be with Dad. My gut had filled with the shame of it all back then, and it had never truly left. I'd chosen to get involved with Bobby. I'd brought the money into the house, and I should've known better. A decade later and that mistake was still mine to repair, but it wouldn't happen if I ended up in hospital, or the morgue.

"Okay," I yelled, forcing myself to stop trying to fight back. "I said, all right."

Mel let me go and I clambered to my feet, trying not to wince as I stretched out my arms. The guy was an animal. Tightly wound, desperate for a fight. Waiting—hoping—for me to make another wrong move.

Bobby stood up, leaned over, and patted my cheek with the palm of his hand as he tucked a piece of paper into my shirt pocket. "There's a good lad. You have my number now but we'll be in touch. Don't go anywhere, will you? If you do your dad won't be a happy man."

I watched them turn and leave, couldn't move until I heard the front door close behind them. Breathing hard I raced down the hall to make sure they couldn't come back in, but stopped when I heard voices on the other side. It was Bobby having a conversation, and it wasn't with Mel. What the hell was he playing at? Despite my nerves, I yanked the door open, and Karina spun around.

"Oh, Lucas, hi. What a pleasure meeting your family. Your uncle was telling me they're from…"

"Manchester." Bobby gifted her one of his dazzling smiles. "Well, Stockport, originally. Not as glitzy as London, that's for sure. Our Lucas always was from the posh side of the family. You can tell from his accent. Mine's a little rough around the edges."

"It's no such thing," Karina said. "And it's great to meet you. We've never been introduced to any of Lucas's relatives before."

"Ah." Bobby grimaced with the perfect mix of embarrassment and self-deprecation. "There was a bit of a disagreement in the family for a while."

Karina grinned. "Show me a family where there are no arguments and I'll show you a set of mannequins. But your being over must be such a comfort. Are they staying with you, Lucas?"

"They're only here for a flying visit."

"Well, I certainly don't want to take away from any of it," Karina said. "And I'm so sorry you're visiting under such tragic circumstances, but I'm glad Lucas has more support."

"You never know," Bobby said, before giving me a wink. "Perhaps we'll stick around a little longer. But I've got some business to sort out first, so we'd better be off. See you soon, kiddo. Can't wait to catch up some more. We've missed you."

I didn't notice how tightly I'd clenched my fists by my sides as we watched them get into their car, a shiny black Lexus with tinted windows, until Karina spoke. "Gosh, you look like you're about to keel over."

"I'm fine."

"Are you sure?"

"Yes. Look, I don't mean to be rude, but did you come over for something…?"

"Oh, yes." She held up a bag. "I made pumpkin risotto last night. I brought some for you and Travis. Did you like the cottage pie?"

"Uhhh…"

Karina's eyebrows shot up. "Oh, no. It was too salty, wasn't it? Diane says I use too much, and I'm trying to cut back but—"

"No, that wasn't it. I, uh, it didn't agree with my stomach."

"Really? I'm so sorry. How odd. Diane's fine, so am I. What about Travis?"

"He's okay. It must've been something else I ate." I took the bag Karina still held out toward me. "Thanks very much. I'm sure it'll be delicious."

Another bit of chitchat and I finally got rid of her. The case of the upset stomach had been narrowed down to me only at least, and Travis was a liar seeing as he'd either taken those laxatives himself at some point or shoved them in my food last night. I decided to stop caring about the state of our bowels. There were far more important issues to wrap my head around.

I dumped the risotto in the fridge, let Roger out of the office and went to the back deck for a much-needed smoke. As I lit up my second cigarette, I thought about how my life had suddenly become a minefield over the past few days. Now Bobby had shown up, I had him and Mad Mel to contend with on top of everything else. Once again, my brain whispered I could run. Grab my stuff and get the hell out of here. But I couldn't, not this time, not when Bobby had somehow found out where Dad was. There was no telling how long my father would live if I left.

Time to weigh my options. I could kill Bobby, but I'd have to get close enough, and with Mel around I couldn't see that happening. Finding and hiring Woods to eliminate my wife had taken months of intricate planning, so searching for someone on the dark web to take Bobby and Mel out within the next day or two would be impossible, and Karina had seen them. They could be linked straight back to me.

As I paced the deck, I tried to stabilize what seemed akin

to quicksand shifting beneath my feet. Wracking my brains, I attempted to find more solutions, discarded them all before going around in circles yet again. I couldn't be sure if Bobby knew who Woods was, or if he'd sent the partial photos of Michelle, and as much as I wanted the latter to be true, it made no sense. He wasn't the type to dick around— he'd come straight to my house and made his demands and his threats clear.

When I stubbed out my smoke and looked up, I saw two people walking along the hiking trails at the back of our garden. It was Katie, the newspaper courier, wearing her fluorescent yellow beanie, out for a stroll with her mum. I stopped pacing as a potential solution for one of my problems began to take shape. It was risky, crazy, even. But risky and crazy could be worth it. Risky and crazy were all I had. After all, it was Bobby who'd once told me if you weren't living on the edge, you were taking up too much space.

It was time to push him off.

THURSDAY

29

After one hell of a day, I was at Nora's with her, Travis, Diane, and Karina, giving a full update on the flurry of events that had happened since Bobby had left my house the day before, and which no one had any idea I'd organized. Once my visit came to an end, I'd suggest Travis stay here for a while because I wanted some time alone, and on my way out I'd take another trip to Gideon's wine cellar from where I'd plunder two bottles, because today...well, today called for a celebration of epic proportions.

I shifted in my chair, reminding myself I had to be patient a little while longer. Sit at Nora's bedside as I comforted and reassured the four of them the police were doing everything they could regarding the new developments. "There's still hope," I said, my voice and eyes filled with fake optimism. "I can't believe this all happened today, on our third wedding anniversary. Not as good as her being home, but she will be, I can feel it. It's a sign."

"Oh, I hope so," Diane said.

"We didn't know it was your anniversary," Karina added.

"The traditional gift is leather," Nora said quietly. "Or crystal if you follow the modern theme. Next year's will be appliances although it's linen in the UK. I don't know why I remember these things." She tapped the side of her head. "This is full of useless information."

"Hardly," Travis said, his eyes filling with sorrow.

"It's why you always win at Trivial Pursuit," I said.

Nora managed a small laugh. "True, but you'd best not give Michelle a toaster next year."

"She might chuck it at your head," Karina said, grinning.

"You're right, she wouldn't be impressed." Nora dropped her chin, a shaky hand wiping tears from her cheeks. "Do you really think they'll find her? She'll come home?"

"She has to," Diane said.

"I believe it," Travis added.

"So do I," Karina and I said in unison.

"Detective Anjali assured me they're doing everything possible," I continued. "And I'm still processing what happened. I'm sure we're all trying to understand what it means."

"It's such a lot to take in," Diane said, reaching for Nora's hand, and Travis nodded.

He and Karina had already been here when I'd arrived, and Diane had sat at the little table at the far end of the room, parsing the daily medications into a purple plastic tablet box. I'd offered for her to take a break, but she'd refused, said she needed to keep an eye on her patient. She probably also didn't trust Travis around all those meds. Then again, Nora looked terrible today. Dark circles under her eyes, skin almost translucent and stretched so thin it seemed like it might tear.

She couldn't have much longer to live, and the thought made me feel a lot less buoyant about what had gone down today.

My hastily put-together plan had become a masterstroke, a genius idea I'd be proud of forever, particularly given the speed at which I'd managed to choreograph everything.

After spotting Katie and her mum walking in the woods, I'd taken Roger for a walk and pieced my ideas together at lightning speed. Once certain I'd covered everything, and would be able to execute the details properly, I'd hopped on the Triumph, ridden to a different neighborhood and parked the bike at the back of a Starbucks, where I'd searched a couple of dumpsters, scrounging for newspapers. Satisfied I had what I needed, I rode to various stores picking up glue, scissors, blank paper, a new box of nitrile gloves, and a set of regular envelopes. Back at the house I locked myself in my room, covered the bed with garbage bags, pulled on a fresh pair of gloves and set to work.

I hoped Travis wouldn't be back anytime soon, didn't think so, especially since we'd had the argument about the laxatives. Nora had sent a text message saying he might stay over at her house, and so far the app confirmed his location, but I still had to be careful. Travis's moods flipped faster than a coin toss, he came and went as he pleased, and I crossed my fingers he'd either spend the night there or would soon be in full party mode somewhere else and pass out under a bush.

Some people crack under pressure. Not me. My work was methodical and precise, and I took my time putting another ransom note together, identical in look and feel to the first one I'd composed with cut out letters from the newspapers I'd collected.

FOR MICHELLES
        SAFE RETURN
$1 MILLION IN
$100 BILL
4.15PM THURSDAY
NO COPS OR SHE DIES

I added a specific place at North Station as the drop site. It would be busy as hell on a Thursday evening, packed with commuters bustling and hurrying on their way home. Not a bad spot for a ransom drop, if a little banal and uninspired. Happy with the wording and layout, I rode around to run some errands and dispose of the supplies I'd used for my creation.

Because we lived on a courtyard, none of the neighbors' door cams was pointed directly at our house, but I still waited until it was close to midnight to make my final move. Once I felt certain nobody was on the street, and confident no one was watching the house, I ambled to the mailbox. Upon my return I accidentally-on-purpose dropped my keys and the mail, and as I picked them up, I tucked the ransom note under the welcome mat, making sure it was slightly visible to any-one who came to the door. My plan had been to *discover* it the next morning, but it all changed—for the better, I might add—when Travis arrived at 3:30 a.m., his footsteps thunder-ing up the stairs while he shouted my name, yelling at me to wake up, I had to wake up *now*.

I wanted to punch the air as he thrust the ransom note into my hands. I hadn't expected him to come home, or for him to find it if he was wasted again. But now our fingerprints were all over it. Not only that, but any fibers or trace evidence from my house which might have made it onto the paper despite all the precautions I'd taken as I'd crafted the note would now be deemed to have landed there after he'd opened the envelope.

"We have to call the cops," Travis said, a slight slur to his words, his voice on the verge of hysterical, eyes and mouth wide.

"*No.* They messed things up last time. I'll get the money. Do the drop myself. I can handle it."

"Don't be insane. You're not a cop. You've no idea what you're doing."

We fought. He insisted. I countered. A heated debate ensued. I let him win. He made the call, and Detective Anjali and her colleagues descended upon us in record time. After we'd finished explaining what had happened, she stood in front of us, the ransom note in a plastic bag between her fingers.

"You don't know when this arrived?" she said. "You didn't hear or see anything?"

"Nothing," I said. "I went to bed around twelve."

"I found it when I got back, and we called you." Travis threw me a look. "*I* called you."

"Yuna," Anjali called over to one of her team, a petite woman with a sleek black ponytail. "Take Walker and go door-to-door. Get whatever video footage you can of the street."

"On it, boss."

I already knew they'd find nothing but wasn't about to suggest whoever had delivered the note could've snuck up through the ravine. They'd search for footprints anyway, maybe the ones I'd seen in the garden the other day would be of interest and keep them busy. They were still slightly visible, and it was fun and interesting to see them theorize what was happening, especially when I was the only one who knew they weren't barking up the wrong tree, they were in the wrong bloody forest.

"Let's go over this again," Anjali said, and when I answered her questions for the fourth time in the exact same manner, she seemed satisfied.

"Do you think the note's legitimate?" I said. "Is it from whoever took her?"

"It similar to the last one," she said. "Forensics will give us some insight."

"How long will that take?" Travis said.

"We'll put a rush on it."

Sure, they would. They'd be testing for all kinds of things. Fingerprints and DNA, but they'd only find mine and Travis's, and when they looked more closely they'd see mine were on top of his, confirming he handled the note first. They'd investigate the type of newspaper used to construct the words. The brand of glue to stick them, the paper, the envelope. Suspicions may land back on me but none of the materials were remotely close to anything I had in the house and I hadn't been stupid enough to lick the flap shut. Once again, I was so far ahead of them it was almost unfair. I could've had a rest, allowed them the opportunity to catch up a little, but instead I injected a generous helping of fear into my voice, and said, "But what does that mean, exactly? When will you get the results?"

Detective Anjali took a deep breath. "Not before four fifteen p.m. this afternoon."

"That settles it. I'm getting the money."

She held up a hand. "Whoa, Lucas, hold on. We need to discuss—"

"What's there to discuss?" Travis said. "He's right. We can get Michelle back."

"Exactly. I'm calling Nora. I need her help getting the cash."

"Both of you, please," Anjali said. "Hold on. This isn't a good idea."

"It's not up for debate," I snapped. "I'm getting my wife back, never mind the cost, and save the speech about not negotiating with criminals or terrorists or whatever, Detective. Don't get in my way. In fact, *stay* away. You can't come here and screw things up again."

"Lucas—"

I folded my arms over my chest. "No. I mean it. Believe me, if Travis hadn't found the note and called you, you wouldn't be here."

"It's true," Travis said, and I was impressed how he now seemed fully alert and engaged. "He didn't want me to call you because of what happened last time. What will you do to make sure things don't go wrong again?"

"Everything we can," Detective Anjali said.

I let out a snort. "I've heard that before."

"Look," she continued, her tone a little softer now. "We need to arrange this with you. This isn't something you can do alone. Let my team take over."

"No way," I said, standing tall, extending my full height so I towered above her. I didn't expect to intimidate her, but it was the kind of move a protective and worried husband would make.

"Please, Lucas, this could be the breakthrough we need," she insisted, as predicted fully ignoring my posturing. "You have to understand there's no guarantee this isn't some crank trying to benefit from your situation, someone trying to get money from you."

Tell me about it, I thought. The two partial photographs were an indication her theory could be spot on. I pressed my lips together and waited for her to continue.

"If this is Michelle's abductor," she said, "then this could be our one shot at catching him and bringing her home alive."

"But how?" Travis said. "Last time he didn't even show up."

"We can't be sure he wasn't there and didn't get cold feet. Regardless, we'll surround the area but stay out of sight. It'll be easy for my team to blend in. North Station will be busy—"

"Which means plenty of opportunities for him to slip away," I said.

"We'll block all exits, grab him there and then," Anjali said. "And in case we can't, we'll put a tracker in the money. He'll intend on swapping the bag at some point if he's smart, but it'll be impossible for him to do so at the station. Way too public. We'll follow him, and we'll get him. Give us this opportunity, please."

I pretended to consider her idea but remain unconvinced. "What if you catch him and he won't tell you where Michelle is? If he doesn't talk and we can't find her, she could...*die*."

"It's a risk," Detective Anjali admitted. "But I think the bigger one is giving him the money and expecting Michelle's safe return if he really does have her. We'll do everything we can, I promise. You're not alone in this, neither of you."

I wrung my hands, shushed Travis as he insisted they knew what they were doing, I should agree to whatever Anjali was saying because it was Michelle's best chance of being rescued. After a long pause I said, "Okay, fine, you win. But I want to deliver the bag."

"Out of the question," Anjali said.

"I'm not asking."

"We'll use one of my team—"

"I will *not* allow you to mess up—"

"Same height and build—"

"*No.*"

She raised her hands. "You win, Lucas, but we'll have eyes and ears on you at all times."

"Agreed." I dropped my shoulders. "Can you believe today's our third wedding anniversary? She should be here. We should be celebrating. I should be treating her to a delicious dinner somewhere, not fearing for her life, wondering if I'll ever see her again."

Travis shifted his feet and lowered his head while Anjali spoke. "We're doing everything we can to get her home. Please believe me."

Giving her a curt nod, I wiped my eyes with the back of my hand. "I have to call Nora. We need to get the money organized straightaway." As I pulled my phone from my pocket I moved to the kitchen and dialed. Diane answered, her voice drowsy. I looked at my watch. It was a little after 5:00 a.m. "Diane, I have news. Can I speak to Nora, please? It's urgent."

After I'd explained what was happening, Nora said she'd call her bank manager immediately. She sounded excited, filled with so much hope, and a tiny piece of me hated myself, but not nearly enough to change my plans.

30

Hours later, when I'd been briefed and Travis had left to be with Nora, I found myself in front of the North Station entrance on Causeway a little after 4:00 p.m. As I watched the steady stream of commuters exit the place, all of them looking stressed and grim-faced, I clutched a black leather duffel bag in my hand.

I'd been surprised to find one million in one hundred-dollar bills only weighed a little over twenty-two pounds. Easy enough to fit in a bag without making it seem suspicious. Easy enough to run with, if you needed to make a hasty escape and were relatively fit, although it would undeniably slow you down.

A rush of excitement traveled through my body, as it had when I'd arranged for Michelle to disappear, and again when I'd anticipated hearing from Woods that he'd taken care of things. The sensation was addictive. No wonder adrenaline junkies went hunting for the highest waves to surf, the steepest mountains to climb, and the tallest structures to BASE jump from. None of those held much appeal for me—I'd bungee jumped once and swore I'd never do it again—but this, the knowledge I'd get away with something and solve one of my problems through sheer cunningness and mental agility, would never get old.

I'd agreed with Anjali the cops would surround the drop site, a bench close to a donut shop (my own little joke), and she assured me they'd stay dozens of feet back, in plain clothes and well camouflaged. A multitude of officers were dotted around the area, too many for me to keep track of, and others had covered the exits. More were in cars, ready to give chase and catch Michelle's abductor by any means necessary. Anjali's strict instructions to not use lethal force were unwelcome, to me at least. Maybe someone would make a mistake. Get jumpy and fire their gun. Whoops.

"It's time," Anjali said in my ear. Using comms hadn't been welcome, either, but I'd had to agree. "Walk slowly. Do everything we discussed. I'm here with you."

It was a few minutes before the rendezvous when I approached the bench, the duffel bag still in one hand, carrying a coffee one of the officers had given me in the other so I looked like a regular commuter. I took a seat, lowered the duffel to the floor and pushed it underneath the bench with my foot. Next, I took out my phone, pretending to flick through the news as I counted to twenty, waiting for Anjali's order to leave. When I got to thirty-five and she still hadn't spoken, my foot tapped, and I leaned on my knee to stop it from moving. What the hell was she playing at? It was almost four fifteen.

Finally, Anjali said, "You did great, Lucas. Now get up and walk away. We'll take it from here."

It was an effort to keep my movements slow and natural, and as I did what she asked, I spotted Mel through the crowd. Bobby wasn't with him, which was annoying but unsurprising. Thankfully, Mel hadn't noticed me yet, but all the cops' eyes were on me, and I had to play my next card. I made sure I looked shocked as I hurried in the other direction, away from Mel. Glancing over my shoulder I saw him notice the bag under the seat and reach for it. I wanted to leap up and punch the air, turn around, point at him and shout, "Sucker!" at the top of my lungs. *Calm down*, I reminded myself, *be patient*.

As I'd ridden around disposing of the ransom note materials the evening before, I'd also visited the bus station, where I'd retrieved one of the last few burner phones.

"I'll have your cash tomorrow afternoon," I'd told Bobby.

He had the audacity to laugh. "Well done. We'll pick it up at the house."

"No. We'll meet at North Station. Main floor. There's a bench next to the donut shop—"

"What do you think this is? An episode of *Cracker*?"

"Wrong country. And wrong decade."

"You're funny. We're coming to the house."

"If you want the cash, that's where it'll be at four fifteen."

He sighed. "Fine, Cundy, I'll let you have this one. Don't say I never gave you anything."

"And after *I've* given you what you asked for, we'll never see each other again."

"Well now, see, it's not like me to make a promise I may not keep."

I'd hung up, switched the phone off and tossed it into the river when I'd ridden home. Now, as I glanced over my shoulder and saw Mel who was expecting to deliver two million dollars to his boss, I imagined how I might have ended up neck deep in Bobby's shit if I'd kept on doing his dirty work instead of branching out on my own. No, thanks. I'd kept the old promise I'd made myself that if I messed up and got arrested, it was going to be because of something I'd done for *me*, not someone else. As far as I was concerned, they could put *Didn't play well with others* on my tombstone, if anyone cared enough to make me one.

"Detective Anjali," I said, refocusing as I ran to her, making myself sound breathless and confused. "The man by the bench, the big guy. I know him. I *know* him!"

"Stay here," Anjali said, and before I had time to answer, the team swarmed.

And what a thing of beauty it was to behold, seeing Mel get taken down before he could say *body slam*. Watching him splayed out on his stomach, arms pinned behind his back, in the exact position he'd put me in the day before, the schadenfreude almost made my heart explode. I barely stopped myself from grinning as two cops who matched Mel in height and width, hauled him to his feet and marched him to North Station's exit.

I watched Anjali run back to me, her brow covered in sweat, and decided the way she'd organized and controlled this entire operation had to be commended. I'd been smart to remain wary, should never underestimate her, not when she had the tactical precision of a brain surgeon and her mind worked almost as fast as mine.

"Talk to me," she said. "How do you know that man? Tell me everything."

"Not now." I took a few steps to the car Mel was being piled into, but she grabbed hold of me before I got anywhere.

"Stop. You sure you know him? Who is he?"

I tried shaking her off, but she held firm, her grip tightening. "I want to talk to him first," I said. "I need to know what he's done to Michelle. Let me speak to him, now."

She refused, as I knew she would. A little while later we were at the police station, and I had the pleasure of watching Mel being marched into an interrogation room. Before the door closed, he yelled in a thick Yorkshire accent, "Gerroff me. I'm tellin' ya, I didn't do nowt." His voice was surprisingly high-pitched. No wonder he didn't talk much because when he did, he wasn't nearly as scary.

It took almost two hours of me hanging around before Anjali led me to a room with pea-green walls, a mosaic coffee table that looked so old it was fashionable again, and a squishy pink floral sofa. She handed me a mug that said *10-4 Coffee That*, and spent the next few minutes giving me the lowdown of the situation, finishing with "So, he claims never to have heard of a man called Bobby Boyle."

I figured as much but still took great delight in hearing how Mel had broken out in a sweat, pleading his innocence. He knew what trouble he'd be in if he didn't stay loyal to his boss. If he was in the least bit smart, he also knew there was no way they could link either of them to Michelle's abduction, not easily, anyway. Him being at the ransom drop at the exact time it was supposed to take place could swiftly be deemed a coincidence. Then there was the lack of prints and DNA on the note. Finally, any lawyer worth their height and weight in hundred-dollar bills would argue Mel wasn't in the country when Michelle went missing, although I hoped he had been, because it would solve my problem a little more neatly. For now, though, I'd take what I could get.

"I need you to go over some more things." Anjali tapped the tip of her pen on her scribble-filled notepad. "Make sure I haven't missed anything. You're saying this man, Melvin Davison, came to your house yesterday with Robert aka Bobby Boyle because he claims you owe him money."

"Yes. Well, technically my father did, but Bobby held me

responsible, and men like him never forget a debt. I've no idea how they found me. He knows where my father is, maybe someone there alerted him when I went for a visit, or perhaps they used facial recognition software or something. I'm sure he knows all kinds of people who could do that."

She raised her chin. I could almost hear her brain connecting the pieces together, except she couldn't quite make them fit. "Why didn't you tell me any of this before?"

"Because I didn't think it was related to Michelle's abduction. And I wasn't about to put my father in danger by you paying Bobby a visit. You've no idea what he's capable of."

She crossed her arms and stared at me. "Why do I get the impression there's something you're not telling me, Lucas? There's more to this story, isn't there?" When I didn't answer and looked away, tapping my foot with genuine nervous energy, she continued, "You have to tell me. It may be the only way to help Michelle."

I gave her a succinct overview of my father's gambling habit, the beating Dad took because he'd lost the cash, but didn't disclose I'd worked for Bobby or the fact I'd changed my name. I was hedging my bets on Mel keeping his mouth shut, and if he blabbed, I'd say it had been to hide because I was afraid for my life, which wasn't a lie. Nor was it all of the truth.

"When Bobby came to the house yesterday, he said the fifty grand was now two million American. When I refused to give it to him, Mel attacked me, but I insisted I wouldn't pay."

"And then they left?"

"Yes. But not before threatening to come back. He said my father's debt would increase by another fifty thousand each day I didn't pay up." I rubbed my hands over my face. "Do you think Bobby has Michelle?"

Anjali hesitated. "That's what we're trying to ascertain. Mel's insisting he knows nothing about her abduction, but I'll get to the bottom of it." She tapped both palms on the table. "I'm heading back in. You go home and I'll be in touch as soon as I can, and don't argue with me."

I'd followed her instructions. Now, sitting with Nora, Travis, Diane, and Karina, we'd been over the facts multiple times. There was still no news from the detective, which I presumed meant Mel had kept his mouth shut. I was tired, on the express train to Grumpyville, and I decided it was time to make a move before I derailed. There was, however, one more thing I needed to manipulate first.

"You should stay here tonight, Travis," I said, looking at him. "It would do you and Nora both a lot of good to spend family time together."

"What about you?" Nora said. "You're family."

"I'll be fine," I said. "I need to get my head straight. Go over what happened."

"Please don't feel guilty," Nora said. "If this despicable creature Bobby Boyle took Michelle because of money your father owed, you do understand it's not your fault?"

I grimaced, caught Travis glaring at me, and decided he didn't appear to share his mother's assessment.

"Yeah, it's better if I stay here," he said, his voice dripping with animosity. If I weren't an utter cynic, I'd have believed he'd agreed to sleep in his old bedroom because he hated me and he didn't want Nora to be alone, but I could practically guarantee it wasn't the case. The forlorn face he'd made earlier as he'd looked at his mother, and his incessant offers to get her something to drink, to eat, or to fluff her pillows, were a dead giveaway. Yes, he cared, but he was on the hunt for something more than her well-being. It wouldn't have surprised me in the least if he'd so readily agreed to spend the night because he wanted one of Nora's antiques.

From what she'd told me in the past, it wouldn't have been

the first time a Clarice Cliff vase or a Hummel figurine went walkies whenever Travis was using. Maybe during one of my next visits I'd photograph everything. Make a catalog of sorts. See what disappeared and keep it as leverage against Travis if I needed him in line the few weeks Nora had left. I'd already slipped a couple of smaller items into my jacket pockets over the past month, hoping she'd accuse him of stealing them, but so far, I'd heard nothing. Not that I believed it was because Nora cared about her possessions at this stage, but she certainly would if she thought Travis was using whatever money he got for them to fund his habits.

I pushed Travis and his sticky fingers to the back of my mind and got up. After saying my goodbyes, I headed straight to Gideon's wine cellar where I perused the collection of high-end bottles, congratulating myself on my victory.

Things were being taken care of. With any luck, as soon as Bobby saw or heard of Mel's arrest, he'd left the country. It would be far too risky for him to stay and they'd put a BOLO out for him, including at the airport. Perhaps Bobby might be arrested and brought in for questioning, unless he was somewhere over the Atlantic by now, or on his way to Canada, hoping to make his escape.

Regardless, neither he nor Mel would cause me any more trouble, not for the next while, at least. And if Bobby showed his face again…well, I'd be sure to have a weapon on me.

The stage for killing him and Mel in self-defense had been set.

31

As I drove home, taking deep and satisfying drags on a cigarette, I called the local Italian and ordered some food to be delivered in an hour. Having the house to myself this evening meant I could have the whole night off, and I welcomed the chance to drop my devoted husband act for a bit.

I needed a break. Couldn't wait to kick back and watch a movie, eat a good pizza, and have a couple of beers. I'd save the wine I'd taken from Gideon's stash for another time. The day Michelle was officially declared dead and I became rich would be a great occasion. It might take a few years, but the wine would serve as a reminder for me to sit tight. Much like my situation, the booze would only get better with time.

As I drove along the quiet streets of Chelmswood, my mind went over the events of the day, cataloging the truths I'd interspersed and bookended with lies, making sure I'd never slip up and forget something. I reexamined everything I'd shared with the police, inspecting it for flaws or missteps, but found none. Even under intense pressure, the execution had been perfect, something always so much more easily done when you worked alone.

I wasn't worried about Bobby coming to the house. If he hadn't abandoned Mel and left the country yet—and he was a complete moron if he hadn't—there was no way he'd show his face around my place. No matter how much he was hyperventilating about his guard dog being arrested, I'd have bet my left nut he wouldn't venture within fifty miles of the place in case the cops were posted outside my door. Detective Anjali had offered, but I'd refused, insisting they use all their available resources on determining if Mel and Bobby were involved in abducting Michelle, and finding her.

I'd ended my speech with, "I can take care of myself, Detective. All that matters is you bringing my wife home."

One of her crew had tears in his eyes after my performance. As for the money in the duffel bag, the million bucks had found its way back to Nora's bank account and was safely tucked away, ready to be transferred to Michelle and Travis's inheritance. Final destination: my pocket.

"You're gonna need a bigger pocket," I said in my best Chief Brody impersonation, letting the cigarette dangle from my lips.

I pulled into my street, finished my smoke, and flicked the butt out the window, deciding I may have taken care of Bobby Boyle for now, but I couldn't let myself get complacent. Things were not yet where I needed them to be. Whoever Woods was, he'd gone dark and was no doubt using a different name. I had no tangible way of finding out where he was, the exact point of our clandestine interactions, but now there was a hedgerow of stinging thorns in my side.

Someone out there had sent those partial photos of Michelle, and I'd yet to find out for sure who. My money was still on Woods or Detective Anjali, or some wannabe smart-arse on her team, perhaps, but after today the cops would be off my back for good.

Still, a little bit of elation faded so I reminded myself Mel was in custody and Bobby had been flagged as a person of interest, so at least that threat had lessened for a while. No matter what Mel told them—if he talked at all—once the cops made inquiries with the Greater Manchester Police and learned Bobby Boyle had been on their radar for years, it seemed highly unlikely anyone would believe much of what Mel said. I'd never been caught back home, be it before or while I'd worked for Bobby, much less convicted of anything. I didn't have a record anywhere.

My ex-boss was out of the picture for a bit, which gave me wriggle room. He wouldn't be able to blab to Nora now, I felt confident of that. He knew if he stopped me from getting money, he wouldn't get any either, and if he did take his chances, whatever he said would be discredited. Even if he went so far as to tell her about my name change, I'd say Michelle had known, but had insisted we keep it amongst ourselves because Gideon wouldn't have approved of my father's gambling problem. Nobody could say otherwise.

Still, I couldn't be sure Bobby wouldn't try to hurt my father. He probably knew if he did, getting any cash from me would be off the table permanently, but I wasn't taking any chances. I'd called the home earlier in the day, well before I'd gone to meet Bobby, spoken to the manager, and arranged for Dad to be transferred to another private home under a different name at exactly four fifteen, when Bobby would be distracted. Mrs. Hannigan at first insisted moving Dad and scrubbing all the records late at night wasn't possible, but surprise, surprise, a little financial encouragement made every objection she had disappear. Dad was safe, and I was already looking at moving him again to be sure.

I exhaled slowly. I'd handle Travis soon after Nora's passing. Go to England to visit Dad. In the meantime I'd head back to the dark web for someone who'd get Bobby off my back for good. Paying double to get rid of him instantly would be worth it. My smile returned. After that, all my problems would disappear. Very soon I'd lead the life I wanted, and I couldn't wait to be free from all the hassle and bullshit. Liberated, wealthy, unencumbered. It was what everyone dreamed of.

When I pushed open the front door, Roger stood on the other side, wagging his tail, his face in another lopsided grin. I rubbed his head, decided in six months or so, I'd find another dog at a shelter, give Roger someone to hang out with. Maybe I'd pick up a cat. I'd always wanted pets as a kid, but we couldn't afford the food or vet bills. Therapy dogs for stroke patients was something else I should look into. For now, though, Roger needed a walk before he emptied his bladder on my shoes.

"Let me grab some water and I'll take you out," I said, thinking we'd go before my food arrived, and we hunkered down for the night. At the mere mention of a walk, Roger barked and spun in circles, chasing his tail. I sidestepped to get past his hairy bulk, and he chased me down the hall, all the way to the kitchen where I gave him another pat as he tried to nibble my fingers. "Knock it off," I laughed. "Stop it, you daft prat."

I set the wine on the counter and grabbed a glass from the cupboard, gulping down a pint of water in one go, but when I flicked on the lights and turned to the living room, my heart seemed to miss ten beats as the glass almost slipped from my fingers.

A long black Christian Dior dress, Michelle's favorite, which had cost an absolute fortune and made her look exquisite, lay draped over the sofa. A pair of strappy Jimmy Choos, also eye-wateringly expensive, had been placed on the carpet directly in front of the dress. The way the items were arranged made it seem like my wife was sitting there, waiting for me. One of her silver necklaces with an infinity pendant sat on top of a black clutch and next to it—no, they couldn't be—were those *goddamn* Tiffany earrings.

My mind exploded, a billion thoughts pounding through my brain, but I didn't have time to process any of them, or what I was seeing, because there was more: an ice bucket from the pantry, now standing on the coffee table with a chilled bottle of Veuve Clicquot inside, a white fabric serviette tied around its neck. Time stood still as I watched a droplet of condensation trickle down the outside of the bucket and make its way to the base. My eyes finally landed on the orange envelope propped up against the champagne. One word written on the front.

Lucas.

I grabbed it and ripped it open in a frenzy, yanking out the contents. A dozen or so shreds of paper fluttered to the floor. Dropping to my knees I scrambled to turn them over, immediately certain of what they were. The rest of the black-and-white photograph of Michelle. I arranged the pieces as fast as I could, flipping them over once done. Two words were scrawled across them in black felt-tip pen.

HAPPY ANNIVERSARY

I didn't recognize the handwriting but the entire situation, the bizarreness of it, made my head spin. I grabbed hold of the sofa to steady myself, clenched my teeth so hard I thought they might split. Wracking my brain, I tried to remember if I'd set the security alarm when I'd left this morning, realized Travis had still been at the house. I brushed the thought away because ultimately it didn't matter. There was no mistaking it this time. Whoever had sent me those photos had been in my house. In my goddamn *house.*

My situation hadn't got a little better today. It had become a whole lot worse.

32

Pulse racing, I attempted to comprehend what was going on. My first thought went to Travis. He must have done this. Was this the real reason why he'd agreed to stay at his mother's so readily? My temper came dangerously close to boiling point, and if he'd been here now, I'd have pinned him against the wall and throttled the answers out of him.

"Calm. Down," I said. Travis was the most plausible explanation given the fact he was the only other person who knew how to get into the house. Then again, he was such a blabbermouth, it wouldn't have been a surprise if half of Chelmswood knew the combination. I forced myself to rationalize, analyze. Why would he have done this? What was the point? Wind me up because he blamed me for Michelle's abduction, even more now he believed Bobby had taken her because of something my father had done? I'd given him an update after

Mel had been arrested, so he'd have had loads of time to come back and set this bizarre stage.

My next thought went to the tracking app I'd installed on his phone. I pulled my cell from my pocket and scrolled through his location history, expecting to see he'd come back here at some point during the day, except he hadn't. He'd left shortly after me, spent the day at Nora's, hadn't been anywhere near this house—or at least his phone hadn't, which didn't mean he couldn't have staged Michelle's things in my living room. Either he'd left his mobile somewhere else by accident, or he'd somehow detected the app on his cell, which was unlikely because he wasn't that great with tech.

I slowed down, forced myself to process everything. With a quantum leap of imagination, I supposed it was feasible Travis had done this with Anjali's help. The possibility of me still being their prime suspect remained. They had no others except for Mel and Bobby, and I didn't believe they'd find anything to make those guys stay on their radar for long.

I looked at the display left for me. The dress, bag, and necklace had been upstairs in the walk-in closet, but the earrings… those *bloody* earrings. I'd searched my bedroom and Travis's for them, hell, I'd turned the whole house upside down and hadn't found them anywhere.

Perhaps Travis had hidden them at Nora's weeks ago. Maybe his plan had been to mess with me from the start, either because he suspected I was involved in her disappearance, or because he hated me for not protecting her. Either scenario could have been the real reason why he'd wanted to spend more than a few nights in my spare bedroom. Perhaps I'd underestimated him all along and the guy was craftier than I'd given him credit for.

It had to be Travis. Because if not, and Michelle had worn those earrings the night she'd disappeared, there was only one other explanation. *Woods*. He'd broken into my house to flush me out and get more money. As much as I hated the theory, it made sense and it more than pissed me off.

Red-hot rage billowed inside me as I went over the facts again, trying to determine who else could've been here. Mel was in custody, so it wasn't him. Bobby, then? No. Not unless he'd been leaving the partial pictures to begin with, and while he may have learned it was our third wedding anniversary from going through my wife's social media, there was no way he'd have picked Michelle's favorite dress by coincidence. Or got hold of her jewelry.

Making myself backtrack to Woods, I wondered how *he* would have known about the dress. Had he and Michelle had a cozy little chat while he peeled her like an onion, getting detail after detail out of her before he killed her?

I ran my hands through my hair, trying to think, think, *think*, break down what was going on. The entire world was imploding and exploding at the same time, crushing me before ripping me to shreds.

When Roger let out a bark, I turned around. "Who did this?" I said. "Who came here?"

He stared at me, panting. I was in serious danger of losing it, standing here talking to a dog, expecting an answer. I needed to hold it together. No, forget that. I needed to *get* it together.

As I grabbed the pieces of photograph and shoved them back in the envelope so I could burn them in the sink as I had the others, the doorbell rang. I'd long forgotten about the food I'd ordered, and my appetite had vanished. I pushed the paper deep into my back pocket, deciding I'd forget about the pizza and down as many beers as it took to steady my nerves. Roger trotted behind me as I headed for the front door and yanked it open only to find it wasn't the delivery guy. It was Detective Anjali.

"Hey," she said. "Can I come in?"

I almost told her to give it up already and drop the Columbo act, to stop coming to my house unannounced. Before the words tumbled out, I shut my mouth. She was alone, a sign she still didn't see me as a threat, maybe not even a suspect.

I considered saying I needed time to digest today's events, but I'd taken a while to respond, and my silence was met with an inquisitive expression. No way could I afford to start acting suspiciously now. My mind raced ahead to what she'd think if I let her in and she saw Michelle's clothes and the champagne in the living room. She couldn't come into the house, not unless...

Unless I shifted the outcome to my advantage.

I opened the door, gestured for her to follow me to the kitchen, from where she had a direct view of the sofa, and my wife's things. Her eyes widened a little, and I let a distraught and somewhat embarrassed expression slide across my face, making sure I left it there long enough for her to see. I hung my head.

"Our wedding anniversary." I choked the words out and cleared my throat for effect. "It made me feel as if she was here. I know it's stupid—"

"No." Anjali held up her hands, her expression changing to empathy. "It isn't. I get it, I do. You miss her. You want her home."

"More than anything." I let out a slow stream of shaky breath. "Did Mel say anything? Did you find Boyle?"

Anjali sighed. "Mel still isn't talking. Other than to say he had nothing to do with Michelle's disappearance, he's keeping *schtum*. We checked the records. He arrived in the US two days ago, so we don't have much to go on. His fingerprints aren't on the ransom note and we've put in a request to expedite the DNA. As for Mr. Boyle…" She swallowed, gave her head a shake. "No, we haven't found him."

I sank down onto a chair at the dining table. "Do you think they took her?"

"We can't rule it out at this point."

"But if they weren't in the country, you're wasting—"

"They might have an associate here."

I forced a few tears. "This is my fault. They took her because of me, my father's debt."

"Maybe, but it's also possible they never had her at all."

"What are you saying?"

"It could've been an entirely opportunistic move, coming over demanding the money, you refusing, and them using Michelle's disappearance to get you to pay up."

"Bobby demanded two million. The ransom note said one."

"Better one than none," Anjali said. "And it's a huge coincidence, you showing them the door and getting a ransom note not long after. It wouldn't have been hard to imitate. The first one was all over the news."

"Yeah, because someone at your department leaked it." Nope. It had been me.

"Yes." She looked away. "The department's under investigation, I can assure you."

I waved a hand. "What happens now?"

"We can't charge Mel with the evidence we have. Or lack thereof."

"Arriving at the drop at the exact time isn't enough? What more do you need?"

"It can be argued as circumstantial if it's all there is." She hesitated a while before speaking again. "Lucas… I have to ask you something."

"Okay."

"I hope you understand, but if I don't pursue this line of inquiry, I wouldn't be doing my job properly."

"Ask whatever you need," I said, seeming nervous yet eager to please.

"Did you tell Mel and Bobby to meet you at the drop because you were hoping to get them off your back?"

I'd anticipated this, I'd have been an idiot if I didn't think they'd put two and two together. I changed my expression to one of indignation in a flash, a well-practiced reaction she'd seen me have many times before. "*What?* No, absolutely not."

"Are you sure? Because, according to Mel, that's what happened."

"And you believe him?" When she didn't answer I grabbed my phone and held it out to her. "Check it. Go on. I didn't call him, or Bobby. He's lying. I didn't—"

"All right, okay." Anjali looked at me. "I mean, I'd understand if you did, given the pressure and everything you're going through." Her eyes flicked to Michelle's dress on the sofa. "But you'd be jeopardizing the investigation. You'd have scared the real abductor away today, do you understand?"

"Of course I understand, and I didn't do what you're accusing me of."

"I'm not accusing—"

"I want you to bring my wife home, Detective. Stop wasting my time with these ridiculous theories and go do your job."

"I am, Lucas, I can assure you," she said with a firm nod. "I'll be in touch soon."

We'd made it to the middle of the hallway when the doorbell rang again. Roger let out a loud bark as I stepped past Anjali, reached for the handle, and pulled the door open, expecting the pizza guy. Wrong.

It was a woman I didn't recognize, and she wasn't delivering food. I guessed her to be in her midtwenties, with blond hair cut into a bob, blue sparkling eyes, and a look that suggested we skip the dishes for entirely different reasons. When her face broke into a wide smile I did a double take, almost thinking it was Michelle.

"Hi," she said, her voice low and seductive. Roger barked again. "I'm Josephine. Nice to meet you." Her effervescence faded a little when she caught sight of Anjali behind me, but she quickly recovered. "Oh, hello, there. I thought our arrangements were for two, but it's cool. I'm flexible."

My mouth had fallen open, so I closed it before saying, "You've got the wrong house."

"Lucas Forester?" She rattled off my address. "For a...*special* occasion."

Anjali coughed and patted me on the shoulder. "I'll leave you to it."

"No, wait. Detective, this isn't—"

"Any of my business? No, it isn't. Good night." While Anjali's voice carried more than a hint of indignation mixed perhaps with some mild disgust, as she walked past me, I could've sworn I spotted a smirk.

33

Anjali walked to her car, but didn't turn around, so there was no opportunity for me to see the expression on her face properly. Meanwhile, the woman named Josephine leaned in and lowered her voice to a conspiratorial and unnecessary whisper considering it was now the two of us.

"I'm so sorry to have put you in such an awkward position," she said, batting her long lashes, tilting her head downward and lifting her eyes. A deliberately submissive move, one I'd have noticed blindfolded and three miles away. Quite the turnoff. "I can come back a little later if it's better for you?" she added with an overly practiced pout.

"Later? I don't—"

"Oh, you'll get the same amount of time, of course, don't worry."

"No." My brain gave my voice a kick and I continued more

forcefully. "I didn't arrange for *company*. Not now or for later. I told you, you've got the wrong guy."

Shaking her head, she brushed a lock of hair from her face, slid an elegantly manicured finger across the screen of her phone and held it up to me. "This is the correct address. See? I didn't make a mistake. I'm booked to be here all night with Lucas Forester."

"What are you talking about?" I peered at the screen, saw my name, my address.

"That's what was requested." She glanced over her shoulder. "Maybe we should go inside and talk?"

"No, not happening. Requested by whom? Who sent you?"

Her eyes widened as she gave a small shrug. "I don't make the bookings, so I presumed it was you."

"Except it wasn't."

"And you *don't* want me to come in?"

"Uh, that's a firm no."

"Obviously, something went wrong somewhere. I'll contact the agency." Josephine bit her lip and wrinkled her nose before giving me a slow and purposeful once-over, all the way from the top of my head and down to my toes. "Shame…and I apologize for the trouble. Maybe another time?"

"Still a no, but thanks."

She smiled tightly, her voice losing some of its sugariness. "Okay then. I'll call an Uber. Have a good night."

Roger had already lost interest and disappeared into the house somewhere, but as I was about to close the front door, I pulled it open again. "Excuse me, Josephine? Wait."

She spun around, her expression transforming back to dazzling and professional in an instant.

"Can you tell me who made the payment?" I said.

She suppressed a sigh, let her shoulders drop. "Like I said, the agency handles the details…but let me see if I can find out for you. I'll call them." She moved a little farther away, whispered into her phone for a minute. "Prepaid credit card," she said after hanging up. "It happens a lot so there's no trace on any statements. But as I said, probably a communication error."

Unease tugged on my gut. This wasn't a mistake. Crazy as the thought was, Josephine arriving while Anjali was at the house seemed calculated. Too well-timed not to be deliberate.

"Is there anything else you can tell me?" I said. When she hesitated, I gave her my best smile. "Were there any other instructions? Maybe my friend did this. He's always staging pranks."

"Expensive prank," Josephine said before pointing to her eyes and twirling a lock of hair around her index finger. Blue contact lenses and a blond, chin-length bob.

Exactly like Michelle.

"And the—" I made air quotation marks "—special occasion?"

She shifted from one foot to the other. "A wedding anniversary?" It sounded tentative, as if she were asking a question because an admission might cause trouble. "This whole situation is weirding me out. I'm calling an Uber."

I took a step back, held up my hands. "Yes, yes, of course. Thanks for your help."

Without another word, Josephine turned and bolted for the road in her sky-high heels. I went back inside the house, pulse thumping in my neck, but only made it ten steps before the doorbell rang again. Who the hell was it this time? Hannibal Lecter? Norman Bates? Good ol' Darth Vader?

Thankfully just the pizza guy, who apologized profusely for being late. Zero clue how much I tipped him but judging by the delighted look on his face, it was generous. Door closed once more, Roger jumped up and walked over, sniffing at the cardboard box.

I went through the automatic motions of feeding him before

opening the patio doors and letting him out into the garden. Still on autopilot I put the pizza in the fridge, mind racing in deranged loop-de-loops, veering off in all and any directions it could think of as I tried to grasp what was happening, and, most importantly, who was pulling the strings.

Most of the things that had been going wrong recently… taken in isolation they were no big deal, and while I might have brushed some of them off as misfortune and coincidence, when I put them together it became increasingly clear someone had been trying to screw with me from the start. Not *trying*. *Succeeding*. My head was a mess, my focus shot again. If this was the cops' way of trying to get me to freak the hell out and make a misstep, they were increasingly close to getting their wish.

As my brain kicked its activity and efforts of self-preservation up a notch, I thought about the burner laptop and phones I'd stored at the bus station. Those were the only items with my DNA on them and which, if found, could link me to my activities. Potentially to Woods.

I didn't want to destroy them as it would also cut my method of communication with him, except he hadn't responded to any of my messages so far, and I didn't have a choice. It was time to get rid of anything implicating me, and in an instant, all my anger turned inward. For God's sake, I should've done so the moment the first picture of Michelle arrived with the flyers instead of assuming it was a goddamn printing error. Never, *ever* assume. Rule number one in the Bad Guy's Handbook.

Feeling the urgency to act immediately, I called Roger inside and went to the kitchen cupboard to retrieve the locker key from the tea tin, my heart still pounding. I decided to take my phone with me this time. If anyone asked, I could easily explain stopping at a random bus station to use the bathroom.

After I'd hastily shoved a few essentials into my backpack

and swept the Triumph for tracking devices, I fired the bike up and took off, reducing my speed when I saw I was going almost twenty over. It would not be wise to get stopped by the police this evening, and definitely not once I had the devices with me.

My brain jumped ahead, planning where I'd dump the laptop and burner phones—in two or preferably more locations—and I was halfway to the bus station before I remembered I needed to take a few detours and shortcuts to ensure nobody was following me. Jesus, this situation really was messing me up. Not only that, but Josephine showing up at the house while Anjali was there... I wouldn't have been surprised if the detective was following me herself.

I debated whether I'd made the right decision by letting her see the dress and the shoes in the living room. If Anjali hadn't organized Josephine's arrival, she'd no doubt presumed the outfit had been intended to help me fantasize about my wife during the encounter. This was not good for my caring husband persona and I needed to fix it, although whether the detective would believe anything I said about the situation was more than debatable at this point.

When I'd ridden around long enough, I headed for the bus station, stopping dead as I walked to the row of lockers. An older man with a Santa belly, and dressed in blue overalls, stood a few rungs up a ladder, screwdriver in hand, installing what looked to be security cameras. I yanked a Red Sox baseball hat from my backpack and pulled it low over my face, nodding to the man as I walked by. He had a direct view of all the lockers, but I didn't want to come back later.

As I turned the key in the lock, I held up my backpack, planning on sliding the contents into it without the man seeing what was inside.

When I opened the unit, my heart stopped.

The locker was empty.

34

Empty. The locker was fucking *empty*. How was this possible? I examined the key in my hand, as if doing so might explain the situation, hoping I'd somehow opened another unit. Except I hadn't. The number on the locker door and the key were identical. Unit 23. I hadn't made a mistake. I wasn't dreaming. I hadn't slipped into a strange parallel universe, which would've been quite welcome at this point.

Somebody had stolen the laptop and burner phones, and it could've happened at any point since I'd been here last. Had my locker been targeted, or had the thief broken into multiple ones and taken whatever they could find? I slammed the door, examined the lock for signs it had been damaged or tampered with, but it looked fine.

I turned to the man on the ladder. "My stuff's been stolen."

"Oh, sorry, man, I'm just the tech." He pointed behind

him with his screwdriver. "Customer service is back there, I think. Guess you could report it. Shame these cameras aren't working yet."

"Did you see anyone open this locker?"

He gave a small shrug. "Sorry."

There was no footage for me to get my hands on. The lack of it had been why I'd chosen this location in the first place, but I needed to get my things back, to destroy them and not only because they were covered in my fingerprints and DNA. While I was reasonably tech savvy, there was no way I'd hidden my digital tracks well enough to ensure the governmental cyber-geeks who might examine the devices wouldn't be able to see exactly what I'd done.

Rage and frustration shot through me as I hurried back to the bike, my brain trying to kick itself into damage control. I kept asking myself who'd done this. Mel and Bobby? Not possible. What about the cops? Were they examining the laptop now? Waiting for me at home with a warrant for my arrest? Was that why Anjali had smirked?

As I tried to unscramble the possibilities, another thought zoomed into my head. If it was the police, they'd have needed some kind of warrant to get their hands on my gear. I stormed back inside and marched up to the customer service desk from where a middle-aged woman with a mop of macaroni-shaped curls, three silver nose rings and a name tag that read Betty glanced up from her *US Weekly* and beamed.

"Hello, sir."

"Hi, Betty," I said in an Australian accent after mustering some fake enthusiasm. "How's your evening going so far?"

She waved a hand. "Slow'n'boring, sweets, slow'n'boring. As usual. How can I help?"

I leaned in a little, mirrored her body language. "Well, I work for the *Boston Herald*."

"Oooh, are you a reporter?"

"I am indeed."

"How exciting."

"It is, but this is my first week. Not entirely sure I know what I'm doing, to be honest." I made a self-deprecating face. Betty giggled, and I could already tell she enjoyed a good gossip, so I rolled my eyes. "The boss sent me out on an assignment about bus station safety in the area. Sounds pretty ridiculous, huh? Nothing ever happens in these small towns."

"Oh, I don't know," Betty said. "It can get a little hairy around here at night."

"Really? In this charming place?"

"Oh, yes, definitely. Small towns can be evil. It's where murderers and serial killers hide, leading regular lives, pretending they're normal." She made big eyes. "I've seen it on TV."

"Gosh, I'd never thought of that. You mean they're hiding in plain sight."

"Exactly."

"But does anything ever happen here at the station? I had a look around. Saw security cameras by the storage lockers are going up."

"Oh, we'd been waiting for ages. Funding came through at last."

"Does a lot of stuff get stolen from the units?"

"A few times a year. But it's mainly bicycles out back, to be honest. We get the occasional mugging."

"Anything recent?"

When Betty said she hadn't seen anything suspicious forever, that nothing exciting had happened in her life since her pet gerbil, Mr. Nibs, had escaped from his cage and almost been sucked into the vacuum cleaner (he'd survived, phew), I cut her off and changed tack.

"But I'll bet all kinds of things get forgotten in those lockers."

"Forgotten and abandoned," she said. "No Picassos yet though. I wish."

"Oh, but wouldn't that be fun? Do the cops ever ask you to open them?"

"The lockers?" She glanced left and right before leaning in closer. "One time they busted a unit open and there was a pile of silverware and expensive watches." Betty widened her eyes again and whispered, "Stolen. Worth at least two thousand dollars."

"Wow. Unbelievable. But no cops breaking into anything recently? Nobody complaining about any locker thefts or something I could write about to get my boss off my back?"

"Oh, if only, it would brighten my evenings, for sure. Uh, I mean, I'm not wishing harm on anyone, of course, but no."

"You sure?"

"Uh-huh. I'm here six days a week so I'd know."

A dead end. I thanked her and headed back outside. The cops might not have been here, but someone had got into my unit. I had no idea how, though, because the lock was intact.

Rubbing a hand over my face, I still had trouble believing Travis was the brains behind all of this. Which left me with Woods—but who the hell *was* Woods, and how did he anticipate my every move? How would he have known about the locker, and the key in my kitchen cupboard? There was no way, not unless...

I tripped over my own feet. Son of a bitch. He hadn't only wandered around my garden, or broken in to stage a few clothes. He was watching me from *inside*.

It was the only explanation. Whoever it was, Woods or the cops, they'd put a camera in my house.

I'd been so focused on the vehicles, never taking the Triumph out without checking it first, never driving anywhere that had anything to do with Michelle's disappearance in the Mercedes. I'd been so cocky, so goddamn self-assured, and certain I had the upper hand, I'd forgotten to secure my own home.

As I was about to jump on my bike, race back and do a full sweep of every floor, my phone buzzed with an incoming text. Pulling the cell from my pocket I saw it was from Primrose, unusual seeing it was the middle of the night in England and Dad wasn't even there anymore. My heart made its way into my throat. Messages at this hour were never good news. My finger slid over the screen, a frown deepening as I scanned the words.

AUTOMATED NOTIFICATION—URGENT ACTION REQUIRED

Dear Mr. Forester,
Regretfully, the payment for October fees is in arrears. Please contact Accounts Receivable between 9 a.m. and 4 p.m. GMT to rectify the situation.

Thank you.
Primrose Living Finance Team

A patch of sweat collected under my armpits. The payments for Dad's care were automatic. I set them up ages ago, a direct debit five days before month end. I hadn't changed the details, and always received acknowledgment of receipt from Primrose via email the day after. I tried to remember when the last one had arrived but couldn't get there. I'd been too preoccupied, and when I'd spoken to the manager earlier, Mrs. Hannigan hadn't mentioned anything. Then again, she hadn't looked at Dad's billing. She'd been too busy driving up the price of what it would cost me to move him.

I opened the email app on my phone, sifted through both my inbox and deleted items, hunting for the message confirming the payment had gone through. There wasn't one. The banking app, then, that's where I'd find proof the transfer had been made, except when I examined the monthly transactions, there was nothing there, either.

"What the hell is happening to me?" I whispered, the intensity of the chatter in my head increasing tenfold, shouting at me to pay attention. Dad's payment mishap wasn't an accident or clerical error. It was deliberate. Whoever was behind all this knew me and my routines. They had access to the house. They knew where I went to the gym. Where I banked. They'd got into my work emails.

A barrel of pennies dropped, and I gripped my phone as the understanding of what was happening erupted from the pit of my gut. It wasn't one person screwing with me, it was *two*.

Travis quietly blamed me for his sister's disappearance, not because he thought I was involved, but because he felt I hadn't protected her, that I'd let her down. Hell, for all I knew he was projecting his guilt on me and taking it out with petty shit. He'd keyed my car, messed with my gym membership, got into my work email, put laxatives in my food, and cancelled my dad's care home payment somehow, perhaps when I'd popped to the bathroom and he'd pretended to be asleep in the den. Spiteful actions to piss me off.

In the meantime, Woods or the cops were sending me partial photos of Michelle, trying to trick me to see if I was guilty of hurting my wife.

And I was sick and tired of being played.

Taking a deep breath, I now felt I had a better understanding of my situation. I could handle the cops by continuing my charade. The same with Woods, in theory, but either way things were escalating, and he was a slippery little fucker I hadn't been able to locate yet.

Heinz had once told me the best way to win a war was by picking the battles you knew you could win. Sorting out Travis was the obvious choice, and I knew exactly how to test my theory about his involvement in making my life a misery. I flipped to the tracker app, saw his last destination had been Nora's house, and got back on my bike. When I arrived at my mother-in-law's I knocked on the door until Diane opened up, her expression turning from surprise to worry when she saw my thunderous face.

"Lucas? What's the matter? What's happened?"

"Is Travis here?"

"He went out about an hour ago."

"Are you sure?"

"Uh, well, I fell asleep, but—"

"I'm going to check with Nora."

"It's almost ten. She's exhausted."

"I'll be quick." I pushed past her and headed for the hallway, darted up the stairs two at a time with Diane somewhere behind, saying she was certain Travis wasn't at the house and could I please leave Nora be, she'd had a sedative and was sleeping.

I didn't listen. Walked into the bedroom hoping to find Travis with his mother, but as per usual, he wasn't here. Nora lay in bed asleep, as Diane had said. She seemed worse than ever. Sunken features, raspy breath, and the way her bony arms were stretched out by her sides, they could've been a pair of matchsticks. It reminded me of my father when I'd snuck to the nursing home a few months after he'd had the stroke. Back then I'd wondered how he was still alive, how his heart kept beating when everything else seemed so utterly, irreversibly broken.

"Nora." I put a hand on her shoulder, shook her lightly and whispered, "Nora, wake up. Do you know where Travis went?"

"What in God's name do you think you're doing?" Diane snapped, charging up to the bed and trying to pull me away. "She's sick. She needs to rest."

I opened and closed my mouth a few times, trying to think of an excuse, a better reason for my intrusion. Acting fast, I slumped into a chair. "I'm sorry. I can't reach him and I'm worried. His relapse is bad and I promised Nora I'd look after him. I'm terrified—"

"Terrified, huh? Who was the woman who came to your place this evening?" When she saw my startled expression, she continued, "Karina saw her. She'd only just got home and did a double take because she thought it was Michelle."

"Uhm…"

"Who was she?"

"It was a mix-up."

"Mm-hmm," Diane muttered, one eyebrow raised.

"I need to go, I'm not thinking straight," I said, truthfully. "My brain's fried. When Travis comes back, please let me know he's here and that he's safe."

"Sure."

I didn't believe her. And that meant I'd have to go searching for him myself.

35

Before I got back on the bike I checked the app, saw Travis had reappeared at a bar downtown, and chances were he'd be there for another little while. I patched myself into his phone but couldn't make out any distinct conversations. Now I knew where he was I regrouped, decided it made the most sense to deal with him later, wait until he was properly wasted. While he was out drinking, my priority was to go home and search the house for bugs and hidden cameras, a task best done without Travis around.

In the short time I'd been at Nora's the skies had filled with clouds, which, as sod's law dictates, burst open before I'd made it fifty yards down the street. I swore at the raindrops smattering my helmet, cursed the ones hammering the back of my neck. The whole day was going from shit to shitstorm. Make that the entire week. Nobody, I decided as I raced down the road, jeans already half-soaked, *nobody* would get away with messing with me.

I got home faster than I should have given the weather conditions and the speed limits, and parked the Triumph in the garage, but when I tried to put the key in the lock, it wouldn't fit. At first, I thought it was because my hands were shaking so badly, both from the cold and my temper, but my brow creased further when I still couldn't make the damn thing work. I turned the key the other way around, put my intense struggle with the most basic of tasks down to my scrambled mind. Still didn't work. Letting out a string of expletives which would've made Bobby spontaneously combust, I stomped out of the garage and straight to the front door.

The key didn't fit there, either.

"You've got to be kidding me," I yelled, tilting my face to the skies.

"Lucas?"

I spun around. Karina stood a few yards away, clutching an oversize paisley umbrella in one hand, her bright pink wellies splashed with rain.

"What are you doing here?" I snapped.

She recoiled a little, eyes widening. "I heard the bike. I thought I'd check on you. Diane called. She said you seemed upset, and—"

"I *am* bloody upset. I can't get in my house."

"How did you lock yourself out?"

I gave her a sarcastic look and held up my keys. "The lock isn't working."

"What? That's strange. Let me try."

"I'm not an imbecile. I can handle it."

"I thought—"

"So you keep saying. Stop thinking and leave." I turned my back, fiddled with the lock and the door handle again, cursing some more as I failed to get inside. My *friendly neighbor* mask slipped farther and farther down my face, twisting itself around my neck, pushing against my windpipe, threatening to strangle me.

"Well, good night then," she said tightly, before scuttling off.

I didn't bother acknowledging her departure. Once she'd gone, I tried both locks again three times before going around the back of the house, hoping either Travis or I had left a window or the patio doors unlocked, but everything was shut tight.

If I wanted to get into my house quickly, I had two options: shatter a window or call a locksmith. I didn't have time to deal with the former, so I pulled out my phone, ran a search and called the first company that came up.

"The tech will be there in about twenty minutes," the dispatcher informed me.

Too much time to get more riled up. "Tell them there's a bonus if they get here faster," I said, and hung up without waiting for a reply.

I looked over at Karina's place. A little earlier, Diane had mentioned Karina seeing Josephine at my house. She'd come over when Bobby and Mel were here as well. I hadn't realized she was such a nosy neighbor, but perhaps she could be useful. I strode to her front door, forcing all my anger down deep, and deeper still, as I reminded myself to stay calm.

"Oh, hi," Karina said when she saw me. "Did you manage to get in?"

I tried not to shiver as the warmth of her home breezed past me, the rich scent of cooked chocolate and spices making my stomach rumble. It had been hours since my last meal. "No, I called a locksmith."

As she nodded, I studied her face to see if she had something to do with what was happening to me. I almost laughed. Karina wore her heart on her proverbial sleeve, and more than once Diane had joked about how her wife was incapable of lying. "I never ask Karina if my butt looks big anymore," she'd said. "Her expression will tell me everything I don't want to know." Karina had argued she couldn't help it, she'd been brought up not to tell lies.

Sure enough, she tilted her head to one side, her face in a sympathetic expression. Perhaps she thought I was losing my mind. Maybe she was right.

"I'm sorry about earlier," I said, my voice smooth as I added an embarrassed grimace to make my hollow offering seem solid. "The way I spoke to you was out of order. I apologize, Karina, really."

"It's fine, honestly. You're under a lot of stress."

"Yeah…uh, listen… I know you saw a blonde woman stop by the house earlier." I let out a small cough. "What a mix-up that was. Anyway, did you see anyone else?"

"With her? No."

"What about before she arrived? Was someone else around?"

"Not that I remember. I'd only just got back, anyway."

"You sure? A courier, or a utility van? Anything?"

"Positive. Why?"

I opened my mouth but closed it again when I heard a car crawl past and pull into my driveway. "Must be the locksmith. I'd better go."

"Oh, great, that was fast. Good luck," she said, already closing the door.

I jogged back to my house, waving at the technician as he got out of his vehicle and grabbed a tool bag.

"Thanks for coming so quickly," I said.

His face lit up. "They told me you were in a hurry. I'm Rory. Locked yourself out?"

"Something like that."

"Well, let's take a peek." Rory rearranged his green ball cap and pulled the collar of his rain jacket up to his neck. "Before I do anything, I need to verify you live here."

"Course I do."

"Company rules," he said, holding up his hands. "There'll be a whole lot of trouble if I break you into somebody else's home, you know what I'm sayin'? Got your driver's license and another document? I need two."

"Fine, fine." I fished my license from my wallet and went to grab the registration papers from the car, thrusting them so close to Rory's face, he took a step back. "It's me. This is my address. See? Can we get started now, please?"

He gave me a curt smile, which I loosely translated into *wanker*. "Yes, thank you, Mr. Forester. I'll get to work. I'll be as quick as I can." Walking to the front door he said, "Have you had the locks changed recently?"

"No."

"Only, it wouldn't be the first time a client had a new lock installed but forgot to swap out their keys. It happens—"

"Let me guess, all the time? No, I didn't."

"Okey-dokey, then." He knelt and removed some tools and a flashlight from his bag, examined the lock and let out a loud whistle. "I see what the problem is. Silicone."

"Excuse me?"

"Silicone, it's for—"

"I know what it is."

"Well, your lock's stuffed with it."

"Are you kidding me?"

"Nope. Seen it many times. Been doing this for years, family business. Worked with my dad since eighth grade. He started the company way back in—"

"You're sure it's silicone?"

276

"Yup. Let me see if I can clear it out so I don't have to change the lock."

"Actually, I'd prefer that."

"For me to change it? Might not need to."

"I said change it, please."

Rory looked up. "Okay, got it. You getting married anytime soon?"

"What? No. Why?"

"This guy I know, his friends did this to his locks as a joke while he and his wife were honeymooning. Jamaica, I think it was. Maybe Aruba. Somewhere hot. Man, I wish I could go there." He sighed. "Anyway, they weren't impressed when they came back to that mess."

"I can imagine."

"It's generally teenagers who do this. People don't realize in some cases you need a brand-new lock because…"

I tuned his incessant chatter out and when he took a breath, made my excuses and got into my car to wait. As soon as the front door was fixed, I showed him the lock in the garage and left him to it.

Once I found myself back inside the house, I called out to Roger, registering for the first time since I'd got home that he hadn't scrabbled and barked at the door as soon as he'd heard me arrive. He was probably asleep, had to be starving and busting for a pee, and yet, once I'd made it six feet down the hallway there was still no sign of him.

"Roger?" I called out. "Where are you, boy?"

I froze midstep. Something was wrong, and the overwhelming sensation someone had been inside my house again wrapped itself around my lungs. I glanced at the alarm keypad by the door, but it wasn't armed. I'd been in such a hurry to get to the bus station I now realized I hadn't changed the code. But I'd set it before leaving, hadn't I? I was almost certain I had, and when I'd searched for Travis's location on the tracking app earlier, I'd noticed he hadn't returned, so he hadn't disarmed it, not unless he'd switched off his phone again but there was no way he'd have beaten me here.

I stood still, listening. Could somebody else be in the house?

As quietly as I could, I opened the hall closet and grabbed an umbrella. Not the best of weapons but it was all I could find. I flicked the hall light on and stopped moving, but all I heard was the sound of my own breathing.

Moving slowly down the hallway, I made sure the powder room was empty. Everything appeared as it had before I'd left. I continued, silently putting one foot in front of the other, sneaking through my own house as if I were the intruder. Reaching the stairs and creeping up them, I checked the bedrooms and bathrooms, but they were all empty. Back on the main floor, I peered into the mudroom, family room, and the den before moving to the living room, dining area and, finally, making my way into the kitchen. Nothing had been displaced. Nobody jumped out from behind the curtains, the pantry or from under a table.

I was alone, no noise except for Rory whistling "Let it Go" on the other side of the door leading to the garage. I was about to call out to Roger again, wondering how he'd slipped past me, when my eyes landed on the knife block sitting on the counter, specifically on the empty space where the largest butcher's knife was supposed to be. My gaze went to the floor. A puddle of red. A ruby trail. Smears across the pristine white tiles.

Something had been dragged from the kitchen to the patio doors.

Not some *thing*.

Roger.

36

"Roger," I yelled, lunging for the patio doors, and yanking them open, bellowing as loud as I could. *"Roger!"*

Stepping farther onto the terrace, I tripped the motion sensors, the lights illuminating the garden and the trees backing onto the ravine beyond in an instant. I called my dog's name, frantically searching the ground for more of his blood. Spotting another smear and a few large drops leading into the grass, I let out a roar.

Anger churned as I followed the trail to the garden shed on the right side. Getting closer, I saw a mass of something on the ground. Dark red and glistening. Not big enough to be Roger, but plenty to know he was hurt.

I took another step, saw the pile was made up of internal organs and intestines. The rancid smell made my stomach lurch as I took in the fly-covered flesh, and the missing butcher's knife discarded by its side. As I reached for the shed's door handle, my stomach lurched again. There was no way Roger could've survived such a vicious attack, and I braced myself for what I was about to find.

I pushed the door open, and fumbled for the light switch, saw Roger on a mat in the corner next to a bucket and the hedge trimmer. Falling to my knees, I clutched at his fur. When he jumped, I did too, watching in shock and disbelief as he leaped up, stretched, and let out a bark before yawning and wagging his tail. He wasn't hurt. There wasn't a single trace of blood on or anywhere near him. Not a drop.

I pulled him to me before sitting back on my heels, weaving my torso left and right as I ran my fingers over his body, making sure he hadn't been harmed. There were no cuts, scrapes or injuries of any kind. What the hell had happened? And where the hell had the pile of innards come from?

I didn't have time to contemplate the last question because when Roger moved out of the way, I looked down and my breath caught.

It was another goddamn orange envelope.

Fingers trembling, I snatched it up and tore it open, reminding myself to breathe as I slowly removed the single sheet of paper inside.

Another photograph of Michelle, one I remembered from my Instagram search. She'd turned to the camera for this shot, her face beaming, teeth white and perfect, lips slightly parted. I flipped it over, read the words: *I KNOW WHAT YOU DID.*

White fury filled every fiber of my being as I scrunched up the envelope and picture, crushing them tight. My mind whirled, throat running dry as the entire shed began to spin, making me feel as if I were about to pass out or throw up.

When I was calm enough to hold a thirty-second conversation, I took Roger back to the house where Rory was finishing up with the other lock. I paid the bill and gave him a huge tip as fast as I could to get rid of him, all the while wondering if I'd find my credit card had mysteriously been blocked, but the payment went through.

Once Rory had gone, I locked the front door and headed for the kitchen where I cleaned the butcher's knife and scrubbed the floor. Next, I went to the bathroom. After I'd searched it thoroughly for hidden cameras and bugs, I put down the toilet lid and took a seat. Tried to unscramble my brain. I needed to *think*.

I may have forgotten to set the alarm earlier, but whoever had swiped my stuff from the bus station locker would've had to have followed me despite my precautions and seen where I'd hidden the key. Following me wasn't impossible although I'd been careful, but I ran through everything again, and a third time, checking my logic, came to one undeniable conclusion. For them to have found the locker key so easily, a hidden camera had to have been planted in the kitchen or my living room.

From all my research, I knew spy gear came in different shapes and sizes, which made things tricky for me because I didn't want to alert whoever was watching they'd been found out. As much as I felt the urge to examine my surroundings, check if there was anything new or out of place, remove every single wall socket, switch plate, smoke detector or ceiling light, there was no way I could do it without being obvious.

Taking a few gulps of air to steady my pulse, I walked back to the kitchen where I filled a glass with water and discreetly scanned the cupboards and open shelving, where I found nothing. I sank down at the kitchen table. The angle from the living room bookcase offered the perfect vantage point for anyone who wanted to see what was going on here, at least in the open plan area of the main floor. It offered an unobstructed view of the kitchen, living room, even part of the hallway, and if the camera was streaming sound, it was quite possible they could hear me leaving the house.

I tried to picture what else was on the shelves aside from books. A set of cast iron elephants, which Nora had given Michelle, a ship in a bottle she'd made with Gideon. Another sentimental object was an old stuffed toy, a mouse in blue shorts she'd had as a kid, about ten inches tall. The digital photo frame, a gift Michelle had given me, preloaded with photos of us, our entire three-and-a-half-year relationship displayed on an incessant loop. I'd switched it off when she'd disappeared, told Travis the memories were too painful.

Any of those objects were an ideal spot to hide a camera. The ones I'd seen online were no bigger than my fingertip. I wanted to walk over and prove my theory right, but I couldn't, not yet. Whoever was watching me still needed to think they had the upper hand. And I knew exactly how to get Travis out of the way while I went after them.

Things were about to get ugly.

FRIDAY

37

It was a little after midnight, and although I'd spent the last few weeks sleeping only a few hours each night, I was now fully alert. Awake, running on adrenaline, and fucking *pissed*.

I'd gone through all the Wi-Fi security settings of the house a little earlier, checked for any newly connected devices I hadn't authorized. There weren't any, and any hidden camera in my house was no doubt running off one of the neighbors' networks. Karina and Diane's settings were tight—I'd helped hook up a new router—but the family's on the other side were lax. They had a Wi-Fi booster, so their network was well within range, and I could've streamed every single Hollywood blockbuster since *Jaws* without them noticing. But I couldn't go over there and demand to comb through their setup, nor was I technically good enough to hack their password, and on the one hand it didn't really matter. Even if I'd discreetly located the camera, I'd have left it on to keep up the charade of not knowing I was being watched, never mind how much I hated the feeling.

After a covert and careful examination, I'd established with a good level of certainty my en suite bathroom wasn't bugged. I couldn't be sure of any of the other rooms, though, and to be safe, I now stood on the main bedroom's balcony, which overlooked the back garden, huddled against the wall and trying to avoid the incessant, frigid rain. A few swipes on my cell and I'd logged into the tracking app to find Travis. His last known location was the same bar he'd been at earlier, but that had been a few hours ago. I called his cell, which went straight to voice mail, and trying to listen in didn't work. It seemed he'd switched his phone off. He wasn't making my life any easier but one of the only good things about Travis was his predictability. It made him quicker to find.

In the short time I'd been outside, the weather had gone from bad to atrocious. Raindrops moved horizontally now, belting the walls, spraying the bottom of my jeans. Trees swayed and bent, the last stubborn leaves whipping through the air, and somewhere in the distance I heard the ominous rumbling of thunder.

I went back inside and changed into a dry pair of jeans and a thicker sweater before going downstairs and updating the house alarm code. The digits I chose were a mixture of two of the street numbers I'd lived at with Dad before I was ten, something nobody would guess. This was my first barrier of defense. The next was making sure the patio doors and the one to the garage were properly locked, before double-checking all the windows. Next, I lowered the indoor electric blinds. I'd have much preferred if they'd been the old-fashioned ones on the outside, but Michelle hadn't wanted those because they got dirty. Not that either of us cleaned anything in the house but that bit hadn't factored into her equation.

As I pressed the various buttons and the blinds slid down to the windowsills, effectively shuttering me in from the outside world, for the briefest of moments I thought about packing a bag, getting Roger, and walking away. Not a chance. I wanted to know for certain who was behind all this mayhem and take them down. If I was going to run like a coward, I should've done so after the last ransom drop, somehow lifted the bag with the million bucks and disappeared. Except I'd constantly been watched, hadn't put together an effective plan for a disappearance, not to mention the cash wasn't nearly enough. No, the urge was too great, the primal need to find out who was pulling my strings…and taking great delight in using them to strangle them with.

Taking the bike in my search for Travis wasn't an option, not only because of the weather, but also because I wanted to have Roger with me. No way would I leave him at the house, not after what had happened when I'd got home. Front door locked and secured, and with Roger in the car, I drove into the night, windshield wipers going high-speed.

The closest stop was Nora's in case Travis had opted for an early night and gone there. His car was nowhere to be found, and although I supposed he may have got an Uber, I bet he was partying somewhere. Travis hadn't missed a heavy Thursday-is-the-new-Friday booze session in weeks and was definitely still out somewhere. Mind made up, I headed for the bar he'd been at last, but he wasn't there. I drove to the strip clubs, stopped at the nearest one before heading to Eden.

The place was jam-packed, a crowd I pushed my way through as I scanned the room for Travis's face. I thought I spotted him at a table with a group of guys, but when I got close enough, I saw it wasn't him. I kept moving, toured the entire place three times to make sure I hadn't missed him. I checked the bathrooms, stopped a couple of hostesses to ask if they'd seen Travis, but no one had any recollection of him being here all night. Jaw clenched I weaved my way through the hordes of patrons to the exit. Finding Travis so soon would've been too easy, and it seemed *easy* was a word I should ban from my vocabulary.

Back in my car I rechecked the tracking app, called him again, but Travis's phone was still off. Cursing loudly, I drove in the direction of Boston's Shawmut Avenue where I knew he enjoyed spending a lot of his time and most of his money.

It took me almost an hour and six different places before I finally located him. He sat alone in a booth at the back of a small bar, half slumped against the wall. His rumpled shirt had a collection of stains down the front and judging by the set of empty bottles and shot glasses in front of him, he'd been here a while.

The beer in his hand told me he wouldn't agree to going anywhere soon, and the drunker he was, the faster and more easily I'd be able to manipulate him. I hung out at the corner of the bar, observing the room. A tall guy hovered by the hallway leading to the bathrooms. Long blond hair pulled into a ponytail, designer beard. Expensive-looking jeans, crisp fitted white shirt, a leather jacket casually slung over his arm. I knew people like him, had seen them countless times when I'd worked with Bobby. There was always at least one in these places.

Sure enough, in the time I spent watching him, a few people approached and shook his hand. While the guy was slick and had clearly been dealing a while, his customers weren't all so gifted, one of them even dropping the little plastic bag on the sticky floor. Ponytail didn't seem concerned about the bartender or owner seeing what he was up to and I guessed they were taking a cut.

Now I'd identified who had what I wanted, and where he kept it, I headed to the bathroom. As I got closer to Ponytail, I pretended to trip and crashed straight into him. Within a heartbeat I'd lifted a bag and a vial from his coat pocket.

"What the hell?" he said, pushing me away. "Watch where you're going, dumbass."

I apologized and slunk off to the bathroom, where I first examined the little baggie I'd stolen. Tablets. Ecstasy, probably, which wasn't going to be much use, and I dropped them in the toilet. The vial contained something much more promising: white powder. I couldn't be sure, but judging by the amount, I'd have bet money on it being heroin or some other opioid, which Travis had admitted to using in the past. I wiped the vial down, wrapped it in tissue paper and stowed it safely in my pocket before flushing the toilet and heading to Travis's table.

I sat down, my most approachable, trustworthy, and reassuring expression sliding over my face. "Hey," I said. "How's it going?"

"Lucas." He smiled, said my name as a long, drawn-out *Loooocuuuush*. Most of the time, Travis was a friendly drunk like my dad had been, easily amused, happy to see anyone who didn't rattle his cage, including me in this instance, his anger from our last encounter all but forgotten. Bars were, after all, his happy place. "Great to see you, man," he added, his words slow and slurred. "Get you anything?"

"No, thanks, I don't—"

"Oh, come on." He waved a hand and beamed. "Imagonnagetyouadrink." As he attempted to push himself up, his elbows buckled, and he fell onto the bench, almost sliding off and disappearing underneath the table. He giggled like a kid as he clawed himself back up and tried to get to his feet again, lowering his voice to a stage whisper. "Whoops."

I reached for his shoulder and pushed him down. "I'll go. Beer?"

"Sure. And a bourbon." He tapped a drumroll on the table with his fingers and waggled his eyebrows. "A bo-bo-bo-bo-bourbon!"

I pressed through the crowd to the bartender and ordered Travis's drinks, adding a club soda for me. As I waited, I glanced over my shoulder at Travis, making sure he didn't disappear. Not only could he have a teddy-bear persona when he was drunk, but also a tendency to wander off. At one of Gideon and Nora's parties, Michelle had found him at the far end of their estate near the duck pond, pissing in the water. When she'd told me the story I'd silently wondered if she'd been tempted to push him in. I would've been.

I approached our table as Travis was fiddling with his phone, which he'd plugged into a socket on the wall to charge. It seemed he was attempting to enter his pass code. I stood still, watched his clunky fingers move slowly, deliberately across the screen. The numbers were easy to recognize, even easier to retain. Michelle's birthday.

Acting as if I hadn't seen anything, I handed Travis a pint of lager and the shot of bourbon and settled in to sip my water. The drunker Travis became, the faster he guzzled his booze, and I knew before long he'd declare it time for another round. Not happening. I needed him inebriated, not passed out, and without knowing how much he'd consumed before I'd arrived, or what else he'd taken, it was tricky to judge.

"Come on," I said, hauling Travis up when he put his second empty glass down. "I reckon we should call it a night."

He made a feeble attempt to brush me away, protesting as I

led him from the bar to my car where Roger patiently waited for my return. I practically poured Travis into the passenger seat and buckled him in like a child. By the time we got to the house he was snoring loudly, and it took a fair amount of effort to get him to walk inside.

I put on a show of helping Travis out of his jacket and shoes, talking to him gently but hoping the predominantly one-sided conversation would get picked up on the suspected hidden camera, even if we weren't onscreen. I followed him as he wandered into the living room, got there in time to see him trip on the rug by the sofa, and fall onto his knees.

"Dude," he laughed, "I'm okay, I'm okay. I'm not wasted."

"Yeah, right." I helped him up before half-coaxing, half-dragging him to the spare room where he collapsed on the bed with a loud grunt.

"Thanks, Lucas," he mumbled. "You always look out for me. Michelle does, too." His face crumpled and he covered it with his hands as he let out a sob. "I can't believe she's gone." Crying harder now he added, "She's dead. Oh, my God, my sister's dead."

"We don't know that. We have to stay strong. Wait here. I'll get you something to help dilute the alcohol."

Back in the kitchen I grabbed a tub of Gatorade from the cupboard, dumped a scoop into a glass and filled it with water. With my back turned so a hidden camera couldn't pick up on what I was doing, I retrieved the plastic vial I'd lifted from the dealer. Very carefully, I sprinkled some of the powder into the drink, making sure none of the stuff touched my skin, and went upstairs.

"Here you go, mate," I said, setting the glass on the bedside table.

Travis didn't reply. He was well out of it. I wondered if I

should try to wake him up and force him to take a sip, but decided against it, biding my time. I switched off the light, took the vial from my pocket, wiped it down again with my shirt, pressed his fingers over it, and set it next to the glass. Travis didn't move. Didn't even flinch.

And I intended to make sure he stayed that way.

38

It was well after three by the time I got to crash. The rush of adrenaline had long subsided. My limbs were heavy as logs, my eyelids prickled as if they were on fire, and despite not having had a drop of alcohol, I seemed incapable of walking in a straight line.

I had a quick shower and pulled on a pair of track pants before stumbling to bed, and although I tried my hardest to stay alert, I kept dozing off only to twitch and jerk awake a few seconds later. This was going to be one hell of a long night.

It had seemed as if I'd closed my eyes for a half minute at most when a dull thud made me jump. Brain groggy, vision blurred, I grabbed my phone, realizing it was gone five. Another moan, another thump, the sound of glass breaking—all of it coming from Travis's room. No sense pretending I hadn't heard the noise. Everyone knew what a light sleeper I was. Michelle had often joked she could snooze through an earthquake and feel well rested the next morning whereas I'd hear a fly land on the outside of the window. I'd pretended to laugh along with her, never said it was because I'd always slept with one ear open when I was a kid so I could stop Dad from choking on his own vomit.

Another noise, muffled this time. That was my cue to get up and investigate. I grabbed a shirt and pulled it on, heading into the hallway with a mix of excitement and elation. When I got to Travis's room and flicked on the light, I knew I'd struck gold. He was sprawled out on the rug, facedown, still dressed in the clothes he'd gone to bed in. His bedside lamp had shattered on the floor. The glass I'd spiked was still on the bedside table, but was now empty.

Rolling him over, I saw a trickle of blood oozing from a half-inch gash on his forehead. Must've hit the corner of the bed frame on his way down, which lent the situation even more authenticity, and I gave him an A+ for his unwitting participation.

"Travis?"

I grabbed his chin between my thumb and fingers before giving him a slap, but he didn't move. Looking around, I spotted the little plastic vial of powder I'd left next to his glass. It had fallen on the carpet, the cap open. He must've sprinkled in more. *Idiot.* I slapped him again.

"Hey. Wake up. Come on, man. Stop messing around." When he still didn't reply I grabbed his shoulders. "Travis! Wake up. Can you hear me?"

His eyes opened briefly before rolling straight into the back of his head like a pair of marbles. The guy was well and truly messed up, his breathing already shallow. I wanted him in hospital, incapacitated, out of the way, but I didn't want him dead. Not quite yet, not when it meant his money would go to Nora and she might donate his inheritance to charity.

"Travis. *Travis.* Did you take something? Shit. *Shit.*"

I ran to my bedroom, grabbed my phone, and dialed 911, explaining the situation as I continued trying to wake Travis up. The dispatcher told me the ambulance would be there in a few minutes. "I'm not sure he'll make it," I urged, and I meant it. "He's in a really bad way. Can you hurry? Please?"

I figured maybe I *had* gone a little heavy on the drugs. I filled his glass with water from the bathroom tap and held it to his lips, but he was too far gone to take even a sip. I stayed with him, monitoring his pulse, trying to wake him up. Doing all the things an innocent good Samaritan without any ulterior motives would do. When I heard the sirens in the distance, I ran downstairs to the front door, shouting at the paramedics to hurry and they bustled in, equipment in hand, high-visibility jackets slick with rain.

"I'm Ulla," the woman said. "This is Bolin. What's your name?"

"Lucas." I gulped in air as I layered on the fake panic.

"It's okay, Lucas," Bolin said. "Keep calm. Tell us what happened."

"My brother-in-law Travis. He collapsed. He's upstairs. Please, hurry."

We thundered up the stairs, and as soon as we arrived in the bedroom, they got to work with speed and efficiency. "Travis, can you hear me?" Ulla said as she checked to see if he was breathing. "No respirations," she said to Bolin. She placed the tips of two fingers on his neck to check for a pulse, and I wondered if it was too late.

Meanwhile, Bolin pulled out one of those bag and mask combos I'd seen in the medical dramas I detested but sat through for Michelle's benefit as Ulla lifted Travis's shirt, placing the leads of a cardiac monitor to his chest. Bolin attached a small oxygen cylinder to a tube he connected to the resuscitator bag and handed it to Ulla before looking up at me.

"Tell me what happened," he said, and after I'd explained how I heard Travis fall and found him on the floor, he continued to pepper me with questions. He wanted to know Travis's medical history, allergies, medications. Whether he was a diabetic, had any known health problems.

"He's allergic to bees, I think," I said, remembering Michelle had mentioned he'd been stung once and had looked like a blowfish. "I don't know about meds, but..."

I watched as Ulla placed the mask over Travis's mouth and nose, slowly squeezing the bag. Was any oxygen moving into his lungs? If he didn't die, would he have brain damage? I imagined Travis confined to a wheelchair the way my father was, and something small inside me shifted, a sense of disquiet I tried to ignore but couldn't brush aside. Dad had ended up that way because of what Bobby had done to him, and he'd been twice Travis's age. It wasn't a life I'd ever wish on anyone, including Travis. Incapacitated now so I could test my theory about him messing with me, and put a stop to it, yes. Dead at some point for my financial benefit, definitely. But not trapped inside his body like my dad.

"Lucas?" Bolin called out, snapping my attention back to him. "You mentioned Travis has used drugs before?"

"Uh, yeah..."

"Pupils are pinpoint and nonreactive," Ulla said, pulling out another device I'd seen the nurses use at Dad's care home. She held it to Travis's finger and within a few seconds added, "Blood sugar's within normal range."

"*Lucas.*" Bolin's voice was sharper now. "What drugs has Travis taken in the past?"

I rubbed my forehead. "What *hasn't* he taken. Weed, coke,

ecstasy, harder stuff. He's been drinking a lot. Anything he can get his hands on, basically. He's been in rehab a bunch of times. It's been a lot worse lately."

"Were you with him tonight?"

"I didn't see him take anything, if that's what you're asking."

Ulla gently said, "Tell us what you know so we can help him."

"I told you, I found him at a bar and drove him home. He was really drunk, probably high. I heard him fall, saw him on the floor and called 911. I don't know what he took."

"Ulla," Bolin said to his colleague, who was still mechanically ventilating Travis with the bag. He gestured at the little plastic vial on the floor and they exchanged glances, eyebrows raised. "Narcan," he said, turning to his kit and removing what appeared to be a nasal spray. He placed it inside Travis's nostril and squeezed.

"What's that?" I said. "What are you giving him?"

"It's naloxone," Ulla said. "For suspected opioid overdose cases."

"*Opioids?*" God, I was good at this. "What the hell do you think he took?"

"Judging by the little plastic vial over there, I'd say fentanyl or something like it," Bolin said. "We can't be certain, but if it is, the naloxone will help him."

"Will he be okay? Is he going to recover?"

"We're doing everything we can," Ulla said, turning her attention back to Travis, continuing to feed air into his lungs. After another dose of Narcan she shook her head. "Still unresponsive. We need to get him to the hospital. We'll get a stretcher and—"

Voices in the downstairs hallway drowned out the rest of her sentence and I headed for the door. Karina and Diane were halfway up the stairs, both dressed in pajamas and sneakers.

"Lucas," Diane gasped. "We saw the ambulance. What happened?"

"Travis." I moved out of the way as Bolin bounded down the stairs, presumably to fetch a stretcher. "I think he overdosed."

"What?" Diane said. "What's his condition?"

"I'm not sure. He wasn't breathing and they're ventilating him. Gave him something—" I pointed to my nostrils "—up his nose."

"Narcan."

Karina looked at Diane. "I thought he was spending the night at Nora's."

"He was supposed to go back there," Diane said, "but you know Travis."

"Weren't you on night shift?" I said to her.

"I was. I just got back."

"But—"

"Never mind that," Karina said, turning to me. "Were you with Travis? Did you see him take anything?"

"For God's sake," I said and raised my voice because she was seriously starting to piss me off. "No, of course I didn't. Why does everyone keep asking—"

"Then how do you know he overdosed?"

"I don't for sure. Jesus, Karina, I told you he wasn't breathing. He was wasted when I brought him home. God knows what he took. The paramedics found a vial next to his bed." I indicated to Bolin as he moved past us. "They think it's fentanyl or something."

"What? Oh, man," Diane muttered. "This isn't good."

"No, it isn't." I dropped my shoulders, hung my head. "I told you earlier I was worried he'd end up doing something stupid. And I was supposed to take care of him. How could I let this happen on my watch? How will Nora cope if he—"

"It'll be okay," Diane said. "Trust me, they'll do everything they can to help him."

"That's what they said, but what if…" I ran my hands over my face. "What if he dies?"

While neither of them answered, their expressions said everything their mouths didn't. They would hold me responsible. I shifted from one foot to the other as we waited in collective silence until Ulla and Bolin brought Travis downstairs. The color had drained from his skin, reminding me of how bad Nora looked when I'd seen her last night. It was hard to imagine how he'd survive being carried over the threshold.

"Where are you taking him?" I asked Ulla.

"BMC."

Diane looked at me. "That's Boston—"

"Medical Center," I said. "I know."

"We'll all go," Karina said.

"No, I don't want to trouble you. I'll keep you two up-to-date and—"

"Don't be crazy," Diane said. "We'll run home and get dressed. It'll only take—"

"I'm going right now," I said thinking if by some miracle Travis woke up anytime soon, I wanted to be there, explain how he must've brought the drugs home and put them in his drink in case he remembered otherwise. "I'll call Nora."

Diane put a hand on my shoulder and squeezed. "Why don't we wait until we know what's going on? We shouldn't put her through anything more than absolutely necessary."

"You're right," I said. "I'll wait."

Once they'd all left, I ran upstairs to change, grabbed my wallet and keys, set the house alarm and charged outside, but not before I'd shoved a chair under the handle of the garage door in case Woods or whoever the hell tried to get in again that way.

I drummed my fingers on the steering wheel as I drove to the hospital, hoping the smaller oddities that kept happening would stop, seeing as Travis was indisposed. Woods had to be my focus now, and I tried to rationalize who else may have hidden a camera in the living room, and I kept going back and forth between him and the cops until another theory emerged.

For all I knew, a device had been there for ages, and my wife had installed it for some reason that escaped me. I'd never given her any cause to doubt me. From the start, I'd made sure our relationship was close to perfect. She needed independence, I backed off. She wanted affection, I gave her plenty. I'd carefully played this role, made sure our marriage was *close* to perfect because everyone knows the saying about things being too good to be true. I'd kept them real, ensuring when Michelle got together with her friends, she had a few things to gripe about. Leaving socks next to the dirty laundry basket was a classic, and harmless if I didn't do it all the time, so was *forgetting* to empty the mailbox when I drove in, buying the wrong toothpaste when I got the shopping. Banal things, which, when she expressed her frustration, her girlfriends would laugh at and say if those were her only complaints, she should take a seat.

Hell, perhaps my wife had installed a camera to keep an eye on the cleaning staff, or possibly even Travis, but why wouldn't she have mentioned it to me? It seemed unlikely, and I had no way of knowing for sure if there really was one or how long it had been sitting there and there was still the unanswered question of who had plundered my bus station locker, and how.

I wracked my brain, retracing my actions and movements in my home over the past four weeks since the abduction. I'd been careful outside the house, and with Travis around I was confident I'd kept up my act on the inside. I admired method actors. Daniel Day-Lewis, Christian Bale, and Reese Wither-spoon were all fine examples. Like them, I was a big believer in staying in character for as long as possible, preferably at all times. As far as I was concerned, it was the only way to get the job done properly, and never slip up, which meant if someone had watched me at home to see if I had anything to do with my wife's disappearance, they'd been fumbling in the dark.

I frowned. What about those partial pictures of Michelle? I'd burned them both in the sink. Would a camera have captured what they were? Did it matter? Uncertainty gnawed at my bones.

As I sped to BMC and my hands gripped the steering wheel, I wished I could put them around the neck of whoever was fucking with me instead.

39

Ever since Dad's stroke, I hated hospitals. The smells, the sounds, the despair. All of it unsettling and a reminder my father would never live a normal life again.

When I arrived at BMC I wished I had the time to sit in the parking lot and have a smoke before entering the building but instead I hastily made my way to ER. Early Friday morning, and the place was hopping, an array of injured and sickly individuals of all shapes, sizes, ages, and backgrounds sitting in the drab, fluorescent-lit waiting area.

A guy pressed a blood-soaked dishcloth to the side of his head while the one next to him held his hand. A kid of about ten who was dressed in dinosaur pajamas, and whose entire face was a peculiar shade of green, had his head in a young woman's lap, and a bucket close to her feet. He pressed a hand over his belly, wrapped the other around the neck of a stuffed tiger. Poor sod. Seemed like he was about to throw up, and I suspected a few other people feared the same as the seats on either side of them were empty.

An elderly couple hovered at the front desk, and before I had a chance to play the white privileged prick card and demand to see someone right away, they were shuffled off and it was my turn.

"I'm Lucas Forester," I said to the man behind the desk. "I'm here for Travis Ward. He arrived by ambulance not long ago." I leaned in a little and lowered my voice. "Suspected opioid overdose. I'm really worried. I need to see him right away."

"I understand. Let me find out what the situation is." He tapped a few keys on the computer. "Travis is being attended to by our emergency physician right now and—"

"I want to see him."

"Not just yet, I'm afraid. Are you a family member?"

"Brother-in-law."

Within minutes I was whisked away to a separate room, informed I'd be provided an update on Travis's condition as soon as possible. I paced up and down, stopping only to observe two cops walk by with a woman who had her hands cuffed behind her back. When more paramedics walked past the room with an elderly woman who looked frail, helpless, and frightened, I turned away because she reminded me of Nora. Yes, I felt bad about what I'd done. Not toward Travis, but *her*. With a bit of luck, he'd have the decency to hang on until she passed first.

I needed an update, couldn't hang around any longer. I wanted to know if he'd regained consciousness and, if so, what he'd said, but before I could take a step out of the room, Diane and Karina rushed in, their faces pink, voices high-pitched and, frankly, more than a little shrill as they fussed over me.

"How's Travis?"

"What did the doctor say?"

"Did they give you a prognosis?"

"How are you doing?"

"Do you need some water?"

"Shall I get you something else?"

The verbal onslaught made me want to stick my fingers deep into my ears. "I haven't spoken to the doctor yet. They said they'd come and find me as soon as they have news, but I was just about to—"

"Leave it with me. I'll find someone who'll give us information." Diane was in full-blown nurse mode, but Karina held her back.

"We should all wait here. How many times have you said how difficult it is when the family freaks out and presses you for info you're not yet ready to share?"

Diane rolled her eyes and sank into one of the armchairs. "I hate it when you're right."

"And I love you, too," Karina said, settling down next to her.

"You stay here if you want," I said. "I'm going to find out what's happening." Without waiting for their answer, I was in the hallway. Three minutes later I found myself back in the family room. A nurse had at first kindly and then very directly told me I had to wait. No, there wasn't an update. Yes, Travis was still unconscious, which was the only reason why I did as I was told.

I needed to distract myself, wanted to flick through the copy of *Car and Driver* sitting on the corner table but it wouldn't have fit with my stricken look so I resumed pacing the room instead. We barely spoke for the next little while, all of us apparently lost in our thoughts about Travis's condition. A thousand bucks said mine were a whole lot more sinister than theirs.

Almost a full hour ticked by until a doctor arrived. He was

a few years older than me, half a head taller, slim and broad-shouldered, big brown eyes adorned with thick lashes my wife would've killed for. Judging by the shadows beneath them, his shift had started a long time ago.

"I'm Dr. Mendoza," he said, and as I shook his hand, I noticed a tattoo on his wrist, an ECG line with a heart and the words *buena salud* underneath. "You're Mr. Ward's family?"

"Yes, I'm Lucas, his brother-in-law."

"Good to meet you," Dr. Mendoza said, a flash of something crossing his face, and I wondered if he recognized me from the news when I'd been pleading for Michelle's safe return. If he had, he didn't mention it. Probably never had time to watch TV, anyway.

I made some more quick introductions, finished with, "How's Travis?"

Dr. Mendoza interlaced his fingers, rested his hands against his stomach. "I believe the paramedics informed you they suspected an opioid overdose, more specifically fentanyl?"

"Yes," I said. "They gave him some stuff to wake him up."

"Narcan," he said, which I remembered perfectly well, but stress—real stress—could make you forget details. "Depending on the amount of drugs in an individual's system, Narcan can be extremely effective."

"But not for Travis?" Karina said.

"Unfortunately, not in Travis's case, no," Dr. Mendoza said. "He wasn't breathing on his own when he came in. We put a tube down his throat and—"

"You intubated him? He's on a ventilator?" Diane gasped. When she saw the look of surprise on his face, she added, "Occupational hazard. Twenty years in hospice. What about tests? You've ordered a full tox panel?"

"Yes, and a chest X-ray and CAT scan," he said calmly before turning to me. "The chest X-ray was to make sure the tube is in the right place, and the CAT scan will allow us to check for damage to his brain such as a—"

"Stroke," I said. "I'm familiar."

"That's correct, and a tox panel is a whole battery of blood tests. We're doing a urine test, too. Basically, we want to determine what drugs are in his system, and how much alcohol he consumed. I understand he was drinking?"

"Heavily," I answered.

"And did you see what drugs he took?"

"No. When do you think he'll wake up?"

"I'm afraid we're not ready to make that call yet, Lucas," Dr. Mendoza said.

I decided I liked him. He was direct but not cold or cocky as the doctors in England had been when Dad had his stroke, and especially after they'd found out he was an alcoholic. Seemed to me those guys didn't believe my father was particularly worth the effort. Mendoza was different, didn't appear to judge Travis's lifestyle choices in the least.

"But…he's going to wake up, right?" I said.

"That's going to take some time to determine," Dr. Mendoza answered, and Karina grabbed Diane's hand. "My biggest worry is his brain having been starved of oxygen, but we're not sure how long for, or how much damage might have been done. We'll have a clearer picture over the next few days."

"Days?" I said, and when Dr. Mendoza gave me a nod I added, "Basically, it's a waiting game?" This was excellent, better than I'd imagined. If the Narcan had worked, Travis might have walked out of here tonight and potentially tried to mess with me again. Now he'd be where I could keep an eye on him.

"We'll move him to the intensive care unit as soon as possible," Dr. Mendoza said. "You'll get word when it happens. I'll be back as quickly as I can."

More waiting and pacing followed. More hanging around the family room, more pretending to be worried about Travis for innocent reasons. I ducked out for a while to use the bathroom, went to grab coffees for the three of us for something to do. When we finally saw Travis, I had to admit I felt sorry for him. His face was puffy, and the tube disappearing into his mouth made me want to claw at my own. A multitude of machines were positioned around him, beeping and hissing. Was this going to be where it all ended? It was a path he'd chosen, one he'd been off and on for a while now. I'd given him a little push, but by adding more fentanyl himself, he'd taken a huge flying leap.

A couple of hours passed, and my frustration levels increased. I didn't want to hang around here all day. I needed to make use of the time I had alone in the house and work out how I'd get to Woods. Then again I didn't want to leave Travis here alone in case he woke up and said something while I was out of earshot.

I had a brain wave and got up. After glancing over my shoulder I searched through his things for his phone because if I could stash it somewhere close to him, I could use the tracking app to turn it on and listen to every conversation going on around him. Within seconds it became clear his device wasn't here, it had to be back at the house, and that meant I needed to go there as quickly as possible, find it and return. I walked softly toward the door, but as it opened it let out a loud creak and Karina jumped.

"Are you leaving?" she said, rubbing her eyes as Diane yawned and stretched.

"I feel useless. I'm going home to get a few things for him. You sleep. I won't be long."

Diane nodded. "Shouldn't we tell Nora what's going on?"

"Yes." I wasn't looking forward to making the call but given the fact I was the one who'd helped put Travis in a coma, there was some sense of duty. "I'll do it on my way home."

"Or we can go see her now," Diane said. "This kind of message is best delivered in person, and then we can all come back and stay with Travis."

Duty, schmuty. "Thank you," I said. "You're being so thoughtful."

We walked to the parking garage together before going our separate ways. I expedited the overdue payment for Dad's care, then made a quick call to make sure he'd settled into his new place. Once I had all the reassurance I needed I let myself breathe for a moment before my mood darkened again.

The rain still hadn't let up. It now fell in a steady stream from the gray skies, the wind whistling through the trees, playing an eerie, ominous tune. If I hadn't known any better, I'd have thought Death stood on the front step, was reaching out a bony knuckle, ready to rap on my door. I shuddered. Thank fuck it would be Travis's and Nora's instead.

40

When I got home and parked the car in my driveway, the lack of sleep made me half walk, half stumble to the front door. Now I'd reset the code, and although I knew my house should be safe, I still had some trepidation simply by being here, but when I set foot on the front step and Roger let out a loud bark, my shoulders dropped.

I unlocked the door and stepped inside, switched off the alarm and listened. Going from hunter to potential prey was excruciating. This wasn't supposed to happen. It had been so simple, so clean. Find a killer-for-hire. Get rid of Michelle. Have her declared dead. Cash the check. Live wealthily ever after. That had been my plan, not this monstrosity of a gong show.

Roger followed me as I walked farther down the hallway, and I glanced at the door leading to the garage. Although the chair I'd shoved under the handle sat untouched, I did a quick sweep of the main and upstairs level as discreetly as possible before heading to the basement. Nothing seemed out of place anywhere. Good.

Back upstairs, Roger let out a bark and wagged his tail. "Not now, pal," I said. "No time for a walk." I pressed the button for the automatic blinds and opened the patio doors as soon as there was enough room to let him out. Next, I quickly grabbed his bowls and filled them with fresh water and food. I was about to set them on the floor and call him back inside, but when I turned and caught sight of the window, the containers dropped from my hands.

While I'd been gone, the entire back window had been plastered with black-and-white pictures. Dozens and dozens of photocopies stuck to the glass, a chorus of letter-size pages fluttering in the wind.

I stepped closer, my heart thumping.

MURDERER

The word was scrawled across every single one of the pages in big red letters. *MURDERER MURDERER MURDERER MURDERER MURDERER MURDERER MURDERER MURDERER MURDERER MURDERER MURDERER MURDERER MURDERER MURDERER MURDERER MURDERER MURDERER MURDERER*

The picture was of a man dressed in white coveralls, kneeling on the ground, a black backpack by his side. All of it more than a little blurry, but I knew who it was. *Me.* In the woods. With Michelle's body.

"Mother*fucker*," I whispered through clenched teeth, saying the word over and over, louder, and louder, until I thought the force of my voice, and the intensity in my body might shatter the windows.

Someone *had* been in the forest that night. The noises I'd heard hadn't only been animals. Somebody had watched me, followed me, taken pictures of me. Somebody *knew*.

Woods.

He was the only one who'd known that exact location. He'd led me into a trap. Must have suspected if he pushed enough of my buttons, at some point I'd go verify my wife was dead, especially after he'd sent the partial photos with the cryptic messages on the back. The guy was smart, had to have all kinds of surveillance gear. All the precautions I'd taken when I'd gone to the conservation area had been pointless. He must have set up motion sensor cameras in the forest, it was why he hadn't needed to follow me there. All he'd had to do was wait until I showed up.

As for the dress he'd draped over the sofa, either it was a lucky guess or he'd questioned Michelle before he'd killed her, got all kinds of details from her in exchange for the promise he'd let her live, things he put to great use to destabilize me because that had been his plan all along.

It would've been so easy for him to copy her set of keys so he could get access to the house before returning them to her bag and dumping it in her grave. He'd set up a nanny cam in the living room, watched me, goaded me, messed with my brain, and manipulated me into doing exactly what he wanted. Showed him I was guilty.

I made my mind retrace every step I'd taken the night I'd dug up my wife in the forest, walked myself through everything I'd done in minute detail. Before, during, and after my expedition, I'd implemented all the precautions I could think of to leave no trace. I'd worn different shoes, put on coveralls, gloves, and a mask. I'd got rid of those and thrown the GPS navigator in the river, donated the boots. The only possible evidence was the tread on the tires of my Triumph, but it wouldn't be enough to charge me, let alone have me convicted.

I peered more closely at the pictures sprawled across my

living room windows. They were blurry, and because of the distance and angle, you couldn't make out the face well enough to be sure it was mine. *I* knew. *Woods* knew. Nobody else would if he sent them these, but we both also knew it wasn't a gamble I'd be willing to take.

My rage searched for an outlet and I wanted to punch something, but remembered the potential camera, the fact I was probably being observed, studied like a caged animal at the zoo. Woods was expecting a knee-jerk reaction, and I couldn't show him another.

Hurrying outside, I ripped the pictures down, my blood pressure rising with each one I removed. After bundling them into a giant ball, I stuffed the wad of paper in the covered firepit, retrieved a lighter from the kitchen and burned the lot. Watching the images blacken and curl wasn't nearly enough to calm me, the thoughts of what I'd do to Woods when I found him, how much pleasure I'd take in inflicting maximum damage, sent waves of anticipation through me.

A bazillion thoughts raced through my mind as I calculated each angle of the situation, analyzing, rationalizing while I detached myself emotionally, forcing myself to look at everything from the outside in so I could remain objective.

In drawing me to the forest, Woods had flushed me out. By now he had to be a thousand percent certain I'd hired him, but he hadn't made direct contact yet. Almost a week had passed since the first partial picture of Michelle had arrived, and I had no doubt he'd try to extort me soon enough and demand a significant chunk of cash. He was probably waiting for Nora to die. Everything else was his way of letting me know he was coming for me.

I didn't believe he'd try to frame me for Michelle's murder yet, that wasn't his approach. Money was his top priority, and now he'd made it crystal clear he knew what I'd done, he'd crawl out of the darkness at any moment, and make his demands. He had me by the balls and was squeezing them tighter and tighter, sending me pictures and breaking into my house to make me lose focus and slip up. It had worked.

Whatever amount he demanded, I'd have to agree to pay, lull him into a false sense of security. Somehow, I'd have to find out who he was. Take a knife and bury it deep inside his chest. I pictured shoving him to the ground, the cool steel piercing his skin. He'd picked the wrong guy to fight with. He thought I was just a suburban idiot who wanted his wife gone, a pathetic husband with no criminal background, knowledge, or expertise. Wrong, dead wrong.

Once again, my blood felt as if it were burning me from the inside out, the anger building. I had to calm down, maintain a level head until I could fix this. I was about to head back inside when Roger trotted over with a mud-covered ball in his mouth and dropped it at my feet.

Aware I might still be on camera, I bent over to retrieve the toy. As I straightened up, I glanced through the window and into the living room. From my vantage point I could see a little way underneath the sofa, and there, next to the back leg, was Travis's phone, the one thing I'd come home for and had since forgotten, but which I still needed to plant at the hospital.

Back inside I cleaned up the mess from Roger's bowls, and grabbed Travis's phone, thinking I'd flick through it to see if there was any evidence of him messing with me. My banking information saved somewhere, search history that indicated he'd been looking for ways to lock me out of my home, maybe a message from his friends telling him to use silicone. A minute later I was in the bathroom, pass code entered, scrolling through his emails, none of which were of particular interest. I flicked to WhatsApp where the conversations mainly consisted of hookups and *Duuuuuude* messages from his fair-weather mates, joking about their escapades. None of it yielded information to prove my suspicions.

Text messages were up next. More communications from a variety of friends, a few irate notes from his former bosses threatening to fire him. Breathing hard, I went through his photos, found nothing of value there, either. Not ready to give up I opened his Notes app and the third one down leapt out at me so hard, it may as well have punched me in the face. Three words.

ceremonies cleared tote.

Anyone else might have disregarded the note as pure gibberish, random words strung together, but I'd seen this type of combination before. Heart beating faster, I checked his apps, and there it was, buried in his Media folder.

what3words

Fingers trembling, I plugged in the combination, zoomed in on the map. It was a location not far from here, northeast of Chelmswood, a road out in the middle of nowhere between the I-495 and a place called Clinton.

I stared at the phone, blinking hard, once, twice, three times. I'd felt so certain two people had been fucking with me: Woods and Travis, but individually, and without the other knowing. I'd been wrong. Travis was somehow involved with Woods. They had to know each other. But how? And since when? With his inheritance and financial freedom hanging in the balance, I didn't think Travis would have needed much convincing if Woods had posed as a cop, asked him to help figure out if I was behind the hit on Michelle, told him to keep quiet. But…no, it would've been too much of a risk, he could easily have mentioned it to Anjali.

My mouth dropped open. I couldn't help it. Because if Woods hadn't approached Travis after Michelle had been taken, that meant they'd known each other from before. I shook my head, but the thought wouldn't let go. I knew Travis had hung out with plenty of shady characters in the past, and he'd spent time in juvie as well. We had no clue Nora was dying before Michelle was taken. That meant he hadn't realized he was about to inherit a large sum of money from his mother.

Had Woods contacted Travis once he'd learned Michelle was the target? Could the real reason why Travis derailed so hard when his sister disappeared be the guilt from knowing she was going to be killed, and having to go along with it because he needed the cash he could get by extorting me afterward?

The more I thought about it, the clearer the picture became. Travis couldn't have been the instigator or the architect behind everything, but he might have been a willing participant. He loved his sister, but maybe not as much as the money and financial freedom he could gain by her disappearance. After all, it was what we both wanted.

The question was, what were Woods's intentions? If I were him, and whatever the history between them, I'd have no problem killing Travis once there was no more use for him, and that meant by getting Travis to overdose, I may have done Woods a favor. He'd lost his inside man, but he didn't need him anymore. Did he?

I checked the map, read the three words again, and headed for the door.

41

I sped off into the rain on the Triumph, only half bothering to check if someone was on my tail. My phone buzzed in my jacket pocket and when I stopped, I saw a message from Karina.

Hey Lucas. We're staying with Nora a little longer. You back at the hospital?

I typed Almost and switched my phone off. Nobody needed to know where I was going.

Back on the road, I put my head down and went faster, racing out of town and into the countryside, down the deserted streets. I stopped a few times to check for directions on the remaining handheld GPS navigator I'd got at Jeffreys and which I planned on getting rid of long before I went home again.

My mind kept running through what I'd found. Travis and

Woods were collaborating somehow. I should've paid more attention to the details, not dismissed Travis's potential involvement because he'd started using again. He'd jumped at the chance when I'd offered for him to crash at my place after Michelle's abduction, around the same time as Nora had been diagnosed. He'd got me to believe her cancer had been the reason for him staying with me, and I'd bought it. All of it.

This entire time he'd wanted to get close. Not a doubt remained in my mind: he and Woods had sent those partial photos, keyed my car, canceled my membership at Invicta, stuffed my locks with silicone, stolen my gear. I still had no idea how they'd pulled off getting into my online banking to delete the payment for my father's care, or how they'd shifted the client meeting with Jeffreys in my calendar. Maybe those really were coincidences or Woods had contacts who could've hacked into my computer. Either that or he'd got some information out of Michelle before he'd killed her.

Their threats had been escalating, making me unsettled by an unseen enemy to profoundly mess with my head. Staging the anniversary outfit, getting the hooker to my house at the exact time Anjali was there. Making me dig up Michelle's body so they could get photos of me with her corpse. Christ, they'd made it seem like they'd hurt my dog, and given Woods was a killer and Travis obviously was all out of principles, I supposed I had to be thankful they'd let Roger live. My brother-in-law was a lucky bastard. If I'd found all of this out yesterday, I'd have poured the entire vial of fentanyl down his throat.

Jaw clenched, I focused on the road, slowed down when I got close to my destination. A small lane veered off to the left, flanked by dense bushes and trees on either side. I abandoned the bike and decided to cover the rest of the distance on foot. Three steps in and the skies burst open, dumping a deluge of rain on top of my head. I ignored it, along with the smell of damp leaves as I pulled up my collar and headed about ninety yards down the road where I noticed an old farmhouse.

The place looked ready to be torn down. A gaping hole in the roof had been halfheartedly covered with black plastic tarp fluttering in the wind, and the rest of the shingles were patchy, leaving a few rafters exposed. Any windows which weren't boarded up were mostly broken, and what had to have once been fire-engine-red exterior paneling was now a flaky, dusty shade of pink. The porch had seen better days, and most of the railing lay on the ground in rotting heaps. All in all, it was an ideal place to hide. Dilapidated, deserted, inconspicuous. Somewhere nobody would ever come looking. Nobody would see you come and go either, especially if you did so quietly, in the dead of night. If this was Woods's hideout, the place he and Travis had met to put together their plans, I congratulated them on a choice well made.

No vehicles were parked in front, and I decided to approach the house from the side with the least number of windows. I snuck around back in search for an easy way in, ducking under each of the windows until I reached the door, but it was locked.

An old rusty hammer lay in the grass and I picked it up, wishing I'd perhaps been a little less impulsive and had come better prepared. Woods was a killer-for-hire, and most probably armed, but with my strength and the element of surprise on my side, I hoped it would be enough to overpower him if he was here, and the hammer would come in handy to get him to talk. I wanted all the details. I needed to know I was right, and then I'd go back to the hospital and take care of Travis once and for all, Nora's potential charity donation be damned.

I stood still, took my time as I listened for movement or sound of any kind coming from inside the farmhouse, but there was none. The only noise was the rain, the *swish-swish* of the tall grass and the squawking of a few crows overhead.

As I cupped my hands over one of the dusty windows and peered inside, I could make out a square room. A dark wooden rocking chair stood in one corner, and an empty, stained mattress lay shoved against the left wall. I tried the window, but it was locked. I considered taking off my jacket and punching in the glass, but I couldn't be sure I was alone. I didn't want to risk alerting anyone inside, not when I was so close to finding Woods, and dealing with him for good.

I shimmied the pane again until it gave way beneath my fingers, and slid it to one side. When the gap was wide enough, I climbed through as fast as I could. If Woods walked into the room while half my body dangled from the frame, I doubted he'd invite me in for a chat and a plate of Jammie Dodgers.

Once in the farmhouse, I waited a while before taking a cautious step forward, wincing as the floorboards creaked and croaked beneath my weight. I made my way through the house, examining each room, the hammer clutched between my fingers as I pushed open the doors, ready to strike. No clue how long it took for me to execute a full sweep, but by the time I found myself back in the room with the mattress, I knew for sure I was alone.

Kneeling down I took off my biker gloves for better dexterity and examined the items strewn around the mattress, searching for clues. There were some cleaning supplies, including a bottle of bleach, which struck me as odd when the entire place was a rodent magnet. A few granola bar wrappers had been tossed into a cardboard box, but I found nothing else when I dug around inside, and there wasn't anything underneath the mattress. I'd read somewhere serial killers often took items belonging to their victims and kept them as trophies and souvenirs. Locks of hair, jewelry, driver's licenses. One psycho had even taken their eyeballs, another their heads. No clue if killers-for-hire did the same, but there weren't any mementos here.

As I turned around in a circle, surveying everything in the room, a small bag caught my eye—a dark green carry-on suitcase with silver trim, tucked away behind the rocking chair. Squinting, I thought it seemed vaguely familiar, and as I got closer, I saw a rip on the left side of the zipper. This was *my* bag. Michelle had wanted to throw it out but as it was still perfectly usable, I'd put it back in the basement storage room. Travis must've taken it.

I opened the zip and peered inside, pushed jeans and T-shirts away. Digging deeper, my hand closed around something else. A laptop. *My* laptop, and underneath, my remaining burner cells from the bus station.

There was another device, but this smartphone wasn't mine. I switched it on, tried to determine to whom it belonged. There were no emails or messages, no contacts or call history. I thought the phone had never been used until I read the name of an app I'd seen before when I'd halfheartedly looked at security cameras to demonstrate to my wife I was doing the homework she'd assigned me.

Sure enough, when I tapped the screen and it sprung to life, I had a direct view into my living room. A bloody camera, hidden exactly in the spot I'd suspected. There was another, this one in my hallway, angled at the house alarm keypad. The Dynamic Duo had hidden a second one. Even if I'd thrown Travis out and changed the alarm code a million times over, they'd have always been able to get in. I flicked back to the view showing the living room, and my breath caught.

Movement.

Not Roger. A person. Tall, lithe, dressed from head to toe in black, complete with a balaclava pulled over his face, and patting Roger on the head.

Woods was in my house. Instead of freaking out, I laughed. This time he had no idea he was the one being watched.

42

I stared at the screen, watched Woods sneak through my living room and out of view. I wanted to reach in through the phone and grab him by the neck. Next best thing? Delayed gratification. Get home as fast as possible and hope the canny fucker was still there.

Before hastily leaving the farmhouse the way I'd come in, I threw everything back where I'd found it, except for the laptop, burner cells, and the phone with the spyware. Until Woods or Travis—if he recovered—returned and found them gone, they wouldn't know anyone had been here. Maybe they'd accuse each other of taking the one thing they could use to extort me. Perhaps they'd turn on each other, and if I was truly fortunate, kill one another in the process.

I went out through the window and ran to my bike, mind humming about how I could salvage the situation, turn everything around to my advantage. Even if my house intruder had gone, Travis knew who Woods was. I needed him to recover as fast as possible so he could lead me to his accomplice. First, I'd kill Woods, which was bound to terrify Travis, then I'd take care of my brother-in-law. Another overdose would be highly effective and simple to pull off, and this time I wouldn't call the ambulance.

An anonymous tip would bring Woods and Travis's collaboration to light. Speed was of the essence, and this would probably all happen before Nora died. I'd be by her side as she wept, console her as she tried to comprehend her son had teamed up with a criminal to kidnap Michelle and get ransom money, but that things had gone wrong and his sister had died.

Nora would be sure to disown him. Leave her entire fortune to the only person left. Me. I very much doubted there'd be any more talk about charitable donations and if there was, I'd make sure it was the smallest amount possible. Pinning everything on Travis and Woods would be worth whatever paltry sum I'd lose.

There wouldn't be anybody left to contest Nora's will, either. I'd stop facing Anjali's scrutiny, which meant I could speed up the process of having Michelle declared dead. Man, this was getting better and better, and although I wanted to return to my house as swiftly as possible to make good on my plans, I needed to dispose of the laptop and burner phones. If Woods was still in my home when I got back and I *accidentally* killed him, I couldn't have them lying around when the cops arrived.

I took a quick detour along the Sudbury Reservoir and threw the devices into the water. Satisfied they'd never be found, I hopped back on my bike and gunned it down the road and all the way to Chelmswood, breaking every speed limit.

There were no vehicles I didn't recognize on our street,

but it was all too clear Woods had got into my home on multiple occasions without being seen, more than likely sneaking through the back garden, so I slid the key into the lock and pushed open the door. The alarm was set, there were no sounds or noises coming from anywhere except Roger—happy and unharmed—who trotted up with the usual enthusiastic wag of his tail. He was the worst guard dog I'd ever met, and once all this was over, I'd look into getting him trained.

I crept around the house, making sure we were alone, and when I reached the living room, I saw another orange envelope on the coffee table. Now I knew Woods was leaving them for me, it had far less of an effect. This time there wasn't a whole, partial, or cut-up photograph of my wife inside; it was a single sheet of folded paper with a phone number.

Idiot. Me, not him. If I'd kept one of my burner phones instead of chucking them in the water, I'd have been able to contact Woods straightaway. Now I had to find a corner store somewhere and buy another. I didn't care. Knowing I finally had the upper hand, I would've ridden to Mars on a unicycle naked to get what I needed.

Clothes changed and dry, and back outside, I raced off again, thankful the rain had finally let up and the sun had decided to break through the clouds. I headed about five miles out to get a burner phone, well away from my house, and once I'd paid for the device, I went to a coffee shop, grabbed a drink, and let the phone charge a little before going back outside. I dialed the number and a man answered.

"Hello, Lucas." His voice was low, tinny, and slightly mechanical, probably plugged into an interface on his computer.

"Woods. What do you want?"

He let out a small laugh. "Your money. Three million in crypto."

"No way. If you want money, we're going to have to meet in person."

"You don't have a choice."

"Try me."

I waited for his reply, thought he'd hung up but finally he said, "Call me in two hours."

I punched the air. I'd tell Woods I wanted my burner phones and laptop in exchange for the cash. He'd argue he didn't have them. I'd tell him he was full of shit. And when he returned to the farmhouse to get them, he'd walk straight into my trap.

43

I tucked the new burner into my pocket, got a little closer to the house before stopping to switch on my regular phone. I had three missed calls from Nora, a raspy voice mail asking me to contact her immediately.

"Where are you?" she said as soon as she picked up. "I couldn't reach you."

"I'm so sorry. I was struggling with what happened to Travis and needed to clear my head, then my phone ran out of battery. Have you spoken to the hospital? I was about to go see him."

"There's no change," she said, her voice strangled. "He hasn't woken up."

"Are Karina and Diane still with you?"

"No, they left a little while ago. I needed to be alone, too."

"I don't know what to say," I whispered. "This is all my fault."

"Nonsense, you saved him," she said. "Nobody blames you for anything, Lucas, but his actions have made my decision about the management of his money a lot more pressing. I simply can't wait anymore. I can't watch him do this to himself, I can't."

"It's okay, Nora, I understand. How can I help?"

She took a few slow breaths. "Do you remember Mr. Danton?"

How could I forget? He'd put together the blasted prenup for me and Michelle. His skill in drafting contracts Houdini couldn't have extricated himself from were legendary, but this time he was on my side.

"Yes, of course," I said. "Good man."

"He managed to rearrange his schedule and can be here in thirty minutes for us to go through my will and the power of attorney, and I'll sign them immediately if you agree. We can discuss potential donations as well. I know it's short notice now, but I'd feel so much better to have it done. Can you come? Would you mind going to see Travis afterward?"

"I'll come straightaway," I said, forcing the smile from my voice.

My mind barely registered the cold as I rode to Nora's because my veins had filled with euphoria. I was about to end up with more money than I'd ever dreamed of. I could feel it. Taste it. It would all soon be mine, and Dad's.

When I'd met Michelle at the art gallery, I'd thought a few million would be coming my way, but with Gideon's death, Nora's cancer, and Travis's upcoming demise, I bet I was about to have almost ten times that at my disposal. I could do whatever I pleased as soon as I wanted, since there'd be no waiting years to have Michelle declared dead.

First off, Jeffreys and Richard could suck it. Never mind the new care home Dad had been transferred to, I'd immediately move him to a state-of-the-art facility, where only the best doctors would treat him. While I was at it, I'd find a way to contact Robert Downey Jr., convince him to pay Dad a visit dressed up as Iron Man—he'd get such a kick out of that—hell, maybe I'd arrange for the entire cast to come. And very discreetly, I'd make sure my one remaining problem, Bobby, was taken care of, permanently.

I made it to Nora's on time, but there wasn't another car in the driveway. Typical. Philippe Danton was a pompous arse. No doubt he'd show up late, making us wait before he graced us with his presence.

I rang the bell. When nobody answered and I found the door unlocked, I went in and jogged up the stairs, taking them two at a time.

Wiping the smile from my face I walked to Nora's bedroom and knocked. The door was slightly ajar, and I peered through the crack at first, then around the side, expecting to see my mother-in-law safely tucked up, but her bed was empty.

I leaned over and noticed the en suite door was closed, the noise of running water and voices coming from the other side. Strange. As far as I knew she had a catheter, and I thought the nurses helped Nora shower in the morning. There must've been an emergency. It was why nobody had come to the front door, and I'd have to reprimand Diane's counterpart for not locking the bloody thing. Anybody could've strolled in and robbed Nora blind.

Deciding it would probably be best to wait in the hallway until my mother-in-law was done, I was about to leave the room when I heard a creak behind me. I spun around, stopping dead in my tracks as I came face-to-face with Anjali, wearing what appeared to be a pair of Diane's soft-soled shoes. Those didn't confuse me as much as the gun in her hand.

"Detective," I said. "It's good to see you. I didn't hear you ring."

"That's because I didn't."

Her face was neutral, but something in her tone made me frown. I looked at her clenched jaw, the gun aimed right at my chest. "What's going on? What are you doing?"

Anjali blinked, long and slow. "I know you tried to get Travis to overdose."

My feet felt as if they'd grown roots. Thick, gnarly, twisted ones that had instantly busted through the soles of my shoes and tied me to the floor. My heart thumped faster, and I barely managed to keep my voice even enough to whisper, "What are you talking about?"

"And I know what you did to Michelle. You hired a hit man to kill her."

It took a nanosecond to react. Lunging forward, I slammed into her stomach, knocked the gun from her hand and sent it skidding across the floor. Both of us tumbled to our knees, but I got up faster. I was stronger, and soon had my hands wrapped around her neck as I tried to figure out how she knew, if they'd found Woods, maybe Michelle's body, and somehow linked it all back to me. My grip loosened a fraction. Maybe *she* was Woods. Wouldn't that be fucking ironic?

What was I going to do? Nora didn't know Anjali was here, she hadn't seen her, the detective had clearly only just arrived. Anjali dug her fingernails into my hands, and in response I squeezed harder, watched her face go red as I calculated how I could get rid of her.

They say someone with nothing to lose is the most dangerous among us. Incorrect. It's the person who has *everything* on the line, who's so close to realizing their dreams, and who'll stop at nothing to make sure they come true. *Me.*

I yanked Anjali to her feet as she kicked and struggled, but when I went to drag her from the room so I could decide what to do with her, something cold and hard pressed against the back of my head.

The detective's gun.

Instinct made my hands drop, and Anjali spun around and took a swing at my face. The impact made me lose my balance, and as I stumbled, I caught sight of the person who was now holding the weapon. My mouth dropped open.

"Surprise," Michelle whispered.

I couldn't speak, could barely blink as I stared at my wife standing in front of me. She looked incredible, wearing tight black jeans and a fitted white top, a bomber jacket I remembered from her wardrobe. She looked healthy, hair swept back, face made-up, skin glowing. Not how I'd imagined a person might appear if they'd been held hostage for a month.

And wait a second. She hadn't been held hostage. I'd seen her body teeming with bugs. She'd been in the ground. Because she was *dead*.

"You look confused, babe. Aren't you happy to see me? Aren't you relieved?" Her words weren't filled with anger and hatred, in fact, she seemed so calm and serene I wondered why she was still pointing a weapon at me. I lifted a foot.

"Stay where you are," she said, her voice still soft.

The gears in my mind clicked and whirred as I shifted to the role of a lifetime, saw everything I needed to do mapped out in front of me like Keanu Reeves in *The Matrix*. Everything else, including finding out what the hell was going on, would have to wait.

"My God, Michelle," I said. "It's really you. You're alive. What happened? Where were you? I've been frantic." When she didn't answer, I turned to Anjali. "Detective, help her. She's suffering from some kind of psychotic break. Tell her to put the gun down."

Michelle laughed.

"Anjali, please," I continued. "I didn't mean to attack you. You accusing me of hurting Travis and my wife. The stress. Not sleeping. I have no excuse—"

"Enough," Michelle said. "We. Know."

"Know what, sweetheart?" I said, mind racing. "You've been through a terrible ordeal. Do you know who took you? Did they hurt you? I can't believe you're here."

"Take a seat," Michelle said, and I glanced at Anjali, who shrugged.

"She's the one with the gun. I suggest you do as she says."

I thought about bolting for the door but my wife looked like she'd put a bullet in my head if I didn't do as she said, so I sat down, immediately wishing I hadn't when Anjali removed a set of white plastic zip ties from her pocket.

"What are you—"

"Shh." Michelle put a finger to her lips, and within an instant Anjali had secured my arms to the chair and got to work on my feet. Once she was done, I could barely move my fingertips.

"You tried to have me killed," my wife said, handing the gun back to Anjali. "You ordered the hit on me."

"That's not true. It's insane. I never—"

"Save it," Michelle said, sweetly. "As I wrote on the back of those photos, *I know.*"

"I don't understand," I said, which was the truth. She'd sent them? It had been her all along? She'd done all of this? *How?*

"Do you have any idea what it was like," Michelle continued as she cocked her head to one side, "being bundled into the back of a van by a stranger? Held for hours before walking through the forest in the middle of the night, knowing you're about to die? Seeing your grave and hearing the person tell you not to worry, they've made preparations so the animals can't get to you?" She took a breath and smiled again. "Can you imagine hearing that and not understanding why? What you've done to deserve this?"

"I had nothing to do with your abduction. I didn't—"

"I begged him to let me go," Michelle continued. "I cried and I begged. Promised I wouldn't tell a soul even though I'd seen his face. And I meant it. I said I'd do anything—*anything*—if he let me live. I told him he didn't have to do this. I had a wonderful husband who loved me, and my family would be devastated. I begged and I begged, and I *begged*." She held up her hands. "He refused, even when I offered him five times whatever the person who'd hired him had paid, he said no."

"Big mistake," Anjali said. "Big. Huge."

Michelle let out a laugh. "Oh, he was gentlemanly about it. Apparently, it wasn't personal. Said he had a reputation to maintain. Can you believe it? A *reputation*."

Anjali waved a hand. "Good work ethics can be so overrated."

Michelle turned to me. "I bet this is eating you up inside. You're wondering how I got away, where I've been, how I tricked you." She laughed again, and this time it was a cold, hollow sound. "Unfortunately for you, this isn't an episode of *Scooby-Doo*, but I will tell you one thing: the hit man you sent after me had a primal fear of cats."

"I know you've told me that," Anjali said, "but I still find it weird. They're adorable."

"In his defense, a bobcat jumping at you from a tree is terrifying," Michelle answered. "But I was a bit surprised a ruthless killer gets scared so easily."

"Good thing he did, and good on you for shooting the asshole, by the way."

Michelle bowed a little. "One fewer scumbag in the world,

although he was quite docile as he bled out." She turned to me, tapped her lip with one finger. "He had no clue who wanted me dead. Said he was supposed to send a photo of my corpse with three words to a number on his phone."

"Smart getting him to talk like that," Anjali said.

"Oh, it's amazing what he shared when I promised I'd get help, and what he confessed when he realized I'd lied, and he was dying. He'd killed eight people, in between his regular job as an auditor for a bank. Apparently, he liked the excitement more than the money, the precision of blending their graves into the landscape so they went unnoticed. Can you believe that?"

"I can," Anjali said. "Real life is stranger than fiction, believe me."

I realized I hadn't been far off with my assessment of what Woods did for a living, but I didn't say as much. Anjali had obviously helped Michelle stage Woods's body. Planting the bag, shoes, and her phone. Dressing him in yoga pants and a shirt similar to the one my wife had, pouring the drain cleaner over him, waiting weeks before making their move to ensure the corpse had decayed beyond the point of recognition. I almost wanted to give them a standing ovation but I kept quiet, processing my thoughts and the bizarre banter between the two of them, letting them play with me before finally deciding it was time to speak.

"I have absolutely no idea who or what you're talking about."

"Well, that's just not true, is it?" Anjali said. "And we have lots of photos of you with his body, Lucas. Plenty to pin it all on you."

I wanted to yell they had no evidence, nothing that would stick anyway, but I wasn't going to admit to anything. These were intimidation tactics. They were trying to scare an admission out of me, and they weren't getting one.

The sound of footsteps came from the hallway. Anjali must've called for backup. I bet she and Michelle had been hoping to get me to confess but I'd kept my mouth shut. It might take a day or two but very soon I'd be a free man again. No richer, unfortunately, but free.

When the bedroom door opened, instead of it being more cops, it was Karina, Nora, and Diane, who was dressed from head to toe in black, and I couldn't stop my head swiveling toward the en suite, from where I could still hear running water and the sound of muffled voices.

My confusion must have made it to my face because Nora chuckled, walked to the bathroom, and shut off the taps. When she returned, she held a phone in her hand, tapped the screen, and the voices stopped. "Diversion tactic," she said. "Guess you should've paid more attention to the crime shows Michelle enjoys."

As they all glared at me, what struck me the most was Nora's face. No longer pale, but a healthy pink sheen, and her eyes weren't surrounded by dusky shadows. She was still bone thin, but on her feet, moving with her usual grace. And there was a fire in her eyes I hadn't seen in a month. What the hell was going on?

"Has he admitted anything?" Diane said.

"Nope," Michelle answered.

"Taken responsibility?" This came from Karina.

Anjali snorted. "I don't think that's in his repertoire."

"What about Gideon?" Nora asked. "Did you ask him about that?"

"I don't think there's much point," Michelle said. "Neither of us believe that day was an accident anymore, do we?" She walked behind me and slowly slid her hand into the back pocket of my jeans and removed my wallet. "I know you think you're the smartest, but you weren't clever enough to find the tracker we disguised as a library card, were you?"

My jaw clenched as I pictured myself checking my Triumph, feeling so smug for outwitting them with everything I'd done. My wallet! Of all the things I hadn't bothered checking when it was the one item I carried on me no matter where I went.

"You got a warrant for that, Detective?" I said. "My lawyer's going to have a field day—"

"Looks like he didn't have a clue," Karina said, crossing her arms. "I'm not surprised. Anjali's wicked smart. It's what attracted me to her when we met on safari."

My eyes widened. "You know each other?"

"Our holiday romance was the reason I moved to Boston," Karina said. "Didn't work out, in the end, work schedules can be a bitch."

"All right, ladies," Anjali said, clapping her hands like a schoolteacher to get her students' attention. "Let's get moving. Diane, do you have—"

"But you're sick." I turned to Nora, the thousands of questions about what was happening—and how—rushing to the forefront, almost making my head explode. "The doctor said you had a few weeks left. You wanted me to manage Travis's money. Philippe Danton's supposed to be here any minute. You wouldn't have done that if you didn't trust me, Nora. I swear, I'm innocent. You have to believe me."

The five of them looked at me, and each other, before erupting in laughter.

"You're not the only one who can pretend to be something they're not," Nora said, wiping a few tears from her cheeks. "You saw what we wanted you to see, helped along by Karina's makeup talents and my strict liquid-only diet. God, I can't wait for a big fat steak."

"I won't give you a hard time about it," Michelle said with a grin. "Seeing as distracting Lucas with the promise of money was your idea." She looked at me and smiled. "Turns out greed was your downfall, especially when you believed you'd get everything."

"But… Travis," I said. "You let him stay at my house. You wouldn't have done that if you thought I was guilty. You trust me."

For the first time since she'd entered the room, Nora's triumphant look slipped, a pained expression taking over her face instead. "It was a gamble I had to take and, believe me, lying to him wasn't an easy decision, but we couldn't tell him what was going on and—"

Michelle grabbed her hand. "It's okay, Mom, he'll be okay. We're going to get him into rehab now, I promise." She turned to me. "We tried to get him to leave the house but he wouldn't. Even the scratch in your car and the laxatives weren't enough for you to throw him out."

"And I was there in the background," Karina said. "Checking up on him as often as I could."

"I didn't think you'd hurt my son," Nora whispered, "not with the threat of giving his money away, but you caused the overdose, didn't you?"

I pressed my lips firmly together, raised my chin and said nothing.

"How does it feel?" Michelle said. "Realizing you've been lied to, messed with, manipulated by those who you believed love you? Having everything you are twisted and turned and used against you? Tell me, how does it feel, *Michael*?"

"How did you…?"

"Me?" She put a hand to her chest. "I'm an art curator. I wouldn't have known where to start digging up your past."

"I did," Anjali said. "Amazing what you can find with the

right contacts, even overseas. Not always legitimately, but you don't seem to have a problem with illicit arrangements."

I looked at them, determination flowing back into my body, filling my stomach, my lungs, every square inch of me. Once again, I reminded myself they had zero evidence, nothing remotely tangible to go on. Even the name change was something I could defend and as for everything else—deny, deny, deny, and stay the course.

"Go ahead and arrest me," I said. "You're wasting your time. I'm disgusted you think I'm involved in this. I'm innocent and there isn't a shred of proof to back up a single one of your allegations."

"We know," Michelle said with a deep sigh. "You've been very clever, and we bet you got rid of the laptop and phones we let you find."

I leaned back in my chair. "Untie me because I've got nothing to say except this—I want a lawyer. Tell your colleagues that when they arrive, Anjali."

"Colleagues?" she said, a mock-confused expression on her face. "Looks like you're having trouble reading the room. This is my day off." Her eyes twinkled, her lips twitching. "I'm not even here."

I frowned at her, a flicker of panic making its way up my throat. "What are you—"

"We're teaching you a lesson," Michelle said, her voice soothing again, gentle as a lullaby. "You see, we're not like you. We don't think we're invincible. We understand strength in numbers and what we can accomplish by working together."

My heart started to thump as I watched Diane remove a little black case from her back pocket. Slowly, methodically, she took out five syringes filled with clear liquid, and handed one to each of the women.

"What's that? What are you doing?" I whipped my head

around, struggling against the restraints, but they wouldn't budge. Was it heroin? Fentanyl? Whatever it was, this was their revenge. They were going to shoot me up and let me die.

"Relax," Anjali said. "Or don't. It'll hurt much more if you put up a fight."

"But you're a cop. You can't do this. You—"

"Listen to me, *sweetheart*," Michelle said as they came closer, needles aiming straight for my neck. "We're not lone wolves. We hunt in packs. And when you go after one of us—" they spoke their next words in unison as they pierced my skin "—you feel the wrath of us all."

SATURDAY

44

With what went down, I must admit not waking up dead came as a surprise. Yet here I am, in a bit of a predicament, it would appear, although the day's still young. The room I find myself in, completely alone, is about fifty square feet, has a dented green metal door with a round silver handle. It opens outward. No doubt a strategy to keep its occupants, such as myself, from loosening the hinges and trying to escape.

The faint smell of burned coffee lingers in the quiet air despite nobody having offered me any. A bright neon light hangs overhead, a little out of reach, the eggshell frame covered in a thick layer of dust. The place is boxlike, no windows or two-way mirrors, and the white paint on the brick walls is scuffed and marked, a random pattern of black and gray streaks and smudges mixed with what might well be an occasional trace of blood.

I'm sitting on an uncomfortable plastic fold-up chair which is making my arse sweat, in front of an aluminum table cool to the touch. Obscenities and random words scratched deep into its surface offered a short distraction, but I've gone over them three times now and I'm bored.

An old TV sits on top of a smaller table at the back of the room, an anomaly, I reckon, although I'm not entirely sure. There may be some obscure and new rules about detainees needing entertainment, but I'm not privy to those details seeing as I've never been detained, let alone arrested. The power to the telly is on, but the screen's filled with static, and I can't see the remote control anywhere, so I do my best to ignore the constant black-and-white flickering, which is giving me a wicked headache.

I've resisted the urge to get up and turn the channel by hand or bang on the door and demand to see someone, shout about how well I know my rights. I'm not stupid. I know they're watching me. I can tell from the camera high up in the left corner, its little red light shining, observing my every move.

I can hardly wait to speak to my lawyer. He won't be impressed with the treatment I've received, and I'm going to make excellent use of the multiple strikes the cops have provided me with already, especially that bitch Detective Anjali Dubal. She brought me here unconscious. I've not yet been cautioned. Left alone for I've no clue how long. Judging by the pressure in my bladder, which I'm determined to ignore as well, it's at least been overnight with nothing but a bottle of water. I haven't touched it. It's on the table in front of me despite the burning in my throat.

By leaving me here with nothing to do, they must think it'll make their job easier, I'll relent faster. I'll confess. They still don't know who they're dealing with. During all the time they've let me stew here, I've done a lot of thinking.

I lean back in the chair and stretch out my legs, pull on the collar of my shirt, trying not to wince as I graze the sore spots where the women plunged the needles. I don't mind sitting here for another while. Actually, I'm grateful for the peace and quiet, the time provided to go over what happened this past week as often as possible. I'm examining every tiny detail. Plastering over each crack and fissure. Thinking about everything leading me here. How I can bend the truth. How no one—*no one*—has any proof of my involvement in anything. Even if they fish the laptop and burner phones from the reservoir, they'll be dead, and without them, they've got nothing.

I'm going to walk out of here. I bet they know it. It's why they've delayed talking to me. Anjali's probably out there arguing with her boss, trying to convince him or her they have enough to charge me. They don't.

When Michelle and those four other traitors plunged their needles into me, I thought for sure I was going to die and end up thrown into a grave or on top of Woods. Glad that didn't happen. I couldn't have spent all eternity with the imbecile. He had one job to do. *One.* And he got scared by an animal. If it weren't for a big cat, everything would've worked out, and I take a lot of pride in the fact.

Curiosity whispers in my ear, and I let myself wonder about which police station they brought me to, and how Anjali will explain why I wasn't taken to hospital instead. My neck feels stiff, and while the grogginess has worn off, my body's heavy from whatever drug they gave me. I hope it's still in my system. The blood test I'll demand is something else I'll add to my arsenal. I grin, and mutter, "I'll have your badge for this, Detective."

The TV flickers and the picture clears, making me sit up straight and pay attention. It's WHDH, the local news station, informing me it's exactly 10.02 a.m. Saturday morning. The ticker runs across the bottom and I catch the last few words:

MISSING LOCAL WOMAN FOUND SAFE

An elegant, silver-haired reporter I recognize appears on the screen, her blue eyes becoming wider as she speaks, her voice serious and low. "This really is an incredible story, one of courage and resilience and, quite frankly, something you might see in a Hollywood movie, not real life. A young woman, Michelle Ward-Forester, who was abducted in a parking lot more than a month ago was found safe late last night, and—" she touches her earpiece "—I'm told we're heading to the live press conference now. Let's listen in."

My jaw drops a little as the feed cuts to a different room with a long mahogany table, a few chairs, and microphones set up at the front. An audience watches, as I do, while Anjali, another cop I don't recognize but who looks senior in rank, Michelle, and Nora slowly walk into the room and take a seat. I'm unable to move until the cop I don't know gives Anjali the go-ahead.

Anjali reaches for the microphone, adjusts the height, and speaks. "Last night, at approximately eleven fifteen p.m., Michelle Ward-Forester walked into the Clinton Police Department, safe and alive. After being abducted thirty-seven days ago and spending the last five weeks bound, blindfolded, and gagged, she escaped from an as-yet undisclosed location in the Clinton area. She successfully guided us to said location, which was immediately surrounded and searched. Her abductor wasn't at the premises, but we recovered copious amounts of forensic evidence." Anjali pauses and stares directly at the camera. Directly at *me*.

Undisclosed location? She means the decrepit farmhouse. Michelle, Anjali or whoever planted the coordinates on Travis's phone, and which were obviously intended as a trap for me, led me straight to it. And...*shit*. My DNA is all over the place. On the bottle of bleach I picked up and examined, which, incidentally, I'm now sure one of them took from our home gym. I touched the box with the cereal bar wrappers as well, and I'm certain they lifted those from my garbage bins. I hadn't taken any of my usual precautions. Had removed my gloves. I'd been too eager to search Travis and Woods's hideout, which the cops were only going to find if and when I led them to it, and had first swept it clean.

Fuck.

Anjali continues. "We can confirm Mrs. Ward-Forester's husband, Lucas Forester, is the prime suspect in this case."

The reporters blurt out questions, but she raises a hand and waits for the hubbub to die down before talking again. "It's alleged he coordinated the abduction of his wife while he was abroad and kept her alive to extort money from her family. We're searching for his accomplice, but according to information Mrs. Ward-Forester has provided, we suspect Mr. Forester may have killed the man he was working with."

As I realize they're pinning Woods's murder on me, more noise erupts from the gaggle of reporters, one voice louder than the next.

"Who's the accomplice?"

"Where's Lucas Forester?"

"What are you doing to find him?"

"Is Forester responsible for Travis Ward's overdose?"

Anjali remains composed, stoic, and focused as questions fly at her. She waits again for the room to fall silent, and leans in. "All I'm prepared to say about Travis Ward is that we expect him to make a full recovery. We don't know who the accomplice is, or Mr. Forester's current whereabouts, but we're making every effort to locate him."

Huh? What's she talking about? They've arrested me.

"Are you saying you've lost Forester?" a reporter near the front says.

Anjali narrows her eyes. "We believe he fled once his wife escaped. A significant manhunt is underway. Roadblocks are set up, bus and train stations, as well as airports, are all on high alert."

"He has a head start then?" someone else yells.

"Yes, but I'm sure it won't last." As Anjali takes a sip of water, I feel a trickle of sweat sliding down my spine despite the cool temperature of the room, especially when she looks back at the camera. "This is a message for Mr. Forester. Make no mistake. We *will* find you. You can't hide forever."

I wonder if I'm on the batty bus heading to Crazy Town. What does she mean they'll *find* me? And then I know, and it makes me let out a groan. They're going to keep me here, wherever I am, for a while, hide me away so it appears I've been on the run, which will increase the optics of my guilt, boost the chances of a conviction when I'm miraculously found.

Without the laptop and burner phones, they need as much evidence as they can fabricate. And, Jesus, they thought of everything. Every last detail to nail me to the wall for Michelle's attempted and Woods's very real murder. My mind spins, generating the lies I'll feed the cops, trying to find a way to be released on a technicality.

I push my bewilderment aside, focus on the TV again. A reporter asks how Michelle's doing. She's as good an actress as Anjali, her voice small and frightened, not at all sounding like the astute and assertive person I already knew she was, or the cold-blooded woman she revealed herself to be yesterday. Her face is makeup free, her shoulders hunched, but right then, all I can think is she's so fucking smart, it's turning me on.

"I'm…coping, for now," she says bowing her head a little. "I'm glad it's over."

"What can you tell us about your husband?" a female reporter asks. "Did you have any idea what he'd been planning?"

Michelle shakes her head, quietly says, "None. I thought he loved me."

"Nora, Nora! How are you feeling?"

Nora squeezes Michelle's hand. "I'm beyond grateful my daughter's home."

"Is it true you're sick? Can you confirm you have cancer?"

"Yes, but we just found out the treatments are working after all. It's a miracle."

Miracle, my arse. The reporters blurt out more questions, and one catches my full attention.

"Michelle, have you spoken to your husband's family?"

My wife shakes her head, lowers her eyes. "No, and I'm worried about how this will affect his father. He's not well and he lives in England. He's got nobody left. I'll have to take care of him."

Any lingering attraction to her evaporates. "Take care of him? What the hell do you mean, Michelle? What are you going to do to my dad?"

None of the journalists think to clarify the statement because as far as they're concerned, there's no need. I can't work out if it was a threat or not, if she's going to hurt him, or Roger, the dog she wanted to have put down. It's an effort to concentrate on the rest of the press conference, during which Anjali commends Michelle for her bravery, and the Clinton cops for their swift action. As the screen cuts back to the regular news, the TV returns to static, and I'm left in silence while I piece together the rest of how they did it.

After Michelle shot Woods, she went to Nora, and they came up with a plan to find out who tried to kill her. Oh, to have been a fly on the wall during those conversations. Did they immediately suspect me? Decide that between the possibilities of some random stranger and the husband, it had to be a case of Occam's razor, and the simpler explanation was correct? Was it the first allegedly bungled ransom drop that tipped them off? Knowing Michelle was supposed to be dead, and Woods hadn't made those demands? Or was it after they'd roped in Diane, Karina, and Anjali, and the detective had dug into my background? Maybe they'd been through my gear in the bus station locker weeks ago.

As Diane is a nurse, assisting Nora to convincingly fake her illness was easy, especially with Karina transforming my mother-in-law into a terminal cancer patient, making her look sicker each day. Thinking back, I realize I never saw any doctors. Not once had I met another caregiver, was always told they'd arrive for a shift soon or they'd already left. And their *pièce de résistance*, the tracker cunningly disguised as my library card. They'd always known exactly where I was, taking turns breaking into my house, staging the clothes, messing with my food, leaving envelopes. Working together, they devised a strategy and pressed my buttons well after I'd been to what I believed was my wife's grave, even though that's when they knew for certain what I'd done.

I marvel at their ingenuity, the level of dedication and collaboration it took for them to pull this off. They make Danny Ocean and his crew look like a bunch of kindergartners and as I think about Michelle's deviousness, my anger rotates, shifting and turning into something else. Not lust. Definitely not love. It's admiration.

The sound of footsteps outside the door makes me sit up straight. The press conference has ended. I might be in the same building, this could be Michelle coming to visit me, to gloat, and I welcome it. The anticipation of seeing her face again almost kills me. I have so many questions. I want her to tell me everything. I need to know every last detail about how she tricked me, and if my assumptions are correct.

A key turns in the lock. I haven't taken a breath and still don't as the door swings open.

It's not Michelle.

Not Anjali.

Bobby Boyle.

Mad Mel stands by his side. They're dressed in white coveralls zipped up to their chins, and there's a roll of plastic sheeting tucked under Mel's left arm, an electric saw with an extension cable in his gloved hand. I stare at them, mouth dropping open as I understand this is where my story ends—with a man who, I was once warned, despises all forms of violence against women, and always keeps his word.

They step inside the room. Mel slowly bends over and puts his materials on the floor. Lines them up neatly, taking his time.

When Bobby speaks, his voice is low, raspy, filled with palpable excitement.

"Hello, Cundy," he says. "The missus says happy belated anniversary."

Cluck.

★ ★ ★ ★ ★

ACKNOWLEDGMENTS

Never will I ever tire of saying the book community is like no other, and during what have been more than challenging times, it became a lifeline. And so, it's an incredible privilege to put together another list of tremendous people to whom my boundless gratitude extends.

First and foremost, and as always—thank you to you, the reader—whether in a professional or "just-for-fun" capacity, thank you for picking up *Never Coming Home* and taking this journey with me. I hope you had fun and will come back for more.

To Carolyn Forde, my amazing agent who knows what's what and brims with brilliant input and expert advice—thank you for your guidance and support, and everything you do.

To Emily Ohanjanians, my extraordinary editor—you always, *always* surprise me with your insight and ability to bring a manuscript to a whole other level. It's an honor to work with you and be one of your authors.

To the incredible (and I mean *incredible*) Harlequin, HarperCollins, HTP, and MIRA teams, including Cory Beatty, Peter Borcsok, Nicole Brebner, Audrey Bresar, Randy Chan, Jennifer Choi, Eden Church, Heather Connor, Monica Espinoza Chavez, Lia Ferrone, Emer Flounders, Heather Foy, Olivia Gissing, Miranda Indrigo, Amy Jones, Sean Kapitain, Linette Kim, Ana Luxton, Ashley MacDonald, Leo MacDonald, Lauren Morocco, Lindsey Reeder, Alice Tibbetts, and colleagues: you are out-of-this-world wonderful, and your support means everything.

To HarperAudio, BeeAudio, and Alex Wyndham (who could read me the phone book without my ever getting bored), thank you for making fantastic audio versions of my novels. To Brad and Britney at AudioShelf—thank you for being champions of books, including mine.

A huge thank-you to fellow author and retired Detective Sergeant Bruce Robert Coffin who helped me get away with fictional murder *again*, and to Forensic Detective Ed Adach who happily assisted in covering up said murder. I know it sounds weird to be grateful for discussions that include outsmarting the cops, maggots, and decomp, but I am. Please don't turn me in.

Huge thank you also to Drew Murray for the tech advice and rather unsettling chats about the dark web. Because of you I'm still sleeping with the lights on. Don't worry, I'll get you back. Massive shout-outs to Steve Urszenyi and Morgan Hillier for your stellar medical advice. Even bigger thank-yous for everything you do and have done to keep your communities safe. You are heroes. Cheers to Mark Bull for the recruitment refresher. Hope we get to see each other sometime this decade!

Thank you, my dear friend and First Chapter Fun partner in fictional crime, Hank Phillippi Ryan, for input on an early version—I hope you enjoy your cameo. Hugs to cool A.F. Brady for pointing out a few manuscript flaws (my lips are sealed as to which ones), to PJ Vernon for making sure I got things right, and to Sonica Soares and Candice Sawchuk for all your feedback, excitement, and enthusiasm about my work.

Waving at all my GTA author-pals, including Sam Bailey, Karma Brown, Molly Fader, Jennifer Hillier, Natalie Jenner, Marissa Stapley, and K.A. Tucker. Love & hugs all round.

To every single one of my author friends from near and far, I'm so grateful for your friendship. I can't wait for us to meet in person again (maybe we already have by the time you read this in which case I apologize for almost hugging you to death). You make this community what it is—a fantastic place I never want to leave. Thank you.

To Dad, Joely, Simon, Michael & Oli—thank you for always supporting me. To my in-laws, Gilbert and Jeanette and my extended family everywhere—thank you for reading my books, snapping pictures of them, and insisting your friends read them. Lots of love to Becki, my BFF. Through thick and thin, indeed.

And finally: to Rob and our sons, Leo, Matt, and Lex, who always make me laugh no matter what, and who never doubted my creative abilities, even when I did—thank you for being there and putting up with me not only as I disappear into my creations, but also for sticking around when I resurface and tell you about my crazy research. And, Rob, when you first suggested moving to Canada in 2009, it was one of the hardest decisions we'd ever faced as a couple, but I have you to thank for kick-starting my writing career. It was the right move (see, now you even have it on paper). I love you all so much. You are my everything.

NEVER
COMING
HOME

HANNAH MARY McKINNON

Reader's Guide

mira

1. What did you think of Lucas? Did you at any point in the story think what he did to Michelle was somehow, even a tiny bit, justified? Why, or why not?

2. What do you make of Lucas's statement: "I don't adhere to the logic parents are responsible for their offspring's mistakes for all eternity"? Do you think Lucas's father was somehow responsible for how his son turned out? If so, why?

3. How do you think Lucas may have grown up to be as an adult if his mother and baby sister hadn't died? Was that the life-defining event for him or were there others along the way?

4. Do you believe Lucas was searching for something other than money and more advanced health care for his father? If so, what was it? Was there any nobility in his endgame?

5. Did your allegiances shift at any point during the story? Toward whom, why, and when? Did Lucas have any redeeming qualities, and if so, what were they?

6. What scene was the most pivotal in the story for you? How would the novel have changed if it had been different, or hadn't taken place? What did you expect to happen?

7. What surprised or shocked you the most? What didn't you see coming? What was obvious?

8. What did you make of the collaboration between the women? Is what they did acceptable? Why or why not? What might you have done in Michelle's situation? Do you think Nora favored one child over the other?

9. How do you feel about the ending? Was justice served and if you think it was, what did you make of its delivery? Was it fair?

10. What do you expect will happen to Lucas? Do you think there's a chance he might escape, and would you want him to?

11. If you could choose for any of the deceased characters to live, which one would it be and why?

This is your sixth novel. What was your inspiration for _Never Coming Home_?

Instead of a news article or a radio segment, which is typically where the inspiration for my books comes from, for Never Coming Home _the character appeared first. I wanted to write about someone who was evil, despicable, but also relatable on some levels, and definitely funny—and whose enemies were even worse. Cue Lucas and Bobby Boyle. The story evolved from there, so it was very much character driven, and writing from the antagonist's point of view was a completely new experience. I had so much fun, and thoroughly enjoyed crafting another novel entirely from a man's perspective. While I probably shouldn't admit to this, despite his many flaws, I enjoyed spending time with Lucas because I found him hilarious._

Did the story end up the way you first imagined it or did it evolve along the way?

My stories always shift and evolve as I write, and even as a plotter I can't—and don't want to—foresee every little twist. I knew the major beats, and those didn't move that much from plot to final version, and the ending is exactly how I'd imagined it, including the very last word. Out of all my books so far, Never Coming Home turned out the closest to my initial vision and was the smoothest to write and edit. I fully expect the next one to whoop my backside.

Do you have a favorite chapter or scene?

More than one! I loved writing the scenes with Bobby and Lucas, especially the banter between them, and Heinz was my favorite tertiary character. I think he'd make a great protagonist for another book. The scene in the forest was creepy and unsettling to write, and I'm glad I did so with the lights on. I'm a visual person, so I was describing what I pictured in my head, which was a little gruesome. To counterbalance that, Lucas's one-liners and wry sense of humor made me chuckle, and he kept pushing me to explore his character further. But if I must pick a favorite scene, it's the one close to the end, when Lucas realizes who's been messing with him. As much as I liked him, writing his downfall was hugely satisfying.

What research did you do for this novel?

This book took me to some very strange places. First of all, I needed to understand the dark web, and I listened to several podcasts about it, which were both fascinating and disturbing. I had to spend a lot of time thinking like a criminal, all the way from pickpocket to murderer. I also spoke to the former commander of Ontario's Emergency Medical Assistance Team and an emergency physician to get the medical details right. As always, my go-to policing and crime scene advice came from retired Detective Sergeant and fellow author Bruce Robert Coffin, and Forensic Detective Ed Adach. I swear they keep helping me get away with fictional murder and we have a blast doing so.

Do you have a writing routine? Do you let anyone read early drafts, or do you keep the story private until it's finished?

I have three teenage sons so often my schedule needs to work around theirs. Flexibility is a big part of the job description but I write full-time and work most days, depending on the stages of my projects. As for my early drafts, no, nobody will ever see them, those are for my eyes only as they're basic and require a lot of work before I'm comfortable sharing. Typically, I'll have one or two people read the manuscript when it goes to my editor, and perhaps another one or two after the structural (large) edits but before the finer embellishments. People are so generous with their time and always have incredible suggestions. They always make the novel so much better.

Do you read other fiction while you're working on a book, or do you find it distracting? Do you listen to music while you write?

I'm always with a book in hand (or headphones in my ears taking my audiobooks for a walk) and it would be awful for me to not read when I'm writing. To me, books aren't distracting at all, but music is. I need silence when I work. My preferred writing spot, at least to draft my initial manuscripts, is our small spare bedroom with its dodgy Wi-Fi connection and an old laptop. I leave my phone downstairs, so I'm not tempted to check emails, the news, or go on social media. When I do that my productivity at least doubles.

How did you experience writing during the pandemic?

It was difficult and I limited my news consumption to thirty minutes a day because I couldn't cope with more. Never Coming Home was plotted and written in its entirety during 2020/2021, which was also the year my lovely mum passed away. Because of Covid, traveling to Switzerland to see her and be with my dad and sister was impossible, and so I was forced to say goodbye from thousands of miles away. A gut-wrenching, guilt-inducing experience if there ever was one.

During all this, the book community and working on Never Coming Home kept me sane. It gave me a place to hide, somewhere to try to escape from my grief and a space where I could take out my frustrations and despair on my characters when I couldn't get away otherwise. In many ways this is my darkest book to date, but it's also my funniest. Lucas is a despicable character, yet he made me laugh, which was exactly what I needed when everything else felt so hopeless.

What can you tell us about your next novel?

Book 7 is another psychological thriller. It's about a woman named Frankie who has some anger issues, and writes a list of people she could work to forgive as a therapy exercise. She thinks nothing of it when she loses her list in an Uber, until one by one the individuals become victims of freak accidents. Frankie desperately tries to determine if the tragedies are indeed accidental, and if not, who's behind them before someone else gets hurt, especially as one of the names on the list is her own... I'm so excited for this next novel and can't wait for you to meet Frankie and the rest of my cast.